TARNISHED
CHORDS

Steve

hope you enjoy
the
read.

best wishes

TARNISHED
CHORDS

FELIPE GUERRA

Matador
5 Weir Road
Kibworth Beauchamp
Leicester LE8 0LQ, UK
Tel: (+44) 116 279 2299
Fax: (+44) 116 279 2277
Email: books@troubador.co.uk
Web: www.troubador.co.uk/matador

ISBN 978 1848764 781

British Library Cataloguing in Publication Data.
A catalogue record for this book is available from the British Library.

Typeset in 11pt Galliard by Troubador Publishing Ltd, Leicester, UK

Matador is an imprint of Troubador Publishing Ltd

Printed in Great Britain by the MPG Books Group, Bodmin and King's Lynn

To Sue.
Always full of kindness, and a rare ability to help the lost and perplexed

CHAPTER | ONE

      With palpitations and a deep sigh, Manny Rodriguez stepped forward. In this most anxious of moments, he still could not help but notice the attractive and elegantly dressed woman waiting patiently behind him. His ego threw her a grin and it pleased him that she responded coyly.

With a prayer he apprehensively inserted the card into the mouth of 'the old enemy.' Deep down, however, he knew the outcome and there seemed, once again, very little chance that ignorance would be accompanied by bliss on yet another depressing start to the week. This was becoming all too frequent for his liking. The familiarity of the same routine was grinding him down. He punched in his pin number and entered the least amount of cash available for withdrawal. Fearing the inevitable, he positioned his body in an attempt to shield the screen.

The cold, grey and blustery morning reflected his mood and only added to his increasing desire for money and the temporary warmth it could bring. He privately chastised himself for his own recklessness and complete lack of foresight.

He waited. Time seemed to stand still, though his debts continued to dominate his thoughts. He self-consciously glanced behind him at the lengthening queue and found it a real challenge to act calm whilst at the same time continue with the subtle flirting. He failed miserably at both.

He turned back around but could sense her eyes searing into the back of his head, making him feel totally inept. On another day in a different place her stare would have been most welcome.

However, on this cold Monday morning outside the train station, he was downcast with the disheartening thought of not having the money to pay his rent.

The cash dispenser digested the information and made all the usual teasing noises before declining the request with the dreaded words *'insufficient funds please refer to branch'* bellowing across the screen. Even the well rehearsed 'just checking my balance' routine was cruelly denied him by the heartless machine as it decided, in full view of those waiting next in line, to withhold his only card.

"What now?" Manny asked himself. His chances of getting to work on time looked bleak. Standing motionless over the machine, he tried to think. He lacked the enthusiasm for another game of hide and seek with the over zealous ticket inspectors. He had to act fast. Damage limitation was now a priority. He decided he could not face a day of teaching. It was fast approaching eight o' clock. This left the school with barely enough time to arrange a replacement for him and meant even less time for him to plan and e-mail in work for the poor unsuspecting person who would end up taking his first lesson. The furious face of the head of department receiving his hastily arranged cover work forced its way into his head. The vision of her storming into his unkempt classroom and stumbling across all the unmarked work and unwritten reports whilst furiously rifling through his fathomless filing system filled him with dread.

He felt a sense of guilt towards his colleagues too. It meant more work and stress for them. They would silently curse his name, turning the staffroom air blue, thought Manny. The familiar scene played out in his mind. The angry looks on their faces when they first noticed their names up on the dreaded cover board informing them that instead of having a brief moment of calm they would find themselves thrust back deep into battle against the unruly students in his most challenging classes. But he quickly shrugged off the guilt, remembering how many times he had had to step into the breach for others that term. Yet the memory of how resentment could easily grow when stepping in for an absent teacher during a demanding cover lesson did not rest well inside him.

He pondered his limited options before having his train of thought interrupted by a voice projecting its way from the waiting queue. "Come on, mate! Hurry up, I've got a train to catch!" a man moaned.

Manny walked away and wearily sat himself down on a bench. He felt the sense of powerlessness return that had been pursuing him of late. The gravity of his financial situation was weighing him down. Too many debts and decidedly too little money to pay them.

He looked up just in time to observe the attractive and now unattainable woman withdraw cash from the dispenser. His dark eyes followed her. He admired her dark straight hair and trim build and his eyes continued to follow her as she made her way into the station. This time to his disappointment she never looked his way. He rhetorically inquired within why it was that he hungered for the things he could no longer afford. He suddenly felt the morning chill.

He got up from the bench and headed for the high street café. Once there he searched around for a place to sit. Finding a table in the corner, he sat down and ordered a double espresso as he passed the waitress.

He tried to find the will power to phone work and leave a message. A quick glimpse at his watch and the decision was made for him. It was too late. By now the school cover manager would be at her desk, next to her phone, with the answer machine switched off, which for him on this particular morning was bad news. He didn't have the stomach to begin the day yet again with a bunch of white lies and attempts to sound ill whilst fending off probing questions over the background noise. Determining to face the flack when feeling in a better frame of mind, he decided to do nothing. The truth was that he had found himself once again, just after payday, flat broke and with his biggest expenses yet to be paid.

He motioned to the waitress who came over and removed the empty cup. Gloomily counting the change he dug from his pocket, he smiled ironically as he discovered that he had enough for another. With a silent nod she acknowledged his request. As he felt the caffeine from the first cup kick in, he took the opportunity to ride its waves by toying with far fetched ideas that would instantly make him rich, successful and happy. He didn't want much, he reasoned. A home that he could call his own in a nice part of town. Nothing too big. A decent car, again nothing too flash. A job that would earn him a far healthier salary than his stressful teaching career could ever hope to pay. When he had first started teaching, he'd found it rewarding. His new career had played a major role in rebuilding his shattered confidence after a failed romance which had opened old wounds, causing him to spend a vast amount of time and money after the break-up looking for ways to deaden the pain. With bad company and drink contributing to his slow deterioration, it had taken a great deal of effort to get his life back on track. Discovering that he could teach had helped to restore his self-esteem.

Look at me! Fast approaching 30 and still I find myself bunking off school with just enough money in my pocket for a warm drink. His thoughts were interrupted by the arrival of the waitress placing his coffee on the table.

"Are you having anything to eat?" she asked.

"No, you're all right. I've already eaten," he lied needlessly.

The truth was he felt hungry and he reluctantly thought of the empty fridge that waited for him at home. He looked around the busy café and tried to assess the age and financial situation of those around him. It was a game he often caught himself playing but never winning. In this typical London café, he had a wide range of clientèle to attempt to pigeon-hole. As he was wearing his favourite suit, he mentally allied himself to those who looked and seemed to act in a manner that suggested that they were doing reasonably well. This made him feel slightly more worthy on the surface at least. Unfortunately, even this shallow comfort was denied him when he noticed a man, dressed in similar attire to his own, and roughly of the same age, nonchalantly leave the waitress a generous tip. Manny leaned back, placing his hands behind his head, looked up to the ceiling and exhaled loudly. He needed to find the courage to face his present plight. But he did not know where to look for it.

Straightening up, he looked around the little café in search of a free newspaper. To his approval the café did provide some, keeping them on a rack towards the back. Reaching out, he grabbed the solitary paper there and, leafing through to the classified ads section, began to browse. "I need cash and I need lots of it now!" he told himself firmly. He had exhausted the patience of friends and family a long time ago. As for the banks, asking for another small loan was a non starter. The days of the banks' and credit card companies' generosity had come to an end. It had been easy at first. Banks and other lending outlets had made borrowing relatively simple, providing you were in full time employment. Manny had put a lot onto his credit cards under the illusion that he'd be able to pay it off over time. That time had now arrived with vengeance. Credit card companies were ruthlessly demanding their money back – and he was able to predict their answers to his applications for further credit with a grudging ease. He had enough rejection letters hidden in his drawer at home to prove that times had certainly changed. In the past, the credit companies had allowed him to borrow more than he could possibly hope to pay back. He knew that the blame lay with himself for his lack of self control and discipline, but still he felt irked that he had been allowed to borrow so much.

In this state of mind he failed to see what else his six years of working as an English teacher in a high school qualified him to do. How he wished he could make a clean break and start again in a more lucrative profession. He struggled to live on his current salary despite not having any dependants to provide for. He completely understood why it was that so many teachers were fleeing the profession, men in particular.

But establishing himself in a new career would take time and time was something that his financial situation would not allow him. Also, the school term had just recommenced after the Christmas break and for a teacher the next opportunity to leave was still another seven weeks away. This also posed a problem for him. Though he was disillusioned with many aspects of the teaching profession, he remained sensitive towards the needs of his students. Yes, they could play up frequently but he had established his own set of rules which the majority of his students tended to abide by. They responded well to his firm, friendly but never over-familiar style and he had never really experienced the kind of bad behaviour he had often witnessed in the classrooms of some colleagues. The cold stare he had perfected during his years in teaching had served him well and often prevented the most unruly of students from stepping over the line. He could look a 'hard bastard' when annoyed or angered, people often told him. He did not mind the comment and would often use the persona when the situation demanded. Anything that made his job easier he endorsed.

People would often remark on his smile and by now he had established that this was a very useful tool in making others do what he wanted them to do. A part of his charisma he did not reserve purely for his students.

Leaving his more senior classes before the start of their exams sat awkwardly with him. It was an unwritten bond between teacher and student he would rather not break. To give up on his teaching career would not only mean turning his back on a job he knew he did well, perhaps better than most of his colleagues, it would also mean undermining a role which provided a sense of self-worth whenever his inner demons attacked.

He skimmed and scanned the employment pages in the hope of finding a solution to his problem. With a mixture of amusement, resentment and alarm, he pondered over just how much some people could potentially earn. It made him feel that he had somehow fallen far behind in a race he had first set out to win. This raised more inner conflict about the way he had been living his life. It annoyed him that he'd never been able to manage his money sensibly and he was now seriously regretting borrowing so much from the all-too-accommodating banks. It was an internal conversation that he'd rather not engage in again. Instead he silently decided to concede defeat to the irritating voice of hindsight. Bravely, he made an effort to remain realistic while he pondered his options. But again, Manny found it hard to fend off all his unrealistic dreams on how different life could be, for him, if he only had more money at his disposal. He drank the last of his coffee and was about to close the paper, resigned to the probability of spending the rest of the day drifting further and deeper into the realms of his depression when a small advert on the bottom of the page caught his attention. He felt the hair on his forearms and back of his neck stand to attention. "My God," he gasped. "That's it. That could be the answer." He looked at the bottom of the page again.

Perfect Company
escorting services
our aim is our name
call for the perfect service
01717 45537389
male escorts urgently needed
call Virginia
Excellent earning potential for right person

Pulling out his mobile phone, he punched in and saved the details of the advert. He paid for his coffee and left without having enough change to leave for a reasonable tip. He simpered at the waitress and quickly departed the café with glimmerings of hope that just maybe he had found a way out of the quagmire of financial hardship that he was sinking in. With fresh verve he decided that he had a very important call to make. A male escort? His heart suddenly caught fire and jumped into a higher gear at the possibilities and experiences the job would provide. He strode purposefully the quarter of a mile back to his bedsit. Yes, he might bump into Anna, his landlady, who'd be demanding all the outstanding rent he owed. There would be more final demands to add to the growing pile impatiently awaiting his attention. But he had felt a resolve rise inside him. A resolve that demanded that he start taking back some kind of control. A resolve that was telling him to start living life and not just existing. A feeling that had been lying dormant for far too long.

Manny was pleased not to see his landlady's car sitting on the drive. He let himself in and headed straight for his room. He stretched out on his unmade bed and plugged in his ipod. The music helped smooth out his racing thoughts as he searched for answers to his questions. Was he really thinking straight? Could he be a teacher during the day and escort by night? There were contrasting answers swimming around his head. It did seem a bit fanciful. Rather unreal. However, he did not need to remind himself that his financial problems were very real and with this thought he decided that in making the call he had nothing left to lose. He was bound to feel a bit afraid but his situation demanded that he act now with courage before everything become unmanageable. What could be more difficult than taking out a few lonely women and showing them a good time? For once he felt it was a position that he was more than qualified to fulfil. Little did he know just what a tortuous and turbulent path he was about to embark on. Some hard lessons were waiting for this teacher to learn.

Manny finally stopped fretting and made the dreaded call in to his work. He told them that something that he had eaten over the weekend had not agreed with his sensitive digestive system. He then apologised for the lateness of the call and added it was due to feeling so ill. He'd fallen into a hallucinatory state that had made him oblivious to time. The long pause at the other end of the phone enabled him to take on board the school secretary's silent scepticism. He proceeded to inform her, trying to create a more upbeat note from the feeble sound coming from his mouth, that the doctor had prescribed him some medicine, that when taken with plenty of rest, should allow him to resume work within the next couple of days.

The only utterance she made during the brief conversation was a robotic reminder to him that if he should be off work longer than the protracted five working days, he would need to provide the school with a valid doctor's certificate or his pay might be affected. Before hanging up, Manny faked a couple of coughs and then sarcastically thanked the sterile voice on the other end for her genuine, caring concern.

He stretched out on his bed and thought about the next call he was about to make. Feeling nervous, Manny assured himself he could handle any questions that they were likely to ask. Seeds of doubts were waiting to enter his thoughts and test his resolve. He felt an impulse to fast dial the stored number and to act quickly before any of the more insistent doubts filtered through. Pressing dial, he grabbed a pen and a sheet of paper and waited for the call to connect. He felt that he had nothing left to lose. As he waited for the call to be answered he felt his heart beating forcefully and was embarrassed by his fears of talking to someone he had never met nor was ever likely to. Expecting an answer machine to intercept the ringing, he was caught slightly unprepared when he heard a bright voice on the other end answer. His felt his tension swell.

"Good morning. Thank you for calling Perfect Company. This is Monica speaking. How may I help you?"

Manny remained silent. Unable to find his voice.

"Hello? Can I help you at all?" she repeated calmly.

"Er… yeah, good morning, can I… or is it possible to speak to Veronica please?" He finally mustered in an awkward manner.

"Veronica? I'm not sure we have a Veronica working for the company. Are you sure you don't mean Virginia?"

Manny nodded, silently chastising himself for making such a basic error.

"Sorry. That's right. What an idiot. I meant Virginia."

The mistake instantly removed the tension from his voice and in a funny way made him feel more at ease.

"We're expecting Ms Griffin in around midday. May I ask what it's regarding?" she enquired with a sympathetic titter hidden in her tone. He could not help but be impressed by the girl's accommodating style and thought her manner was more in keeping with a five star hotel, rather than a sleazy escorting company. Her friendly tone helped persuade him to distance himself from his anxiousness.

"It's about the advert I saw in the paper. It said you needed male escorts and I guess I wanted to find out if you're still looking and whether or not I'd be suitable." He paused and a short silence followed. Feeling his confidence seep out with every passing second, he thought about hanging up and forgetting the whole idea. He took a deep breath and gave it one more shot.

"Look. How do I go about this? Do I send in a C.V with references or what?"

"I take it you haven't done escorting before?" She did not wait for him to answer and calmly continued. "But that's cool. Not a problem. What usually happens first is this: If we like the sound of you, Virginia invites you in for a chat and of course likes to give you the once over!" She sounded positive as she uttered the last sentence with a slight tease in her voice, "Then, if she feels that you have potential she will most likely get you to take out one of the other escorts, who work for the agency, for a drink or a spot of lunch, something like that just to get a bit of feedback and a second opinion if it's needed. How does that sound to you so far? Doesn't sound too bad, does it? It's well worth coming in to see us and finding out more about the company." She added encouragingly, "Any further questions?"

Manny nodded approvingly. Nothing that he couldn't handle so far, he reasoned.

"Yeah. You said something about if you like the sound of me. Who decides whether they like 'the sound' of me?" He was pleased to be feeling slightly more in control of his nerves.

"Generally it's the person who first takes the call. So that would be... mm mm let me think now ... oh, that's me," she said in mock delight.

He allowed her sense of importance to fade, remaining quiet before asking the obvious question as to whether he sounded suitable enough to continue.

"Well, apart from getting the boss's name wrong, you're not doing too badly," she joked. "What's your name?"

"Manny. Manny Rodriguez."

"Is that a Spanish name?"

"Yeah, that's right. Spanish father, English mother."

"You don't sound very Spanish but that's cool. What's the Manny short for? It's not Manuel, is it?" She laughed.

It was not the first time he had been asked this, so he took the opportunity to seize the moment and silently waited for her laughter to subside.

"Yes, it is actually," he retorted sternly. There was an

uncomfortable silence coming from her end this time, which he allowed to continue for a few more seconds before bringing her embarrassment to an end.

"No, it's not 'Manuel'. Which is good news for you. Isn't it, Monica? It's actually short for Manolo. I was named after my Spanish grandfather, luckily."

"Why luckily?"

"Because, my English grandfather was called Horace."

She laughed because she thought he was kidding.

A more relaxed atmosphere entered the conversation as Manny continued to provide her with brief details about himself. However, he could feel the tension beginning to return when she asked him if he would be willing to come into the office later that day to meet Virginia.

"Would three o'clock be OK?" she asked. "Ms Griffin will be out of her meeting by then."

Caught slightly off-guard by the question, he wondered why she had reverted back to the formal way of addressing her boss. However, Manny promptly agreed to the time. She then proceeded to give him the address of their office and how to find it. He was surprised to hear that the company was located a short walk away from Bond Street tube station, off Marylebone Lane and close to St Christopher's Place with all its boutiques and trendy restaurants. Nothing sleazy about the location, he thought.

Monica suggested that he dressed smartly and warned him not to be late. He thanked her for her help and tried to discover if she herself would be there later. Picking up on his subtle probing, she confirmed that she would still be at the office around three. He could not decide whether this was a good thing or not. He closed his phone and exhaled loudly, not quite believing the pace that things were moving at or what exactly he was getting himself involved in. But he was able to keep his apprehension in check by constantly reminding himself that he could back out at any moment should things get too uncomfortable for his liking. He failed to see the harm in just turning up and meeting this Virginia woman for a brief chat.

After all, he had survived two Ofsted inspections at work and nothing could be as bad as that, he reasoned. Anyway, he had grown curious as to how these kind of companies operated and if nothing else it would be a good story to tell Andy Moran, his work colleague. Manny ordered himself to remain light hearted about it all, and not to lose his nerve or more importantly his sense of humour. There were still a few hours to kill before he had to make any decisions. He decided to visit his local gym and have a workout which always provided him with some quality time to think things through. The gym was an excellent place for resolving any internal dilemmas – of which lately, he admitted, there had been far too many.

After his workout and jog home Manny found that a note had been pushed under his door. He knew straight away who it was from and what it was about and it gave him very little pleasure to be right on both counts. His landlady wanted all outstanding rent paid up in full by the end of the week. She told him in no uncertain terms that enough was enough. He felt bad and full of guilt. Anna was a decent woman who relied on his rent to make ends meet. With the note, all doubts disappeared from his mind. He would go and speak to Ms Virginia Griffin not out of choice but out of necessity. He must pay his landlady. She had always been kind to him and deserved better. All other debts would have to wait.

Manny stripped off his sweaty gym clothes and took a long, hot shower. He wished it was possible to wash away the slight guilt he was feeling. When he was done, he wrapped a towel around himself and used another to clear the mist off the small mirror so he could shave. He noticed that his money troubles were beginning to leave reminders around his eyes. He looked tired. Manny also acknowledged the fact that he was having to shave further and further up his face. He wondered while removing rebellious hairs from his nostrils if this Virginia from the agency would find anything attractive about him. He decided not to stand so close to the mirror. He stepped back into his room to get dressed and worked harder than ever to keep his insecurities at bay.

Feeling he had nowhere left to turn, the thought of working as a male escort carried the sweet taste of promise. A taste that had been absent for too long.

Manny stretched out on his bed, plugged in the ear buds from his iPod and tried hard to compose his thoughts before the all-important meeting with Virginia. He had experienced interviews before but struggled to remember a time when he had felt so unprepared. Without the aid of a job description, he tried to imagine the kind of questions he would be asked but soon gave up. Manny was wise enough to know that he needed to remain calm whilst thinking fast on his feet and only when the situation demanded display a discreet allure. He got up from his bed and went over to his makeshift wardrobe where he weighed up his limited array of clothes.

Little time was needed in deciding his choice of wear. He reached for his only suit – the one that whispered class. An ageing number by Paul Smith, in charcoal grey, usually reserved for the odd wedding, interview or funeral even, together with a crisp white shirt. He didn't feel the need to add a tie. He grabbed a clean pair of boxer shorts from his clothes pile and quickly finished dressing, stepping back to catch a glimpse of himself in the mirror. With only his doubting eyes to judge he vainly searched within to try and recall any complimentary remarks he had received of late regarding his looks or appearance. He concluded that lustful stares from dinner ladies and sixth form girls finding their flirtatious feet did not really count. There had been moments when he had allowed himself to bask in any admiration that shone his way but the dark memories from his childhood ensured any light soon faded away.

Manny looked at his watch and decided to walk the distance to West Hampstead Underground. From there he would take the tube to Bond Street which was only five stops away. The journey would take him less than twenty minutes, leaving him with an hour to kick his heels in town. But his first priority was getting his hands on some money to cover his fare. He knew that Anna kept a jar of change in a kitchen cupboard. It was not the first time he had dipped into it but he was always careful to replace the money before it rattled her attention. He would remember to apologise and come up with an excuse later, should one be needed. He guiltily dipped in his hands and counted out £10 made up from pound coins and fifty pence pieces and made his way out of the house. Walking briskly, Manny had an inkling that things were going to get better. The thought cheered him. The wind had died down and he no longer felt the chill from earlier. Instead the weather was displaying a deceptive calm.

CHAPTER TWO

Manny made his way to the address in Marylebone Lane and stood outside the impressive building that Monica had described. He looked at his watch and felt apprehensive. It was almost three. He stepped to one side to view the names on the intercom. He saw the sign for *Ms. Virginia Griffin Consultant.* There were two other signs below hers. One was for an accountancy firm and the other appeared to be a solicitor's office. Two firms that provided a respectable service, he thought. He wondered again if the choice he was making meant that he was sinking to a new level of desperation. The memory of how he could not afford to travel in to work that morning and how he'd had to raid Anna's money jar just to get there soon served as a stark reminder to him that he had already reached a new low. He felt a wave of guilt. His modest teaching salary alone was unlikely to provide any short term solutions to his financial ordeal. Manny flinched at thought of the gloomy consequences which would be bestowed upon him if he failed to take drastic action. *I can't keep living like this*, he thought irritably. At once he understood what he had to do. Without further deliberation he pushed the buzzer determinedly.

A voice he recognised from earlier answered. Manny announced himself.

"Hello. Come on up! We're on the third floor. Push the door." The door was unlocked and he walked in. He anxiously made his way up the stairs to the third floor. He knew that he had to lose the defeated expression he'd been wearing of late.

He slowed down as he neared the top and tried desperately to compose himself. Feeling the adrenaline still chasing through his veins, he heard the buzz of conversation get louder as he approached the door at the top of the stairs. There was a smell of an open fire coming from somewhere and he could also smell fresh flowers. Manny exhaled forcefully when he reached the door. This was it, he thought. He knocked solidly a couple of times before entering the room where he saw a pretty but overly tanned girl sitting behind her desk working on a computer. She smiled instantly. An older and more sophisticated looking woman, probably in her late twenties Manny guessed, attended a photocopier in the corner. Both motioned for him to come in, inviting him to take a seat on a large blue sofa.

"Hi. I'm here to see Virginia," he announced with a modest amount of confidence.

The older lady made the first move by walking over, offering her hand and a warm smile.

"You must be Manny? Nice to meet you. I'm Louise and this is Monica whom I hear you have already spoken to." Monica smiled and waved and he found himself waving back in the same silly manner. "We both work for Virginia who's in a meeting at the moment."

She pointed to a heavy, white adjacent door as she mentioned the word 'meeting'. Manny assumed this to mean that Virginia was in there. "She shouldn't be much longer. Can I get you anything to drink?" Louise spoke with a deep, rich voice that sounded well-educated and warm. *I really could do with a drink. Maybe a glass or two of red wine*, he thought, just to calm his nerves.

"A coffee would be good."

"Milk and sugar?"

"Yes please."

She smiled politely and left the room. He was conscious that the sofa made him look small when he sat back. His feet barely reached the polished wooden floor. He decided to sit on the edge and tried his best to look at ease. Monica had not taken her eyes off him from the moment he walked in. He was thinking of something witty to say before the silence became uncomfortable for him. He needn't have worried.

"You got her name right this time then?" she beamed with girlish charm. She had a high, pleasant-sounding voice, and tiny hands that she kept on the desk in front of her, busy fiddling with a pen. He also noticed that she wore no rings. Her skin colour suggested that she used fake tanning lotion or indulged in the odd sun bed. She wore her highlighted blonde hair tied back. Manny saw her as a fun girl to meet during a wild evening out without ever wanting to give her his phone number towards the end of the night.

"Yeah. I've been practising it all day. You didn't tell anyone, did you?"

"No. But I did tell them about the cruel joke you played on me. You had me there. For a horrible moment I thought your name was 'Manuel'. I almost died." She paused and looked him up and down with a worried frown on her face. "What happened to the dressing up and looking smart?" Her expression was serious. Manny felt a sudden panic as he looked down at his chosen outfit, automatically reaching towards his top button, in search of his absent tie.

The sound of her laughter made him look up and at once he knew she had him. He smiled in appreciation at the way she unwittingly calmed his nerves.

"I'm sorry about that but it had to be done. I had to get you back. You do look smart, honest." There was a note of triumph in her voice.

The playfulness was interrupted by her having to answer the phone. Just then Louise returned with his coffee and delicately placed the tray onto the table by the sofa. At the same time a smart-suited older gentleman carrying a brief case came out of the office. A dignified-looking fellow, Manny thought as he watched him stride purposefully out of the reception. The man gave him a mock salute as he passed by. He had a tough-looking face and a heavy, solid frame. A man who probably used brawn rather than brain in his younger days, Manny guessed. He looked at his watch. Three-fifteen. A slight resentment started to build that he was being made to wait. Monica was still dealing with an inquiry on the phone as Louise made her way into Virginia's office. He felt a knot tighten in his stomach. Stroking his cropped hair nervously with one hand, he exhaled loudly. Monica looked his way and sent him a reassuring smile as she continued with her conversation, miming and indicating with her hand just how much the person on the other end of the phone was jabbering on. Manny looked away, too nervous to raise a laugh. He studied the two framed pictures that hung on the walls. He immediately recognised one of the prints. It was called '*Women running on the beach*' by Picasso. An aunt in Spain had the same print. The naked breasts in the picture had always been a great source of amusement for him and his sisters when they were children. He remembered this particularly because laughter was scarce back then. He rubbed his face and calmed his mind as he sensed his thoughts start to drift in a different direction. This was not the place to lower his shield. The moment of weakness was over. A lot depended on what happened inside that room and he admitted to himself that this was an unusual situation even for him. Manny reminded himself sternly that he was free to walk out at any time. He would have to find another way, that's all. Despite all the self reassurance, he felt his heart racing.

Louise came out of the room and invited him in.

"Virginia can see you now." Holding the door open, she ushered him in.

He strode forward, taking a firmer grip of his nerves. Monica mouthed the words "Good luck" as he passed her desk. He winked back in her direction. Simple smiles were exchanged as he crossed paths with Louise. The decisive moment had arrived.

Manny entered the stylish-looking room where a log fire burned proud. It was the only reminder of the building's illustrious past. Bunches of fresh flowers were scattered in vases around the room. Towards the end of the room sat a solid-looking desk that dominated the space. Behind the desk there was a black leather chair which was occupied by a woman with long fair hair. He was unable to see the whole of her face due to the fact that she was talking on the phone, her hands cupped over the receiver. She motioned with her eyes for him to take a seat on one of the chairs in the corner. She wore glasses with thin black frames. As he took his seat he could tell that she was studying him. He made sure that he felt and looked comfortable sitting in the deep leather seat before looking up. When he did, their eyes locked. Virginia was the first to look away after several seconds had passed. His eyes fell onto her ample breasts, he wondered if they were real.

He then took a look around the room as she continued with her call. The classy furniture and pictures were probably as expensive as they looked.

"That sounds ideal. Thanks, Monica. Did he really? Make sure you make a note of that... Yes, I will. Can you send it out tonight?" He tried hard to avoid listening in on her conversation. But he was drawn in on hearing Monica's name. It was extremely likely that they had been discussing him. He hoped that he'd done enough to hide his insecurities during the time he spent sitting out in the waiting area.

"Yes, all right, I'll bear that in mind. Must go now because I've kept him waiting long enough and he will think that we're rude and we don't want that now, do we?" The way she looked and smiled at him was all the confirmation he needed that he'd been right. Good teamwork, he thought.

Putting down the phone, she got up from behind her desk and walked over to him. She held her hand out to greet his, not allowing him the time or space to stand up himself. Her dominant manner impressed him slightly more than it bothered him. She sat in the armchair opposite. She appeared to be in her early forties. She did not look as Manny had expected her to look. He'd expected an older-looking woman. The name Virginia had led him to assume that she'd be several years older than she was. He doubted that it was her real name. She had sharp features with clear blue eyes and could easily be considered beautiful, but he did not search for evidence of her beauty for too long. Pretty women always made him feel self-conscious and he needed to show confidence. Instead he tried to find fault behind her make-up. He thought he had detected evidence under her eyes that there had been moments when life had been a struggle. But it was a feeble argument and could easily be put down to tiredness.

"Hello, Manny. I'm Virginia. Sorry to keep you waiting but it's been one of those days, I'm afraid."

"Don't worry. It's good to hear that you're busy."

"We are, thankfully. January always seems to be a really busy time for us. People tend to assess their life more after Christmas. They seem to want to take back some kind of control early in the New Year, I guess. Now, I gather you're here to see me about the advert in the paper. Is that correct?"

"Yes. That's right. I suppose I want to find out a bit more really." He remembered what she had said and used her words in building his answer. "I guess I have assessed my life and I want to take more control."

Her next question caught him off guard.

"Want to or need to?"

He paused before answering. He debated whether telling the truth meant he was revealing too much and proceeding too fast, so early in the conversation. He was quick to remind himself that this attitude was in stark contrast to the interviews he'd attended in schools for teaching posts. His approach in this case had to be very different.

"To tell the truth, Virginia, I need to make some money. When I saw your advert I saw it as an ideal solution to my problems." He was about to continue but she jumped in forcefully.

"I appreciate your honesty but there are many ways to make money. Why escorting? Have you done it before? Have you ever used an escort yourself?"

"No. No way. Never." The minute the words left his mouth he silently cursed himself for not pausing to think before he spoke.

She leant back in her chair and threw him a piercing look. Her body language demanded that he continue. He knew that his response had carried a disapproving tone that made it sound like he had issues with the escorting business. A business that she worked in, and judging by her appearance and the location of her offices, a business that she had done remarkably well in and had obviously invested a lot of time and effort in building up. Manny knew he had placed his head into the noose and the executioner was ready and waiting to end his misery.

"Look, I suppose I have always thought like most people that it was a sleazy business for sleazy old men who could no longer attract the ladies. But times have changed. I have read articles in magazines and I've heard about the odd TV programme. Escorting is a more acceptable service nowadays. There are other ways of making money, that's true. But I have to be realistic about my options. I'm committed to my teaching until the summer. I don't mean to disrespect anyone but I can't really see myself doing telesales or bar work in the evenings or at weekends. Those types of jobs require that you put in plenty of hours just to earn peanuts." Manny lightened his tone. "I know Monica thought my name was Manuel but I'd make a lousy waiter." He saw a smile replace the frown and he felt the noose loosen slightly from around his neck.

"Virginia, my situation demands that I make some money. I'm here because I know how to show someone a good time. I'm fun to be with as I hope you'll get to find out. I'm sure if I'm making money then you're making money too. Give me a chance. You won't regret it. And to clear up any misunderstanding. I meant to say that I have never needed the help of an escort agency because I've always backed myself," he boasted. It was a remark intended to lighten the atmosphere and he allowed the comment to hang in the air for a short while before realizing that what he had just said was not entirely true. "Until now, that is, of course."

She allowed some time to pass before getting up to fetch two glasses of sparkling water from a dispenser placed in a corner of the room. He silently admired her shapely legs as she walked away. On coming back she bent down to arrange the drinks on the glass table beside them. Manny watched her. He lowered his gaze as she turned around. Her smile suggested she had guessed his thoughts. He felt embarrassed. She sipped her water and seemed to be composing hers. He liked the way she presented herself. Her mannerisms were polished and elegant as she answered his questions with an assured smile. He noticed the ring that she wore on her wedding finger. Her silence was beginning to make him feel uncomfortable, confusing him. Manny was about to take a sip of his water when she finally began to speak.

"You might think it sounds sleazy but I think you'd be surprised at just how worthwhile it could make you feel. Not everybody finds it easy to play the dating game, you know. Many of our clients are professional people with precious little free time on their hands. Others are working through issues that make dating and meeting strangers a difficult experience. But they still desire and need intimate company and rightly so. We all need someone to give us permission to shine, don't you agree, Mr Rodriguez?" She didn't wait for a reply.

"That's why I started 'Perfect Company'. Our role is to help certain types of people. Your job would be to make people shine. Can you do that, Mr Rodriguez? Can you make people shine? Have you the gift of being able to listen and make the person speaking feel refined, radiant and beautiful while allowing them to believe that they're the most precious gem on earth as you subtly slip them their bill?"

This time he did sip his water as he witnessed for the first time the ruthless streak that explained her company's success. Her soft manner was belied by the fire in her eyes which told him that she had a monstrous appetite for making money.

"I can do that. It's part of the requirements for the job I do now. It's the one thing I tend to do well, make people shine and feel better about themselves."

"Why? What do you do for work at the moment?"

"I teach English at a secondary school. I believe teachers become teachers because they tend to have caring natures and like to build up their pupils' confidence. I know that I do."

"An English teacher?" She quickly pulled away her glass and he thought she was about to spray out the water in surprise. A smile broke out across her face.

"Really? You don't look like an English teacher. I bet your lessons are interesting – poetry and Shakespeare in a cockney accent?" She looked at him more closely; he had her full attention now. He noticed her eyes were green, not blue. "Where do you live and where's your school?" She reached across her desk, grabbed a pen and a note pad and began taking notes. He took this as a positive sign that she was beginning to take his application seriously. It often amused him how people reacted when he informed them of his profession.

"I'm renting a room in a house in West Hampstead at the moment. The school that I work at is in St Albans. Just a few stops away on the Thameslink."

"A teacher living in West Hampstead? No wonder you're broke." There was a teasing tone in her voice. He didn't know how to respond because her words were true. She picked up on his silence.

"Don't take it to heart I didn't mean it to sound so flippant. I understand. I had a couple of friends who were teachers. I know the pay's not great and, boy, were they stressed." The use of the past tense was not lost on him. "Listen, Mr Rodriguez, you seem bright and you've clearly got guts to come here. The girls out the front like the look of you. You have certainly made an impression on Monica and in a very short time which bodes well. You're a good-looking guy with a smile that will sell. You obviously look after your body and you certainly have charisma. You're a little bit short. We usually don't take on men below six feet tall and it's also a shame that you don't have a Spanish accent like your name would suggest. Can you speak Spanish?"

"Yes. Yes I can."

"That's good, we can use that. We have very high standards here. Our clients expect quality. If we decide to take you on, part of the terms and conditions require that your profile and photo appear on our web page which only our members are able to access. Of course you could use a pseudonym but for you, a Spanish name would work well. Louise oversees and updates our web page and has set up our online membership system. She'll explain it in more detail to you later if you want. Would you have a problem with that?" He shook his head but the thought of a friend, family member or, even worse, a student stumbling across a website featuring him posing in nothing but his briefs trying to sell himself sent a cold shiver down his spine. The consequences were simply too horrific to consider. He made a mental note to share his fears should they progress that far.

"When accepted, we provide all escorts with a mobile phone and for the more successful escorts, a personal laptop. You'd be expected to liaise with your client base and keep a track of all your bookings using the Internet – do you have access to the Internet?"

"Yes," Manny replied.

"We also provide cars if necessary. With or without a driver depending on the situation. Do you drive?"

"Yes. Yes I do but I'm without a car at the moment."

"I thought as much. I may need to see your driving licence. We also cover all expenses for work-related items such as clothes, food, drink, toys etc. Nothing comes out of your own pocket and if it does, provided you've kept the receipts, the company will usually reimburse you. Monica deals with that side of things. I have to warn you that some parts of the job, although financially rewarding, can be rather tedious." He tried to suppress his excitement on hearing the words 'financially rewarding'.

"Spending a few hours in the company of somebody you would usually choose to avoid, whilst having to make them feel special, is an unenviable task at times. Other aspects of the job will present you with some moral dilemmas, I'm sure. But don't worry, I'm always here to help and advise you on those. I always find that money plays a major role in helping us reach the right decisions. Anyway, let's not get ahead of ourselves. Tell me, Manny, do you have a partner at the moment?"

The question caught him by surprise. He shook his head. He didn't really enjoy reviewing or discussing his ill-fated romantic record, even less so with total strangers.

There had only ever been one meaningful relationship in his life to date and that was with a girl he had met while attending an evening class at college. Lucy Randell, to this day, had been the only girl to really touch his heart. After inviting her out for a drink one evening, he decided that he had found the girl he was going to explore the universe with. He recalled how his heart would burn in a blazing fire whenever she looked at him deeply with her passionate eyes. They both shared a desire to travel to Australia and other exotic locations. Naively, he believed she was a girl worth taking risks for and he secretly set about securing a couple of loans and credit cards in order to turn dreams into reality. Despite the financial recklessness he still thought that those two years had been the happiest of his life. During their travels, they'd met many fellow travellers living out the same dream, all independent and free from responsibilities. The dissolving of their romantic relationship started near the end of their adventures when they both befriended a slightly older man at a party in Australia. Falling for the more emotionally mature man, Lucy slowly began to drift away from Manny and into the arms of the smooth-talking man from Surrey. Manny was left with loans and credit card bills to pay back as well as having to deal with a broken heart. He had not seen or heard from Lucy since. In moments of darkness he still found himself invoking her name but he would never admit to anyone the pain she had caused him.

The longer he looked at Virginia the more beautiful she seemed to become. She reminded him of a babysitter he had had when he was about ten and living in Spain. He didn't understand it back then. All he knew was that he would look forward to the warm sensation that stirred in his loins whenever she sat on his bed to read to him. He would tell himself that his love of books developed from those precious moments with her. Unknown to her she had given him his first glimpse of the secret gifts that women possessed. He tried to re-focus. He was getting hungry as he had not eaten much that day and he could feel his concentration begin to waver.

"The fact that you're a teacher tends to suggests that you're probably quite caring and teachers tend to be trustworthy as they'll have been CRB-checked." Manny remained quiet. "That could be useful." She looked down at her watch and stood up. "Is there anything else you need to know?"

He wondered what she meant by this but decided to leave that for another time.

"How much is it possible to earn in a night?"

"I like you, Mr Rodriguez. We have something in common. A thirst for money. I recognise that look in your eyes when the word money is mentioned." She smiled at him.

"It's always difficult to predict the earning potential for a rookie. But if you're as good as you say you are and you're not too fussy, then I can see you earning anything up to six hundred pounds per night." Virginia waited a few moments, allowing the quote to sink in and register in his mind. She knew she had him. "The look on your face tells me you're still interested. If you do go on to earn that sort of money, Señor Rodriguez, then you're going to make your boss a very happy girl indeed."

Manny thought about the possible riches that awaited him and gave up trying to suppress his excitement. He refused to listen to the inner alarm system that sounded inside his head. He sat on the chair lost in thought, the silence in the room failing to trouble him. She went back and sat behind her desk. He knew the conversation was almost over.

"What happens next?" he asked as he stood up.

"We usually send applicants out on a dummy date with another escort. Call it a second opinion if you like. I shouldn't really be telling you this, and please don't repeat this to anyone but we only tend to do that if we're not quite sure about a person. As I'm sure you already know, there are a lot of strange people out there. But you don't need to worry about that, Mr Rodriguez. I've got a good feeling about you. I can see you have the potential to make money. We'll be in touch to let you know how your application is progressing."

She never looked at him again. Putting on her glasses, she picked up the phone on her desk. "Hi, Louise, can you come and show Mr. Rodriguez out now please?" She had already become absorbed in her next task, staring straight ahead at her computer screen. As Louise escorted Manny back to reception, Virginia called out to tell her to take down his details. Things were gathering pace and he felt the twinge of anxiety return. Monica stopped typing and took the opportunity to congratulate him. "I think she likes you. I've never seen her make her mind up about someone this quick." He liked Monica: she was good for his ego. "Are you going to do it?"

Manny nodded. "If I get in, that is. Nothing has been confirmed yet."

"That's great if you do. We'll be seeing some more of each other then. I did put in a good word for you but I doubt if it was needed. You look like her type of bloke." He looked at her in the hope that she'd elaborate but she didn't add anything else and continued with her work instead. Louise then gave him a brief summary of what would happen next, giving him a form so he could fill out his details. He allowed the conversation to die away before saying goodbye. Both girls hinted that they'd be in touch at some stage. On leaving, he found himself mock-saluting the two girls in reception in the same way the tough-looking man had done earlier. He realised that he actually felt excited. He wondered what would happen next. Probably nothing. Discarding that pessimistic view, Manny instead thought about the money that had been mentioned. He had to admit that everything had gone better than he had hoped. The excitement was there bubbling again. That, he could not deny.

CHAPTER THREE

Manny arrived back at the house feeling acute pangs of hunger. He would have liked to have stayed up in town and made use of the wide range of restaurants and snack bars at his disposal. Unfortunately, his lack of funds left him with only one sensible option: to return to his dismally dark room and prepare for work the next day. The choice hardly filled him with joy.

On opening the front door, he saw Anna, his landlady. She was sitting on the bottom of the stairs in the hallway reading her mail, still wearing her outdoor coat. As usual, she looked pale and tired. Anna was in her early forties and in the time he had known her she had always worn the look of someone who had been dealt a rough hand in life. She had told him, over a bottle of wine more than a year ago, that she was in the middle of agonising divorce proceedings. Her husband had left her and had set up home with another woman. The experience had left her feeling devastated, draining her of all her energy and self esteem. Manny understood something of the pain that caused her paleness. His own mother had displayed the same exhausted look. He also knew about Anna's daughter who was currently taking a year out of university to travel around Asia. The daughter would call the house once in a while and, judging by the conversations he could not help but overhear, she was usually calling to require some kind of help with one problem or another.

"Hello, Anna, good day at work?" He didn't wait for an answer. "I'm pleased you're in. I wanted to catch up with you and talk about the money I owe and about the note you left. I've got some good news. I went for a second job today, a part time number. I think I might have got it. It does mean working some evenings though, but that's fine because with the extra cash it means that I can start paying you back the outstanding rent."

He was pleased that he had been able to approach the tricky topic first, creating a positive base to start from. Having been expecting a verbal roasting, he was caught completely off guard by her sombre response.

"Hi, Manny, that's great, I'm pleased." Her tone was flat and distant. The letter she was reading seemed to have hypnotised her. Her vacant stare told him that she had finished reading but the words on the page were taking a long time to register and form any kind of understanding within.

"Are you all right?" he asked, concerned.

"Yeah, I should be," she frowned. "My final divorce settlement. I should be delighted really. I've been waiting ages for this moment but I feel totally numb. Twenty-two years of my life closed, over, finished, just like that." Anna had still not looked at him. Instead, her eyes remained staring into that same distant place.

Normally he enjoyed their discussions and small talk but ever since he had begun falling behind with his rent, he had been doing his best to avoid her, silently creeping in and out of the house trying to remain invisible. On the train home the prospect of bumping into her had filled him with dread. Manny knew he had to face up to the possibility of her giving him his marching orders. She was well within her rights. The need to approach the subject with some diplomacy was crucial, he told himself. Now he felt that her bad news could provide an opportunity for him to exploit. He felt bad about turning her pain to his advantage. Somehow I will learn to live with my conscience, he pledged. Making a mental note to make amends to her when he was in a better place both financially and psychologically, he acknowledged that his moral compass seemed to be failing him more and more during this troubled time. Survival instincts were leading the way. Manny could feel his guilty thoughts written all over his face. He sat down next to her and joined in with her silence, tenderly rubbing her back. He allowed a few minutes to pass before heading into the kitchen where he took a bottle of red wine from the rack. He opened the bottle and poured out two large measures, ordering her to take off her coat and join him at the table for a glass of wine.

She did as she was told and sat down with a deep sigh.

He then proceeded to tell her that this was a reason to celebrate. That good times were waiting to make an appearance and that she was now free to wander in the fields of flowers where in time the thorns that pierced her heart would be extracted by the gentle hand of a future lover. As the wine flowed, the more flowery his words became. He could see a smile and some colour slowly return to her face. It pleased him.

"You do talk some shit. Anyway, you bugger, where's my rent?"

"Anna, I'm really sorry. I've got myself into debt and I just can't breathe at the moment."

"What the hell are you spending all your money on? You only have to provide for yourself."

"I just don't earn enough to cover everything. You'd be surprised. The more time I spend in teaching the more in debt I find myself. I have to get out at the end of this year. Start again and do something different. But the good news is that I should be starting a part time job soon, so I will be able to pay you back and get back on top of things."

"You mentioned that. Well done by the way." She raised her glass to him. "What will you be doing?"

"Oh, nothing major. I went for an interview at a college in central London. Teaching English to adults for a couple of evenings a week." The lie left a bitter taste. "I've agreed in principle but I'm just waiting for written confirmation. It's really good pay for easy work." He gulped down a mouthful of his wine but it failed to wash away the bitterness. He ruefully acknowledged that it was a lie he might have to get used to telling. The wine and his attentiveness helped soften her stance and she agreed reluctantly to allow him some more time to pay the rent. Manny allowed her to talk some more while he simply listened and subtly reassured her whenever her self-doubt re-surfaced. Anna confided in him that although she had benefited financially from the divorce she felt all the poorer. He found himself having to suppress his excitement once again as he told her he would be around any time she needed a chat and that one evening, on account of her being such a sympathetic and understanding landlady, he'd make her a special meal. Cooked and prepared from a secret family recipe his Spanish Grandma had passed down to him.

"You're quite sweet really. I bet your students love you," she replied before adding that he could also come to her should he need any help or advice. Manny allowed the conversation to slide away before asking if she could possibly see her way to lending him a "few quid" until he got paid. He promised to pay her back in full.

CHAPTER FOUR

It was nearly 7.00am on Tuesday morning when Manny first stirred. He woke up feeling fully rested. Usually he'd be awake wrestling with his demons as early as 4.00am. He would then struggle to get any more sleep, meaning that he always began the day fatigued and battle-weary. Feeling a jolt of happiness that he had slept so well, he hoped that the wind of change had started to blow softly in his direction. It was certainly a positive sign. He showered and dressed, choosing to wear the same suit that had served him so well the day before. He picked a clean but creased white shirt from the bundle of washed clothes that was piled in the corner of the room. Finally, he put on a tie, grabbed his laptop, headed out of the house and made his way towards the station. He thought about having a coffee at his local café, Barrissimo, but decided against it. Instead, he chose to visit the mini-market to buy some coffee, milk and biscuits for his unsuspecting work colleagues. There was a rota pinned to the English department office noticeboard informing them as to whose turn it was to supply the refreshments, but Manny was unsure as to when exactly he had last bought some.

The generosity and kindness Anna had shown him the night before was contagious. With the £100 she had loaned him he felt he should treat his colleagues to some decent biscuits for a change and he'd been sufficiently observant during their weekly staff meetings to be aware of their preferred choices. The price of a decent brand of coffee confirmed his belief that indeed it had been a while since he had purchased any coffee for the department.

Quick to remind himself that he hadn't solved his money problems just yet, Manny opted to buy a cheap brand on this occasion.

He arrived at school with plenty of time to spare. The staff car park was relatively empty and the students did not enter the school grounds for another forty-five minutes. Apart from when the bell sounded at the end of the day, this was usually his favourite time of day. He liked the sound of silence and the smell of the clean building. The peaceful setting was in stark contrast to the scenes that waited to be played out during the course of a hectic school day.

After tidying his desk he made his way over to the staffroom, where he proudly placed the coffee and biscuits he'd bought that morning in the department's cupboard. He was hoping that his thoughtfulness would help sweep away any bad feelings that lingered over his calling in sick the previous day. The first morning back after having time off ill was always an uncomfortable experience. Fridays were usually a better day to be off as people tended to forget about his absence over the weekend. Manny expected the usual doubting looks and sarcastic comments as he feebly tried to explain away his illness. More people seemed to notice if you were off at the start of the week. There would be the probing questions from members of the senior leadership team perfectly worded to sound more concerned than suspicious. Manny was also expecting fierce words from Maureen Baxter, Head of the English department, on account of his not phoning or emailing through any work for his classes in accordance with official school policy. He congratulated himself for arriving early so that he had more time to prepare for any issues that were likely to flare up.

Further evidence that his luck might be changing presented itself on entering the small staffroom kitchen. An empty jar of coffee of a far superior brand than the one he had just purchased sat on the side, waiting to be recycled. Looking around the sparse staffroom, he ensured that no eyes were upon him. Swiftly, he poured his coffee into the empty jar and disposed of his own.

Fortunately at this time of morning it was unusual to find many people around. He made himself a cup of coffee and took his seat in his usual corner of the room where he liked to listen to the early morning banter that was swapped between teachers just before the Head and the rest of the senior leadership team entered, ready to begin the morning briefing. He used to welcome the conversation with certain colleagues as they arrived ready to face another day of teaching but lately he'd been finding it all a bit of a strain, wanting only to get another day out the way.

He sat drinking his coffee in anticipation of the barrage of questions that would undoubtedly fly his way. The ones loaded with ridicule, asked by those colleagues he was closest to, were not the problem. It was the more genuine questions that troubled him the most. He knew he'd have to sit tight and see out the worst of the early morning storm. He hoped the interrogation would not last long. The staffroom could at times resemble a bear pit, he thought idly. Full of gossip and laced with character assassination. He'd always believed that it would never affect him but now he was no longer sure. As he sat there, he tried to recall the last time he'd actually felt calm inside but soon gave up. *I've been in teaching far too long*, he thought. *I'm becoming institutionalized, always feeling the need to look happy and in control.*

Dom Bonner was the first person he saw walk through the doors into the room. Bonner was a technology teacher who also happened to be responsible for organising the daily cover. It was a role Manny would not want to do. He often saw Bonner under pressure trying to find enough teachers to cover the lessons of those who were absent.

"Morning, Dom."

"Mr Rodriguez. Are we feeling better?"

"A bit better thanks, Dom. Sorry about the short notice. I was in a bad way." He rubbed his stomach and grimaced, hoping his actions would explain.

"It's not me you should be apologising to. You didn't leave me much time to find a supply teacher so I had to ask some of your colleagues to cover your lessons. They weren't too happy. Andy Moran especially. I heard that he had a torrid time trying to control your Year Tens. He never got any work out of them."

"Really? The little bastards. I've got them first lesson, I'll have a word with them." His concern was genuine as was his ⌐

He considered Moran to be a trusted staff room comrade. Teachers who were dedicated to improving the lives of their students instantly won his respect.

As he pinned up the day's cover list, Bonner turned towards him with a sinister grin.

"What? What is it?" he asked impatiently. "You can't have used me for any cover. I'm teaching all day today." Manny knew that Bonner would have been more apologetic if he had indeed used him for cover. His curiosity grew but he suspected that he already knew what it was all about.

"Don't worry. You'll soon find out."

"I know. It's Baxter, isn't it? Was she angry about not receiving any cover work from me?"

Bonner nodded. "Angry? That's putting it mildly. Breathing fire, she was. Pleased I'm not in your shoes and I don't think that was the only reason she was gunning for you."

Manny jerked his head and raised his eyebrows. "That woman is on a mission to destroy me."

Other members of staff started to arrive, sitting in their usual seats in time for the morning meeting. Andy Moran came over and sat next to Manny. He taught art and had entered teaching at a later stage than most. Manny was two years younger but had gained more experience in teaching. He had helped Moran to settle in at the school after he'd experienced a rather difficult initiation period. Moran liked to confide in him about all matters. Work as well as personal. Manny was happy to listen but preferred to draw a line when it came to discussing his own private life. His early experiences had warned him to trust no one. Manny understood that this way of thinking was flawed but he felt powerless to change it. He knew it made him the poorer person. He believed that he had his parents to thank for embedding him with this character defect. The emotional debris he had been exposed to during their violent and very dysfunctional relationship had wounded him deeply. They had lived in Spain at the time due to his Spanish father's reluctance to settle in England. Eventually his mother, who was English, fled her violent husband's drunken rages all the way back to the sanctuary of her parents' home in England. Regrettably, she was only able to take her two daughters with her. To this day Manny never knew why. Apart from his father spouting his bitter views, nobody had taken the time to explain to him why it was on coming home from school one day a little boy was unable to find his mother and sisters no matter where he searched or how loud he'd shouted. The wound had never been dressed. But now was not the time for self pity.

"You made it in then? I was cursing you yesterday. I had to cover your period 3. What a nightmare I had. How do you cope with them? They're awful. So rude. So disobedient."

"Yeah, so I hear. I'm sorry you got lumbered. Sounds like I owe you a pint later."

"A pint? You owe me more than a pint. They acted like I wasn't even there. Especially Sarah Godfrey and Kamran Ahmed. Honestly, mate, they made my life hell. I was trying to get my Year Nine reports done. Maureen came in at the start to settle them down and set them some work. They were okay for a bit, but then all hell broke loose! Kamran started throwing pencil cases around the room. I tried to give him a detention but he just laughed at me. Then Sarah decided to start writing the names of boys she loved all over the board. It didn't matter how loud I shouted she just wouldn't return to her seat." On hearing this, Manny felt let down by his class and was determined to let them know of his hurt. He could instantly tell by the tiredness around Moran's eyes that it had troubled him through the night. His face was ashen, eyes bloodshot, hair more wild than usual. It was hard to switch off from work after experiencing a lesson where you'd lost control of the classroom. Manny remembered the early days when he would get home and head straight for his room, shutting the door on the unruly world. He would lie on his bed paralysed with doubts wondering whether he would ever win back control. He felt guilty. Andy was a decent man who gave freely of his own time to help the students achieve. He'd often run school art clubs and would help them out with their projects and coursework.

"Listen, mate, I'm really sorry you had to go through that but I will sort them out. I promise."

He wanted to do more to help Moran.

"Most of them were reasonably good it was just those two who spoiled it. It was bad. I was bad," he said rubbing his tired eyes. "I should have chosen a different career. I sometimes feel like I'm in the wrong film."

Manny felt a sadness come over him. He recalled how much energy and joy Moran had shown when he'd first started working at the school.

"Anyway, are you okay?" Moran asked.

"Yeah, I'm fine now cheers. I had to sort some business out." Manny decided it was best not to elaborate. A short silence followed and he knew Moran was waiting, wanting to hear more.

He told him about the prank with the coffee jars instead. He hoped it would help cheer him up. Moran did indeed find it funny and they both began to laugh.

A stern yet familiar voice interrupted the laughter.

"Pleased to see that you're feeling better, Mr Rodriguez."

He looked up to see Maureen Baxter standing in front of him with her arms folded giving him the hard look that she normally reserved for the students.

"Hello, Maureen, I was just…"

She never allowed him to finish

"Are you free anytime today?"

"No. Sorry, Maureen, I'm teaching all five lessons today. I don't have any free periods until tomorrow."

"Then I need to see you in my office at break time today please. There are one or two matters I urgently need to discuss with you."

"Sure. No problem. I'll bring some coffee and biscuits, shall I?"

Moran tried to stifle a laugh.

Baxter cast her gaze onto Moran and furrowed her brow. "How are we today, Mr Moran?" He sat back in his chair in an attempt to escape her burning glare. "Can I remind you to collect work in and leave the room tidy next time you cover a lesson in the English department? We're trying to raise standards here at the school not lower them." Baxter looked straight at Manny before continuing. "While we're on the subject of standards, Mr Rodriguez, can I see your Year Eleven's coursework folders together with their grades and remember to bring along your Year Nine reports which were due in last week." She marched off to find a spare seat without waiting for a reply. Manny and Moran looked at each other mouths open in exasperation. Manny was first to speak.

"I will hand in my resignation at the end of this term. She can go to hell. That woman talks to me like I'm one of her students. It's unbelievable."

"How long is it before she retires?" Moran asked, slowly shaking his head.

"Good morning, everyone. Any messages today?" the head teacher asked. A sign to everybody that the morning briefing had begun. Manny didn't listen to the messages being announced around the room that morning. In his mind he was still having a heated discussion with Baxter. It was always the same. Words and clever responses always came to him too late. The woman terrified him. He would bide his time and wait for the right moment to tell her what he thought of her and the lack of faith she'd had in his teaching. He sensed that the moment was not too far away.

The staff football team had a match that Friday after school. It was the only message that he bothered to listen to. He didn't hear the beginning of the announcement so he was unsure whether they were playing home or away. But that never worried him. Manny enjoyed these matches that had been arranged against staff from other local schools. He gave the thumbs up to Phil Young from the P.E. Department to confirm that as usual he was able to play.

With briefing over, the staffroom emptied. First lesson was ten minutes away. Manny headed back to his classroom. He still had a bit of time to prepare for the busy day ahead. Feeling hurt and bitter, he knew he wanted out. The motivation he needed to face the day had once again evaporated. He hoped to hear from the agency soon.

The eruption of noise coming down the corridor told him that first lesson was on its way. Manny exhaled loudly, stood up and waited in the frame of his classroom door.

"Come on, Year Tens, hurry up and line up quietly please."
He allowed a certain amount of laughing and talking to continue,
choosing to ignore all the 'good mornings' and questions that
they bombarded at him. Still standing by his door he continued
to allow the chattering to continue. The students wrestled and
pushed to get in line. He frowned menacingly. Some of the
students were quick to read his body language and stood still,
waiting to enter the room politely. More followed suit but a few
of the boys at the end of the line were slow to pick up on the
message that Manny's silence was sending out. He carried on
frowning, looking towards the back of the line. The students
warned each other to keep quiet and stand still. Now the whole
class stood in silence. He looked down the line and made eye
contact with Kamran Ahmed. He held his stare for a short while,
making the boy feel uncomfortable. Kamran looked away with a
silly grin on his face.

"Right, that's five minutes you have kept me waiting. Don't
waste any more of my time," Manny warned. "Now, I want you to
go in quietly, sit down and get your books out. I want to speak to
you all." The students began to enter his classroom in single file.
Manny was hoping for somebody to make a noise. He didn't have
to wait long. A couple of students started talking to each other.

"I SAID QUIET! Jones, take that scarf off now!"

The class knew that something had upset him. Manny would
usually adopt a more friendly approach but not today and he
guessed that they'd know the reason why.

"Can you get out your Anthology books please and turn to
page 72. Can you also open your exercise books and underline
the work you did yesterday and neatly write today's date with the
title 'Comparing Poems'. He wrote the date and title onto the
board for them. He then put down his marker pen and stood in
front of his class. "I'm sorry I wasn't here yesterday but I was on
a course. Nicky, can you tell me what you had to do yesterday?"
Nicky was one of his more able students. He knew she would
give him an accurate account.

"Yes, sir. We had to finish reading the poem that we started
with you on Friday and then answer some questions."

"Thanks, Nicky. Can I see your book please? He walked over to her desk and checked her work. "Not bad but it's unlike you not to have completed all the questions, isn't it?" He had expected her to do some of the work, if not all of it, even with a disruptive atmosphere. She was an honest and reliable student.

"No, sir. Sorry, sir." He saw her cheeks begin to burn so he moved on.

"In fact, can you all open your books so I can see and check the work that you did for me yesterday?"

A couple of students raised their hands to tell him that they had been absent. He made a note of the names and told them he would check on the register. This would deter anyone wanting to use the same excuse.

"Kamran, what did you learn in yesterday's lesson?"

Silence filled the room.

"Come on, don't be shy. It's not like you not to have anything to say."

Kamran Ahmed was a big, powerful lad who liked to intimidate those around him. Manny walked over to his desk looked at his book.

"Kamran, were you here yesterday?"

"Yeah."

"PARDON?" The bark made him jump.

"Yes, sir." This time he answered with more respect and Manny had not only his attention, he had the attention of the whole class.

"Well, in that case would you mind telling me where your work is?"

Kamran lowered his gaze, shrugging his shoulders.

"Don't ignore me, young man! I'm waiting for an answer."

"I didn't do it, sir."

"Tell me, Kamran, why do you think your mum and dad work so hard?" Manny knew that his parents owned and ran a successful local printing business. "Come on, Kamran, speak up. When they're at work, working hard, what do you think they're hoping that you're doing?"

"Learning stuff, sir."

40

"What would they think if they saw how you behaved in yesterday's lesson? Sara, were you here yesterday?"

"Yes, sir."

"It's just that I can't see any work from yesterday in your book. In fact, tell me, Sarah, did you do any writing yesterday?"

"No, sir. Sorry, Mr Rodriguez. I didn't write anything because I didn't know what to write. I couldn't understand it."

"Sarah, look at me." For the first time she looked straight at him and he could tell she was close to tears. "I'm going to ask you once more because I'm getting fed up with this. Did you do any writing yesterday?"

Sarah finally knew where this conversation was leading. She didn't want to go there. Manny had an excellent relationship with most of his students and he was hoping that they would see and feel his disappointment. He always showed his students respect and he expected the same respect back. To him, this provided an opportunity for a short lecture on the subject.

Sarah finally spoke up. "Yes, sir. I did write. I was writing on the board... sorry, sir."

The silence he allowed gave each student a chance to contemplate his or her own behaviour.

"Kamran and Sarah, I will speak to you both later. I can't begin to tell you just how disappointed I am in you all. Why did nobody stop the troublemakers? What gives you the right to act like that when you have a different member of staff? Kamran? Sarah?"

They silently shook their heads.

"You wouldn't do it to me. I heard about everything you did yesterday. Shocking. I was looking forward to seeing your parents again later this month, at the Year Ten's parents' evening. I wanted to tell them about the good progress you've been making in English this year. I don't know what to say now. I even said to Mr Moran that he would not have any trouble with you. I told him that you were one of my favourite groups. I'm really feeling bad now. Mr Moran is a good bloke. He's on your side. Do you want all the good teachers to leave? I suggest to you all that you make time to say sorry to him. He's here because he wants to

41

help you get somewhere. An honest man trying to earn a living. Well, I hope you never find yourselves working in a place where the people there make your life hell. It's only a year and a half away before you leave. Do you think you're ready? Anyway, I've said enough. I don't want to hear another sound for the rest of the lesson. Make sure you finish the work from today as well as the work from yesterday. I'll be collecting your books at the end of the lesson to see how much you've done. I can't be bothered to speak to you today. I'm far too upset with you all." *That's enough, I don't want to overdo it*, he thought. He could sense by the atmosphere that the message had hit home.

For the rest of the hour they all tried to show him how sorry they were. They either tried to catch his eye with an apologetic smile or they would pretend to stretch or lean back so he'd be able to see how much work they had done. Manny knew that they were not bad students. He understood that young people preferred to know where their boundaries were. They might moan when he set them lots of homework and then get upset if he ever had to tell them off and give them a detention for not doing it. But, without knowing it, he suspected that they actually wanted the discipline. It somehow meant that someone cared.

Manny soon got back into the routine. He enjoyed the rest of the day teaching lower school and his lessons seemed to fly by. Luckily, Maureen Baxter had put off their meeting at breaktime due to a fight breaking out in her classroom just beforehand. She did find time, though, to write him a long list of the things she was disappointed and concerned about. She had rescheduled their meeting for the following day. This allowed him a bit of time to try and get on top of things. On his way home he turned on his mobile phone and found that he had one message. It was Louise from the agency asking him to contact them at the office when he could. Not for the first time Manny wondered what he was getting himself into. He felt the anxiety and excitement start to bubble up.

Manny sat on his bed for a few moments, wishing he could lie back and have a sleep as he normally did after a full day's teaching. But he knew he couldn't. He got up and paced around his room. There was a phone call to make. It felt like he was having to make a call to ask a girl out on a date when not being entirely sure of hearing the right answer. He shook his head in disbelief at his indecisiveness. When and why had his confidence diminished? Had he ever had any in the first place?

Manny sat back down on the edge of the bed, the phone waiting on his bedside table. His plan of getting his school work into some kind of order in time for his rearranged meeting with Maureen now looked doomed. His priorities kept changing. He suddenly remembered something Virginia had mentioned. *She was right*, he thought. *Money does play a role in helping us to reach a decision*. Manny picked up his phone and made the call to the office. Louise answered and thanked him for calling back. She informed him that Virginia was happy to move on to the next stage.

Louise asked if he would be able to email over a couple of recent photos of himself so she could upload one onto their website. He stood holding the phone to his ear, trying to recall her face. He dropped his eyes just to check he'd got his laptop with him before confirming that he could. Louise seemed to sense his apprehension. She assured him that only their members would have access to the site. Manny nodded but he still didn't like it. The thought of his image being on a website for an escort agency stirred up considerable anxiety. He wondered if things were proceeding too quickly.

CHAPTER
FIVE

Dr Sasha Harrington left her office and headed for the university car park. Her busy day was not quite over. Before she could relax in the comfortable surroundings of her home she had another challenge to face. The busy London roads. Sasha smiled to herself. Deep down she felt a vague sense of relief. The difficult part was over. Scaffolding and dust sheets were now a thing of the past. The money had been well spent. The desired results had been accomplished. She had been able to put some distance between herself and her painful past. New fixtures and furnishings had altered everything, both literally and metaphorically. She embraced the sanctuary her home now provided.

There was one disappointment at the completion of the work, however. Sasha had to admit that she missed the flirting with the burly builders. Their cheeky behaviour and witty comments had often made her laugh. Having men around the place had been a novelty she had thoroughly enjoyed. She had not always been able to enjoy the company of males. The boys at the boarding school she had attended had made her life a living hell, and the anguish that this had once caused her was still able to filter through, despite all the efforts she had made to try and forget.

For someone with such a meticulous nature, living for the best part of a year in a building site had been a severe test of her sanity. In the past she would have easily succumbed to the stress. But not any more. She had changed.

Her initial thought was simply to sell the house which she had inherited from her parents and travel the world, living on her inheritance and the money raised from the sale of the family home. She was the only child and sole benefactor of her wealthy father's estate which for her had been both a blessing and a curse. Sasha had envisioned living her life the same way as a migrating bird. Constantly in search of warmer climates where she would be free to travel and become a wise spiritual wanderer. In idyllic settings, she would continue to indulge her passion for the works of Rumi, the 13th century Persian mystic poet. But during the time spent in rehabilitation and sessions with her psychologist, she had come to recognise that these were romantic yet incoherent thoughts made during a time of desolation. She was a new woman now. Stronger and more self-assured. She had stumbled across a way to manage the torment she suffered due to the fact that her father had barely acknowledged her while he was alive. He had never made any attempt to hide the obvious disappointment she had been to him. Consequently she had spent many fruitless years in search of love and acceptance, hoping to fill the void her absent father had left her.

The impulsiveness she had felt on cashing in on the property had for now subsided and it delighted her that she had been able to carry out her plans. Like the house she had also undergone a metamorphosis. She could not help but wonder whether her father would have approved of all the changes she'd made. She very much doubted it. But his fears of her destroying herself on account of the riches his death would bring had been unfounded. He had left strict instructions and certain conditions in his will. Controlling to the very end, she thought. One condition he stipulated in his will was that she could access her trust fund only after reaching the age of thirty. Even her mother had come to blame her for her father's slow demise. She claimed that the years he spent worrying and living with the shame of her 'immoral behaviour' had taken a profound toll on his health. Sasha still carried a heavy heart that neither of her parents were around to witness the accomplishments she'd achieved in her life. The money they had thrown at her and her education had not gone entirely to waste. Achieving a doctorate in Persian literature, she liked to believe, had proved that. Although reluctantly she could still hear the disapproving voice of her father questioning whether 'announcing oneself as an historian on the rather vague topic of mystical poets' warranted the same title that had been bestowed upon himself for his medical expertise.

The renovation performed on the house had helped to conceal the bleak memories of her past and she rejoiced at the fact that at last she had found some peace. Whenever she grew tired of the world, she was able to find sanctuary in long walks on the common, losing herself in its wild beauty. She would often do this during her earlier years when she was home from boarding school. During those confusing years at the school, she had been helped by the warm words of a teacher she had once confided in. He had told her that the walks were a good thing for her to do and that she was not to worry about crying as her tears would help the flowers to grow. It was the same teacher who had introduced her to the poet Rumi. Sasha would always be grateful. Growing up, the words of the mystical poet, the surrounding wetlands and the views of the River Thames had all played an important part in saving her from the inner demons that at one time threatened to destroy her.

Sasha threw her keys on the kitchen counter and checked the phone. No messages. She took a shower and put on fresh clothes. She poured herself a large glass of wine and lit a cigarette, ignoring the silence and the emptiness of the house. Sitting in her favourite chair, Sasha looked out across the riverside view and gave herself permission to sink deep into thought. This was always a good time for her to unwind and reflect on the events of the day. It had been a tough time for her of late but things were improving. The malicious gossip at work was beginning to subside and she believed that the majority of the people there were understanding. A vast improvement on her previous place of work, although it bothered her that her colleagues had been slow in inviting her to join any of the social gatherings which regularly occurred. But she understood why. Her psychologist had forewarned her that it might take time for her to be accepted and he had been proved right. He had also encouraged her to be patient and brave when developing new social networks. People would eventually become sympathetic towards her needs, he would constantly reassure her.

It had been some time now since she had been out on any proper dates for fear of experiencing further rejection. Instead, she opted to devote most of her free time devouring volumes of Persian poetry, preparing her work in isolation. She would fret that her life was passing her by and, although the thought of growing old alone was for her inconceivable, in her wisdom she realized that it was becoming ever more plausible. It confused her that she was able to deliver talks and presentations in front of large audiences yet had to pay someone to accompany her out on a date. She was growing tired of all the excuses she had offered herself for using the agency. The truth stared her in the face. It was an arrangement that in the beginning had seemed to work and had many advantages. It had started as a safe way of boosting her self-esteem at a time when she was getting to know herself all over again. But lately a sense of shame had entered the debate which would rage inside her soul the morning after. She would swear to herself that it would not happen again. That she would be like all the other lonely people her age. From somewhere she would find the courage to date men using the more traditional methods women used.

Sasha poured herself another glass of wine and headed for the sanctuary of her study where she switched on her computer and checked on her forthcoming agenda. Sasha liked wine not just for its taste but because it provided her with temporary confidence in her own worth – something she only really felt under the influence of drink or when sharing her knowledge of Rumi. Both had the power to liberate her. Work dominated her time during the days, as usual, but there wasn't anything of a more personal nature to get excited about booked in for the coming week. This fact subdued her. Ignoring the feeling, she focused instead on the talk she had agreed to present at the London Metropolitan School of Philosophy the following Tuesday. She sighed. It was not the talk that worried her. She felt honoured that her knowledge warranted an invitation to deliver a talk on the topic of Shams' influence on Rumi and his poetry. The evening was part of the school's celebration of Cultures Week and she felt enthusiastic at the opportunity. The fact that her presence had been specifically requested was enough to delight her. She had delivered several similar lectures in the past and it was something she took great pride in. In a strange way she felt most at peace discussing her favourite Persian poet. Rumi's life story was full of intrigue and drama mixed with intense creative outbursts. She could identify with the mystical poet's words when he spoke of his pain and longings through his poems. She'd felt a deep connection with him from the very first time she'd read his work.

It was the social gathering arranged for after her presentation that troubled her most. The invitation stated that she was welcome to bring a guest to the private bar for the post talks gathering. Sasha was becoming more and more self-conscious whenever she attended these gatherings alone. She so much wanted to show her peers that her personal life was as much of a success as her professional status. Her profession often brought her into contact with handsome men and it irked her that she had never been romantically approached. People were keen to discuss her work and praise her presentations but that was as far as it went. She sighed wearily.

Lighting another cigarette, she picked up her wine glass and stood looking out of the window. The winter darkness was already beginning to cover the surrounding grounds for the night. She stood staring out for a long time, then went back to her desk. She could feel the alcohol start to take effect. Tapping a pencil on the desk, she pondered a short while. She had promised herself and her psychologist that she would work harder in not resorting to this type of behaviour any more. Her eyes gazed vacantly at the computer screen while she considered the consequences of repeating her behaviour patterns and acting on her impulse. Clicking onto her favourites, she scrolled down the list in search of Perfect Company's web address. The website came up instantly and she proceeded to enter her eight digit membership number. It was easy to recall. Clicking onto the heading titled 'male escorts', she waited for the images to appear. This time she wanted a younger one who looked and sounded tougher. A character who was more manful in his mannerisms. Moody. She had been disappointed with the last man the agency had sent her. Too well groomed and far too gentlemanly, she had furiously emailed her feedback to the girls in the office. She had expected better for the amount of money she had spent over the last couple of years. The ones who were too eager and keen to please simply reminded her that she had indeed paid for the service of their company, thereby clumsily shattering the fragile illusion and inviting the inevitable guilt and turmoil to arrive prematurely.

She spent the next few minutes lingering over the images of the male escorts the agency had at their disposal. She was considering a couple of guys that she had used before when she became aware of a new image emerging onto the screen. Sasha flushed excitedly. She clicked onto the gorgeous image that had presented itself and read through his profile. *Sounds perfect*, she thought. Feeling a growing pleasure, Sasha unhesitatingly dialled the office and asked to be put straight through to Virginia.

The cheerful receptionist recognised her voice and obliged instantly.

Virginia listened to Sasha's request before telling her a bit about the man in question. She went on to tell her that because of her loyalty and the fact that the escort was new to the company she would offer her a slight discount on the first booking, in return for some feedback of course. If she was happy with his service and decided to proceed with a second date then the standard rate would have to apply. Virginia ended her side of the conversation in her customary manner and said that she would be in touch soon. Just before the call ended, Sasha added an urgent plea that the agency would act promptly in confirming her request. She could feel her expectations swell as she began to fantasise about the potential date with the attractive stranger who'd appeared on her screen. Sasha hoped Virginia would be able to deliver. She switched off the desk lamp and remained sitting in the dark, ready to ride the upsurge of energy that always greeted her whenever she decided to dance with danger. After a short while she got up from her desk, took down some books from the shelf and headed for the sitting room where she stoked the fire before reclining back on the sofa as she tried to focus, making notes in preparation for Tuesday evening. She felt invigorated. It had been a long time since she had felt like this and she revelled in the feeling. She hoped she would not be made to wait for confirmation too much longer.

CHAPTER
SIX

"There is much more to teaching than being able to deliver interesting lessons and having strong classroom management techniques, Manolo. I agree that these are tremendous qualities to have. But it's also imperative that you're competent enough to display good administration skills. It's vital that your record keeping is kept up to date and in reasonable order. I have to admit that I was horrified upon entering your classroom on Monday. Year Nine reports were unfinished, attendance figures for the first part of the academic term had yet to be completed, schemes of work were simply stuffed into your drawers and NOT filed in their appropriate folders. Your Year Ten and Eleven coursework folders have not been graded using the appropriate marking criteria as discussed at the last meeting. Ah. Yes. How silly of me. You weren't there, were you? When was the last time you actually attended one of our departmental meetings? Oh, and before I forget, I strongly advise you stick to the calendar the school provides for you. I don't really think that a copy of FHM's hottest babes calendar is at all suitable for a classroom teacher to keep on their desk. Do you?"

"I was disgusted on discovering where you've written your personal reminder for the Year Ten parents' evening. This is a school, Manolo, not a mechanics garage."

The scheduled Wednesday meeting with Maureen Baxter, head of English, was in full flow. Not once had she given him a window of opportunity to answer her questions. Manny lowered his head and allowed himself to shrink into the chair. He felt like a naughty schoolboy as she savagely tore off the remaining strips of his credibility.

For the second time that week he felt hurt and bitter. But he decided to ride the storm out and keep quiet. He would have his moment one day soon, he reminded himself.

"Is that it, Maureen? May I go now? I have lots to be getting on with."

"Yes, that is all for now. Oh, before I forget, thanks for the coffee and biscuits that you brought in on Tuesday. So unexpected. Your choice of coffee cannot be faulted. It tasted as coffee should taste: rich. Remember to finish your reports and all your marking tonight. See you tomorrow."

He was still upset when he got home. In his mind he continued a heated discussion with Baxter. Again, as always with her, it was only after the bollocking that he was able to come up with the clever, witty comeback lines that he struggled to find at the time. The woman angered easily and could be unpleasant to both students and colleagues. Manny had lost count of how many times he had entered her classes and noticed the students either stifled with boredom or stiff with fear. Never did he witness the happy, healthy learning environment the school inspectors constantly harped on about. Her manners and methods were beginning to drive him to despair.

He went into the kitchen to make himself a sandwich. He looked in the fridge. Old tomatoes and some hard cheese were the only items that belonged to him. He heaved a deep sigh as he recalled his present circumstances. Helping himself to Anna's milk and cereal, he poured them both into a large mixing bowl. Just as he was about to start eating, his mobile rang. He struggled to get it out of his pocket. It was the agency.

"Hello, is that you, Manny? It's Virginia Griffin from the agency. Are you free to talk?"

He swallowed hard and felt the knot tighten in his stomach.

"Yes, of course. How are you, Virginia?"

"I'm very well, thank you. Listen, I'll keep things brief. Are you available for work this Friday and possibly next Tuesday? It's with a respected client of ours. She liked the look of you and was impressed by the profile Louise posted on the web page. Basically, she wants you to pick her up from her home in Barnes and would like to get to know you over a meal on Friday night. If that goes well, then she needs you to accompany her to a talk she has to attend this coming Tuesday evening. You would be expected to remain by her side for the evening, acting like the doting boyfriend. Easy money really. This is it, Manny. What do you say?"

Manny thought about what she had said. The moment he had been waiting for had arrived. He did not know how to respond. The feeling that things were proceeding too fast for his liking resurfaced. He felt unnerved. Virginia instantly picked up on the reasons for his silence.

"Look," she continued, "you're either interested in making money or you're not. But please don't waste my time or anybody else's. I can find plenty of willing workers to fill the booking, it's not a problem. What's it to be? I'm far too busy to be dealing with indecisive time wasters. You're either available or you're not. This is the only chance you're going to get. Do I make myself clear?"

"No, it's fine. I'm just a bit surprised to hear from you so quickly. Don't get me wrong. I'm glad you called."

"Take it as a compliment. We don't mess around here. Louise is very good at her job. You have the opportunity to earn good money. It seems someone has taken a shine to you and as far as I can see it shouldn't really be a difficult assignment."

"I'm available on both nights." He made a mental note to take a look at Louise's handiwork on the website for himself.

"Excellent. Louise or Monica will be contacting you shortly to fill you in on all the necessary details. Dr Sasha Harrington is the client's name. Very well known to us. Wealthy. A historian of sorts, I believe. Into poetry of some kind. With you being an English teacher, you should find that you have plenty in common. Play your cards right here, Manny, and you could be onto a winner."

Manny thought about it. It sounded perfect. Despite his initial doubts, he couldn't foresee anything that he would not be able to handle.

"Great. Thanks, Virginia. I will not disappoint," he announced with a little more assurance.

"No. I'm sure you won't. Just think of the money. She pays very well. There is one small thing that you should know about Dr Sasha Harrington."

"Is there? What's that?"

"She's a transsexual."

CHAPTER
SEVEN

Manny woke with a start. At first he thought he had overslept but a quick glance at the bedside clock calmed him. It was only 5.15am. Falling back against the pillows with a familiar weary sigh, Manny closed his eyes in an improbable attempt to steal some precious sleep, but his mind was determined to revisit the dark thoughts, laced with insecurities, that had plagued the night before. He'd hoped that things would feel different come the morning.

Despite it being early he decided to get up and make use of the time. Lifting the pile of school folders that had been waiting, some time now, for his attention, he placed them on his desk and searched for the enthusiasm to begin the laborious task.

Before making a start, however, there was something more urgent that needed clarifying. The argument with himself had penetrated his mind late into the night, blatantly delaying his sleep. The tournament of words and questions seemed to bounce around inside his head constantly throughout the night. What did being a transsexual actually mean? That was the question that still lingered from the night before.

Switching on his laptop, he went in search of the definitive answer. After a short while he discovered that he'd been right. On this occasion however, that gave him little satisfaction. The amount of links and adverts he found devoted to the subject managed to surprise him. Also, some of the images made him recoil like a scolded pup.

With a tense curiosity he clicked onto a couple of the links.

Immediately the laptop screen was ambushed by all kinds of transsexual paraphernalia. Manny then spent the next fifteen minutes frantically trying to erase all evidence of the sites that he'd just visited. Some of the images only served to heighten his fear of what he was considering doing in order to transform his money woes.

It occurred to him that he might not be able to find the courage he needed if he was to execute his plan. A depressive cloud soon overcame him. Once again his outlook looked bleak. He sat there with a perplexed look on his face.

For now, the best thing I can do is not to think about it, he ordered himself. A tough day of teaching still lay ahead before any difficult moral decision had to be made.

Picking up his pen, he set about trying to ease his bulging workload. He was able to focus for about an hour before deciding to get ready and to set off for work.

On entering the staffroom he headed for his usual seat in the far corner. The place was beginning to fill and he witnessed all the commotion the morning usually brought.

Older women sat in a cluster, gossiping happily to each other, awaiting the start of the morning briefing. The more senior members of staff sat in distant pairs, busily whispering in quiet undertones.

Dom Bonner was busy dealing with the usual rumpus that always greeted him whenever he pinned up the day's cover list to the board. Nobody wanted to find out at the beginning of the working day that they were required to stand in for an absent colleague's class. Having to forfeit a brief moment of calm during a turbulent day was never easy to accept without a desperate fight. Manny could afford to sit back on this particular occasion, not needing to get involved. A full day of teaching lay ahead without any free periods.

The wearier looking teachers sat slumped in their chairs, staring vacantly into space, desperately searching for the spark that would allow them to get through another torturous day. Manny thought he understood a little of what it was they hoped to find when they peered intently into the void. Memories.

Memories of how they had once been free and fearless, with endless possibilities opening before them. He smiled as they remained in a trance-like state even when their younger colleagues approached them with their endless energy, eager to discuss work-related issues. He recognised the sound of their silent cry whenever he heard a sigh.

Manny wondered for a fleeting moment whether he'd ever been guilty of revealing the same expression of hopeless dejection that he was clearly able to see etched onto a number of faces scattered around the room. If he hadn't yet, he sensed that it was on its way. He was more fortunate than some, he acknowledged. Age was still on his side. Manny also knew that many had families to provide for and mortgages to pay. Responsibilities which meant that they remained firmly and somewhat reluctantly chained to the job. Even their age was starting to turn against them. It helped explain the morose look they wore. Their dejected mood evoked his sympathy.

Others seemed all too keen to display their importance to each other, talking excitedly and gesticulating wildly with their hands. For them, life still held significance and made sense. The position they held within the school gave them a status that succeeded in making them feel that they had achieved something in their lives. He could not help but wonder as to what it would feel like to be so content.

A vivid picture flashed into his mind that made his heart twitch. A picture of him walking into the packed staffroom one morning, aware that every single pair of eyes were fixed upon him. Tutting and shaking their heads in disbelief, mouthing the word 'disgusting' at him, all of them aware of the proposed plan to change his fortunes. The fear of the disgrace that would befall him if word ever got out about him becoming a male escort caused his inner self to flinch. Feeling increasingly paranoid, he wished that he had not been so quick to email Louise at the agency a recent photo of himself for her to add to their website. A knot tightened in his stomach.

"There you go, son. Get that down your neck!"

The forcefulness of the words snapped him out of his

pondering state. He jumped slightly, causing Moran to smirk.

"What's the matter with you? Baxter hasn't just made a pass at you in that English office, has she? You look petrified."

Moran, carrying two coffees, had come over and sat down in the empty seat next to him.

"No, don't be daft. Just got things on my mind, that's all."

"Girlfriend problems?"

"Yeah, something like that." The irony was not lost on him. Manny seldom talked about personal matters in front of his colleagues.

"Could you imagine having to wake up next to her though, every morning?" Moran said, nodding towards Maureen Baxter. "Her husband's a braver man than me. She's obviously the dominant force in that relationship. Poor sod," he added with a genuine sense of pity. "He should get a medal for services to mankind. Here, listen to this: I was reading one of my girlfriend's magazines the other day. Do you know what I read?" He never allowed any time for a guess so Manny simply shook his head and waited for the influx of insignificant knowledge Andy often liked to share. "That when you're feeling a bit depressed, smoking a cigarette or having a drink is not always such a bad thing. Best of all, this article said that making love really helps to lift the depression. Honestly, straight up. I asked my girlfriend whether she had read it."

"And had she?" Manny inquired, not really caring for the answer.

"Yeah, she had. But she's a top girl, my Jane. She told me I had nothing to worry about because she wasn't feeling depressed and so therefore there was no need to put the theory to the test."

Manny laughed, thinking that it was a joke.

"I can't see the sex bit working for everyone, mind," Moran continued. "A drink and a smoke maybe but imagine having to make love to some of the women in here? No way, José! Not even for a grand. No chance. I think I'd rather be depressed."

Manny shook his head in disbelief. Andy's genuine naivety and moments of vulnerability were part of the reason he liked him. He was no longer sure that Andy had meant this to sound like a joke.

Not far from them, sitting in another part of the room, sat an attractive young woman whom Manny had not seen before. She had long, fair hair and dressed fashionably. He liked the look of her energetic face which also happened to display perfect, delicate features. Something inside him melted and he briefly forgot about feeling forlorn.

"Moran, who's that girl sitting over there?"

"Where?" He looked around the room before following the direction of Manny's eyes. "Oh, her. She's the new geography teacher. Now, I can understand someone like her being able to cure depression. About bloody time this staffroom had a bit of eye candy. I'd gladly give her one."

"Good morning, gentlemen. Although I use the word 'gentlemen' loosely." Maureen Baxter's sudden arrival startled them both.

"Good morning, Maureen. I did not see you standing there."

"Do you have your diary on you, Mr Rodriguez?"

"No, not at the moment. It's in my classroom. Why? Is there a problem?"

"No, not yet. I have some dates for when I and another senior member of the leadership team would like to observe you teach. We will need to see your planning folder, an updated list of interim grades and levels for all those whom you teach. I assume that they're kept up to date?"

"Yes. Of course they are," he lied. "Is it just me you're observing?" he added, trying not to sound rattled.

"Don't fret, Mr Rodriguez. Internal audits are being carried out across the whole school in all departments. As mentioned at the last staff meeting. The school is committed to raising standards and expectations. I will be coming in on the…now, let me see…" She looked down, tapping her pen on her list. "Ah, there we are. This Friday, period 4, and first lesson next Wednesday. Do you think you will be able to remember that or would you like me to write it down for you?" she asked in a patronizing tone.

"No. I think I'll be able to manage, thanks, Maureen." Manny compressed his lips to suppress his annoyance. As she turned away to head for her seat, both Manny and Andy raised their middle fingers at her. They thought she had finished talking to them but they were wrong. They failed to disguise their actions in time and both were forced to pretend to adjust their ties.

"Oh, before I forget. There is one more thing," she continued. "Could I have photocopies of your lesson plans, together with a copy of the resources that you will be using? Thank you. Have a good day now."

"That woman terrifies me," said Moran. "She makes me nervous. How long do you think she was standing there for?"

"I don't know or care. But I did hear you say 'Sorry, Miss' to her like a naughty little boy."

"Shit, I didn't, did I? What has she done to me?"

"I don't know. But I do know that I'm sick and tired of constantly having to jump through hoops for this crap job."

Manny caught the new geography teacher quickly looking away, her eyes smiling silently.

He wondered how much of that ear bashing and dignity-sapping lecture she had overheard. He hoped that she hadn't seen the raised middle finger. He instantly discarded the feelings that stirred when he looked at her.

The head teacher together with his leadership team walked in fussily through the doors, ready to start the morning briefing.

"Morning, everybody," he bellowed. "Silence please."

Immediately, the hubbub of men's and women's voices slackened.

"Thank you." The head teacher waited for the whispering to fall silent. "Any messages?"

At once an army of people raised their arms, waiting for permission to speak. *We act just like well-behaved schoolchildren*, Manny thought.

He found it hard to listen rationally to the announcements ringing out around the room. He was feeling frustrated. It troubled him sorely that he had to sit there and listen to a female colleague's eloquent tones informing everyone of exactly how much money had been raised on the cake stall the previous day. Another female teacher asked whether all staff could be sympathetic when dealing with the troublesome Jessica Atkins of class 10KR. Her mother had contacted the school to confirm that her daughter's rabbit had passed away during the night and Jessica was feeling extremely upset and really resented coming into school today. And could teachers write in her diary the details of any homework that they set. She had trouble reading her own handwriting. Manny's face wore an expression of despondency as the other announcements faded into the background. He sensed it was going to be one of those days. The question "What am I doing here?" took up residence in his head. His mood darkened. Today everything sounded trivial but there had been a time when he used to be more empathetic.

He decided he would consider doing anything to free himself from the mental oppression that was hounding him. Nothing could be as bad as this, he quietly remarked to himself. Teaching had helped him rediscover his self-esteem and sense of self-worth but on its own, it no longer seemed enough.

Manny knew he used to be, and still was, a great teacher. Not only was he able to relate to his students and the problems they might face, but young people quickly established that it was better to keep on the right side of him so they would choose to work hard and follow his advice. Manny had gained a reputation as being someone who could actually help them with their problems. However, this came at a price. The distraction of having most of his free time and energy taken up with other people's problems meant that there was little time for him to deal with and face up to his own issues. In the past, he had welcomed the distraction, but the time had finally arrived when his own desperate situation was begging for his own individual attention.

CHAPTER
EIGHT

By the time she closed the well-thumbed research book and stretched, it was after 9.00pm.

Sasha felt calm and contented. She read through her work again before saving it onto her computer. The talk was going to be a success. She could feel it. The selection of poems that she had painstakingly chosen would help the audience to understand the longing Rumi had developed for Shams, the wandering wild holy man who could not be caged. From her years of research she'd been able to deduce that Rumi was a charming, wealthy Persian nobleman, a genius theologian and a brilliant scholar with many keen followers. Shortly after meeting Shams of Tabriz, a dervish or wandering mystic, walking the path of love, he was instantly transformed from a sober and bookish scholar into an impassioned seeker of the truth and love. His devotees were left dismayed at their teacher's recklessness. At the time it had been socially unacceptable for a man of Rumi's status to be seen socialising with such a simple wanderer. Shams may have been a powerful spiritual figure in Rumi's eyes but he was still considered poor, homeless and not from the 'elite class'. Their relationship severely stretched the social boundaries of the time, causing Rumi's pristine reputation to be ruined. After receiving repeated death threats, Shams decided to flee Rumi's home town, leaving his *grand master student* to fall into a deep state of grief, following which he spent the majority of his time outpouring his pain and loss into over 70,000 verses of poetry which he named in honour of his mentor and close spiritual friend. The book, titled *Divan-e Shams-e of Tabrizi and Massnavi*, had been a personal favourite of Dr Sasha Harrington for many years now. Rumi's words had always managed to console, pierce and lift her heart during her own fruitless search for the true meaning of love. The fact that her greatest passion had become her life's work filled her with pride. Bringing Rumi's teachings to the awareness of others had always been more than just a job to her. It was her mission. She saw it as a divine gift which could have been delivered straight from the hands of the poet himself. Tuesday night's talk was likely to be attended by other experts in the same field as hers. It was vital that she delivered with panache and style.

A memory crowded into her mind. She hoped that she was not going to be disappointed with the escort from the agency the following evening. Virginia had been very convincing in selling the new Spanish recruit. She lit a cigarette and paced the room, glancing occasionally at her computer. It was a childish game but she was feeling playful. The screen saver had not yet appeared so she left her study to fetch another glass of wine. On her return she paused to look out of the windows of the balcony doors. Sasha dearly loved that particular view which looked out across the river. She opened the doors so that she could hear the rhythmical sound of the river. The cold chill of the night pinched at her face. The view alone was worth the price of the house, no matter how many millions that was. The decision to keep the house and refurbish it had been one of her better ones.

Into the silence she began to recite one of Rumi's poems:
'I've had enough of sleepless nights,
of my unspoken grief, of my tired wisdom.
Come my treasure, my breath of life
come and dress my wounds and be my cure.
Enough of words.
Come to me without a sound.' [1]

Finishing her cigarette and sipping some more wine, she returned to the desk in her study and glanced at the monitor. He was there. She felt the adrenaline surge through her as she stared into the computer screen. He looked perfect. She noticed a slight reluctance in his dark, smouldering eyes to pose for the camera.

The cropped hair complimented his dark complexion and she liked the way his full lips framed the most gorgeous of smiles. The indent on the bridge of his nose added to his brooding quality. Using her index finger, she gently outlined his features and sighed deeply as she tried to get her heart to beat back to something like its normal pace. She smiled guiltily at her own recklessness and thought of what her psychotherapist might make of the set of circumstances that had caused this feeling of invigoration to grab hold of her emotions. She needed to cut down on her drinking. The ashtray was also loaded with butts and a blue smog was forming around the desk. Sasha stood up and went to the window to let in some fresh air. She lit another cigarette. Taking a few long drags, she stared out into the distant chill of the night sky. She felt a desire tugging at her. Not long to go now. The alcohol was once again achieving the desired results in temporarily masking her deep, inner wounds and silencing the self disgust and loathing that lingered in the dark recesses of her mind. She decided that she would allow herself another small glass before trying to get some sleep. Tomorrow she had a long day ahead of her.

CHAPTER
NINE

Manny Rodriguez was lying on his bed, sweating profusely. He'd been having a nightmare. He felt disorientated. The dawn light filtering through the gaps in the blind helped him to regain some sort of composure. On ascertaining his whereabouts he let out a sigh of relief and allowed a dry smirk to break out across his face at the insanity of it all. The dream had left him feeling disjointed and for a horrible moment he had feared the worst. That he'd not been having a bad dream at all. He remembered dreaming about how he was at work, being observed as he taught a lesson to his naughty Year Tens. The observers sitting at the back of the room consisted of the head teacher, Maureen Baxter, the attractive new geography teacher and, rather oddly, Virginia Griffin from the escort agency. They all had their pens poised ready to jot down any mistakes that he might make. He remembered feeling triumphant as he entered the classroom because for once he had found time to plan and prepare thoroughly for the lesson. All was going well as he stood confidently in front of the class, expertly addressing his students. However, as he turned his back in order to write on the board, the classroom erupted with laughter. To his horror he discovered that he was not wearing anything apart from a novelty apron with a caricature of a man's suit printed on the front and from then on everything happened in slow motion. The head teacher looked at him with rage as he tried to comfort and revive a shocked Maureen Baxter. The new geography teacher stared wide-eyed and open-mouthed before deciding to hide behind her clipboard. Virginia was standing up applauding with delight. The students were simply howling hysterically in their chairs, banging their desk tops and pointing at him. Full of shame and embarrassment, he made a strenuous effort to shuffle his way out, towards the classroom door, desperately trying not to reveal any more of his bare backside to the watching world.

The dream itself had been so bizarre he was unsure whether to laugh or cry. He did neither. The cause of the dream was easy to work out. He put it down to all the debating he'd been doing with regard to the escorting work. Friday had arrived quicker than he had hoped and the supposed date with the transsexual was drawing nearer, causing his anxieties to rise.

He lay very still with his eyes open, looking at the shadows in the room. He tried to recall the last time he'd gone to bed, slept well and had awoke feeling alive. The answer arrived promptly. He hated to admit it but it was during the carefree time he'd spent travelling with Hannah. The memory caused a flutter deep in his chest.

He decided to take control of the situation before his indecisiveness took over and paralysed him. If he had not heard from the girls in the office by lunchtime that day then he would call them and cancel.

The money Anna had lent him on Monday was beginning to run low and the promise of him settling up with her by the weekend was once again looking dubious. She was going to be furious. He feared that she was going to ask him to leave.

His thoughts drifted back to work and the observation Baxter had scheduled for period five that day. He had not yet prepared for the lesson. The courage he needed to face up to the task was deserting him. A normal day of teaching he could handle but the added pressure of having to deal with Baxter's pedantic methods was simply too much to cope with today. There were moments he detested his job and this was one of them.

A wave of desperation came over him followed by that familiar sense of powerlessness. He felt the onset of a headache. Manny wanted to pull the covers other his head and simply disappear. He wished that he had someone with him who could put their arms around him and make him feel better. Instead, he sat up on the edge of his bed and held his head in his hands, rubbing his face and frantically feeling his cropped head. He squinted at the clock. It was fast approaching seven. The sound of his phone made him jump. He grabbed his mobile by the side of the bed. The name and number were listed as unavailable which only added to his curiosity

"Hello." Manny answered, instantly alert.

"Excuse me for calling so early. I tried to contact you yesterday evening without much joy, I'm afraid. Is that you, Manny?"

At first he did not recognise the woman's voice on the line.

"Yeah."

"It's Louise from Perfect Company. I'm calling to remind you about and discuss the date that you're booked in for tonight with Dr Sasha Harrington. I thought it better that I spoke to you direct rather than just leaving a message on your voicemail and because it's your first booking I didn't really want to email you the details without talking it through with you first. The booking was made quicker than we'd expected. Well done!"

A silence followed.

"I take it that you are still available?"

"Actually I'm pleased you called, Louise. I was planning on calling the office later this morning." He took a deep breath before continuing. "I'm not sure I can do it tonight."

She instantly seemed to pick up on his state of agitation.

"Look, wait there a second," she said before all went silent on the line. Manny found the silence discomforting. He wondered where she was calling from and what was happening. It seemed to him that he had been put on hold. Whether it was to talk about him or whether she just wanted to find a better place to talk, he could not know. He sank back onto his pillows and stared up at the patchy ceiling, waiting for her voice to continue with their discussion. Several moments passed before she recommenced with the call. She seemed to take forever.

"Manny? You there?"

"Yes, still here."

"Look, don't make up your mind just yet. Why don't you let

me take you out and buy you breakfast or treat you to some lunch? We can talk this over. Honestly, try not to worry. Tonight will be easy. Trust me," she soothed.

He closed his eyes and thought for a moment. It was a tempting offer. He liked her tone and he needed to talk to someone desperately, just to help him make sense of the doubts pounding in his head. She could be the perfect person, he felt.

"I'm meant to be teaching all day today."

"Look, give me your school's number. I'll call in for you and say that you're not well. Who do I ask for? I'll say that I'm your devoted partner and that I've ordered you to stay off work as you're not feeling too good. I'll make out that I'm also really concerned that you'll spread the virus onto your students. Come on, give me the number. Leave it all to me. Get yourself ready. I'll meet you inside St. Pancras Station, say ten? There's a café opposite Marks and Spencers. Meet you there. Oh, and Manny…"

"What?"

"Cheer up. You're about to make lots of money. Promise me we will talk again before you make any decisions."

Manny was captured by her directness. He liked the way she was organising him. It felt good. He provided her with the school's number and promised that he would speak to her again. Her voice and manner had pierced the gloomy bubble he was wallowing in. With renewed emphasis he got out of bed and headed for the shower.

To his surprise, Anna was already up, dressed and eating a bowl of cereal at the kitchen table.

"For Christ's sake, Manny, will you put some clothes on! I'm trying to eat my breakfast here."

"Sorry, Anna. I didn't know that you were up."

"Obviously."

She covered her eyes with the cereal box, not too dissimilar to the teacher in his dream. He ran into the downstairs bathroom, trying hard to conceal his manhood. He could hear her still complaining behind the closed door. He turned on the shower in the hope of drowning out her moaning.

"Did you hear what I just said, Manny?" she asked whilst banging angrily on the door.

"Yes. I hear you," he lied. "Don't worry, I will have the money."

"And I mean ALL of it. Or else. Oh, and while I'm at it, leave my bloody food alone and stop helping yourself to money out of my change jar. Honestly, it's like living with a flaming magpie. I'm not your mother, you know!"

Manny didn't reply. He heard the front door slam forcefully. She had every right to be angry, he told himself. Anna would be the first person he'd pay back. The first question he would ask Louise would be "How soon do I get paid?"

Thirty minutes later he was shaved, showered and feeling fresher. He headed into town to meet Louise. There would be plenty of time to worry and feel guilty about missing work for the second time that week over the course of the weekend.

Manny arrived at St Pancras with a bit of time to spare. He walked around and admired the newly refurbished station. The wine bars, shops and restaurants gave it much more of a cosmopolitan feel. He liked the way the station had also kept many of its original features. The city's early morning rush was in the process of settling down. He stopped to look in a shop window while keeping an eye on the café. He saw Louise coming up the station, walking purposefully. He watched as she went into the café. Manny waited a while before he followed her inside.

As he opened the door of the café, he was immediately hit by the smell of fresh coffee. Louise was sitting at the table in the corner busy texting on her phone. She closed it the moment she saw him approach and stood up to greet him, planting a kiss on each cheek. He wondered to himself whether the new surroundings played a significant part in making people greet each other in the same continental manner.

"Hi, Manny. Good to see you. Come and sit down. What would you like?"

He could smell, as she kissed him, the same scent that he'd picked up on before. "I would love a coffee," he said. "And a croissant, if that's okay."

"Sure. Very continental. I like it."

"Did you phone my work?"

"Yes. Relax, it's all good. I spoke to a Dom something or other."

"Bonner?"

"Yes. That's it. A nice man. Told me to wish you well and I was to tell you not to worry. He said that he would be brave and would take care of the fire-breathing dragon. Not sure what he meant by that. But I think I can guess. I work with one too," she said with a smile that suggested she understood.

He smiled and nodded to show his approval at the way she put distance between herself and the boss and in recognition of her people skills.

Louise went up to the counter and ordered. When she paid, he noticed that she asked for a receipt. She came back to the table carrying a tray with his order and an extra coffee for herself.

"Now. Did you remember to bring that smile of yours?" she asked playfully.

He smiled at the comment, finding it increasingly hard to look straight at her. He was beginning to feel some kind of attraction to her but he wasn't sure if that was because of the way she was fussing over him. She looked like she was in her mid to late twenties, which would make her younger than him. She had a soft, attractive face with serious brown, almond shaped eyes, which Manny liked. She wore a skirt that finished just above the knees, a jacket in a matching shade of green and a white collarless blouse. The colours complemented her olive-coloured skin. Her dark hair was in the same tied-back style that she had worn the first time they'd met. She didn't bother with much make-up, which he also agreed with. She didn't need to. He looked down at her dark hands as he automatically did with all attractive woman, and saw no rings on any of her fingers. He wondered if all men did this or was it a sign that he longed for someone of his own?

"Right, Mr Rodriguez. What's happened to that confident, handsome man who strolled into our office that day boasting that he could make himself and our company lots of money? You know something? Since putting your photo and details onto our web page, the phones have been exceptionally busy. There is lots of work waiting for you if you can handle it. Most escorts have to wait some time before receiving as much work. You have real earning potential."

Manny could see why she was regarded so highly by Virginia. It was easy to like and believe her. She was very good.

"I know it's hard to think clearly when you first start and I guess you're not as sure now as you were when you first approached us. There is a big difference between thinking you can do it and actually doing it. We did not have you down as somebody who was all talk, Manny."

Her last comment, if she really did mean it, worked. He frowned at her and this time he had no trouble meeting her gaze.

"Hang on a minute, Louise. I appreciate what you're trying to do. The problem is, I wasn't expecting to be asked to entertain a transsexual on my first booking. I was hoping that you would take into consideration that it was my first time."

"Manny, what did you expect? We're an escorting agency not a dating agency. There is a big difference. What were you expecting? To be working with a load of attractive young girls? I hate to be the one to tell you this, Manny, but pretty, fit and attractive girls don't always require our help. Of course there is always the exception and in this game you quickly learn that nothing should surprise you."

Manny was annoyed but he tried not to show it. He chastised himself for deliberately blocking out his initial doubts about the business. Once again his desire for money had silenced his early concerns and glossed over the reality of what the work would involve. Shaking his head, he smiled at the ability he had to camouflage the truth even from himself.

It was one of those moments when silence took charge. He felt her trying to read him in the silence. He started to feel jittery and he hoped that it was because of the coffee. Louise was the first to speak.

"Listen. I know that what I'm about to say might sound odd. And I'm not trying to make light of your anxieties but this booking really is the easiest introduction that you could possibly wish to have. Yes, she is a transsexual but she also happens to be intelligent, wealthy and very sensitive. Not to mention lonely and confused. She cares a lot about what people think about her. If you think about it, you're nothing more than an expensive decoration she wears on her arm. You're there to make her look good not necessarily feel good, if you know what I mean?"

Manny nodded. He knew what she meant.

"Sasha is consumed with her image. She's the best type of client. You meet her, greet her and for most of the time you'll be by her side in public together at one of her highbrow functions. That's what we provide, company. Don't forget, our clients usually pay us a fixed fee before the date. They will have filled in a request form informing us of their required needs. We will find the appropriate escort willing to fulfil those needs. Obviously we talk it through with you first and if there is something that you're not happy about, we will try to rectify and adjust accordingly. We will charge them extra of course if they for some reason detain you or the driver against your will, preventing you from meeting another of our clients on time. But, should they want to meet you or get you to stay longer and it's in your own free time, then that is strictly between you and the client, a personal arrangement. You will always be in control, Manny. You never have to do anything that you're not happy about. Anyway, I thought you needed to make money? All you have to do tonight is charm her and eat her food. She has paid for a car with a driver. He will pick you up outside the office at seven. The driver knows where she lives and will show you the way there. He will collect you too. It's all paid for and confirmed. Len will pay you at the end of the booking. Sasha just wants to meet you tonight, just for a meal and a chat at her house. It's easy. If all goes well, she has provisionally booked you again on Tuesday, to accompany her to a public function."

There was no anger or pressure in her voice, merely a quiet confidence. She was showing him the ability she had to read people. He was impressed and, despite himself, felt a shiver of excitement run down his spine.

But he sensed that something was amiss.

He looked at her as she finished her coffee. She noticed him looking at her and it was the first time that she seemed at a loss as to what to say. Louise looked down at her cup and showed him that it was empty.

"Do you want another coffee?"

"Yeah. That would be good."

He watched her make her way to the counter to order and pay for two more coffees. This time she didn't ask for a receipt. He knew then what it was that was bothering him. She was a very confident person whilst talking about the business. She had done a tremendous job in reassuring him, and he felt certain now that he would proceed with the booking and other work if it should come his way. But, with all his concerns, he had failed to find out anything about her on a personal level.

With his mind now made up, he was going to relax and enjoy his second cup of coffee. As she came back over to the table with the drinks, behind her pretty face he felt sure that he could sense a loneliness. He was sure that, despite her show of confidence, a mystery of some sort hid behind her polished veneer. He decided to turn the conversation around to her one day, but not now. It would sound too clumsy. He would get to know her another day.

CHAPTER
TEN

Manny sat in the window seat of the wine bar across the road from the office, drinking a citrus flavoured vodka with a splash of tonic. It was his drink of choice when courage was in short supply. Louise had spent the rest of their meeting filling him in on the details of the booking.

She told him that Len, the driver, would be picking him up outside the office at 6.45pm in a black Audi A4. Len would then give him a mobile phone 'purely for business use of course.' Also, providing all went well, it would be Len who would be handing Manny his first wage packet, providing the booking had reached a 'satisfactory conclusion.'

The conversation with Louise had provided him with some insight as to how things worked at the agency.

Len, the driver had been on the payroll from the very beginning. He was a long term associate of Virginia's. Louise had told Manny that driving and looking out for the female escorts had always been his main role, but he also carried out a number of other small assignments. Manny was wise enough not to ask what those other 'small assignments' entailed. What he did learn, however, was that after his military career had ended, Len had spent a bit of time working in the security business and Louise had informed him that despite his intimidating, blunt and prickly manner, he was a very loyal team player who nursed something of a soft spot for Virginia.

Manny looked at his watch. Five minutes left before he should start thinking about making his way outside. He nervously played with his phone, deleting all unwanted text messages. Moran had texted him earlier to warn him of the avalanche of anger that had greeted another one of his 'no shows.' He also wanted to know who the 'posh bird' was who'd called in and spoken to Don on his behalf. Manny deleted the message, downed the rest of his drink and headed outside without responding. For he had now embarked on a passage of his life that he was determined to keep wrapped and sealed forever in secrecy.

Louise had not been exaggerating in her description of Len. He was the same man that Manny had seen coming out of Virginia's office on the day of his interview. He remembered the silly salute.

The fixed frown that he wore could be conceived to be intimidating. But Manny was too lost in his thoughts to be at all bothered.

His strong, well-built frame suggested that he still regularly partook in rigorous workouts and, despite his advancing years, he presented a formidable force.

On seeing Manny he got out of the car and opened the rear door, inviting or insisting that he took a back seat. Manny happily obliged, hoping that it was because Len, like him, also lacked the enthusiasm to engage in small talk during the course of the journey.

He spoke with a boom that derived from somewhere deep within his chest. His tone demanded instant compliance.

"Manuel? Hurry up. Jump in. I'm Len, your driver. How's it going?"

"I'm good thanks, Len. It's Manny by the way."

"What is?" he asked as he got back behind the steering wheel.

"My name. It's Manny. Short for Manolo, not Manuel."

"Yeah? You sure? I could have sworn that Monica told me that it was Manuel."

Manny smiled in recognition of Monica's playful attempt to keep their game alive. He made a mental note that he should speak to her soon.

Len reached across, opened the glove compartment and took out a mobile phone

"Here. Take this," he said without turning around. "It's yours. Call me or text me if there's a problem. But that's very unlikely. She's quite a sensible lass, is your Sasha."

Manny belatedly stopped trying to frown at the back of Len's bald head. Instead, he took up the challenge and stared back at the small brown eyes that scowled intently in the driver's rear view mirror.

"My number is already stored in the phone. I'm supposed to pick you up at around midnight. Just before she turns back into a man," he added dryly. "But should you be 'otherwise detained', make sure you give me plenty of notice. There's other business I could be attending to."

Manny was unsure what disturbed him most. The comment itself or the fact that Len had failed to laugh or smile even at his own attempt of humour.

"You're a funny bloke, Len. My sides are splitting back here. Do me a favour can you put some music on. Preferably none of your old Englebert Humperdinck collections though, eh?"

This time Len did manage a smile of sorts and played music that Manny was not familiar with.

Not many more words were exchanged during the rest of the drive to Barnes. Manny spent the early part of the journey trying to fathom what he would be talking to Dr Sasha Harrington about. He also wondered what on earth she would look like. He soon gave up and spent the majority of the time staring out of the window, fighting with his fears.

As they drew closer, Manny had time to register the luxurious looking buildings with all their plush surroundings. There was very little doubt that he was in one of the more affluent parts of the city. He tried to dismiss the fact and concentrate on the task at hand as they turned into a long drive in front of one of the imposing houses. Swallowing hard, he felt his heart beat faster. A nervous, gnawing sensation was stirring deep in his stomach. *This is all so wrong*, he thought to himself. Immediately, waves of doubt came hurling towards him. They hit him hard and for the first time he knew that he was in deep. Two small brown eyes were observing him from the driver's rear view mirror, watching him begin to slowly drown. Holding on firmly to the arm rest he tried, miserably, to act calm.

"Hey, Manuel. Relax. Here, take this."

Without turning around, Len handed him a thick brown envelope. Manny took it. He could feel the bundle of money inside. His money. Money he desperately needed. Now he had the money, the situation felt slightly more reassuring. He put the envelope into the inside pocket of his jacket and acknowledged that a pivotal moment had arrived.

"Now, listen," Len looked at him intently, and spoke in a low voice. "I'm trusting you that you will not let Virginia and the girls down. I don't really fancy having to come and pay you a visit at your school. Never liked schools. Something about them always brings the worst out in me. They always seem to make me want to misbehave. Know what I mean?"

Manny simply nodded to show that he understood. The threat was unmistakable.

"I will pick you up at the time we mentioned. Use your mobile if there's a problem. Have fun tonight." Manny found the timing of his sarcasm, along with his grin, irritating. The comments he'd just made about visiting him at school started to slowly sink in. Len had touched a raw nerve. Manny temporarily forgot all about his fears and doubts.

"Hey, Leonard. Maybe going back to school would do you some good. You could take up drama lessons. They might help you learn how to act like a proper hard man. I find some of my younger students more intimidating than you." With fire in his voice, he continued. "Don't ever threaten me again!" Manny fixed Len with one of his special stares, the one that displayed his anger. A short silence followed as both men looked at each other searchingly. Manny was the first to speak again.

"I will call you when I'm done here." He opened the car door, ready to get out before stopping to add, "You're thinking the wrong kind of thoughts about me, Len. But hey, that's understandable and I can forgive you for that as you hardly know me. It's quite simple really though. Look after me and I will be kind to you. Upset me and you might end up regretting it." With those last words, he got out of the car, making sure he shut the door forcefully. Len simply looked away, shook his head and muttered something inaudible to himself before spinning off, disturbing the gravel along the way and leaving tracks of dust in his wake. Manny stood watching him disappear, feeling the cold. He was not sure whether he would be seeing Len later that night. The chilly air reminded him that he was now on his own. It was the dreadful feeling of abandonment that was distressing him the most.

Stepping onto the curved wide path that led towards the steps of the front door, he simply stood there, aware that he was allowing the insecurities from his past to take control of him. A soft music started to sound from inside the house. He wanted to run, not knowing where or to whom. He hesitated and pretended to look around and marvel at the riverside views, an act intended to borrow a bit more time. He sensed that the eyes of the house were upon him, witnessing his uneasiness.

The Friday afternoon traffic had been slightly lighter than usual. She hoped that this was a positive sign, suggesting that the evening ahead would also reveal some pleasant surprises. She quickly chastised herself. Sasha knew by now that the best thing she could do was to keep her expectations in check. But how could she? Virginia had mentioned that he was an English teacher. This suggested that he would have a thirst and a flair for literature, just like her. Surely it was fate. The handsome stranger must also have a passion for enlightening young hearts and minds. It was never easy to know how to appeal to the hearts of those that were reluctant to open. Understanding how to do so would make him different. Maybe a kindred spirit even. She would need to revisit her notes for Tuesday and ensure that she emphasise the importance of the role a teacher plays.

Sasha paused for a moment on the steps of her house and sucked the cold fresh air into her lungs, ordering herself to be calm. Reaching into her coat pocket she pulled out her keys and let herself in. The house smelt clean and fresh. She walked around and surveyed the downstairs living quarters. Isabella, the housekeeper had done her job well, as always. She was a discreet, loyal and meticulous employee who had served the family well over a number of years.

The champagne was on ice, waiting, and the food had been splendidly prepared. All she would need to do later was to take the tapas dishes out of the refrigerator, heat up those that needed heating, and place them, as they were, straight onto the table. With time on her side she decided to have a warm bath. There she would enjoy a soak, sip some champagne and lose herself for a short while, reading some of her favourite poems.

Bathed, dressed and feeling wonderfully alive, Sasha turned up the volume of her stereo. 'Saltwater', by Chicane, had always been a tune she loved to get ready to. She added some final touches to her make-up, making a mental note to arrange for Manny to take her out clubbing one night. She would enjoy that. It had been a while since her new body had graced a dance floor. Suddenly her thoughts were interrupted by the beams of light that had been projected onto her walls. Instantly she jumped up to peer out of the window. *My God*, she thought, *he's here already*. She saw the car door open. The man inside was about to exit the car when he suddenly stalled and stayed put. Her heart missed a beat as her thoughts began to predict the worst. He seemed to be talking to the driver. Finally he got out of the car. The way he slammed the door implied that he was unhappy about something. His body language revealed quite a lot about him. More in fact than any of the words that were to fall from his lips. That night or any other night.

The wandering friend had arrived looking lost and forlorn as he stood motionless on her path. He seemed unsure whether to take the next step. She gasped as she saw him begin to waver and without a further thought she flew down the stairs to open the front door so she could greet, help and steady the dark stranger.

CHAPTER ELEVEN

"The views are even more delightful when the sun's out."

The solid wooden door had been partially opened and in the door frame stood a dark figure. Due to the lack of light and his reluctance to look up, he observed very little of her features. He hoped that he was wrong but she seemed very aware of the process of deliberation he'd been agonisingly putting himself through.

He wondered how long she'd been watching him and whether or not he was doing enough to conceal his indecisiveness and state of agitation.

"Why don't you come in? You must be freezing."

Manny saw that he was frantically rubbing his hands together, more to do with nerves than any attempt to keep them warm. The voice sounded strong and was delivered in a low pitch, oozing a gentle undertone. Her tone and sympathetic manner had answered his internal question. It was not the answer he wanted to hear. He had no idea what to say.

She beckoned him forward and swung the door wider, implying that he should come in. He walked forward towards the steps of the porch, looking around once more at the dusky scenery in another desperate attempt to compose himself and delay having to make any eye contact.

"Thanks. You live in a beautiful part of the city. Stunning views round here."

"Yes. I feel most fortunate. There are some splendid walks to enjoy. Do come in. Here, let me take your jacket." Her voice had a gravelly quality which suggested she enjoyed a good smoke. Rich, velvety and strangely enticing, is how he would come to describe it.

Manny took off his jacket and handed it to her, still avoiding any eye contact. Instead, he busied himself looking at the pictures and selection of framed verses which hung on the walls of the oak-floored hallway. They intrigued him. The framed stanzas were masterfully enscribed in a calligraphical style which he believed to be a form of Arabic. The frustration he felt at not being able to comprehend them gnawed at him. He was unsure whether the frustration was born out of a genuine curiosity to know or the fact that he was denied the ideal opportunity to begin an intellectual discussion with the educated doctor.

Louise and Virginia had both mentioned to him what it was she did for a living. Again he chastised himself for his poor listening skills. Instead he stared, admiring the clever, artistic work, wondering if she had taken the time, care and skill to enscribe them with her own hands. Manny desperately wanted to say something meaningful, but for once words were not forthcoming. He cursed inwardly at not having been more thoughtful during the drive over. The journey had taken just under an hour and, instead of wasting time gazing out of the back window at the city, he could have been giving more thought as to how he was going to manage and approach this unfamiliar situation. He made a mental note to find out more details about the client next time. If there was a next time, he nagged himself. Louise had mentioned some things to him about Dr Sasha Harrington but he'd been far too preoccupied with his doubts to gather and store any of the what now seemed extremely useful information. Feeling ill-prepared, Manny was starting to think that the whole thing had been a terrible mistake on his part. But she seemed to realize his dilemma and politely pointed him down the hallway, telling him to take a seat and relax whilst attentively hanging up his jacket. With her back turned, he allowed his eyes to cast their first proper glance at her. With a furrow on his face, he reluctantly noted that everything looked normal. She appeared to be as a woman in her late thirties or early forties should look.

She had long, wavy, dark hair that hung loosely, a tall, slender body, stylishly wrapped in an electric blue dress. A complete contrast to the image of the burly drag queens that had been terrorising him in his sleep for the past couple of nights. Before she had rotated fully back into eyeshot he'd managed to reach the large sitting room where a sumptuous Persian rug did its best to elegantly cover the finely polished floorboards. The room was warm, welcoming and, he had to admit, beautifully furnished. A sweet yet subtle scent of burning incense hung in the air. An Eastern fragrance, he decided. A quick look around at the artwork displayed throughout the room told him she had a penchant for historical artefacts. That fortunately helped trigger a memory that her work involved reading Persian literature, so that made some sense, he readily acknowledged. He took a seat in an inviting leather armchair that was positioned to provide the occupier with a picturesque riverside view. He tried his best to feel comfortable and look at ease. Suddenly hit by a wave of guilt for not having greeted her nor introduced himself in a proper manner, he wondered if he had done this subconsciously in order to avoid the dilemma of whether he should kiss her or offer a firm handshake. Manny shook his head again at the dismal start that he had made to his life as a male escort. *Some 'escort'*, he thought, *I don't even know how to greet a client.* He came to the conclusion that a polite kiss on each cheek, continental style, would have probably been the appropriate thing to do. Depressingly, he sensed that his new money-making venture was another of his far-fetched ideas destined to be shortlived. He was tempted to send a message to Len asking whether he'd be able to come and pick him up soon. He would give back the envelope containing the precious money that mentally he'd already handed to Anna, his exhausted and long-suffering landlady.

"Can I get you anything to drink? Some coffee, water or maybe something stronger? A beer, wine? I'm having a glass of champagne," she asked, heading for the kitchen.

"Champagne sounds perfect," he replied, grateful to her for taking the lead role. "You have a very nice home by the way," he added lamely.

"Thanks. It was my parents'. They left it to me, fortunately. Quite a bit of work has been carried out to make it more modern looking and I've also tried hard to infuse my own warm and enchanting personality around the place." She laughed girlishly at the last part of her comment. Manny guessed that he had detected the first trace of nerves in her voice too. He heard her getting out the glasses and pouring in the champagne. It gave him time to think and compose himself. He stared out through the sliding glass doors into the darkening night sky, grappling with himself to find the resolve that would allow him to turn the situation around. He needed that money and the only way he was going to get to keep it was if he was to hold his nerve and promptly start performing with a measure of self-confidence.

He was still rubbing his hands anxiously when she walked in a few minutes later, holding two flutes of champagne. She handed him one and then took a seat on the sofa opposite. He saluted her with the glass without looking up and absent-mindedly drank half of it before putting the glass down on the small table beside him. He felt her eyes upon him, taking their time to examine him more closely. He sensed her calling silently for him to do the same. But, again he chose to look out of the window, focusing on the city lights that shimmered in the night outside, squirming at his own uneasiness. Realizing that he could no longer avoid her gaze, he decided to give it a go just for tonight. He had nothing left to lose, he dejectedly reminded himself. Manny reached for his glass and took another sip, this time positioning his body in a way to inform her that she now had his full attention. What he saw astonished him. Her eyes were dark, warm and sincere. She certainly did not fit with the image that he'd been seeing in his mind's eye. Her full, moist lips which were partially open could be considered appealing. Her soft facial features hinted at beauty. She wore a lot of make-up which added a hazy effect that reminded him of the leading ladies in the old black and white films. Manny guessed that the heavy use of make-up was to hide the minor scarring that might have been left by the surgeon's scalpel. Altogether, however, she was surprisingly easy to look at. Her forearms, hands and shoulders did look slightly masculine, despite their smoothness, if he looked hard enough. What little he could see of her legs revealed that they were still quite muscular and taut. He felt that maybe he was being a bit harsh in a stubborn and unfair attempt to find fault. The problem that was now arising inside him was totally unexpected and one that he'd not even considered. He was not supposed to find anything about her attractive, yet he did. Manny felt something in him begin to ease up. Both of them then just sat there for a moment and stared. He realised that he had a smile on his face. Nerves, no doubt.

Noticing that they had finished their drinks, Sasha headed back out to the kitchen to fetch them both another. She also changed the music that had been playing quietly in the background to a faster pace.

"When you're hungry, let me know, and we can come out here and eat."

"Thanks, but I'm fine at the moment," he replied despite the fact that he was starving.

Sasha walked back into the room with her head perched high and bosoms thrust forward. On this occasion there was no need for him to wonder. He knew for sure that they would be false. She handed him another flute of champagne. Manny instantly took a couple of large gulps, tasting it properly for the first time and presuming that it was top quality and expensive like most of the other things in the house. He felt the effects of the champagne start to work and his courage start to rise.

The graceful way she moved, her eloquent voice, her title, the house and the material things inside it, all pointed to a privileged and well-educated upbringing, both hugely significant in helping her reach such a high status in life, Manny believed. Why she needed to pay for an escort was a question that he intended to find out indirectly

"Virginia tells me that you work as a teacher. Is that correct?"

"Yeah. That's right."

"Do you enjoy it?"

"Some parts I do but other parts are beginning to grind me down."

Sasha listened to him attentively as he explained away his patchy professional life to date. She laughed at his funny comments and showed real empathy and understanding when he spoke seriously of the challenges, difficulties and fears that he faced working in a tough comprehensive school. He found it a novelty that he was able to talk so easily, openly and honestly with a complete stranger. When he looked into her deep, dark eyes, she seemed genuinely interested in what he had to say. Excluding Lucy, he struggled to recall the last time he had spoken with so much honesty and lack of self-awareness. Sasha did not interrupt him once. They laughed at the fact that they had not introduced themselves properly. This time he stood up, kissing her on each cheek and introducing himself proudly by his proper name. Sasha willingly did the same. They took it in turn to make jokes out of each other's names. He was pleased that she failed to link his name in any way to 'Manuel', the long-suffering, comical and fictional Spanish waiter from Barcelona.

The stress and strain that he'd been suffocating under seemed to disappear the more he laughed. It had been so long since he had felt so lighthearted that at first he tried to pin the fleeting moment of happiness on the drink and lack of food.

This prompted them to head out into the kitchen and consume the Spanish delights that had been prepared. Manny was amazed and touched at her choice of dishes. It was almost as though she had taken the time and trouble to contact his family back in Spain, asking them what kind of food he really enjoyed eating as a young man. For a brief moment, the sight and the smell of the food made his bottom lip quiver. He had to ask whether she'd had any inside information before preparing it. She responded in the coy manner of a woman who had just been deeply flattered. Something seemed to catch his attention as she did this, although it did not register with him at the time.

All his favourite Tapas were laid out in front of him on a solid wooden tabletop: Tortillas, chorizo cooked perfectly in a red wine sauce, potatoes in salsa, a small dish of seafood paella, salads, hams, cheeses and more. They sat at the table enjoying the food and drink. Manny loved it. They didn't talk much as they ate because they didn't need to. The silences had now become a comfortable place for them both to be. Manny felt the drink working on him, allowing him to temporarily forget about his money and work related problems. This is just so good, he kept on saying before finally finding himself full to the brim. Sasha seemed both happy and relaxed, confessing to him her vice for smoking as she got up from the table to grab an ashtray and her cigarettes from the window sill. She offered one to Manny who politely declined with a shake of his head, motioning for her go ahead and light up.

When she was making the coffee, he noticed how well equipped the kitchen was with all its machines and modern gadgets giving it an almost lavish feel. The furniture, new and old, combined well with the room's more antique features. Manny thought that the time-worn furniture added a certain homely charm, a charm he hoped to be able to create in a house of his own one day. That day he feared was a fair distance away.

Finally he was able to turn the conversation on to her. He could sense a loneliness about her and, after the effort she had gone to in making him feel good about himself, he felt a pure and unselfish desire to hug her, as he would a friend, and tell her that she was perfect as she was, and that she deserved the very best. But he didn't act on it.

Her name was Sasha Harrington. She talked a little about her life growing up although Manny could see by the distant look in her dark eyes that it was a memory she didn't enjoy revisiting or talking about.

He led her back onto safer ground by encouraging her to explain to him what it was that she did for a living. She told him how she concentrated most of her life on her work and the passionate and enthusiastic manner in which she spoke about it confirmed to him that her work was also her true love.

"Tell me more about this Rumi and Shams," he asked after noticing the glimmer in her eyes whenever she mentioned their names.

"No," she said forcefully. "You will just have to wait until Tuesday night."

She began to tell him all about the event that was happening on Tuesday night and what would be expected of him. Manny was surprised to find himself actually looking forward to seeing her perform. He was intrigued to learn more about her and the story of the mystical poets. He found the fervent way in which she had briefly explained their story to him compelling. It felt like she had disturbed something inside him that had remained dormant far too long.

Manny was feeling much more secure with her and it was turning into the most pleasant evening he'd had in a while. But when he enquired whether there had ever been anyone special in her life, not including the escorts, he saw the light vanish from her eyes and by the way she pulled on her cigarette he instantly knew that he'd made a mistake. Sasha answered his question despite the look of discomfort that had appeared on her face. There was nobody special in her life right now. She then stubbed out her cigarette before she had finished it, making sure it was out in a strained and very deliberate manner before taking a long drink from her glass. A shadow of unease darkened her face. For the first time that evening he thought that she had unknowingly shown him a glimpse of how she would have looked if she had remained a man.

Manny simply nodded, wishing that he had not wandered off track and had stuck to the script. He was back to not knowing what to say. He realized that he was not here to talk about her personal history. Not once had she mentioned or asked him anything about his being a hired escort. She had mentioned Virginia once earlier but had referred to her as an ordinary mutual friend of theirs. He believed that at that very moment he had learned the first golden rule of his secret role. Never do or say anything that will remind the client that you're nothing more than hired goods on temporary loan. Manny hoped that his clumsy mistake wouldn't cost him too dearly. The sound of his mobile going off was the second mistake he would not repeat. He knew who it would be and so did she. He felt disappointed that an enjoyable evening had come to a messy end and decided to rescue the situation the only way he knew how. Give her something real of himself. He grabbed her hand and in a hesitant move leaned over the table and kissed her quickly on the lips. He could taste coffee and cigarettes. What he didn't taste was a woman. Trying hard not to dwell on that thought, he continued with the rescue operation.

"Look, I have to go now. My ride home is here. I've had a brilliant time and really hope I can see you again on Tuesday night. In the meantime I will leave you my mobile number. Call me any time."

He saw the light return to her face as she went happily to get a piece of paper and pen. He read out the number that had been stored on his phone. They both laughed as she playfully wrote the name Shams above the number although he felt a bit uneasy as he made his way out to the waiting car and assumed that he'd drunk too much coffee. She stood by the front door to wave him off. He saw her blow him a kiss as he climbed into the back seat. Judging by the irritating grin on Len's face, he'd seen it too. Sasha stood in the doorway waving until they were out of sight. During the drive home it belatedly came to him what it was that failed to fully register at the time. Sasha been very convincing in her ability to act coy after he had paid her an honest compliment on her choice of meal. But from previous experience he had learned that, when women really feel, hear or sense something special, they tended to blush. Sasha didn't or rather couldn't. He felt nothing but pity for her.

Len was silent during most of the drive back, busy listening to his music that was playing quietly. This suited Manny as it allowed him time to sit with his thoughts. He sank back into the seat, yawning repeatedly and smiling at the words of the song that was playing. It was 'My Secret Life' by Leonard Cohen and he hoped it was nothing more than an ironic coincidence. He hadn't noticed Len's eyes watching him out of the rear view mirror which suggested that it was not another of his poor attempts at humour.

Feeling the small wad of money in his jacket pocket went a little way to putting the events of the evening into perspective. The prospect of more work, earning more money still carried a taste of promise for him. But Manny knew he would have to toughen up emotionally. He also knew that with more work there came a risk of bumping into a friend or, worse, a colleague whilst in the company of a client. But for now it was a risk he was willing to take. His debts demanded it.

Sasha poured herself a glass of brandy and sat down in the living room. She had trouble concealing her contentment and borrowed the words of Rumi to express her emotion:

'My soul heard something from your soul
my heart drank from your spring
I drowned and the flood swept me away.' [2]

They had come together unaware of each other's difficulties, yet she'd felt, as the evening unfolded, that she'd been able to recognise a deep wound in the handsome stranger's soul. For the first time as a woman she had been able to feel a close connection to someone. So close in fact that words had sometimes not been needed. Sasha was even prepared to overlook the streak of naivety that he had innocently shown during the course of the evening.

She could hardly wait for Tuesday to arrive. At last a fellow searcher of truth and wisdom to accompany her at what she hoped was the start of a new journey. Those attending the event would be curious and intrigued to find out more about the strikingly handsome wanderer who would be standing silently at her side. They would want to know all about him and the details of their mysterious relationship. The gossip would slowly begin to build, covering them in the same veil of controversy that Rumi and Shams once had to endure. Tuesday night's talk had taken on a whole new meaning for her. She made a note to contact Virginia first thing in the morning to confirm the booking. In fact, she would email her office now.

CHAPTER TWELVE

Manny lay in his bed listening to Anna, his landlady, thump about upstairs. For a Saturday morning she was up and about at an unusually early hour. A quick glance at his clock told him it was only 7.10am. The noises coming from above briefly made him wonder whether she had someone with her. Manny found himself staring into his past, ambushed by disconcerting memories of life with his father as he listened out for evidence that would help explain the sounds. After hearing her footsteps run up and down the stairs a couple of times, he thankfully ruled out the possibility that she might be having sex. The muffled moans and groans that he'd been able to hear had an entirely different cause. Manny sat up and waited for the images of his past to fade. As a boy, his father would often use him as an alibi and selfishly take him out on his booze-fuelled nights, duping Manny's mother into thinking that they were off visiting friends or relatives. But he could remember how they always ended up in the home of one of his father's cheap girlfriends. There his father would aggressively make love to his grateful lover while Manny waited in the next room, drinking pop and reading his comic, trying desperately not to listen to the awful sounds, wanting desperately to be home with Tigger, his toy. During the drunken early morning drive home, his father would concoct a story for Manny to learn and recite back to him in preparation for his mother's probing questions regarding their whereabouts and his father's choice of company for that particular evening. After a long stretch the unpleasant memories were quick to evaporate, leaving just the doleful thud in his heart that was always reluctant to leave.

He heard Anna banging about in the hallway outside his room, busily opening and closing doors. She sounded flustered and annoyed.

"You okay, Anna?"

"No, my mother has taken another fall. I had a call from the hospital early this morning. That means I'm going to have to go up to Leeds to be with her," she said, sounding more put out than concerned. "Just what I need, typical. Sorry if I woke you but I had trouble getting a bloody bag down from the top of my wardrobe."

Manny got out of bed, put on some clothes and walked out of his room straight into the kitchen to make some coffee. He noticed a bag packed ready by the front door.

"Don't apologise, I was awake already. Do you want a cup?"

"No, I can't. Don't have much time. My taxi should be here any minute."

"Is she badly hurt?"

"Not really. A bit disorientated and bruised, that's all, but she'll be expecting me to come up and be with her for a bit. I guess I'll be gone for a few days at least. I'll have to miss a couple of days of work too, which I can hardly afford. We're so busy."

"Oh, I've got some money for you. Not all of it but it's a start. I'll go and get it." He walked back into his room to fetch the envelope from the inside pocket of his jacket. He counted out the money onto his bed. It amounted to £400. He took £50 for himself and decided reluctantly to hand the rest over to Anna.

"There you go, Anna. Take this. I should have some more for you later this week," he said sheepishly, hoping that for now the amount he handed over would be sufficient enough to appease her.

"'Bout time too. Thanks. By the way, how did it go last night?" Anna asked as she hastily put the envelope of money onto a shelf in one of the kitchen cupboards.

The question caught him off guard, almost making him splutter in his coffee.

"Sorry, what do you mean?"

"Your new job. I take it that having some money means you've started it. I heard you come in quite late last night. What college are you teaching at? Funny time to run English classes though, on a Friday night," Anna commented as she fastened her coat without pausing for him to answer.

"You'd be surprised. There're lots of people out there with a need to learn English. The college is near Russell Square. I have to go in again Tuesday. Mind you, I'm not going to be doing it for long. Only until I've managed to pay off some of my debts." The ease with which he was able to lie scared him more than it pleased him. Again he thought of his father.

The arrival of her taxi rescued him from his feeling of unease. Grabbing her belongings, Anna headed towards the front door. Manny wished her a safe journey and hoped that her mother would make a speedy recovery. Another lie, he thought. He wanted the house to himself for as long as possible. He felt a twinge of guilt at his insensitivity, for he could see that Anna was clearly under considerable pressure.

"Thanks. You'll have my money later on in the week, you say? Have I got your word on that?" Anna eyed him closely for several seconds. Manny was first to look away.

"Yes. Promise. Go on, off you go, and don't worry!"

She started to say something but stopped. Opened the door and left.

With Anna gone he picked up his coffee and headed back to his room. He sat at his desk and stared out at the rain for a few minutes thinking about the night before. There were many contradictory thoughts rattling around in his head. Grudgingly, Manny had to admit that, the money aside, there had been moments about the night that he'd really enjoyed. It was something about Sasha. There was a warmth in her eyes that had been able to draw him in in spite of himself. She was understanding, sympathetic and had made him feel welcome. That feeling had been rare in his life. He allowed himself to sit recalling the feeling for fifteen minutes or so.

The pile of school work awaiting his attention began to dance before his eyes. He knew that the grip he was barely maintaining on his teaching career could be tightened slightly if he set about getting up to date. Also, it would make the prospect of facing Baxter at work on Monday slightly more bearable. Manny knew then that he would spend the rest of the weekend ploughing through his backlog of marking and writing up unwritten reports. Taking the first folder from the pile, he sat for a few minutes, not opening it, just staring out into the rain and thinking about all the other places he'd rather be. The familiar desire of having enough money to be able to flee from all his troubles and head off to warmer climates where he could start all over again was holding his attention for far too long. He rebuked himself sternly. Manny knew only too well that it was nigh on impossible to escape from yourself. He had done the geographical bit before. Sighing to himself, he opened the folder and scanned its contents, estimating that each folder was going to take roughly half an hour or more to assess. There were fifty-three of them. Manny took a deep breath, opened his desk drawer and stared blankly into it in the forlorn hope of finding a red pen. Failing to see one, he slammed it shut again and allowed his head to slump heavily onto the desk, remaining in that position for quite some time. He eventually found a pen and talked himself into marking the work, reminding himself that he was doing it for his students and not for Baxter. But after completing a mere eight folders, he'd had enough of reading pages and pages of mediocre essays. Poorly written work always made him feel as if it was a reflection on his teaching. He could only wince when students confused their Macbeth with Macduff. At one point he nearly gave up. A student had mistaken the poet William Blake for the 'bloke who did the drawings for Roald Dahl's children's books.' An easy mistake to make for a Year Seven student perhaps, not for someone in their final year of schooling who had been studying Blake's poetry for the past month. Manny threw his pen down onto the folder and watched it bounced off the desk. He didn't get up to fetch it, deciding instead to have a lie-down on his bed and resume with the monotonous task after a short nap.

Manny managed to doze off but was not sure for how long.

He was interrupted by the unfamiliar tone of his new company phone sounding. It was Virginia. She wanted to know if he was available for Tuesday. He confirmed that he was. She congratulated him on his first successful booking, explaining that Dr Harrington was an extremely difficult client to please. The fact that she'd contacted the office straight away to share her approval and delight, instantly requesting his company again, told Virginia everything she needed to know. She instructed him to contact Sasha direct, using his company mobile to confirm all the arrangements. Virginia also informed him that she had some other work for him the following weekend with a different client. Again, Louise would be in touch to provide him with the details of the booking. In the meantime she wanted to wish him good luck for Tuesday and he was to remember that it was a very important evening for Dr Sasha Harrington. Should he have any problems or any other queries he was not to hesitate in calling the office. As Len was not driving him on Tuesday, though he could be contacted if needed, she would arrange for his wages to be paid straight into his bank account by the end of the week. She was about to hang up when she thought of something else.

"Oh, before I forget. I hope you don't think I'm being rude, Manny, but do you have a smarter suit? Preferably not the one you wore to the interview nor the one you wore on Friday night. As I mentioned earlier, it's a big night for Sasha and she needs you to look the part."

"Yes, of course I have," he lied.

"Excellent. I've got a feeling that you're going to need quite an extensive wardrobe for the coming weeks," she said in a complimentary tone. "And don't forget shoes, Manny. Very important. Lots of woman judge a man on the choice and condition of their footwear. You will be mixing with the elite when out and about with Sasha. Okay? Look upon it as a very wise investment. The more dapper you look, the more work you're likely to get."

He was about to ask for a loan to buy some clothes but he hesitated and she was gone. He didn't have the nerve to call her back. It didn't feel right to be asking for subs just yet. Too early, he told himself. But he felt invigorated at the prospect of earning more money. A tingle of excitement ran down his neck. He wondered what the other client would be like next weekend. It also meant that he would get to speak to Louise again. He hoped that they would meet up like last time. Suddenly life seemed good. Manny sat for a few minutes deliberating before getting up to assess the quality and quantity of the contents of his makeshift wardrobe. The feeling of elation soon started to ebb away at the sight of his pathetic collection. He recalled how as youngsters they would laugh and joke about the clothes their teachers would wear when on an excursion. He had become like them. The only thing missing was a tweed jacket with leather patches. Deep in thought, he went out into the kitchen to make some more coffee. Then he remembered that Anna had left his rent in the far cupboard. *Why not?* he thought. *I'll make sure for certain that the money will be put back in time*. The 'need to survive' programme automatically kicked in. It worried him what he was about to do but it troubled him even more that he felt powerless to stop himself. Manny reached up, took back the money and headed into the town centre. Forgetting the coffee, he set off in search of clothing that would help make him look both dapper and quite irresistible.

CHAPTER
THIRTEEN

It was the worst possible time for his mobile to sound. Manny was sitting in the school hall on Tuesday morning during the upper school assembly. Old 'Whistling' Wilson, the head teacher, was sternly addressing the students. His lecture, the Consequences of Improper Conduct In and Around School, was just coming to an end and he'd asked for everyone to bow their heads for a moment's silent contemplation. Like every other teacher standing on the left side of the main hall, Manny frowned as he scrutinised the seated pupils, hoping to find the culprit who had broken a school rule by carrying a mobile phone during school hours. He then realised with belated horror that it was his. He quickly searched his pockets, fumbling around trying to locate and silence the increasing tone. A look of rising panic and sheer embarrassment soon replaced his frown, much to the delight of the students. Finally locating his phone, he switched it off to the background of ironic cheering. Attempting to restore order, the head teacher narrowed his eyes in Manny's direction and threw him a scowling look. Feeling the eyes of the world upon him, Manny tried hard not to look at anything or anyone in particular. He could not help noticing, though, the new geography teacher smiling with what looked like sympathy and the grinning face of the bald Andy Moran. Despite the cool draught in the hall, he knew that his face was flushed.

Weakly, he murmured, "I do apologise for that, Mr Wilson. I'm afraid I had to confiscate a mobile phone earlier. Must've forgotten to switch it off."

Rumbles of 'Sure you did, sir' could be heard bouncing around the hall. The head teacher cleared his throat and waited for the noise to die away.

"Settle down!... Hurry up!... Come on now!... Right, where were we...? Ah yes... Please bow your heads." He was a head who was feared more than he was liked and, much like his lecture, his career was coming to an end. Early in his career he was a fierce games master with psychotic tendencies who enjoyed a smoke. Longer serving staff would often share stories in the staffroom about the head in his younger days. The frantic race to succeed him had already begun with some members of the leadership team already jostling themselves into pole position. Wilson had spent the past twenty-eight years working at the same school. Manny never knew whether to admire or feel sorry for him. After all that time he could not help but wonder if old Wilson, also known as the 'lung' due to his grey and wheezing persona, was able to tell the difference between the older students and his staff. He certainly spoke to them in the same manner, using the same dour tone.

Manny bowed his head, staring down, eyes firmly fixed on his new shoes. He thought about the name that had flashed up on the caller ID while he'd grappled to turn off his phone. Anna had never called him at work before, she usually only sent texts. He felt something in his stomach tighten and hoped that she wasn't home from her mother's already. He would find out at break. There were two tough lessons to get through first.

Moran was the first of his colleagues to pass comment on the embarrassment that he'd just endured. On their way to their respective lessons they met in the corridor outside the hall.

"Your capacity to talk total, utter shite with such a straight face is quite remarkable, Rodriguez... Confiscated phone? Yeah, right... I believe you. Very poor. You should have just kept quiet and 'taken the shame' as the kids like to say. Your excuse made you sound like a pompous prick." He paused to laugh. "Never mind about that, though. I've got a surprise for you later. Catch you at break."

Manny forced a smile but declined to be drawn into yet

another pointless conversation. He could not be bothered. The assembly had not long finished and he was already growing rather irritable at the amount of remarks being launched his way from wisecracking students. *All this reaction*, he thought, *just because my mobile went off*. At an inappropriate time admittedly. But nevertheless, it hardly warranted the amount of excitement that it had generated. It was a bad start to what was to be an important day for him. He only hoped it would get better.

His week had started in exactly the same manner as the last and the many before that: fed up with his work and heavily in debt. The credit crunch had begun to bite.

Apart from his venture into town, where he had purchased a new suit and pair of shoes, he'd laboured for hours over the weekend doing his marking and ensuring that he'd completed writing up all the reports that were long overdue. The benefit of this was that it had briefly helped smooth his way back into Maureen Baxter's good books. She never mentioned his absence on the Friday before, not once. Another unexpected bonus was that she was unable to observe him teach later that day due to a change in her schedule.

He had also taken care of the arrangements with Sasha. He was to be at her house at 5.30pm that evening. Their conversation over the phone had been free of any apprehension and, unlike last time, he was feeling quietly confident. In fact, he was quite looking forward to dressing up in his new clothes and doing it all over again. Manny could feel a tingle of excitement thinking of the money he was about to earn. At least he hoped it was because of the money.

The arrival of breaktime brought with it an opportunity to listen to the message that Anna had left on his mobile. He also noticed that two messages had been left on the phone the escorting agency had provided for him. The reception in his classroom was always poor so he walked across to the staffroom and sat in his usual seat in the corner where he retrieved the message from Anna. His worst fears were confirmed. Anna had indeed returned home early from her mother's and was demanding to know what on earth had happened to the money she had left in the kitchen cupboard. She screamed words at him that he had never heard her use in the whole time that he'd been living there. Her screeching was so loud at times he was forced to hold the phone some distance away from his ear, much to the amusement of those who were sitting near him. He knew that they'd be desperate to find out what it was about. When the message had finished, he calmly shut the phone, put it back in his jacket pocket, pulled the other phone from his trouser pocket and listened to his other messages. Those around him found this very entertaining and Manny could not help but play up to the small crowd, pulling faces and doing his best to laugh it off. The first message was from Louise and he allowed the pleasure to show on his face, giving the thumbs up to his colleagues to inform them that all was well in his world again. She was calling to check that everything was okay for that evening and wanted to discuss the booking for the following weekend. She suggested they should meet up at the same place as last time. He made a mental note to contact her a bit later in the week. The second message was from Sasha. He did not want to listen to a word of what she had to say while others were around, whether or not they could hear what she said. His whole demeanour changed. This was far too personal and private for him to even consider joking about. He didn't know it then but the word he would choose to describe it later would be 'precious'.

This was an area of his life that must be prevented from approaching anywhere near the external boundaries of his school life, at any cost. He cursed himself for even pulling out the second phone from his back pocket. Showing off and drawing attention to himself had been a silly thing to do. *Why do I have to act the wide boy when I'm not?* he asked himself again.

Dom Bonner could not resist making a playful comment.

"I tell you what, Mr Rodriguez, for a man with as many phones as you, have you ever thought about actually using one every now and then? Like when you're toying with the idea of not coming in? Bloody nightmare, he is. He either doesn't call or else he gets one of his harem to phone in for him instead, right at the last minute, just to make my life more difficult. I don't even think we have a proper contact number for the slippery sod."

More laughter at his expense. This time he had asked for it. Fortunately the end of break bell was on his side for once. It quickly dispersed the unwanted attention.

Moran slapped him on the back as he was finishing his coffee.

"What is it with you and phones today? Are you expecting an important call or something? You ain't got a bird, so it can't be that." He looked at him searchingly. "Or have you?"

"No, nothing like that. My phone's been playing up, that's all. I brought the other one just in case. I was just messing about back then, you know, for the lads and that."

"Oh. Okay. That's all right then. Listen, you are coming for a beer tonight after work…? Yeah? I've got a surprise for you."

It was not unusual for many of them to go for a drink after their department meetings had finished. The need to moan to each other about the hassles of the day was therapeutic and seemed to help people to loosen up.

"What surprise? And what do you mean by 'that's all right then'? Am I not allowed to have a girlfriend?" It came out more fiercely than he had intended.

"No, of course you are. I was chatting to that new geography teacher, that's all. Calm down. Blimey, mate, what's up with you?" Moran shook his head before continuing. "Anyway, her name is Emma, and guess what?"

"What?"

"She's only coming down the pub with us all later." He waited to see the reaction on Manny's face. When one was slow in forthcoming, he jabbed him a few times on his arm. "I told her that you'd be there. But, to be honest, I don't think that was the deciding factor. Earlier on I got a feeling in my groin that she liked me," he joked.

Manny's face was still expressionless. He had much on his mind.

During lunch break the day before, he had found himself involved in another meaningless conversation, or rather interrogation, with the excitable art teacher, who was keen to bring some cheer to the face of his despondent mate. Manny had eventually buckled and had agreed that the new teacher was attractive. Moran, without a hint of discretion had then set about trying to discover as much as he could about her. Through certain channels and using Manny's name as a key to open doors, he had eventually been able to establish that she also found Manny to be attractive.

"No! Not tonight, I'm too busy."

"What are you talking about? Stay for a quick drink after the meeting, just to say hello to her," Moran pleaded.

"I'm not staying for the meeting. I've got to be somewhere else."

Deputy head teacher Dan Connelly, one of those jostling in position for the headship, broke up the conversation. Despite the fact that they were the only teaching staff left in the room, he announced in a ringing tone, "Ladies and Gentleman, can I please remind you that the bell has already gone for the start of the lesson. Could we all be making our way to our classrooms please. Teaching time is vital if we are to meet out targets."

They both looked at him and spoke simultaneously.

"On our way, Dan."

Moran headed for the art room, intent on finding out what it was that was troubling his friend. Something wasn't right. He remembered how Manny had helped him through his own difficult times. He would try and do the same for him. He could not recall a time when Manny had ever given up a game of football as well as a drink with a goodlooking girl in the vicinity.

Manny walked to his classroom at the end of the corridor, ignoring the bedlam of noise around him. There had been one or two dates since his last serious relationship, but there hadn't been anyone of real significance. He felt he carried far too much emotional baggage to get deeply involved with anyone again. He had not figured out yet how to deal with rejection. All he knew was that it hurt. Although Louise and the new geography teacher had the potential to defrost something in him, he preferred not to go there. These days he was more thrilled simply by the chase.

He strolled towards his classroom door, stopped when he got there.

"Quickly, Year Eleven! Hurry up and get in line." His class proceeded to do what he had asked. He stood waiting for complete silence before allowing them into the classroom. These were his older students, the ones he never usually minded teaching.

"Sir, was that your girlfriend on the phone this morning, in assembly? I bet she was missing you, sir. I know I would." It was Imani Lewis who felt brave enough to ask him the question. Imani was one of a handful of older girls at the school capable of extracting an impure thought out of him. He'd wake full of guilt, unable to decide whether it was a totally natural thought for a man to have or whether he was a dirty old pervert who should not be allowed anywhere near young girls. Of course, this was far too delicate a subject to be discussed with anyone at school for fear of reprisals. Imani was a light-skinned black girl with stunning green eyes and absurdly long lashes which dominated her face. She certainly knew how to use them too, he'd always thought. The natural corkscrew-curly brown hair with treacle-coloured highlights made her instantly stand out. Most of the boys in the school would drool over her and act submissive when in her presence. The girl was sixteen but her manner and looks were those of a girl three or four years older, mature and comfortable within herself.

It was now proving a struggle for Manny to meet her gaze as he tried but failed not to smile at the remark. He knew it was a mistake. His smile was all the permission needed for other students to chip in with comments and jokes of their own.

"His boyfriend more like." A chorus of laughs followed the comment shouted out loudly by a gawky, unsmiling teenage lad called Tom Rees who irritated Manny at the best of times with his nonchalant approach to life. Rees had a reputation for being sullen and disruptive both in and out of school. The class fell silent when they saw the smile disappear from their teacher's face. The mood turned sombre.

"In you go, quietly please. Sit down and get your books out. Write down today's date, copy down and complete the questions on the board straight into your books please."

He moved into the chair behind his desk and leaned back, tapping a pen loudly on his desk, trying hard to suppress his anger. Sitting back up, he straightened the items on his desk before looking up at the silent faces before him. Searching the room, his eyes rested on Tom Rees as he raised a finger and pointed it in his direction. Manny spoke calmly despite the fire he could feel raging inside him. "Tom, just to let you know for future reference, if you ever say something like that to me again, I'll rip your head off. Fair enough, young man? You're arrogant, aggressive and far too full of yourself. Carry on acting like you do when you leave here and you could find yourself in a bit of bother." They stared at each other unblinking for a few long seconds. Rees looked away first. Manny saw his cheeks turn to a brilliant shade of red and was quietly pleased to see the bravado disappear from the student's eyes.

His behaviour had been unprofessional and not the kind of classroom management that would be endorsed at the teacher training colleges. But Manny didn't care, although he knew that it was out of character for him to have reacted like that and to have taken a student's comment so personally. Doubting whether the rage and frustration he was feeling were entirely down to Rees's loaded comment, he tried to reason with himself and justify his threat. Tom was a few months away from leaving school. He acted like life owed him a future and with his surly attitude somebody in the world outside school was likely to thump him. *I'm doing him a favour really. Students are becoming much more aggressive towards staff, with a complete lack of respect for authority.* He had seen too many teachers leave the profession because of unruly behaviour and the amount of red tape. Yet it seemed to Manny that they were being given less and less power to confront bad behaviour, and the worst behaved students knew this and took full advantage. He felt sorry for the majority of students who also had to put up with those hell bent on disrupting lessons and school life. The job would soon be all but impossible and the lyrics to the Pink Floyd classic 'Brick in the Wall' would need to be completely rewritten. It was a thought that he'd had for a while now. Though challenging, teaching could be a rewarding profession, but it was also stressful and unforgiving. School was a hellish place to be when your private life was in disarray. He wondered if he would have reacted to Rees's remark in the same manner a few months back and questioned why the comment made by Imani had not bothered him. Manny leant back in his chair and surveyed his class. All were busy working. He caught Imani looking at him, her eyes wide and keen. Despite some resistance he eventually met her magnetic gaze. Her smile caused a disconcerting flutter within him. It was his turn to look away first. She was obviously honing her newly-discovered gifts, just role playing, he told himself. Manny stared out of the window, appalled at himself for straying onto that dangerous and forbidden path, the path no teacher should ever tread in these most sensitive of times.

CHAPTER
FOURTEEN

"Jalaluddin Rumi, Persia's best known lyrical poet and mystic, was born on September 30th, 1207 A.D. in Balkh, better known today as modern Afghanistan. Eighteen years later, his family fled the invading Mongols and eventually ended up settling in Konya, modern Turkey in 1228..."

Dr Sasha Harrington was only ten minutes into her presentation by the time Manny was persuaded that she knew exactly what she was doing and was extremely good at passing on her vast knowledge. Also, the fact that a book written by her was on sale in the foyer both surprised and impressed him. The front of house host had greeted them both warmly by the hand, introducing himself as Paul. He'd escorted Sasha off in a different direction while Manny was shown to his seat in the hall by a polite and helpful student of the philosophy school.

From his front row seat he recognised the spark in her eyes and that same contagious sound that he had experienced during their previous encounter. He was full of admiration for her and her ability to hold the attention of the audience as she moved methodically between poems and analyses. The diverse crowd of two hundred or so which had gathered to hear her talk about 'Rumi, his Poetry and Shams' Influence on him' were, like him, captivated. The music and lighting, together with the deep booming voice of the man on stage reciting the poet's work, complemented each other superbly in creating the perfect setting and atmosphere. The candles and incense lent the occasion an Arabian ambiance, similar to the one that he'd felt in her home.

From a distance she looked stylish in her two piece suit and the performer in her seemed to be warming to the task. He could tell that she was enjoying the moment of drama, that she relished telling the story. At times it was easy to believe that she had been there with the two subjects herself, sharing their pain, anguish and longing; her tone of voice rather than her body language holding the observers' attention.

Before her talk, a group of dervish dancers had demonstrated the spiritual and meditative art of swirling, a religious ritual which Rumi had been very fond of, Sasha informed the audience. Manny was mesmerised. This was a different world for him. Tuesday nights usually consisted of beer, bullshit and a curry with colleagues reluctant to go home. Inside the lecture theatre now, he felt a sense of energy and self-awareness that was often absent from his daily life. Those sitting around him seemed wide awake, far less concerned with the pressing demands of work and other mundane commitments to which he usually surrendered. Why else would they take the trouble to find out about these kind of events and make the effort to attend? He sensed that the majority of the people there had an agenda for making their lives more fulfilling, allowing room for light to enter. In stark contrast to his own life in which he'd stumble around constantly in the dark, trying to survive the day like a punch-weary boxer sagging against the ropes. A life devoid of any real meaning. Manny felt envious in a way he'd rather not spend long analysing. Different upbringings. Well-balanced parents.

The events of the day, including the problem with Anna, soon evaporated as he lost himself in the beauty, tenderness and power of the words. The early tremor he'd detected in Sasha's voice was now less evident and he felt a sense of pride and a peculiar yearning to let people see that he was her chosen companion that night. Throughout the lecture he'd find himself nodding, trying to look like he was endorsing everything that she said.

"The central enigma of Rumi's life and the inspiration behind his work is, of course, Shams Tabriz, an enlightened wanderer dervish, who was searching for someone to receive his wisdom -

'someone whose soul was as wide and deep as his own'. Rumi with his thirst for enlightenment found in Shams the perfect mirror of his own soul - his very own beloved."

Manny felt that Sasha was talking directly to him from her lofty position on stage. She stared at him for a moment and he leaned forward in his seat, using his eyebrows as a means to encourage, show anticipation and display his approval.

"They came together in an awareness and understanding of each other's needs..." The drawn-out pause and stare sent a tingle down his back. She had used those words before, he recalled.

"At their first meeting, it is rumoured that Shams pushed Rumi's precious books into a fountain and demanded that, *if it is wisdom you seek, then follow me.'* Rumi relinquished his books and he and Shams began the first of many mystical retreats together. This was the time when Rumi's scholarly words developed the wings of poetry..."

'Seek the wisdom
that will untie your knot
seek the path
that demands your whole being.
Leave that which is not, but appears
to be
seek that which is, but is not apparent...' [3]

"The bond between them was immediate and life-changing. Rumi's students, family and friends struggled to accept or understand the depth of this relationship. Their friendship is one of great mystery and caused much controversy..."

'Hidden from all
I will speak to you without words.
No one but you will hear my story
even if I tell it in the middle of the crowd...' [4]

"Before Shams, Rumi was married twice. His first wife, Gowhar Khatun, died young. She bore two children, Sultan and Allaedin. He also had two children with his second wife, Kira Khatun: Mozzaffer, a son, and Maleke, a daughter. The education of the students who attended his philosophical school suffered during this time. The intoxicating state of love that had been awakened in him by Shams took over his life completely for the next couple of years. This caused heated debate amongst the community. But it was because of this unique relationship with Shams that we are able to admire and appreciate his poetry today. It is the reason why we are gathered here. More than seven hundred years later his words are still able to leap off the page with an ecstatic energy that enthrals and enlightens us all..."

'The secrets are bursting inside me
but to give them away and
expose them to mockery, I cannot.
Something inside me is bursting with joy
but to put my finger on it, I cannot...' [5]

"No one could tell with Rumi and Shams who was the teacher and who the student. Lover, beloved and love become one thing with them..."

"I'm often asked the question whether they were secret lovers and it's true that many people today, both gay and straight, firmly believe that these words of love could only have come from one suppressing and hiding his true feelings. The law, fundamental religious beliefs and the high position he held in the community at the time, would have all contributed in building an imposing barrier around his true emotions. Many would not have understood..."

'I am hopelessly in love with you, no point
giving me advice.
I have drunk love's poison, no point
taking any remedy,
They want to chain my feet but what's the point
when it is my heart that's gone mad...' [6]

"Like one of my fellow historians, the excellent translator and scholar Coleman Barks, I don't know if I agree. I used to believe that they might well have been lovers and I, for one, have certainly been guilty over the years of finding Rumi's poetry containing elements of, let's say, 'erotic fruit.' However, the more I research and study their relationship, I'm led to believe that their friendship reached a divine, spiritual level that far surpassed the physical plane of body and mind. A mystical union in which they drank from a divine source in an eagerness to quench a spiritual thirst. The metaphor of drunkenness is used often, woven into his poetry to help explain the extraordinary spiritual high that they were experiencing. It will become clearer later on as we explore his works that he was in fact searching for a higher love. A love that was not perishable. A love that he had never experienced before..."

Again another sizeable pause and a searching look at Manny. He took a deep breath, hoping that the interval was not too far away. The silence that followed made him feel a touch uncomfortable. He turned his head in the direction of the exit. Her eyes roamed from one part of the room to another.

"Is the mystery of love not the main reason we find ourself gathered in this room?" she asked the audience searchingly. "That one meaningful word we all seek to experience and to understand. Poets write about it, artists paint about it, philosophers talk about it and scriptures of faiths tell us to follow their dogma if we wish to find it. But how many of us have truly felt pure love in all its powerful glory? Does it even exist? Well, for me, Rumi's words tell me that it does. It is my firm belief that, through Shams, Rumi discovered and felt love in all its true essence and form..."

There was a stillness in the room that Manny now found enlightening, stimulating and which spoke straight to the conciousness. He no longer felt the need to fidget. Instead, like the rest, he pondered thoughtfully during the silence that followed, trying to recall moments when love had visited his life. He didn't have to think for long.

"Rumi abandoned all his previous habits, behaviours and beliefs on the strength of Shams' words and teaching style. The essence of his poetry developed from their intense relationship. After Shams' mysterious death or disappearance, Rumi produced some of his best work in honour of his absent friend. For many years he mourned and longed for his beloved friend, never fully recovering from the depression and grief that Shams' sudden disappearance caused within his heart. The next three poems we will hear point to the very moment his ecstasy began to turn into agony..."

An hour and a half before the proceedings, Manny had met Sasha in a wine bar close to the London Metropolitan School of Philosophy in Mandeville Place, central London, the chosen venue for the presentation. Sasha had spent the best part of the afternoon preparing and setting up for the talk with her small team of helpers, ensuring everything was in place and ready to go.

Manny had been feeling increasingly nervous about this evening. In an earlier phone call from Virginia, she'd insisted that he be more attentive to Sasha when in the presence of others. A bit more touchy feely. He should aim to be the strong but silent type, standing confidently by her side, she'd suggested. She'd also informed him that Sasha had not booked a driver for the journey home as she was driving to the venue herself. Nothing was mentioned about his role at the end of the evening. Virginia signed off by reminding him that Sasha had paid good money for his company, now he had to go and earn it, and that Len was on call should there be any problems later on, but she doubted very much that there would be.

"Oh, and Manny? One more thing. Remember to watch your Ps and Qs. You'll be among a lot of educated people later." He heard a trickle of laughter from somewhere in the background.

He felt good in his new attire where he'd been aiming for 'designer scruffy' in a perfectly presentable style. It was the best option for the amount of money he'd had at his disposal. Dark grey tie loosened around an unbuttoned white collar, close cropped hair and a couple of days' worth of stubble added a touch of menace to his unpredictable demeanour. On greeting him in the suggested wine bar, the approval was clearly evident on Sasha's face. This time there was no doubting as to how he would greet her. Holding her firmly by the waist, he planted two kisses on each cheek with the words, 'Wow! Don't you look good?', muttered softly but meaningfully into her ear. He noticed a softening around her heavily made-up eyes. The time had arrived for him to earn his money. He needed to loosen up. Time to go to work. Accepting her invitation for a drink, he sat on the bar stool next to hers. She gave him an outline of the evening ahead, her fears and expectations discussed without reservation.

He was to leave the lecture theatre at the interval and wait for her outside the entrance for some much needed 'fresh air' which he understood to be her cigarette break. After that she was not expecting him to return to the seat that she had reserved for him. Instead, he could head for the cafeteria below, if he liked, where there would be food and drink available for anyone wearing 'one of these.' She handed him a badge with *VIP/guest of Dr Harrington* printed on it. He was to wait for her there. Afterwards he was to spend the time shadowing her movements as she mingled with the other guests. In response to anyone who questioned him directly he was to answer that he was a very close friend of hers who happened to share an interest in her historical studies. All other questions would be handled by her, that was one of the reasons he was to stay by her side as much as he could. Apart from that, he was to relax and enjoy the evening. He nodded as she spoke. Much of what she had said was repeating the conversation he'd had with Virginia earlier that afternoon. It didn't sound too onerous, he thought as he reminded himself that there were far more demanding and arduous ways of earning money. He'd tried and failed at many of them.

Sasha dug around in her handbag for a mirror, in the same way that most women did. He wondered whether he wasn't looking too hard for evidence of masculinity. There was, but the clues were very subtle, well-hidden. Her dark hair was tied back, emphasising a jawline that was stronger than he remembered from the time before, and her shoulders also seemed much broader.

She gracefully made her way towards the toilets. The wine bar was reasonably busy with city workers. Manny had sensed people watching them when they had first greeted each other at the bar. Trying not to feel paranoid, he found himself looking around, searching for clues as to whether the truth of Sasha's gender was obvious to anyone else. Taking a gulp of wine, he dismissed his fear of exposure, reminding himself how many masculine-looking women there were about. A couple of his old aunties as well as a woman he'd once worked with sprang to mind. Virginia had warned him that there would be moments when he'd have to spend time in public with 'someone you'd usually choose to avoid'. He had to admit, though, that Sasha's dark eyes with their long lashes were incredibly seductive and she was very easy on the eye. *Think about the money, Rodriguez*, he said to himself as he looked down at his new black shoes. He nodded, reminding himself to try calling Anna again to explain about the missing money. His calls were being ignored. She had not been at home when he'd arrived back from work. But she had left a note telling him in no uncertain terms to clear off and find another place to live. He'd made the mistake of not disposing of his shopping bags properly, nor clearing away all the other stuff that revealed that he'd been on a mini-spending spree for new clothes. He shook his head at his carelessness: it helped explain her burning anger. But he felt sure that he'd be able to make it up to her later that week. It was regrettable, but he sought comfort in the fact that he was being proactive in doing something about his lack of funds. He only hoped that her initial anger had worn off.

Sasha arrived back from the toilets and sat back on her stool at the bar. He noticed some casual observers eye her up and down, both men and women. They continued to make small talk but he sensed her become understandably more tense as the time for her lecture drew near. He reassured her by saying all the usual positive things but he sensed it was more than just the talk that was causing her anxieties to rise. On probing her further, he discovered that delivering the talk was the easy part of the evening, the anxiousness stemmed from her uncertainty at not knowing who exactly would be there. A problem he could understand, considering her past. They had not yet talked about her sex change; he felt sure that it was a subject for her to bring up and not him. There were quite a few things that he'd like to discuss with her. What most concerned him though was that he knew very little about her past and private life and yet here he was, accompanying her to a talk and a gathering afterwards where she was the guest of honour. Virginia's words resounded in his head: 'the strong and silent type.' Still, while he could be strong and silent, there were questions that he would feel happier if he knew the answers to, such as: how long ago did she have the operation? Was it common knowledge amongst her colleagues and students? Would anybody be there tonight who knew her story? Did she even know that he knew? Virginia would have told her, surely? Guessing that he was about to find out at least some of the answers, he made a mental note to have another chat with Louise at the earliest possible opportunity. Not for the first time he felt a little unprepared.

"Right, time we were off," Sasha said and they walked the short distance to the venue, acting just like a real couple.

A room on the lower floor had been prepared for the reception afterwards. A lavish buffet sat on top of tables covered in crisp white sheets. On the opposite side, tables were still being carefully stacked and arranged with wine, champagne, soft drinks and sparkling glasses.

At one end of the room there was a serving hatch which allowed a partial view into a modern kitchen beyond, where waiters, waitresses and catering staff were busy attending to last minute preparations. A few small tables with seats had been placed around the sides of the room to encourage people to socialise and mingle between the small clusters. Other than the catering team, Manny was the only guest there. The second half of the talk had just got underway.

He'd met Sasha outside the building during the fifteen minute interval, where she'd enjoyed a well-earned cigarette. Their chat had been light and fun with Manny expressing his admiration for her work. He told her about the only time he'd had to take an assembly at his school. "It was going really well despite my nerves," he'd told her. "Everyone seemed to be laughing at my jokes and little anecdotes about how we waste food. I then got on to the serious part of the assembly and everyone was still laughing. Very distressing at the time because I was talking about the starving children of Africa. It was only when one of the teachers there started to wave and point at me frantically that I realised my flies were undone. Funny, I've never been asked to take one again..."

Sasha laughed, grateful for the way his mood had helped her

feel positive and relaxed. It was just what she needed. He continued with his witty encouragement.

"But, honestly, well done, I'm really impressed. You need balls to stand up and talk in front of an audience that size and… oh, I'm sorry, I never meant… I was …" He'd realised the irony of what he'd just said and instinctively raised his hands in an apologetic manner. For a moment there was silence. They looked at each other. Sasha was the first to burst out laughing, much to his relief, and in that moment he thought that he'd caught a rare glimpse of her actually enjoying being her.

"You're very funny. That was a good one. Listen, I must go back in. Thanks a lot, Manny," she said before taking her last lungful of smoke, then crushing her cigarette butt onto a wall.

"What for?"

"Making me smile and feel good about myself." There was another of those drawn out pauses as she allowed her eyes to rest on him. He met her gaze and smiled back. He saw something soften in her.

"Now, go and relax and enjoy the friendly hospitality," she said finally. "The next part should only be about forty-five minutes long. I'll see you afterwards, downstairs. Don't drink too much. Okay?" She leant forward and kissed him full on the lips. Again, he tasted nothing but nicotine. Proudly, he watched her walk away, disappearing through the main entrance. Then he wiped his mouth.

Later, Manny would reflect that that was the moment the ice between them began to thaw. He was beginning to get an understanding of her needs. Things were far more relaxed between them both. Her being a transsexual no longer mattered. Despite all her wealth and academic achievements, he could see a vulnerable person in need of friendship. It pleased him that he was in a position to help make her feel better, regardless of the fact that he was getting paid for it. He'd heard somewhere that it was the least loveable who most required our love. He'd never quite understood what that meant until now. It was the same at school. He'd always make an extra effort with the more damaged, unappealing and friendless pupils. Getting a smile or a laugh

114

from them always made him feel better inside. Before thoughts about his own childhood could assail his emotions, he promptly made his way to the room where the friendly hospitality was being freely handed out.

Manny had about thirty blissful minutes where he could relax, read and sip some quality champagne. Having borrowed a copy of Sasha's book, *'Hidden Passion of a Persian Poet'*, from a kindly lady up in the foyer, now he read the author biog on the front cover sleeve about Dr Sasha Harrington. Disappointingly, the paragraphs only mentioned her academic achievements. The only personal details offered informed the reader that she had been born in 1970 and was currently living on her own in Barnes, London. He was skimming inside the book when a blonde, blue-eyed, fresh-faced waitress asked whether she could get him something to drink. Opting for a glass of champagne, he watched as she strolled away, marvelling at the way her shapely backside moved in her tight, shiny, black skirt before returning to the book.

The sound of movement, laughing, coughing and good deal of muttering coming from somewhere up above told him that the session was over. Manny took the opportunity to stretch out his legs and collect his thoughts. The guests would soon be on their way in to eat, drink and talk. He felt ready to face them.

All was going well. Manny was ensuring that he remembered to laugh in all the right places, always saying very little himself. Stifling the odd yawn was his only battle. There were plenty of people milling around, most of them keen to snatch a word or two with the popular speaker. He was heartened to see people approaching her with a genuine warmth and respect, some were even eager for her to sign copies of her book. The question flared up again in his mind. Why the need for me? Why the need to pay for someone to make her feel good? He could see that the adulation was being handed out for free. They had loved her talk and seemed to like and be in awe of her.

It pleased him to see her enjoying the attention, although he was confused by her humility and humble gratitude. He thought she would have been used to the generous amount of compliments being sent her way. According to the brief biographical note he'd read, she'd been doing this kind of thing for a number of years now and in more celebrated, exotic locations.

All was going extremely well until the arrival of a man in his mid to late thirties. He was wearing a light suit, a spray tan and a hairstyle that seemed to be pushing in opposite directions with the help of a slimy styling gel. He reminded Manny of the male models he'd seen in the pages of his old nan's catalogues in which hunky-looking men would be standing around, chatting and pointing, somewhere in a outdoor location while wearing nothing but underpants. Moran would say that he wore the face of someone that you'd just love to slap not once but twice. The man was powerfully built and walked with a swagger that suggested he knew how to handle himself. Manny was not impressed by the way he butted in and took over the conversation. His presence had darkened Sasha's mood.

"Good to see you again, Dr Harrington. It has been a long time. I must say, I really enjoyed your talk. I see you're still maintaining that your poet Rumi was a red-blooded male. Controversial as ever, eh? That's why we used to love your classes at uni so much. We could never be sure as to which Dr Harrington would be showing up." He made a comment in his friend's ear. They both laughed. Manny felt Sasha tense up and could see the pain that she'd been working so hard to hide. Her eyes were once again staring into that place which she was reluctant to visit. Manny didn't need it spelling out for him. She was being harassed and bullied, albeit subtly. The strangers' arrival had caused a change in the atmosphere. Not for the first time that day he was finding it hard to suppress his anger. He felt another yawn again, this time not bothering to stifle it. The exaggerated yawn achieved its aim and caught the attention of its target. Rather unwisely as it turned out.

"Oh! How rude of me! Gosh, where are my manners? I'm so sorry – everyone… introductions… Yes, please allow me.. My name is Edward, a former student of the noble doctor here, and this is my good friend and colleague, Nicholas. Nicholas, allow me to introduce you to my former tutor, Dr Stephen Harrington. Doctor?... Nicholas Sartain. Nicholas?... Stephen."

Despite the heavy sarcasm implied in his words and the immediate concern that had started to cloud her face, Sasha maintained her dignity, shaking Nicholas by the hand before introducing them both to a few of her associates. The guests to whom she'd just been speaking pretended not to hear or understand what was going on. Instead, they turned their gaze elsewhere or looked down resolutely at their shoes. Manny could sense their embarrassment. This had been Sasha's worst fear. Two narrow-minded idiots turning up from her past, hell bent on making her squirm in order to amuse themselves and anyone else who might care to join in for a laugh. Removing his hand from her waist, Manny decided to take control of the situation.

"Hi. I'm Manny. Manny Rodriguez, the one with the cough and a dear friend of the noble doctor here." He didn't offer them his hand. "Funny that you two should show up and butt in with your witty style right now, we were just discussing the importance a teacher plays in their students' development. We'd agreed that sometimes the downside to teaching is that, no matter how much effort and energy you invest into some students, there are those odd few who, unfortunately, simply never get it. Destined always to stay at the same level of competence they were at when they started school. Shame really. Today they have a label for such students. Special needs, I think they call it." The comment was enough to raise a laugh among the guests around him.

Edward and Nicholas refused to meet his eyes. Instead, they said their goodbyes and moved on over towards the buffet, sniggering as they went. Their mission obviously accomplished. Once again, Manny placed his hand on the small of Sasha's back in an act of solidarity, trying to tell her without the use of words that he'd felt her discomfort.

Fuckers, he thought silently to himself. Despite being tired, he'd been enjoying himself, relishing his role at the side of the guest of honour. The relaxed mood of before never quite managed to recover. He felt for Sasha. The spark in her eyes had disappeared. No matter that he and the others continued to compliment her, he could see that the damage had been done. It angered him but he guessed he had to let it go. *Not your war to fight, Rodriguez...* The evening continued to unfold and, if he was honest, he was starting to grow weary of the same comments followed by the pleasant yet repetitive small talk. Remaining staunchly by Sasha's side, he continued to nod and smile in all the right places, maintaining his role as the strong, silent type, as instructed.

He'd caught Edward looking his way more than once. Each time he would wink and blow Manny a kiss. It was starting to get to him. It had been a long day, after all.

Manny would be unable to explain for some time why he did what he did next. It would take even longer and the help of a good therapist to understand why he'd enjoyed it so much.

Edward finished off his drink and strolled towards the toilets, giving Manny his now customary wink and sarcastic kiss through the scattering of talking heads. Losing the thread of the conversation he'd been listening to, Manny asked Sasha to hold his drink as he needed to visit the gents. He'd fallen into a silent world of his own. All he could hear was the rhythmical beat of his heart. On entering the toilet, he spotted an elderly gentlemen drying his hands under the automatic dryer. The two urinals were vacant so he faked the need to use one. The solo cubicle was occupied. He knew by whom. Perfect. But the old man would not play his game. Time and time again, he pushed the button to restart the dryer, oblivious to Manny's scorn. This only added fuel to his burning anger. His blood was racing, burning through his veins. Finally, the man was done and he slowly shuffled out. The moment he left, Manny pulled up his flies, turned sharply and with all his force kicked open the cubicle door.

"What the fuck...?"

Edward was sitting on his throne looking startled, trousers and pants around his ankles, tissue paper folded in his hand at the ready. Manny was in no doubt that he had to act fast and launched his fist straight at his nose. The natural reaction saw Edward instantly cup his hands together and raise them up in a desperate effort to support his bleeding, shattered nose, ensuring

118

the toilet paper didn't go to waste. Manny was then able to place both his hands on the king's shoulders and push down with all the force he could muster.

Edward found himself squashed down in the bowels of the basin with his feet up high, close to the same level as his petrified eyes. All that remained was for Manny to pull on the chain. The sound of gushing water brought a whimpering noise gurgling from his throat.

"Look at that..." Manny said. "Always the same, whenever you use someone else's toilet. There's always one big turd that can't be flushed away."

"Help!" Edward yelled out.

"If I ever see your cheesy orange face anywhere near me or the 'noble Dr Stephen Harrington' again, as you so eloquently put it, I swear I will bite your fucking nose off!" Manny spat out the words, barely recognising his own voice as he added a final slap around the head of his client's tormentor.

Manny made his way back to Sasha who was busy making small talk with a different set of people but still standing in the same place. In his haste to leave the gents, he'd bumped into the young waitress who'd brought over his first drink earlier that evening. Having apologised and ordered another drink, he wondered whether she might have heard Edward's cry for help and, without thinking through the consequences, he'd explained that there was a man in the gents having a bit of difficulty. He dismissed Edward from his mind and focused on the task at hand.

Now the waitress arrived, carrying his drink. Close behind her was Paul, the front of house manager who had greeted them earlier. His warm smile long gone. Instead, he looked flustered and eager to pull Sasha away from the crowd. It didn't take long for Manny to grasp the seriousness of the situation. A huddle had gathered around the beleaguered and battered Edward who – as he discovered later - also just happened to be the grandson of a founder member of the philosophy school. Not for the first time in his life, Manny felt the familiar feeling of not belonging. He saw Sasha's head bow low as she listened to what Paul had to tell her. He'd failed her. The one person she thought she could rely on had let her down. He felt sickened and angry with himself. He didn't wait to be asked to leave. He would spare them that unenviable task. Kissing Sasha apologetically on the cheek and mouthing the word sorry, he walked straight out of the building, placing his unfinished drink on an empty table as he left. It was only 11.35pm, still plenty of time for him to catch a train back home to West Hampstead. Outside, it had started to rain.

On the tube home Manny did not quite have the carriage to himself, there were still plenty of people with somewhere to go. But for twenty minutes or so he was able to sit uninterrupted as he dissected the events of the night. The earlier part of the evening had been successful in overthrowing his preconceived ideas on Dr Sasha Harrington. He saw in her a vulnerability that he recognised in many of his students. In the same way, it stoked within him a burning determination to help her fight her inner demons. He felt a stirring of sympathy when he recognised that she too was haunted by something in her past.

The incident with Edward was not the stupidest thing he'd ever done. There'd been far worse. On reflection, it was unlikely even to make it into his Top Ten of misadventures. Nevertheless, in terms of timing, it was probably the most unfortunate, and completely unnecessary, and for that he was full of regret and disappointment. He doubted now whether he would even get to see the money or receive any more escorting work. Looking at his hazy image in the window opposite, he silently cursed himself. From that distance he could not see the dejection in and around his eyes, but he knew it was there.

With the money earned for that night's work he could've bought a plane ticket and pissed off, escaping straight into the outstretched, welcoming arms of his loving family back in Spain, leaving behind all this mess. He leant back to rest his head, keeping his eyes shut, allowing himself to wallow longer than usual in this false belief, in a familiar attempt to delay the onset of harsh reality.

Her anger was unmistakable. Manny knew that he'd let Anna down more than once during his time as her lodger, but he could not recall being so hated before. Despite all the times he'd been late with his rent she'd rarely raised her voice. He knew that he was in trouble when he found the front door double-locked and the hall light switched off. Anna had shouted down from her bedroom window above that her mind was made up. He was out. She'd placed most of his belongings around the side of the house stuffed in a pile of black bags. She would leave the rest out in the same place tomorrow. Anna reminded him he'd need to collect them soon because the bin men were due on Wednesday. When he raised his voice she'd threatened to call the police. Also, she told him, her mum was asleep inside, still feeling fragile from her fall. She was staying over for a while. Manny knew that it was pointless to continue to shout out his objections. He would have to try speaking to her again the following day, maybe by then she might have calmed down. The feelings that stirred up inside him were unmistakable. They were the same feelings he'd experienced on the night his mother had done the same thing and kicked him out of her house when he was in his late teens. The comment that had hurt him the most at the time was the one she yelled through the bolted front door that he was just like his father: 'Nothing but a drunken waste of space.'

In the dark he looked through the bags for his most essential belongings but soon gave up and settled for just one bag containing toiletries and a clean pair of boxers. He walked away with his head down and the collar of his new suit turned up. It was cold and raining still. Manny paused at the gate. Their argument had attracted a small audience. Heads of neighbours were peeking between gaps in their curtains. He didn't know which way to turn because he didn't know where to go. Tuesday had spread into Wednesday. It was 1.20am. He was very tired and very worried.

Meanwhile, in her house in Barnes, Sasha sat staring into her dressing table mirror, removing all the make-up from her face, with thoughts of the evening rattling around in her head. A small donation to the school had been enough to appease the ensuing uproar. She lit up and enjoyed a long drag. Holding the smoke deep down she let it out slowly, forming ring shapes of various sizes. She couldn't produce heart shapes. Smiling contently, she felt the excitement bursting in her chest. She could not remember how long it had been since she'd felt such a natural buzz. Who would've thought it? Just like the wild Shams, he'd acted with anger against those educated fools who wanted to pour scorn on her beliefs and criticise their special friendship. Just as Rumi did with Shams, she would open her heart and mind, embracing him and his deep wisdom. It seemed to her that the fiery Manny had more in common with the charming, homeless wanderer than she could ever have hoped. She was tempted to send him a text, but she resisted. He needed time to lick his wounds. His actions were not that of a wise man. He'd be disappointed with himself. Finishing her wine and stubbing out the cigarette into the ashtray, Sasha knew that sleep would be slow in coming. After all, it wasn't everyday that one's beloved arrived. "Faith is the little bird that sings while dawn is still dark," she hummed. This lonely bird had been singing in the dark for some time now. Again she searched her mind for Rumi's words:

'I can be without anyone
but not without you.
You twist my heart, dwell in my mind
and fill my eyes, you are my joy
I can't be without you.' [7]

CHAPTER
FIFTEEN

"Let me get this right. A bloke was winking at you and blowing you kisses so you decided to follow him into the gents...?"

"Yeah. But not for the reasons that you're thinking..."

"I'm only repeating what you told me. Touchy bastard, ain't ya? You were just the same last time... You're a lucky boy. I was on my way home thinking that I was done for the night." He threw Manny a glare to show how put out he was at having to drive across to the other side of the city at 2.30am to pick up someone who'd given him lip on their only previous encounter. Manny was now silently hoping that he hadn't been too obnoxious back then.

Unlike last time Manny sat in the front of Len's car, partly to avoid the latter's eyes peering at him from the rear view mirror and partly in a poor attempt at securing some kind of personal connection with the driver, but Len still continued to look annoyed and inconvenienced.

Without any money and nowhere to else to go, Len had been his only real choice. He had either exhausted everyone else's sympathy or he was too proud to seek their help. Even allowing for the grim situation in which he found himself, there were those in his life who remained off-limits.

There was no way he wanted to involve any colleagues from school. He enjoyed the odd drink and football match with some of them after work but it never went beyond that. His closest friend or the closest thing to it had to be Andy Moran. But Andy had settled down and moved in with his girlfriend, Jane, who never seemed particularly thrilled to see Manny at the best of times, let alone in the early hours of a Wednesday morning. He'd have to concoct yet more lies and, after the character assassination he'd experienced from the furious Anna, he was running on empty, no longer able to find the right words to help dig his way out of another tight situation.

With regret, he'd eventually decided to phone Len from his company phone. There was no one else he could think of to turn to who would leave him alone and not pry into his affairs. Pre-Lucy days there had been a couple of mates he'd knocked about with but he'd never been one for lasting friendships. People came and people went. It was how it was and always had been for him, he reasoned, telling himself that he preferred it that way.

After a great deal of moaning and an audible display of annoyance, Len had reluctantly agreed to come and pick him up from outside West Hampstead station.

Manny had been telling him about the night's events and the trouble he'd incurred as patiently as he could. He was going to need Len's understanding if he was to get some money off him.

"I understand that bit... probably even reacted in the same way, but why has your missus kicked you out?"

"Anna is not my missus."

"Bit of a domestic? Must be hard for the poor cow... working the hours you do... rolling in smelling of perfume and wearing lipstick on your collar. Does she know what you do?"

"She's not my girlfriend, she's my landlady... and as I'm trying to explain, she's kicked me out because I owe her rent." It was a job keeping the irritation from his voice.

Len looked at him as he drove, and gave him one of his leering grins. "Can't you pay her off in kind? I mean...considering what you do...thought that you might have worked something out with her... kind of a special arrangement between ya both."

Manny didn't bother to dignify the seedy remark with a response. Instead, he turned and stared out into the dark, tutting slowly and shaking his head.

"Where do you want dropping?"

The decisive moment had arrived. Manny guessed it was now or never. It could go either way. Len was a hard man to figure out.

"Depends."

"Depends...? On what?

"On whether you're willing to give me a sub."

"A sub? Fuck me... He's been in the job five minutes and the cheeky bastard's asking for a sub." Manny's request had been successful in one thing: bringing Len's piss taking to an abrupt halt. A lengthy silence followed. Len stared across at Manny, weighing him up for the few seconds that the road allowed. All he could do now was sit and wait for his answer. It was now out there. He couldn't help noticing the size of Len's enormous hands. They made the steering wheel look very small. He was a powerfully built man whose many scars suggested that he'd once relished the ferocity of battle. The silence continued as he drove, tapping his fingers on the steering wheel, obviously thinking hard like one of Manny's thicker students. Manny waited as he continued to watch Len deep in thought, pondering and grimacing as he searched for the best answer, not necessarily the correct answer. He finally responded, keeping his eyes firmly fixed on the road.

"From what you've just told me, the prospect of you getting any more work looks seriously in doubt... How are you going to be able to pay me back?... Sounds to me that you're already up to your neck in debt."

"Come on, Len. Have a heart. Don't make me beg... As well as paying you back, I will owe you one... A big one... I shan't forget... I will speak to Virginia tomorrow and try and iron things out with her... You know her well...Can't you also have a word?" He paused before continuing, dropping the persuasive tone. "Besides, as you've mentioned before, you'll easily know where to find me... I don't need much... just enough get me through the next couple of days."

Another drawn out pause, then Len finally replied, "Bollocks... Okay, here's what I'm going to do." He pointed a big finger inches from Manny's face. "And for your sake, don't make me regret it... I will lend you some but I want it back in my hands by this time next week. Wednesday. I'll warn you now though, don't make me come and ask for it. I will be very disappointed. *Comprende*, Manuel?" Reaching into his inside pocket, he pulled out a small brown envelope, the same as before, and handed it across to Manny. It was as thick as last time. Manny had only been expecting £20, £50 at the most. He tried hard not to show any sign of surprise.

"And before you think I'm soft, think again. It's only because the girls in the office seem to like you... Especially young Monica. Fuck knows why though... Where shall I drop you?"

"Cheers, Len. I appreciate it, I really do. Louise told me you were a good bloke really. But don't worry, mate, I shan't tell a soul... I'll jump out near a cheap hotel or at the next B&B that we pass."

"Eh? Can't you stay with one of your mates or a family member?" He raised his eyebrows in genuine disbelief. Again Manny struggled to find the correct response. This time he doubted that it was down to his tiredness. Earlier, Len had pulled over to the side of the road. When an answer was not forthcoming, he put the car back into gear and pulled away from the kerb. The older man's expression had softened. The frown faded, but the lines on his craggy face were still visible. More silence followed.

"I tell you what... I've got a spare room. Used to be my daughter's. You can get your head down there for the night."

"I don't have to lock my bedroom door though, do I? There'll be hell to pay if I wake up in the morning to find my Y fronts on back to front." For the first time both men managed a smile at Manny's poor attempt at humour and there was a brief moment of men being men in the changing rooms after a game, in a lads together kind of way. But he could tell that this act of kindness had caused Len some unease, in having to stray away from his tough guy comfort zone.

They got back to Len's flat in Islington just after 3.00am. The drive home had been a quiet affair, neither man being a fan of small talk. Len listened to his music while Manny busied himself trying to recall the words of the poem that had struck such a chord with him earlier that evening. Unfortunately, the verses were now eluding him, so he gave up.

Len had pointed him into the spare room where the waiting double bed and en suite bathroom were a welcome sight. Manny nodded his appreciation. Both too tired to communicate further.

Manny had to leave for work in less than four hours' time. The thought depressed him. He threw himself fully clothed onto the bed, regretting that he'd taken so many days off sick recently. He really could do with a day off, just sleeping. The way things were shaping up, it looked like he might need to start taking his day job seriously again. It would be hard to secure a decent place to live without a reference from work. One positive thing about teaching was that it tended to be a useful profession when needing to win approval. Trust seemed easier to attain. Allowing his eyes to close, Manny hoped that his mind would soon stop racing. Finally it did and he embraced the ensuing stillness. The words of that poem started to filter through into his sleepy state and suddenly it came to him:

'One day your heart will take you to your lover
one day your soul will carry you to the beloved.
Don't get lost in your pain, know that one day
your pain will become your cure...' [8]

There was a light floating sensation. Then darkness.

CHAPTER SIXTEEN

"All I'm saying is, don't be too hard on the lad. From what he told me, I'd probably have done the same. The bloke sounded a right tosser."

Virginia slowly shook her head in mock surprise in the direction of the two girls who were sitting in her office for their Wednesday morning meeting.

Hope you're minuting this, Monica. Who'd have thought that Len, the hired muscle, would also fall victim to the charms of our Mr Rodriguez? He's a loose cannon. I can't afford for him to come along and wreck things, destroy all my hard work. Are you going soft in your old age, Len?"

"Leave it out, Virginia. You would've needed a heart of stone not to feel for the fella. You should have seen him. He was standing on his own, in the freezing cold, at two o'clock in the morning, teeth chattering, looking dead dishevelled and clutching a binliner with his belongings in. I just think he deserves another chance, that's all. He's better than some of those other posers you've taken on in the past."

"Why didn't he go home?" asked Monica, concerned.

"Couldn't. Landlady chucked him out. Gave him his marching orders. He's fallen behind with his rent. Seems she's had enough."

"So where did you have to take him to? Hope it wasn't too far. I'll take the petrol money out of his wages if it was," Virginia enquired, also concerned but for different reasons.

Len shifted his big frame rather awkwardly in his seat, his discomfort easy to read. He coughed in an attempt to buy time.

"Well, we drove around for a bit, looking for a cheap hotel but we couldn't find one." He coughed again and quickly mumbled his next sentence. "I took him home with me. Stayed in the spare room." He shifted in his seat again, clearly looking uncomfortable and on some level a little embarrassed. He tried hard to conceal it. All three girls looked at each other, wide-eyed and open-mouthed. Len looked down and inspected his fingernails, gruffly clearing his throat. A silence descended over the office.

Virginia was the first to speak. Resisting the temptation to laugh, she permitted herself a rare smile instead. "Leonard, is there something you'd like to tell us? Would you care to elaborate? Do we need to send you an invoice for his services? Louise, did you know about this? I hope he filled out a request form?"

"I'm afraid he didn't. How much should I charge him, Virginia?" It was Louise's turn to poke fun.

"Behave yourselves. What else was I supposed to do?" Len snapped.

"I don't believe that you couldn't find a hotel though. Come on, you're in the middle of London... Well, well, well, we are full of surprises today. One learns something new everyday. I didn't think anything about this job could shock me any more. How wrong could I be! Have you minuted all of this, Monica?"

"Yes, Virginia. Don't be embarrassed, Len. I think that was a really sweet thing to do. Shows that you really do have a kind heart. She leant over and kissed him on his leathery cheek. "Ignore those two, they're just teasing. You should know by now that they love pulling your leg."

Len shook his head and rolled his eyes towards the ceiling, sighing noisily. He muttered something inaudible, annoyance written across his rugged face. Fidgeting with his super-size collar, he loosened the shirt from his thick bull neck. "Can we get on with it please. There are things I need to be getting on with."

"Yes. You're quite right, Len. Sorry. Can we all focus again please? Has Louise given you your list of jobs and gone over it with you?"

"Yes."

"Great. How many drivers have you got for the weekend?"

"Three. Including me."

"Excellent. Right, Louise? Is there anything else you need to say before he can go?"

Len leaned forward, perching himself on the edge of his chair, hands impatiently drumming his knees.

"Nope. That's it as far as I can see," Louise replied, looking down her list. "Thanks, Len. I'll speak to you later. Yeah?"

"Fine. I'll be off then." He stood up, unsmiling, smoothing down the creases from his trousers, then putting on his overcoat.

"Len, one more thing, can you make sure you go to the bank first please and get that money out?"

He nodded.

"And where is the Latin lover now?"

"Who, Manuel?"

More sniggers from the girls.

"I dropped him at West Hampstead station early this morning. Said he had to get to work... Right, I'm off. See you all later. Place is a bloody madhouse." He walked out, shaking his big, sullen face, slamming the office door behind him.

"That Manny has certainly got something about him. First, the good lady doctor herself and now Len. Both singing his praises and defending him to the hilt. Can you ever remember Len speaking up for any of the escorts before?"

"Louise, I would like you to go and see Manny tomorrow. Tell him he needs to control that temper of his. Take him out and treat him to a meal. See how he is. Sound him out about doing a double shift this Friday. If Len's right, he will do it because he needs the money. I'll call him later today. There are one or two things that I need to discuss with our popular new escort. Has Mr Rickmond paid and confirmed yet? Can't we send Nathaniel instead?"

"No. He insists they want Manny. I've already tried to talk him out of it. Also, a few other of our regulars are wanting to book him. He's had quite a few hits on his web page."

"Monica, can you remind me to speak to Dr Harrington later. She's just going to have to learn to share, whether she likes it or not. Highest bidder wins the day, I'm afraid. Our new recruit is hot property. I can see him giving some of our high-earning lady escorts a run for their money very soon." Her cool green eyes flickered onto her computer screen as she stared at her forecast sheet. "I think he was telling us the truth when he said he would make the company lots of money. There's definitely something alluring about him. We need to maximise his earning power. He worries me though. We're going to have to handle Mr Rodriguez carefully, I think. I want him eased in very gently. I'm not sure whether he has the temperament to handle the more demanding jobs just yet. Friday's booking may give us a better indication of his capabilities. Fingers crossed, girls. If he passes that test, then you can expect to meet your bonuses. Don't minute that, Monica." The wide eyes and expanding smile were back on her face.

"Okay, let's move on to other matters. How are we looking for the rest of week? I'm expecting a busy weekend. Lots of bookings have been confirmed and paid for, so we need to make sure that we have few extra ladies on standby. Can you two organise that by the end of the day?"

CHAPTER
SEVENTEEN

Manny stared out at the January gloom from his classroom window, brooding. It was raining and there were still another forty minutes to go until the end of the school day. Exhausted and wearing the same clothes as the night before, he'd spent the best part of the day willing round the minute hands on his watch. Fortunately, the day had been relatively incident free. He'd successfully motivated his classes into completing their assessments in moderate silence. Any student who strayed from his instructions received a contemptuous stare that demanded obedience. The written assessments meant extra marking that evening but they had to be done in order to track his students' progress. It occurred to him late in the afternoon that he'd been wishing the day away so as to get some much needed rest. The irony being that he was still unsure as to where he would be staying that night.

He'd thought about asking Moran for help at lunch but he had been far too eager in filling him in on the events that had occurred at the pub the night before. He took great delight in telling Manny about the new teacher, Emma, and how she'd sloped off with Phil Young from the P. E. department towards the end of the evening. When Manny tried to suggest that there might be a perfectly innocent explanation for this, Moran told him, grinning profusely, that a reliable eye witness had seen the pair tongue-wrestling in the middle of the car park. Manny rolled his head around his neck, trying to create an outlet for the irritation and boredom engulfing him. Pushing himself up from his chair, he announced to Moran that he had some papers to mark, ignoring his friend's mocking shouts that he shouldn't get jealous or upset.

Sitting in the classroom now, he switched on his phone to check for messages. After several minutes he managed to get enough of a signal to read a text message from Louise requesting that he contact her. Nothing from Anna. She was still ignoring his calls. A hot bath and a good night's sleep was what he craved the most. Looking for a permanent new place to live could wait. Instead, he printed off a list of hotels in the area. He was unable to book a room over the phone or on the internet due to his no longer having the use of a credit or debit card.

After work he went to collect his things from the back of Anna's house in West Hampstead. Walking up her path, he could see through the lounge window an elderly lady sitting in an armchair in front of a blaring television. Presuming this was Anna's mother and that Anna was still at work, he didn't bother to knock. Her one act of kindness had been to place his belongings some distance away from the rubbish bins. He decided to stuff only the essentials into two of his sports bags, leaving behind most of his clothes and other items of less importance. With a full binliner in one hand, a large sports bag in the other, and the straps of the large holdall heaved over his shoulder, he made his way to the station, mulling over his dwindling options. It made sense to head back to St Albans and be nearer to his work, so, moving slowly and rather awkwardly, he decided that that was what he'd do.

It was drizzling. The rain wetting his face acted as a reminder of how desperate things had become. A world away from those distant, sunny days he'd spent island-hopping with the beautiful Lucy. How had he been so blind as not to see her and that ponce falling for each other? How many times had she continued to sleep with him whilst wishing she was in the arms of her new love? Pulling his jacket tightly around himself in a vain attempt to shield himself from the draught, he readjusted his grip on the bags and increased his pace. There was no point torturing himself. Somehow or other, he would just have to deal with the blows life hurled at him and concentrate on navigating his way out of his more pressing predicaments.

After coming out of the station at St Albans he joined the queue at the taxi rank. He opted to try a Spa Hotel where he'd once attended a friend's wedding. He knew it would be costly but, after hearing the message Virginia had left on his phone and with the prospect of work alive once more, he'd felt the warm breath of optimism surge through him and his sodden clothes. He was already contemplating the extra money he could earn doing a double-booking that coming Friday. She still needed to talk to him about a couple of things though, she said, so he made a mental note to call her first thing the next day. He'd also spoken to Louise who had suggested that they should go out that evening for a chat and a bite to eat. Despite being desperate to sleep, he felt invigorated at the thought of her company. There was a mystery of sorts about her that he liked and it pleased him that she insisted on coming over to him in St Albans. He was to text her once he knew the address of the hotel where he'd be staying.

On entering the elegant hotel lobby, Manny politely declined the porter's offer to carry his bags. He walked straight up to the reception desk and waited, wet through, his bags dumped at his feet. The lady behind the desk listened as he explained his urgent need for a room, telling her that a pipe had burst and flooded his home, causing hundreds of pounds' worth of damage. She began searching the computer for a single but informed him that they only had double deluxe or executive suites available. The best deal she could offer him was a deluxe room at £139 including breakfast.

"I only need the room for the night. Come on. I'm thinking of holding my wedding reception here, you know?"

She stared at him for a while, nonplussed, before smiling apologetically and turning back to her screen. He noticed the name Bethany displayed on her badge.

"I'll tell you what, seeing as I'm in a good mood, I'll give you a deluxe room at the single rate. Now I can't be any fairer than that, can I?"

"What is the rate for a single?"

"£95"

"With breakfast?"

"Go on then, with breakfast... Oh, and an invite to the wedding," she said with a sarcastic raise of her eyebrow.

Giving her a grateful smile, he took the cash out of his brown envelope and began counting out the money. She looked at him, perplexed.

"Cash...? Don't you have a credit card?"

"No... It's been a nightmare, my room was flooded, couldn't find my wallet. I've got my passport on me though... is that any help? Anyway, I'm a strictly cash man."

After filling in a form and having to hand over his passport, together with another £200 deposit, he finally got a key to his room. It was on the second floor and was positioned at the back of the hotel. The room was modern and spacious. Two large windows looked out onto a darkening backdrop of fields. The double bed looked inviting, as did the bath tub. He wasted no time in hanging up some of his clothes in the hope that at least some of the creases would drop out in time, and placed his toiletries tidily onto the shelf in the stylish marble bathroom. These small gestures helped in making him feel more at home, allowing him to feel as if he still had some control over the situation. He filled the bath with hot water, poured in half a bottle of exotic bath lotion and climbed out of his soaking clothes. Finally he decided to text Louise the address of the hotel.

Having spent the past couple of hours chilled by the rain, he let out a groan of pleasure as he slowly submerged his weary bones deep into the steaming tub. Closing his eyes, he spent the next hour in a temporary state of bliss.

After a shave, he helped himself to a cold beer out of the mini bar, sat on the bed, leaned back against the pile of pillows and checked the time. It was 6.20pm. He was meeting Louise in the lobby at 8.30. There was time for a rest. His eyes were closed for a matter of minutes before the vibrating of his phone disturbed him. It was a text from Sasha, thanking him for his support the previous evening and telling him he was not to worry about the commotion towards the end. It had been dealt with. Also, she hoped that he would be able to meet that Friday. He debated for a while whether or not to reply but decided against. It could wait. For now, he wanted to focus on his night ahead with Louise. He made a mental note of all the things he wanted to ask her about the job: Sasha, Virginia, future clients, money and so on. The one question he would also like to ask but doubted that he would was whether she would care to stay with him for the night. Keep him company. Have sex. He found himself smiling in anticipation at the possibilities, like a euphoric adolescent about to embark on a first date. He considered the variety of responses she might give. Not for the first time that day, he caught himself clock-watching. He searched his bags for a pair of jeans, a decent, clean top and his iPod. Having found them, he laid the clothes out over a chair, returned to the bed, stretched out, plugged in his music and tried to lose himself.

He fell asleep at once and didn't wake until the ringing of the hotel phone disturbed him. In an instant he reached for the receiver and listened to a voice on the other end informing him that his guest was waiting downstairs in the lobby. After throwing on his clothes, he splashed his face in the bathroom sink in an attempt to wash away the grogginess, squirted on some aftershave, grabbed his key and headed out of the door, down the stairs and straight into the lobby.

She smiled when she saw him, rose from her chair, smoothed down her skirt, picked up her handbag and walked towards him. She looked good. Classy. She kissed him on the cheek. With one arm, he pulled her close and returned the kiss, making sure he got a good noseful of her scent. She smelled good, feminine. He held onto her just a touch longer than was usual. Her body language responded positively, in no rush to pull away. This pleased him.

"Hello, Manny. Good to see you again."

"Louise. Brilliant that you're here. Did you have any trouble finding the place?"

"None. Thanks to the age of satellite navigation. What a gorgeous hotel."

"Yeah, it's not bad. Shall we go through to the bar?"

"Sure. Why not?"

They moved into the bar area and made themselves comfortable in a pair of deep, trendy leather chairs. Manny ordered a citrus vodka and tonic for himself while Louise insisted on sticking to sparkling water. The conversation ebbed and flowed smoothly. He discovered that Len used to be Virginia's driver and minder during her own escorting days. The fact that she had started up her company solely with her own 'wages of sin' impressed him more than it surprised him. Then, as the business began to grow, Virginia had hired Louise on the marketing side, her expertise being employed to help the escorting company develop a more respectable profile, being viewed both as a professional and legitimate service. Manny explained again why he'd decided to approach Perfect Company and ask for work. This time he confessed to her the cold reality of his financial situation and how he came to be staying in a luxury hotel despite being flat broke. Although she did not condone his actions, she understood a little of his psychological need to feel like he was calling the shots. She was quick to add, however, that if he continued with this flawed philosophy it would be some time before he escaped the clasp of his debts. Later, he'd admit to himself that he had quite enjoyed the way she rebuked him over his false pride and his reckless attitude towards money. He needed someone to give it to him straight.

He ordered another drink and asked whether she would like a glass of champagne. Louise shook her head, clicked her tongue and rolled her eyes. She asked him why he didn't just move in with a friend for a while? Manny explained his reasons. He could see her thinking, *Why so few friends?*

"Why don't I have a word with Len? I'm sure he would put you up for the short term. Come on... don't look so disheartened! From the interest your profile has generated I'm sure it won't be long before you start to get back on your feet."

Manny realised he'd still not checked out the web page.

"I'll help you to manage your money and try and teach you to become a bit more frugal. A few more bookings and you'll soon be back in credit... Come on, don't give up... Take back control."

He leaned back in his seat and took another sip of his drink, wondering how she would react if he was to tell her what he was thinking. All he wanted to do was lead her up into his room, remove her clothes and lose himself in her femininity.

Her words began to drift away as he imagined her having the power to kiss away all his troubles, temporarily silencing the dull tune of self-pity that played inside him. Part of him wanted to believe that after they'd made love the events that were threatening to engulf him would simply disappear. Unfortunately, the other part of him knew better. He felt a genuine longing to feel safe, to be held. Sex, he thought, was probably the most reliable path to take in order to reach that highly desirable state.

"Manny, are you listening to me?"

He gave a small nod before emptying his glass. Feeling the tiredness creep up on him, he leant forward in his seat. "Tell me about Dr Sasha Harrington."

"Sasha…? What do you want to know?"

"Anything." Through exhaustion and alcohol he began to have trouble articulating his thoughts. Both of them had their attention briefly drawn away by a group of people in suits and evening gowns entering the bar laughing and talking loudly. Louise turned back to face him, taking a sip of her water before answering.

"What is there to know? She's a lonely fantasist desperately seeking love and approval… who seems, by the way, to be developing an infatuation for you. According to Virginia, she sees you through a 'mystical poetic veil.' She went berserk when she found out that you were unavailable this Friday… Oh, by the way, Virginia would like to speak to you about Friday. Excuse me, can I have the bill please?" she asked, turning to the waiter who was busy wiping the tables nearby.

"I'm supposed to be treating you to something to eat. Where would you like to go?" She reached towards her handbag. "Come on, anywhere you want… It's not my part of town so you'll have to pick." She shifted suddenly in her chair to imply that she was ready to leave. The waiter returned with the bar bill which she paid in cash, demanding a receipt. He duly obliged.

Manny sat there motionless throughout, gazing at her with desire in his eyes. A look of bemusement broke out across her face. Several seconds passed before he spoke.

"Can I tell you something, Louise?

"Sure... Go ahead."

He stretched over and whispered in her ear what it was he wanted to do. He felt her fight a shudder as he pressed his lips lightly on her neck.

"What are you doing, Manny? No, stop! Please don't..." Her eyes closed, her words lacked bite. The look of bemusement was replaced by a cloud of concern.

"Stay with me."

"Manny... No... I mustn't... This can't happen." But her body language told him something different.

He stood up and held out his hand. His turn to wait for a response. She stared at him apprehensively, wanting him to understand a little of her dilemma. He saw the struggle going on within her. A few moments passed. He remained standing, hand still held out. The moment she put her hand in his and looked up, he had his answer.

When they got to his room, he inserted the key card in the slot and opened the door. As he was about to walk in, he felt a tugging on his arm. He spun around to look. She kissed him quickly on the lips, followed by a full embrace. Manny hesitated before walking in. Again, he looked hard into her face, wanting to give her an opportunity to back out, half expecting that she would. Louise read him. Then smiled, nodded and led him in.

He wasn't a hard man to find attractive. In fact, she'd found herself drawn to him from the moment he'd first walked into their office. Virginia had described him as the type of bloke women would either want to fuck or mother. She'd wanted to do both. Louise banged the back of her head repeatedly on the head rest of the car seat, cursing. *Jesus, Louise! You silly bitch.* A mischievous grin then spread across her face. Contrasting emotions. It was that look. The one that had passed between them earlier in the evening. Despite the cheeky smile, she'd detected a deep sadness in and around his eyes. Part of her had wanted to believe that she could kiss it away. Heal him. They had made love with an intensity she'd rarely experienced in her modest sex life. Something intimate had been shared in the darkness; the way he'd held her afterwards had only heightened that sense of intimacy. She had tried to discover more about him and the secrets he kept without much success. Rather than open up, he managed to fend off her probing questions with a well-rehearsed smile. He'd admitted that his situation was pretty dire. "However, I'd prefer not talk about myself," he'd said forcefully. There was a certain complexity about him that she found most intriguing. Too intriguing. Her boss had been right... *Oh. Shit. Virginia...* The thought spiked her like a hot needle, her smile temporarily displaced. Virginia was quick to condemn any behaviour which might complicate working relations. She always stressed the importance of being wholly professional when dealing either with clients or escorts. But after her initial fears and a fair amount of lip biting, Louise reassured herself that no one would ever hear anything about their sexual encounter.

Despite the deathly hour displayed on the clock, she felt wide awake, animated. The time was 3.37am. As she drove home along the relatively quite M1, Louise permitted herself another smile. She thought again about the way he'd remained silent after the sex and of the honesty he involuntarily spoke through his eyes and touch, often contradicting the words that *did* leave his mouth. She turned up the volume of her radio as the DJ, Gilles Peterson, played yet another track that seemed to be in tune with her own sensations.

CHAPTER
EIGHTEEN

Trying to ignore the streak of light forcing itself into the room, Manny tightly embraced the pillow on which her scent still lingered. He took in a lungful of her perfume in the hope of prolonging the warm glow of the night before. She'd certainly been a healthy distraction, a warm, sexy and welcome escape from the depressing reality of his world. It was almost time to wake up. Lifting his head from the pillows, he scanned the room with bleary eyes, not liking what he saw: unkempt clothes scattered all over the floor, bags containing his belongings bundled into a corner, and a clock that blinked 7.10am at him. But it was the things he couldn't see that made him sigh and want to lie back down, burying his head deep into the pillows: unpaid hotel bill, precious little money to pay with, no home, a full day of teaching ahead, Baxter, unmarked folders and a thumping headache. How tempting it would be to put everything on hold and stay another night but he didn't have the funds. He was expecting payment from the agency to be in his account the following day (Friday) but most of that was already earmarked to pay back Len.

Manny sat on the edge of his bed, rubbing his hands over his cropped hair, weighing up his options. He squinted at the clock. It was now twenty-five minutes past seven. If he hurried, there might be just enough time to appreciate the hotel breakfast before checking out and heading off to work.

He made a valiant effort to break free from the grip of his darkening mood. Louise had again encouraged him to stay positive, he remembered. Bookings were being made and the work was definitely there *if* he could keep it together, she had said. A big if. His mind returned to the early part of the evening. He'd learnt a lot about Virginia, Len and Sasha, but not a great deal about Louise herself. He'd discovered that she was passionate between the sheets, a good kisser and that she had a tattoo on the small of her back, but not much else. Questions buzzed around inside his head like a swarm of angry bees. Had she been sent by Virginia? Probably, she'd kept the receipts. Did she have a boyfriend? Not sure. Had she really enjoyed the sex? Hope so.

While luxuriating under the steaming water, Manny recalled the conversation they'd had about Sasha. What was it Louise had said? 'A lonely fantasist'? Harsh, he thought. Sasha might have some issues, nevertheless she was a respected historian as well as a gifted writer with the power of being able to inspire people through her passion for her specialised subject. He himself had been surprisingly enraptured by her performance earlier that week. He guessed that Louise had only ever discussed work-related matters with her and any other information she did get to hear about Sasha was probably through Virginia or from the loose lips of previous escorts.

When he'd finished showering, he wrapped himself in the biggest of the towels and as he dried off he found himself singing the words from an old Radiohead song: *"I want a perfect body... I want a perfect soul... I wish I was special... so fucking special... but I'm a creep... I'm a weirdo... I don't belong here..."*

He struggled to suppress a smile as he considered storing the song on his mobile and using it for Sasha's caller ID. Putting the childish thought away, he quickly dressed, grabbed his phone and left his room for some breakfast. On his way down the corridor, he passed a chambermaid who smiled politely and bade him good morning. He returned the cheerful gesture. The smell of fresh coffee hung in the air. He hoped it would get him going. Two nights on the trot with precious little sleep meant that he avoided meeting his own reflection in the surrounding mirrors of the lift. He hadn't drunk that much the night before, but his head certainly felt like he had.

His train of thought was interrupted by the vibration of his mobile, which he'd just switched on. There was a message from Virginia, two missed calls from Sasha and a text from Louise. They could wait. First, he intended to enjoy his breakfast. As he walked through the lobby to get to the dining room he was surprised to see the same girl on reception. What was her name? Bethany. Her face had been freshened up and her hair rearranged but the traces of early morning sat stubbornly under the eyes. She caught him looking her way and gave him a friendly nod.

"Good morning, sir. Is everything okay?"

"Yeah, fine thanks. On my way to breakfast and then I'll be back down to check out."

"Check out? But I thought… I noticed that you'll be staying with us until Saturday."

"Sorry? No… I don't think so…"

She frowned at him for a moment before dropping her eyes onto the computer screen and busily tapping away on her keyboard.

"It is Mr Rodriguez, isn't it?" she asked, not looking up from the screen.

"Yeah. That's right. Why? Is there a problem?"

"Oh, that's strange… I could have sworn… just let me check here a moment." A short silence followed as she studied the screen "Yes. Here we are… I thought so… It says here booked and paid in full up to Saturday including breakfast. Is that correct? The booking was made early this morning. Paid with a credit card which means we're able to give you back your cash deposit. I'll have it ready for you to collect after your breakfast."

Louise! You star! he cheered inwardly.

"The flood must have caused quite some damage."

"Er… yes…yes, it did. A total nightmare. Frozen pipes."

"Oh dear," she said sympathetically. "Well, we hope you enjoy your short stay with us and that it shan't be too long before you're able to return home. Have a nice breakfast and let us know if there's anything you need to make your stay more comfortable."

"Thanks. I will," he beamed before bounding off in the direction of the dining room, reading the text from Louise as he went.

I was meant 2 buy U dinner.
Treated U 2 a couple of nights instead
Be positive. Call me later. L x

He should have felt more grateful but a part of him could not help but brood about whether or not she'd kept the receipt. *What do I care?* he thought while waiting to be seated. Whatever her motives, she had provided him with some much needed breathing space. But inwardly he did care. Something in him wanted or needed to believe that her motives *were* pure. A waiter interrupted his thoughts by asking for his name and room number and showing him to a table. He ordered some coffee, hoping it would help fend off such tired, silly thoughts. He sat alone at a table in the middle of the dining room, assessing the other guests, most of them dressed for business, and gazing silently through the window at the fresh January morning, taking in the beautifully manicured lawns. Calm, crisp and peaceful. The brief moment of meditation was ended by the arrival of a young waitress, bearing toast and coffee. She cheerily took his order and told him to help himself if he wanted any fruit and cereals. He declined, choosing instead to wait for his full English breakfast. While he waited, he listened to the message from Virginia. It was short and to the point, telling him in no uncertain terms to turn on his phone. She'd been trying to contact him and he was to call her before speaking to Sasha. 'It's important,' were her last words. *Sod it, she'll have to wait*, he thought as he switched off his mobile. More pressing matters had to be dealt with first, like the acute pangs of hunger grumbling from the pit of his stomach. All he wanted to do was savour every mouthful of his cooked breakfast. As for Virginia, he would call her on his way to work.

After breakfast, Manny returned to his room feeling energised and in a better state of mind to deal with the day ahead. While inspecting himself in the bathroom mirror he heard a phone ringing. It was the hotel telephone that sat on the bedside table. In some confusion he moved towards it. *Who's this? Louise or reception? Can't be anybody else.* He picked up the receiver.

"Hello…?"

"Manny?" A woman's voice. Virginia's voice. *How the hell…?*

"The whole point of providing you with a phone is so that I can get hold of you when I need to. Did you not get my message?"

"Virginia!" He failed to keep the surprise from his voice. "How the hell did you know I was here?"

"Louise, of course." *What else has she told you?*

"No. I didn't get your message. Sorry, the phone was charging." For a moment or two there was silence.

"I'll be honest with you, Manny, I'm a little concerned right now that you might go scaring away clients instead of generating bookings and increasing our client base. What on earth happened on Tuesday night?"

"Yeah, sorry about that. I've been having a bit of a tough time of late."

"So I hear. We all have our private little battles to win, Manny. I find money tends to help. Start making some. You're lucky Sasha wants to give you another chance. I don't want to hear any more of the self-pity, it doesn't suit you and I can't spare the time. You're still on trial, don't forget, and you still need to convince me that you're up to the task. Cast away these nagging doubts of mine. Sasha explained what had happened, and whether or not that chap deserved a thump is irrelevant. I can't afford to let you bring my company into disrepute. You have a problem while out with a client, you contact Len or myself first. Okay?"

"Yes," he replied reluctantly.

"By a stroke of luck you have a chance to redeem yourself this Friday. A final chance to show me that you're serious and not just wasting my time or anybody else's."

"This Friday? Who with? Sasha?"

"Late part of Friday, yes. But I have a small job for you earlier in the evening with another of our regulars. It shouldn't take long, a couple of hours at most, leaving enough time for you to get over to the 'Dear Doctor' where you can wine and dine her and continue to weave that famous Spanish charm of yours. What do you say? But before answering, it's worth remembering that this could be possibly your last chance to impress and not mess up."

145

"What does this other job entail?"

"Let's talk money first. You could earn in excess of three hundred for the first booking and another six hundred if you decide to spend the night at Sasha's. You know, just to keep her company… any extras are strictly down to you."

He worked hard not to whistle. "Wow! That's a lot of money." Excitement surged through him. He could start taking back control. The last part of her comment was lost on him. He could handle Sasha.

"It certainly is and, from what I've been hearing, you can hardly afford to turn it down."

Not for the first time during this call he had a horrible feeling that she knew everything he and Louise had discussed, as well as knowing exactly what had happened. Sitting on the edge of the bed, he chewed on his lip and rubbed his head.

"What's the first job?"

"Right up your street actually. A young wife. Husband's a rich and powerful businessman. Thirty odd years older than her, though. Bit of a control freak. Unfortunately for him but fortunately for us, he's impotent." She paused for a moment. "I'm sure I don't have to explain the rest."

She didn't.

"You will meet Mr and Mrs Smith for a drink and a chat first. Then, providing that goes well, you're being hired to entertain Mr Smith's wife. If you catch my drift."

He did.

"Take your time to think about it but don't take too long. There *are* others I could turn to."

He thought hard for a long moment before answering. He could hear muffled voices in the background. It sounded like Monica and Louise were in the office with her.

"In cash?"

"I think that can be arranged."

"Okay. I'll do it."

"Excellent. Don't you dare let me down, Manny."

"No, don't worry."

"Your new best friend, Len, will pick you up and drop you

off. I'll get Louise to email you with all the details. Talking of which, whatever did you two get up to last night?"

The question caught him by surprise and he was at a loss as to how to reply.

"She's running late this morning and seems a bit flustered. Most unlike her. I hope you behaved yourself, Señor Rodriguez."

"Of course I did. We just had a drink and a chat, that's all," he said forcefully.

"I'm sure you did. Anyway, I must get going … Oh, Manny? Before I forget…"

Here we go, he thought. *The catch*. He was beginning to see a pattern forming towards the end of her calls. She'd dropped a bombshell, round about now, on the last occasion she'd called him. *Brace yourself*, he told himself, *Make sure you're ready for it this time*.

"Yeah. What is it?"

"Not a word to Sasha about your earlier booking or any of your other bookings, come to think of it. Sensitive subject. I'll explain to you another time. Just make sure you call her today and smooth things over ready for Friday."

"That's okay. I kind of sussed that," he said with some relief. "Anything else?"

"No. I think we're done… I can't think of anything else. I told you about Mr Smith, didn't I?"

"No. What's that?"

"Nothing to worry about really except that sometimes he likes to watch!"

Once again the bomb hit its target. The time was 8.42am and he was already twelve minutes late for school.

Waylaid by Virginia's telephone call and the time he took sitting there afterwards, mulling over their conversation, Manny arrived outside his classroom forty minutes late. The door was firmly closed. Through the glass he could see Maureen Baxter sitting stern-faced behind *his* desk, scrutinizing the work awaiting his attention. She was jotting something down on a pad. His class of students kept their heads down, seeming to be hard at work. All except one. Imani Lewis. She had spotted him looking in and was sitting there with a huge smile. He knocked lightly before entering. A chorus of suppressed sniggers greeted his entrance. Sheepishly, he approached his desk.

"Morning."

"Mr Rodriguez, you're very late," Mrs Baxter said without looking up, still writing. "Lessons started well over forty minutes ago." Her tone was the same as if he were just another student who had crossed her path. Loud and laced with venom.

"Yes, I know. I know. Problems with the plumbing… Frozen pipes. I'm here now, so don't feel that you have to stay… Thanks for covering… Sorry if it put you out." He looked around the class to avoid her glare. "I trust they behaved themselves and are all working hard for you, Mrs Baxter?"

"It's not the students I have issues with, Mr Rodriguez," she said, removing her glasses and putting them away.

"As I said, I'm here now." He leant down and whispered forcefully into her ear, "Can we try and be professional here and talk about this later?"

"Oh, we certainly will be discussing this later, I can assure you of that," she replied in the same venom-laced tone. Somehow he was able to swallow his anger.

Her eyes fell back onto his untidy desk, its surface covered with unmarked work, exercise books and scattered files. For a long and very deliberate moment, she glanced over it, not bothering to mask the look of disapproval etched on her face. "Hmm, professional you say!" She stood up, collected her belongings and abruptly left the room, slamming the door as she went. The majority of the students had stopped working and were looking on, witnessing the burn of humiliation that had spread across his face. Sliding into the chair behind his desk, he tried to recover his composure. In full view of his students it was difficult and he was aware of the uncomfortable silence that had descended on the classroom.

"I should have brought in a note from my mum," he said glibly in an attempt to lighten the mood. He waited for the laughing to subside before purposefully looking at his watch, tapping the face with his finger to indicate that the lesson was not quite over. "Right," he continued, "there's still a few minutes left until the end of the lesson. Can you please carry on with the work you've been set."

"Sir? I don't mean to be rude. But are you sure that your watch is working?" Tom Rees was the first student to speak, much to the amusement of the rest of the class. Manny didn't reply at first. He just smiled, put his head down and pretended to sort through a pile of papers.

"I can do without any more sarcastic comments, thank you."

By mid-morning he'd made a decent effort of ploughing through the mess that sat on his desk, although there were plenty of papers and books still waiting to be marked. He'd responded to the dozen or so emails requesting information on certain students, read up on the minutes from various meetings and entered his class's predicted grades on the school system. It was hard enough keeping up with the relentless box ticking and marking at the best of times, nigh on impossible when you considered what he'd been getting up to in his spare time. He knew Baxter would be going for the jugular later. He needed to do what he could to restrict her ammunition. Luckily, he was free lesson two and was determined to make full use of the hour by getting some marking done. He'd sat there through morning break too, only stopping when he had to pay a visit to the gents. Lessons three and four, the two classes before lunch, he taught the lower school, where he normally liked to interact more by making them laugh with his funny stories. Today, instead, he set both groups a reading comprehension and kept his teacher's input to a minimum, buying himself more time to carry on with the paperwork. He decided not to bother with lunch, opting to stay in his room where he could persevere with the marking. He didn't want to have to sit there and make conversation in the staffroom. Anyway, he would only have to fend off probing questions about his lateness and endure yet more barracking with regards to his lousy time-keeping. No time for interruptions today, he told himself, and resumed his work.

It wasn't long however before he threw down his pen, clasped his hands behind his head and looked up at the ceiling, sighing heavily. He remained in that position for quite some time, losing himself in his thoughts. His mind scuttled back to the earlier phone call with Virginia… *'Sometimes he likes to watch…'* He tried not to think about it, not wanting to give it undue importance. But he couldn't help himself. He countered this by reminding himself of the money Virginia had mentioned. It would make a huge difference. He opened his desk drawer to check his mobile phone and whether it had a signal. It didn't.

I must contact Sasha, he reminded himself. *And Louise. Oh, and while I'm at it, I should try Anna again.* "You never know…" he said to nobody in particular.

"Dear me. He's only started talking to himself."

"What do you want, Moran?" He said it with a smile but there was a touch of seriousness behind his question.

"What's going on? Who are you hiding from?"

"I'm not hiding. I'm trying to get some marking done. Baxter's on the warpath. Loads to get through. Sometimes I wish I taught a Mickey Mouse subject like yours. Bet you hardly ever have to mark."

"Huh, you reckon? Cheeky bastard. I've only come down here to see if you fancy going for a beer and a curry later?"

"Sorry, mate, no can do. Got some running about to do later, a few bits and bobs I need to sort out. As well as trying to get this lot done."

"Mate, come on, tell me what's wrong. You've not been yourself for days now. What's happened? I talked to you when I was having a tough time and I hope that you would do the same with me. You're a mate. I don't like seeing you like this. We used to have a laugh, play football, go for a beer after work, but now…" He left it to hang in the air.

Manny laughed, pushed his books aside and gave Moran his full attention. "There's nothing wrong, I swear. Just got a lot going on at the moment, that's all. Busy. You know how it is with the job and with Baxter always on my case…"

Moran nodded to show that he understood but he was not

yet ready give it up. He sat down on one of the front desks. In the moment of silence that followed a mobile started buzzing. They looked at each other. Moran shook his head.

"It's not mine"

Pulling out his mobile from his desk drawer, Manny saw Sasha's name flashing on his screen. He didn't answer it and switched it off instead.

"Who's that, the bird?"

The question hit a raw nerve but Manny managed to bite his tongue. He ran his hand over his head. Moran was a decent bloke and maybe one day Manny would tell him everything, but not yet. He stood up, walked around his desk and stuck out a hand.

"Look, mate, I appreciate your concern. Let me get through the next couple of days and we'll go for that curry early next week. There's no problem other than work, I swear. If there was, you'd be the first to know."

Moran grinned and shook his hand, seeming happy. Just then, both men's attention was drawn by the opening of the classroom door. The P.E. teacher, Phil Young, swaggered towards them, clutching a list.

"Hello, ladies. Can I put you two down for the staff football match tomorrow night?" Moran nodded while Manny made his excuses.

"Sorry, Phil. No can do."

"What's up with you, Rodriguez? That's the second or third time you've let us down. What is it? Can't you Spanish handle the cold weather?"

Manny remembered what Moran had told him earlier that week, about Phil Young and the attractive new teacher. What was her name again...? Emma. That was it.

"Of course we can. I love my football but given a choice of kicking a ball around with a load of hairy, overweight gorillas or being out with a sexy hot date ... sorry, only one winner."

Young studied him for a moment before replying. "Hot date, eh? Anyone we know?"

"No. I doubt it. But she's a little stunner."

Phil Young smiled, turned and headed for the door. "Okay,

151

don't forget your boots tomorrow, Moran. Enjoy your date, Rodriguez."

"Hey, who's this date?" asked Moran, looking more upset than puzzled.

"Relax. If you're good, I might tell you next week."

CHAPTER NINETEEN

Dr Sasha Harrington, writer and historian, dragged deeply on a cigarette. She exhaled the smoke through her nose and continued to study the blemish on her face in the dressing room mirror. Her mobile phone sat silently beside her. "Little shit," she whispered. "That's the fourth time he's rejected my call." She powdered on some foundation, trying to soften the defined jawline that sat above her thickish neck, and continued to carry out other running repairs. The lines etched around her eyes needed hiding, as did the dark grooves that sat underneath. The minor repairs were becoming increasingly major, this concerned her. Sighing deeply, she set about applying her mascara, noticing that her fake lashes needed doing too. "Oh, for God's sake, what's the point?" She threw down the concealer, stood up and tightened the belt on her bathrobe. The dark shadow of anger and frustration was back.

Her publishers would be expecting her at their office for a meeting in an hour's time. She couldn't cancel again. Or could she? The landline began to ring. Momentarily, her heart flickered with the excitement she reserved only for him. But then she remembered. He didn't have her home number. She hadn't given it to him. "Damn." Maybe she should.

Ignoring the last couple of rings, she reached inside her wardrobe, took out the smart outfit she'd chosen earlier and carefully placed it on the bed. Then she dimmed the bedroom lights, averted her eyes from the mirror, dropped the bathrobe and started to dress. Why had he not replied? she asked herself.

He'd seemed so different to the others. Something about him had made her think that he understood. He'd laughed and joked with her, giving her the impression that he was totally at ease in her presence. Maybe the events on Tuesday evening had altered his thinking, warned him off. Before that, he'd been attentive, fun and seemed to display a genuine interest in her work.

She stood a few steps back from the full-length mirror and smoothed down her skirt. The suit she wore fit snugly. Too snugly, she thought in her present state of mind. Adjusting her cuffs and collar, she turned sideways for a final look. It would have to do.

She marched into her study where she collected her manuscript and other documentation she needed for the meeting and stuffed them frantically into her briefcase. Finally, with a great deal of haste, she grabbed her phone, reached for the bunch of keys that hung from the rack, marched out of the door and down the steps to the garage. While waiting impatiently for the garage doors to slide open, she checked her mobile phone once more. At last, a text message from him. She hesitated before opening it, feeling the knot in her stomach tighten. *Don't cancel on me. Not today, not now.*

Hi, sorry I've not been in touch.
Work hectic and have had to move out of home.
Don't ask!! Will explain Friday.
Can't wait to see you. M x

The hard lines on her face softened and fell away as she scrolled down the text, no longer feeling the mid-January chill or noticing the afternoon gloom. Everything in her world was bright and warm again. Sasha backed out the silver Mercedes and headed off to her meeting with a happy heart. All her dark thoughts banished. Something only he had the power to do.

By five o'clock Manny was back in his hotel room, stretched out on the bed. As he'd expected, Sasha had responded to his text almost immediately.

Thanks, appreciate your honesty.
Let me know if I can be of any help.
Looking forward to seeing u too. X

Her text raised two minor questions in him. How did she know he was being honest? And why, in fact, had he been honest? After all, he'd found out earlier that he couldn't speak the truth when pressed by Moran. But not with her. Easier in a text maybe? *Whatever the reason, there's no point dwelling on it*, he thought. So he didn't. He put his mobile on the bedside table and closed his eyes for a few moments, welcoming the onset of a short nap. But his moment of tranquillity was denied him by the sound of his mobile. He regretted not turning it off. Another text message. This time from Len, inquiring about his money. After work, Manny had made time to go into his bank branch and withdraw the wages Virginia had paid him before the bank swallowed it up. He was mightily relieved that she'd agreed to pay him in cash next time. It would save him a lot of hassle with the bank. Basically, if they saw an influx of money coming into his account, they were likely to reclaim a lot of it, if not all of it, as they did with the salary from his school, in order to pay off his debts. Being paid in cash would enable him to control things better, more on his terms and not theirs. 'If you're sensible with it, that is.' Louise's words not his, although he was quick to acknowledge that she had a valid point.

He confirmed to Len that he had his money and that he was welcome to come over to his hotel in St Albans to collect it, never really expecting that Len would agree. But he did. Also, Manny was not sure what to make of the fact that Len didn't need any directions and already knew the name of the hotel where he was staying. Louise must have told him, he guessed, or Virginia. They agreed to meet in the bar around 7pm.

Shortly after 7pm, Manny walked into the bar where he had no trouble spotting the formidable and rugged-looking man that was Len, his large frame squeezed into one of the bar's trendy chairs. He was sipping the froth from his beer. He stood up and held out his large paw when he saw Manny approaching. They shook hands.

"Manuel," he said dryly.

"Leonard. Good to see you again. Still cracking the same gag."

"You daft sod. Why are you throwing your hard-won earnings away by staying in a place like this?" He looked around, shaking his head. "Louise said you had a problem."

Manny shrugged and waved over the waiter. "I'll have the same as him please. Do you want another one?" he asked, pointing to Len's glass.

"No, thanks. Got to make this one last. I'm working tonight."

They were both silent for a moment. Listening to the tedious background music, both nervously tapping while they waited for Manny's beer to arrive.

"Ah, your money." He reached into his back pocket and handed over the same brown envelope that Len had handed to him just a few days before. "It's all there. Cheers, Len. Really appreciated that."

"That's okay. If I'd known you were going to squander it all to stay in a place like this, I might have had second thoughts." He put the envelope straight into the inner pocket of his black leather jacket, not bothering to count its contents. "Look, I'm not going to mess around. Why don't you stay with me for the time being?"

Manny looked at him quizzically, furrowing his brows.

"Only until you get yourself sorted out. You know, back on your feet. The girls tell me that you're proving to be popular with the punters and soon the money will be rolling in."

Manny wasn't sure he liked Len's choice of vocabulary. The word 'punters' didn't sit well with him. He let it go.

"At your place?"

"Yeah, why not?"

"What, me and you?" He hadn't meant it to sound so flippant.

"Yeah. Think about it. I've got a spare room and you need somewhere to stay. Makes sense. Not to mention that the rent would come in handy." He took a long gulp of his beer before wiping his mouth and continuing. "We do work together." Manny looked around for a while, rubbing his head, giving himself time to consider how he felt about Len's proposal. He knew that he was not going to find an answer while Len sat there waiting for one. Manny had never been able to operate like that.

He needed to mull things over in his own indecisive way. Len read the concerns on his face.

"Don't get thinking anything stupid now. I'll be expecting rent every week. You'll have your own space and room. In fact, I'm hardly ever there. There is the odd weekend and evening when my daughter comes to stay. Then you can piss off and do what you like. Stay in your swanky hotels for all I care. But at least by then you'll have some money in your pocket to play with and can look upon it as a treat. What you're doing now is plain nuts. You'll never get ahead. I presume you're doing the escorting for a reason and not just to put on your resumé?"

Manny raised his eyebrows, then frowned in a mild warning to Len to stop trying to read him. "Why are you doing this, Len? Have the girls in the office put you up to this? You know, so that they can keep an eye on me while I earn them their bonuses?"

"What do you mean? No. Look, if you think that I'm a..."

"How did you know I was staying here, by the way? Who told you?"

"Louise did. Hey, relax. Stop being so paranoid. It's okay. You're a lucky bastard. They like you. Be grateful that they want to help."

"Yeah, right. Why do *they* want to help me? They hardly know me - and why do you want to help me?"

"I'm not. I'm helping myself too. I need the rent. You may not have noticed," he said with a touch of humour, "But I'm getting on now. Need to slow down, just a bit, mind. The girls know that too. They're just trying help, solve a problem for both of us. They're like that... if they like you, that is ...Yes, you're new but...take it as a compliment. I've been moaning non-stop to them of late about the need to let out my spare room. You're not the only one who dreams of getting away, you know." He paused for a moment and stared into his beer before adding,"Or needs the cash."

Manny nodded to show that he understood. Earlier, he'd tried to contact Anna in a final attempt to get his old room back. He had been unsuccessful. She was not taking his calls. It seemed clear to him that that particular road was now firmly closed.

Shame, he thought. He had neither the money nor the time to get a deposit together and he waved away the idea staying on where he was for the same reason. Len's offer all of a sudden seemed increasingly attractive.

"When do you have to check out by?"

"Supposed to be by eleven this Saturday."

"Where's all your stuff? Is it still at your old place?"

"No. It's upstairs. All in my room."

"Go and grab what you don't need. I'll stick it in the boot of my car if you like. Leave it at mine until you decide what to do. Save you wandering around having to lug it everywhere with you."

"Cheers, Len." Manny thought for a moment before giving him a nod. "How much would you want for rent?"

"Oh, I don't know, say eighty pounds per week, including bills and a lift to the station some mornings?"

"Okay, you're on."

Len stood up first and slapped him hard on the shoulder. "Great. Let's go and grab some of your stuff." The awkwardness of earlier was long gone.

After Len had gone, Manny sat up at the bar for a bit, enjoying a light snack with a glass of wine, weighing up the pros and cons of his new living arrangements. Overall, it made sense. Yawning, he headed for his room, took off his clothes and fell into bed, remembering this time to turn off his mobile phone.

He was awakened by a knocking on his door. He jerked open his eyes and looked at the clock. 11.36pm. Swearing quietly, he pondered for a moment as to who it could be. More gentle knocking. Suddenly he knew. Springing out of bed, he pulled on his trousers, walked over to the door and opened it. He was right. Louise was standing there, glancing back down the corridor. Hair pulled back, she was wearing a sports top with jogging bottoms and no make-up. The look suited her. Sexy but cute. In a quiet, husky voice, she said hello and asked whether she could come in. Without a word, he opened the door wide to suggest that she could. She looked deep into his eyes for a moment.

There was something familiar about the way she was staring at him, but right now he couldn't place it. Boldly, she pressed her lips firmly against his and jostled him backwards until they both fell onto the bed. Sitting on top of him, she lifted her arms and pulled off her top. She wasn't wearing a bra. Instinctively, he placed both his hands on her breasts and squeezed. Ripe, warm and real. She lowered her head and began to kiss him, skilfully removing her bottoms as well as his trousers before mounting him. By the time she'd done this and a great deal more, he still hadn't uttered a word. A moan or two, yes. But no words.

CHAPTER TWENTY

The following day, Friday, Manny woke up surprised to discover that Louise was still lying next to him in bed, fast sleep. This troubled him. The previous morning he'd awoken to find her already gone, leaving him to reminisce over the highlights of their sexual encounter. As he lay in the semi-darkness silently staring up at the ceiling, listening to her breathing, he knew which scenario he preferred. Lifting his head, he turned to face the clock. It was 6.20am.

Cautiously, trying not to wake her, he slipped out of bed and crept towards the bathroom. Slowly, he pulled the door shut, lifted the toilet lid and peed, being careful to aim down one side of the basin in an attempt to reduce the noise. Then he spent a few moments leaning over the sink, looking blankly into the bathroom mirror. He widened his eyes, splashed his face with water and checked his reflection again. He didn't look too bad, considering. His eyes were a little puffy and maybe he was in need of a shave, but that was all. He brushed his teeth and decided to have a shower. As he stood in the footwell, washing away the musky scents of the night before, he thought about Louise's late night visit, her 'booty call.' For the second consecutive morning, he found himself speculating over the reason for her visit. He wanted to believe that it was nothing more than her being impulsive, simply reacting to her physical needs. It was also conceivable that she was following her boss's orders, sampling the goods maybe, but he was quick to pour scorn on this conjecture, reminding himself that on the

Wednesday night it had been *him* wanting *her* to see to his needs. Her coming to him, wanting him, had made them equal and he wanted to leave it like that. Embarking on a relationship with Louise at this point would be disastrous. He didn't want to go there. His line of thinking had begun to irritate him. He cursed silently for getting ahead of himself. *Why would she want a relationship with you, Rodriguez?* he asked himself. *You're emotionally inept and carry far too much baggage. She wanted to sleep with you, that's all, and you were happy to oblige.*

However, despite himself, he spent the next few moments considering what he would do right now if he were her boyfriend and they were in a close, loving relationship. He'd probably get back into bed, call in sick for them both, order a champagne breakfast and continue with the lovemaking, exploring her curves, chasing the buzz that only sexual pleasure can bring.

Noticing that he'd become aroused, for a moment or two he was tempted to turn his erotic thoughts into reality. But he didn't. Instead, he continued to shower, shaking his soapy head in an attempt to dislodge the dangerously seductive thought bubbles within.

When he came out of the bathroom, she was awake and sitting up in bed with the sheets scrunched up around her chest. Big brown eyes stared out contentedly at him. That familiar look was there again. He searched his mind as to where he'd seen it before but it continued to escape him.

"Hey, look at you, up and showered already. I didn't think you teachers had such an early start." Silence filled the room. He noticed her eyes were calling him back to bed. But he looked away and the moment was gone.

"We don't… well, I don't normally but I have loads to do today." He groaned inwardly on hearing how inadequate and hollow his words sounded. Avoiding her eyes, he focused, much more than was necessary, on doing up the buttons of his shirt.

"Well, I can't waste any more time lying here either, I need to get going too."

He hoped he hadn't disappointed or hurt her in any way but the way she marched towards the bathroom and closed the door behind her suggested to him that he had. He walked over to window and stared out into the pouring rain. A 'duvet day'. He and Lucy Randell had enjoyed a few of those. Something inside tugged at him. *I need to get away*, he thought, *somewhere sunny and warm. Perhaps I should call on my father in Spain*. It had been some time.

His train of thought was interrupted by Louise reentering the room. She began to dress.

"Are you always this irritable in the mornings?" Her question did indeed irritate him but he tried not to show it.

"No," he answered. "Not always. Only on work days."

He observed her fine figure, recognizing her beauty, admiring those curves. But beauty was not enough. He wanted her to hurry up and leave so he could be alone with his thoughts. He pondered for a short time before continuing.

"Sorry, it's just that I have a really long day ahead."

Louise now had her back to him, using the mirror to rearrange her ponytail.

"Are you okay for later tonight?" Her question surprised him.

"No, I can't do tonight, sorry. I thought you knew that I was working tonight."

She turned around and made a face. "No, you…" She stopped herself, tutted instead and rolled her eyes. "That's what I meant." She slowed down her speech. "Are… you… okay… for… later… with… regard… to… your… bookings? Jesus… get over yourself, Manny!" They broke into a shared smile of sorts. Louise turned back to face the mirror, continuing to arrange her hair, shaking her head in an amused fashion. He felt embarrassed as well as annoyed and ordered himself to lighten up.

"Will you come down and have breakfast with me?"

"I thought you had to be somewhere."

"It can wait."

She smiled at him knowingly. "Why not? You'll have to excuse the way I look though."

"You look great." She did and he meant it.

Ten minutes later, after drinking coffee and eating toast in the hotel dining room, they sat at the table, silently gazing at the other guests around them.

162

Manny checked his watch. It was almost 7.30.

"What time do you need to be at work?"

"I'd better be making a move soon," he answered, trying to sound cheerful.

"Do you need a lift?"

He thought about it.

"Don't worry," she continued. "I won't pull up right outside the school gate or do anything to show you up in front of the children."

Manny smirked. "Yeah, okay, as long as you don't expect me to give you a kiss goodbye in front of everyone," he said jovially. They sat quietly for another three or four minutes, drinking their coffee. There was now a much lighter mood.

"Manny, I don't want you to think I make a habit of doing this. You know, I haven't been with a lot of men in my life."

A cheap joke was there to be made but he let it go, not wanting to interrupt her flow. He sensed Louise was not one to talk about her personal life very often and that maybe he should listen. At least he hoped she didn't.

"I can't explain why I came over last night. All I know is that I wanted to, so I did, and that's very unlike me." He saw by the look on her face that she was probably telling the truth. "I gave in to temptation if you like. But Virginia is..."

He interrupted her to ease her concerns. "Look, Louise, don't worry, I'm not going to say a word."

"It's just that Len told me you were moving in with him, which I think is great by the way, only..."

He put his hand over hers to stop her going any further. "Relax, I'm not going to say a word to anyone. Not even to big Len. You helped me out and I appreciate that. What happened between you and me will stay between you and me." He made sure to use the past tense. "And by the way, sorry about being a bit distant and offish this morning and for getting my wires crossed about tonight ... guess I wasn't too sure how to handle things either."

"Distant? I almost had to call for a search party to help me find you," she said humorously. A much more bearable silence then followed. Both of them seemed uncertain as to what to say next but it didn't matter. Instead they looked at each other warmly. He was going to ask her whether she was in a relationship but he stopped himself. *I don't need to know*, he said inwardly.

Manny was first to end the silence by standing up and announcing that he had better get going. "Am I still okay for that lift?"

"Sure." She stood up too and seemed pleased when Manny walked around the table to give her a hug and a kiss. She responded warmly, although she wanted to hold him tighter and for longer than he really felt comfortable with.

During the brief car journey, Louise had playfully tried to coax secrets from him, mainly about his own personal life and past relationships. He sat in the passenger seat fending off all her intrusive questions with a smile and a shrug.

"What is it, Manny? Why do you never open up? Scared what might spill out?" she teased with an underlying note of seriousness.

He felt that, in time, she might be someone he could be honest with. But not yet.

Eventually, the conversation veered onto the evening ahead and his two bookings. Reassuring him, again Louise was quick to emphasize that if all went well he could expect to earn a significant amount of money in the coming weeks. Off the record, she'd mentioned that he had a growing list of clients wanting and waiting to be introduced to him. But Virginia was being cautious and needed more reassurance that he could cope first, as in her eyes he still wore a rookie badge. However, Louise added that if things ended well later, he'd have credible grounds to hope that the badge might be removed that night. A bolt of excitement charged through his body. The thought that very soon he might have the money to get his old rucksack out again and flee from all that was depressing in his life energized him.

He did kiss Louise goodbye and he didn't care who saw. Manny strode up the steps and into the entrance of the school with a sense of purpose, entering the staffroom a little before eight o'clock. Dom Bonner was pinning the cover list onto the board.

"Blimey. You wet the bed? You're on time for once."

Manny walked over to say hello, making his excuses for his lateness the day before. He winced when he saw his name down on the cover list. But he knew he had no grounds to complain. Checking his pigeonhole for any memos, he found an official-looking letter with his name and the words 'private and confidential' on the front.

Manny shook his head as he read through the letter. It was headed 'Areas for concern' next to his initials and consisted of two sheets of paper containing a list of complaints the senior management team had about him. Teaching, record keeping, planning, timekeeping and so on. Without realising it, he had started to speak angrily and out loud.

"I don't know how much longer I can put up with that woman. I've just about had enough of her meddling. Interfering old..." Gazing around, he saw that the room had begun to fill and his rant had drawn attention to himself. He tried to force down his anger.

Dom Bonner was the first to approach him. Manny handed him the letter to read.

"Looks like Baxter's had enough of you too... And she's letting management know."

Manny looked at him with a mystified look on his face.

"You know, making it official... getting the wheels in motion."

"Wheels in motion? For what?"

"Oh, come on," he said, waving the letter in front of Manny's face. "She wants you out."

Manny swiped the letter back and stuffed it into his pocket.

"Can't blame her really."

"What?" Taken aback by Dom's comment, Manny threw him an angry stare.

"Before I go on, remember your row is not with me. I'm just pointing out to you how she sees things." Dom Bonner was an honest and forthright man. This was the reason why Manny respected him.

165

"She's got boxes to tick, the Head to please, pressure from the county council to improve exam results and so on. She can't afford to carry any dead wood in her department."

Manny bit his lip and frowned, knowing Dom was right.

"Listen, on a good day you're a great teacher and the students here love you. But you have to admit that lately your heart's not been in it at all. Everyone can see that. You're all over the place. Come on, be honest with yourself."

Manny nodded, listening.

"It's still possible to turn things around, but you need to act now. And if you really have had it with the job, then get out... Leave in the summer on your own terms with a decent reference." He scratched his bald spot with a pencil and lowered his tone to a barely audible whisper. "Don't wait for them to make the decision for you. You will come to regret it, believe me. It would affect your future chances in teaching and you don't need that."

Manny turned, patting him on the arm. "I hear you, Dom. Thanks."

"Whatever is troubling you, get it sorted, yeah? Before it's too late. I'm here if you need to talk."

The conversation was ended, the message had hit home. Manny stumbled over to his usual seat, somewhat apart from the others, although at that moment it didn't feel far apart enough, and sat down to reflect on the letter. He felt wounded pride creeping in, the wind being taken out of his sails. He slumped into his seat, failing to conceal the dejection on his face as he read through the letter again. Manny shook his head. He refused to believe it. He knew he hadn't been putting in the effort of late, but he was finding it harder and harder to motivate himself. Yes, Baxter was unpleasant, but she was covering her own back, which he couldn't blame her for. It was all about money. *We have more and more to do*, he thought. *Yet at the end of every month I'm still broke. It's so demoralising. Something needs to change, I can't go on like this. Two or three months of solid escorting work and things might seem better. It's all about money. I need money.* He thought again about his travel plans, 'the great escape,' but noticed at the same time a vague, contradictory wish simmering away at the back of his mind: the desire for a house of his own, some stability. *I want to get off the wheel, stop the constant spinning.*

Eventually, he would have to return from travelling and begin the tedious process of finding work again, teaching no doubt, and sorting out somewhere to live, only this time he'd be older and with another glaring void on his CV to explain.

"Why did you leave your last school, Mr Rodriguez?"

"Well, they didn't want me. Said I couldn't cope with all the planning, marking and stuff. The head of the department was a bit of a dragon actually."

"Oh, I see, so what have you been doing with yourself since then?"

"A bit of travelling and escorting work mostly. I'm sure the agency would be happy to provide you with a reference. I made an excellent male escort, the clients loved me. A real hit."

"A male escort? Do you mean a prostitute?"

"Um, no, I only do escorting."

"Oh, there's a difference?"

Manny concluded that it was best to comply and take heed of the warning. It was far too early in the academic year to be taking his foot off the pedal. Dom was right, if he wanted to leave, he needed it to be on his own terms and with a reference of sorts, plus he owed it to his students, if not Baxter, to do a decent job. He would work harder to keep on top of things and then hand in his notice at Easter, which meant he'd be able to walk away in mid-July with the bonus of getting paid through August too. It made sense not to go burning the one respectable bridge in his working life and throw away a reputation he had previously worked hard to build up. Manny felt himself start to worry. He searched his mind for a job he could do apart from teaching, but failed to find a credible answer. A feeling of insecurity came over him and he wanted to go home, but then he remembered that he didn't have one.

The rest of the morning, nothing significant occurred. His lessons went smoothly and he kept a low profile during the break periods by staying in his classroom where he set about catching up with the paper chase. Only once did he have to deal with

Baxter and that was brief. She came into his classroom to tell him that she'd been looking for him at the end of the previous day. *To hand me the letter no doubt*, he thought. She was surprised to discover that he'd already gone home, she told him, despite the fact that he'd arrived late that morning. Having tried to think of a good excuse, without success, he took her criticism on the chin with a nod and a smile, absent of any warmth.

In the afternoon, teaching his younger students, he felt his mind drift from the class and onto his two bookings that evening. Forcing his mind to return to the classroom, he set various tasks for his young pupils to debate in small groups. This gave him time to pull over a pile of papers to mark, but again he soon drifted away, ending up in a mesh of dark thoughts. Throwing down his pen, he stood up and dovetailed between the groups of children, hoping to be splashed by the innocent fountain of their mirthful youth.

Back in his hotel room, Manny grabbed a beer from the mini bar. The anxiety he'd felt earlier was growing stronger. He hoped he wouldn't suffer from stage fright. *What if I can't...?*

The vibrating of his mobile phone jerked him from his thoughts. It was Len telling him that he'd be over soon to pick him up and to have the rest of his belongings ready for him to stick in the boot of the car.

By half past five, Manny had showered and changed his clothes. The pile of dirty laundry depressed him. He stuffed it into his bags, making a mental note to find time over the weekend to sort it all out. He wasn't sure if he'd be coming back to the hotel, so he collected up all his toiletries before sitting back down on his bed, staring out of his hotel window. He stayed there for some time, watching the rain spatter against the pane. The feeling of being out of his depth was very strong. Manny walked over to the bathroom mirror and studied his face closely. *If I can't do this, I'm in trouble*, he thought. "Don't let me down, Rodriguez," he said to his reflection. "You're a Latin lion, and tonight you're going to roar."

Just then the hotel phone rang, making him jump. It was

reception, informing him he had a guest waiting in the lobby. Manny made his way downstairs with his belongings to find Len waiting for him. Taking Manny's bags and putting them in the boot of the car, Len announced that he needed a coffee before they left.

Len drank his cappuccino. A ring of chocolate appeared on his top lip. Manny smirked but opted not to tell him, thinking it might provide a lighter moment or two during the tense times ahead. He went to pay for the coffees, plunging his hands deep into his pockets and bringing out about 50 pence worth of small change. He looked at Len helplessly.

"No bloody wonder you're doing a double shift tonight." Len thumped the money down on the counter and stomped off towards the car park outside.

Manny sat in the passenger seat, hardly saying a word, quietly listening to Len curse his way through the teeming city traffic. Finally they stopped in front of one of the top London hotels. Manny checked his watch. 7.20pm. Len cut the engine and put his hand on Manny's shoulder.

"Are you sure you're ready for this?" He said it as if he had asked it a million times before. "Give me a call when you're done here and be quick. No loitering afterwards, we don't have the time. Don't fancy upsetting that boyfriend of yours by keeping him waiting."

"Thanks for the lift," Manny said as he slammed the car door.

The doorman had the door held open ready. Entering the hotel, Manny was greeted by soft music and a helpful concierge.

"Good evening, sir. May I help you?"

"Yes please. My name is Mr Rodriguez and I'm here to see Mr Smith, Room 600."

"Certainly, sir. Please follow me." The concierge nodded knowingly, as if he'd been expecting him. He led him to a table in the bar area, signalling over the waiter, who took Manny's order of citrus vodka with tonic.

"I will inform Mr Smith that you're here. In the meantime, please... relax and enjoy your drink." The concierge gave a slight bow of his head and hurried off.

The whole situation is insane, Manny thought, looking around nervously. *Here I am about to sleep with a total stranger in the best hotel I've ever been in while her husband looks on.* In the past, sex with a stranger usually happened after a night on the town, fuelled by alcohol. This felt different, less acceptable. His heart was beating fast and he was starting to feel trickles of sweat running down his back.

Louise had told him that the client had made his money relatively late in life and had celebrated becoming very rich by finding himself a new younger bride.

"We're not in the business to judge," she'd said. "Simply to provide a service." He'd told her that he was unconcerned by the client's background. All he wanted to know were the important bits. How much? And what would he have to do? A couple of days earlier, he'd been confident that he'd be able to do it. Now he wasn't feeling so sure.

At a nearby table an elderly American couple were talking enthusiastically about a play they'd seen and the splendid performance of the lead actor.

Manny smiled to himself. *I must do the same. I am an actor who has to deliver a rock solid performance. Don't think about stage fright.* But he did.

Leaning forward to take a sip of his drink, he sensed the presence of someone behind him. They were here. He put down his drink without taking the sip and stood up to greet them, holding out his hand.

"Hi, I'm Manny."

"Hello, Manny." The gentleman took his hand. "I'm Bill. Bill Smith, and this little beauty here is my wife, Nina," he said boastfully. Manny was sure he detected a slight Antipodean accent.

"Hi, Nina. How are you doing?"

"I'm fine," she said in a sweet, exotic whisper. "Nice to meet you."

She was attractive but not in the aching kind of way. Not the type he'd waste a great amount of time lusting over. She had dark, shiny hair that fell down her back, a centre parting, small, dark, roaming eyes and thin lips. An oriental background, he

170

guessed. She looked young, even younger when standing beside her husband.

As he greeted her with a polite kiss on her cheek, Manny noticed her husband taking a step back, drawing back his head slightly, as if inspecting him, giving him a once over as someone would eye up a new car.

He summoned over the waiter before sitting down beside his wife on the sofa. He flung out his arms to rest along its back, displaying his paunch and drumming his chubby fingers. He was doing a good job in making out that the situation was a perfectly normal thing to be happening. In fact, he was doing it so well Manny was able to recognise his unease.

He was somewhere in his sixties, overweight and with a fringe of grey hair around the edges of his head. His loose jowls gave him an unfortunate hound dog expression. He was dressed in a smart suit with an open-necked shirt. Manny kept eye contact with him to a minimum. The glasses he wore made his cloudy blue eyes look bigger than they were and, although he could have come across as an almost joke-like figure, something about him commanded a certain amount of respect. His wealth probably, Manny thought.

While he was busy ordering champagne from the waiter, Manny looked over at his wife and smiled. She was wearing a little black dress with fishnet tights or stockings. He hoped for the latter. Her dainty body and subtle movements gave her a mannequin-like appearance. They stared at each other a moment. He winked at her and saw something in her stare lighten. The act had begun and, despite the pounding in his chest, the actor had taken up his position on the stage. It made it easier that his male audience was not the rich silver spoon type he'd first thought he'd be. No. Bill Smith was once a common man who had made his own money. The sovereign rings he wore on the last two digits of each hand and the chunky gold chain around his neck told Manny something of his tough working class roots. As they held up their champagne glasses and toasted each other, he'd found small reasons not to be intimidated or overwhelmed by the client. The unusual proceedings maybe, but not by Bill and his young wife. He felt his courage start to rise.

They sat around the table drinking and making polite small talk, seeming to pirouette around the main agenda for a little longer. Finally it was Bill who broached the topic first, suggesting that it might be a better idea, if all were in agreement, to get down to the proper business in his suite upstairs. He leaned into Manny's ear while in the lift and told him he didn't mean to be rude but they had to be gone by ten. They were meeting friends for dinner. *Fine with me*, Manny thought.

It all happened so quickly after that. Within minutes of entering the room, Nina had slipped out of her dress and was ready and waiting on the bed, wearing just her stockings and panties. Her body was skinny and without curves but he'd seen worse. After closer inspection, he decided he'd seen a lot worse. For Manny, sex was about entering into a private world with someone without intruders. Bill was breaking the rules. Trespassing, leering into that private world. Somehow he had to banish him from his mind. But it was difficult. A memory came to him of how he had once ended up in bed with a girl who had a photo of her smiling boyfriend in a frame on the bedside table. He'd felt so bad that when she went down on him he'd leant across and laid it face-down to spare the poor bloke any pain and himself from shame. It had happened a very long time ago, but the memory was there with him now in the room he wanted to flee. He lay next to Nina on the bed where in between kisses they both set about taking pieces of his clothing off.

Kissing her mouth was too personal for him so he wasted no time in moving onto her body. His kisses were rather aimless at first, but somehow he was able to find purpose and direction. Her breasts were small. Very small, But what made them sexy and appealing were her long, erect nipples. He focused on them for a short moment while he tried to block out the intrusive thoughts. The whisper of a light, fruity fragrance encouraged him to explore her lower regions. Hearing the rhythm of her breathing change, he soon felt her shudder. He stayed there, kissing and caressing until she shuddered again. It was this, her wetness and the picture in his mind of Louise's curves that finally made him hard. He was miles away mentally and it was proving a real challenge to keep a certain distance whilst staying hard. She could have his body but that was all. Neither she nor her husband would meet the person playing the part.

Manny found a vibe he could ride. He was up and running but it wasn't long before he was off again. Momentum lost. A light had been switched on and he could hear Bill groaning in the background. Once again he could not do it. His concentration was gone. Manny was on the verge of giving up, but help was at hand. Nina seemed to understand his problem and tried to coax him back to her by putting her hands firmly on the sides of his head, partly covering his ears, holding his head still so he could again focus on her. She helped the cause by touching and kissing him in sensitive areas. Finally, he was ready again and so was she. He reached across to grab a condom from the bedside table and, with her help, put it on. It was painful for him in the emotional sense but he could see that the finishing line was in sight. He paced himself for some time, making sure she seemed satisfied before going for broke himself with a sprint finish to the end. No frills, past caring. They both lay there for a moment, catching their breath. One delighted, the other relieved it was over.

After a short while, Manny lifted his head and was disgusted to see Bill sitting in a chair, sweating profusely, trousers around his ankles and toilet roll in hand. He'd been masturbating.

Nina rolled over to kiss Manny and to let him know that she'd really enjoyed it. Her compliments sounded too well practised to deserve a response. Besides, he was too busy looking at Bill, uncomprehendingly. Virginia had told him that Bill was impotent. "Medical reasons," she had said. But from what he could see, Bill was certainly not impotent. Anger and humiliation flared up in him. He didn't even notice that Nina had departed the bed and was already in the bathroom, showering.

"Well," Bill began, "I must say that you were all that we hoped for and more. I shall let the agency know, of course, that we were more than happy with the service and that we would like to book you again... Shall we sort it now or do I go through the agency? Maybe we can come to an arrangement regarding money ourselves… You know, cut out the middle man, as I like to say in business?"

Manny shook his head and told him to go through the agency. No way was he going to give them his mobile number.

"Look, Bill, that all sounds great, but would you mind doing me a favour first?"

"Sure."

"Pull your trousers back up."

"Oh, yes, sorry, of course." Manny thought he looked sad and a little pathetic as he went about redressing himself. But he soon realised he had no grounds to be critical or cast judgment. He'd chosen to be a part of their private world. He was the one being paid. If anything, his own morals were more questionable than theirs. Manny wondered what they really thought about him as he lay in bed naked, waiting for the pair to disappear. Then he told himself that it was irrelevant what they thought and that it didn't matter. It couldn't be any worse than what he thought of himself already. Nina alone he could handle. The memory of Bill though, thirty odd years her senior, watching and playing with himself, would play on his mind for some time to come.

"If I'd known you were going to do that, I would have charged you extra. A lot extra," he said finally, willing his anger to overcome his shame. But he doubted whether Bill was to blame, and let it go. He made a mental note to speak to Virginia instead and vent his anger on her for the 'little oversight' and lack of information on her part.

"Um, I hope we can do business again. I've already paid the agency but this is for you… A token of our thanks. My thanks." Taking an envelope out of his jacket pocket, Bill placed it on the bedside table. Manny thought he sounded sincere. He wondered whose gratification he'd serviced the most: Bill's or his wife's? *Bill's probably, it's how he gets off. He no longer needs to look at porn mags, or watch porn on a screen at his home and he probably never uses the Net. Wrong generation. What he can afford to do now though, with his wealth, is watch it live. Create it himself. A whole new meaning to the term 'interactive.' He hires the cast, books the location, sits back in his chair and enjoys. No wonder he turned all the lights on.*

A stifling silence broke out between the pair, neither of them knowing where to look or what to say. They were rescued by the returning Nina, freshly showered and changed, apparently ready to leave. She tried to fling her fragile arms around her husband's expanding waist. He in return wrapped one of his arms over her slender shoulders. They looked at each other for a moment, lovingly. It looked genuine enough.

"Right, we'd better be off," said Bill. "Thanks again, Manny, and as I said, I do hope we can all do it again. First time, with introductions, always makes it harder, but I felt we all got on pretty well, considering. If you're having doubts about helping us out again, look in the envelope. Maybe it will help you reconsider. We liked you. Didn't we, honey?" She nodded in agreement. They had their arms around each other still.

"Oh, by the way, you're welcome to make use of the suite. It's paid up until midday tomorrow. Seems a shame to leave it empty. Just go easy on the bar bill, okay?" he chuckled. "Shall we go, honey? See you, Manny, thanks for everything."

"See you, Manny. Thank you," Nina said joyfully, never once taking her eyes off her husband. Manny put out an arm to wave them off, and then called out.

"Hey, Bill, what's your real name?"

They stopped and turned around. "My real name?"

"Yeah, your real name, damn it."

Bill laughed nervously before answering. "It's Trevor. Trevor Rickmond. Why?"

"Thanks, Trevor, no reason. Now go and have a good night." Manny didn't really understand why he had asked the question.

And that was that. With a final wave and a smile they were gone, leaving him alone to fight the repugnant feeling that was busy mauling him inside. He looked around the room, not doubting for a moment that it was the most expensive available. Apart from the envelope that had been left behind, nothing else in the suite was of any interest to him. He had to get out. He was suffocating. The five hundred pounds' tip in the envelope helped, but only a little.

Gravitating over to the window, he stood there naked, lost in thought, watching the traffic below race by. Silence. Total silence. Sound unable to penetrate the thick glass. He leant his forehead against the pane and stayed there for some time, pondering his options. But this was no time for contemplation. Sasha was expecting him and Len was already downstairs, waiting. His world all of a sudden felt very dark and full of confusion. Manny shook his head and went to shower. He wondered what lay in store for him over at Sasha's. He hoped she wouldn't be imposing any demands. The prospect that she might filled him with dread.

CHAPTER

TWENTY-ONE

Sasha stopped in front of the dark wooden door. "Come and see my study or my sanctuary, depending on my state of mind," she winked. "I've been busy too and totally lost track of the time. I've been finishing one or two things for my publisher."

Unlike Tuesday, she seemed calm and free from agitation. It was catching too. He'd felt his own anxiety fall away the moment she'd opened the door. After the cold emptiness he'd experienced a few hours before, a familiar face bestowing on him a warm welcome was much appreciated.

It was gone midnight by the time they had arrived at Sasha's. Over an hour and a half late. The traffic had been heavy, very heavy. Len had spent most of the journey groaning and fretting about Sasha's reaction to their lateness. He was adamant she'd be kicking up a huge fuss, complaining to Virginia. But he needn't have worried. As Manny stood on the front doorstep, at first glance he could tell she was in a happy state of mind.

He followed her into the study and looked around, wide-eyed. There were shelves buckling under the weight of books. Most were leather bound, old and well-used. He raised a hand and let his finger brush across the rows of exposed spines. Another wall was decorated with certificates and other documents that recognised and acknowledged her achievements. He couldn't help but be impressed.

"Wow," he gasped like an awe-struck child. "I dream of having a room like this."

"I'm sure you will one day."

"Ha, doubt it."

She pointed to a battered leather chair and motioned for him to sit down. "Can I get you a drink or anything to eat?"

"No, I'm fine, thanks." He'd lost his appetite back in the hotel room and still hadn't found it. "Actually, a glass of wine wouldn't go amiss... Listen, I'm so sorry for being late and about the trouble the other night. I..."

"Shh," Sasha interrupted while lighting a couple of the candles positioned around the study. "Sit and relax for a moment while I fetch the drinks."

He was emotionally and physically exhausted, but he couldn't let it show.

When she was out of the room, Manny allowed his gaze to travel around the dimly lit study. The only source of light was coming from the candles and a small reading lamp that sat on her desk. It had a calming effect on him. A trace of tobacco mixed with incense perfumed the air. The oak flooring partly covered by a Persian carpet, the floor to ceiling bookcase bursting with a wealth of knowledge and information waiting patiently and gathering dust, all added to the room's character. The study possessed an alluring charm that made him wish he was a wise old scholar. *I would sit and write books here*, he thought to himself. *I'd be held in such high esteem by educators everywhere, my words of wisdom studied, quoted and discussed.* Unable to resist, he went to sit in the large chair behind Sasha's desk and leant back, clasping his hands behind his head, pretending to be someone of importance. Then, with boyish mischief, he swivelled round in the chair. A familiar painting caught his eye. He'd seen it before in a church back in Spain. It was a copy of Rembrandt's *'The Return of the Prodigal Son.'* He knew the parable well. His grandma in Spain often used to read the Bible to him, wanting him to become a good Catholic boy. He leaned forward to take a closer look, adjusting the position of the lamp to expose the painting in a more favourable light. Red and black with iconic gold. *The bearded old man in his dark red cloak, welcoming home his repentant youngest son, while the jealous elder brother looks on.* It held him spellbound for a few moments, the chaos within him momentarily silenced.

"The original painting sits in a hermitage in Saint Petersburg, Russia. I aim to go and see it for myself one day." Sasha was standing in the door frame, holding two glasses of wine. He jumped up out of her chair, slightly embarrassed, but she gestured for him to stay where he was. "It was Rembrandt's last painting. He finished it not long before his death," she added while passing him his glass and taking her seat in the smaller chair.

"I knew who it was by. But I never knew that it was his last piece of work."

"It's a favourite of mine. Sometimes I come in here and just sit and look at it. It calms me. A painting that begs you to sit and contemplate. Have a closer look and tell me what you see."

Manny pulled a face and laughed self-consciously, hoping he wouldn't really have to answer. But she was persistent. He sat forward and looked again, frowning.

"Um, I see a man desperately in need of a new pair of shoes. A bit like me," he laughed. "Also, he has a haircut a bit like me too." The humour was a disguise for the unease he felt at having to produce an answer. What he saw in the painting was close to his heart. Too close. A father's love for his son. He looked at Sasha but her eyes were now fixed on the picture. She was still waiting for his answer, a proper answer, but she wasn't impatient. He felt his discomfort grow the longer he delayed. Sasha's continuing silence encouraged him to compose a more serious response. He looked into the heart of the picture and as he allowed it to take shape and form in his heart and mind, his self-consciousness began to fall away.

"My eyes are drawn to the young man with the shaven head. He's on his knees, looking humble, feeling shame, wanting forgiveness for the way he has lived his life. He's wasted his gifts and talents with reckless ease. His weary head is resting on his father's heart which is a powerful image. The compassionate father is happy to see his son, regardless. Full of joy that he has returned to him, knowing his boy has learnt some hard and painful lessons that will help mould him into a better man.

Offering his son a refuge and sense of sanctuary... a bit like your study. I love the father's big red cloak; it looks warm, soft and comforting. The red velvet folds resemble an entrance to somewhere sacred. It's the way the cloak sits over his shoulders and forms an arch shape; inside, he will find rest and forgiveness. A place to dwell during troubled times. Christ's sacred heart, I guess, seeing that it's a biblical painting."

"Look closer at the father's hands, what do you notice about them?"

He paused for a few moments, examining the hands, trying to trace her line of thought. As Manny leant forward, so did she, closer to his cheek. He felt her breath, heard her breathing. She was now looking at him, but he didn't mind. Time and space seemed to have vanished and he felt an odd sense of intimacy. Her closeness no longer an invasion.

"Um, they seem to be holding the son firmly?"

"Yes, one of them is," she told him. "If you look really close, you'll notice that the right hand seems more feminine, while the left appears to be masculine. The right hand does not hold or grasp. It caresses his shoulder, with a far softer and tender touch. The left hand, however, is firm and strong, holding him steady." A long moment of silence followed as he traced her observation, eyes suddenly opening wider, staring at the image in the candlelight. The flicker of the candles and the harmonious ticking of the clock were the only sounds his senses could pick up. Gradually his mind began to empty itself of the worries and troubles the day had brought.

"Some experts say it represents 'the hand of discipline.' One hand 'confirms, the other consoles'. Commentators also say that the hands of the father represent God. In all forms: man... woman... motherhood... fatherhood."

Manny carried on looking, neither of them interrupting the silence.

"What about the damaged sole hanging from his shoe? Do you think that means anything?"

"Maybe...That's good," she smiled broadly. "I never thought about that... Damaged sole? Is that what you see or what you feel?" Her gaze was penetrating, waiting for his reply.

He wasn't sure how to answer so he merely shrugged.

Eventually Sasha suggested they take their drinks through to the lounge where they would be more comfortable sitting on the sofas. So they did. She stoked the fire and lit a couple of the larger candles. The fire began to crackle and there was an easy silence between them that didn't need to be filled. He sat back on the sofa, silent and watchful. This great sense of peace and calm wasn't something he'd anticipated at all during the drive over to what he'd imagined would be a tricky evening ahead with Sasha. He looked for an excuse to explain it away. *It's because I've not eaten and, on an empty stomach, the alcohol is playing with my mood,* he told himself.

"How did you get on with your father?"

The question yanked him away from his thoughts.

"Do you ever go over to Spain and spend any time with him? He must look at you and feel so proud."

He looked at her quizzically.

"I mean just look at you. You're a work of art. Everything a man should be."

The compliment didn't sit well with him. He rubbed his head and shifted in his seat before reaching for his drink. He took a large gulp, swallowed and gave a nonchalant shrug of his shoulders.

She paused for a long moment, providing a gap for him to comment. He declined, preferring to swirl around the wine in his glass. The first moment of real awkwardness had arrived.

"Sorry, I'm being intrusive and I've also embarrassed you…"

He signalled with a smile and a wave that it was fine, hoping she would drop the subject.

"Whenever my father looked at me, he'd wince," Sasha began. "I think I was a manifestation of all his fears. Camp, insecure and scared of a ball. Every year he'd buy me a rugby shirt in the hope that I'd take up the game. Drove him crazy, it did. Especially when he found out that the only thing I took up were the sleeves… or its length." They both laughed, hers a little more forced.

"He'd be furious when I went out wearing it with nothing else except a belt and a pair of high heels. I can still see the veins at the side of his head exploding with rage."

Her eyes became firmly fixed on a memory from her past. There was still a smile on her face, but her eyes were starting to say something different.

"He used to shout and rant, calling me all the names under the sun. My mother told me once that if I'd been born a girl they would named me Lucinda. When I was in my early teens he'd call me by that name, in a spiteful way. The words 'queer' and 'little poof' were two of his other favourites... 'Whatever will my friends think?' he'd scream at my mother." She stopped to spark up another cigarette, dragging deeply.

"Some father, eh?" she added. In the few moments that followed, Manny felt he was able to understand some of the factors that had led to her having a sex change. For a moment he questioned the purity of her motives before immediately reminding himself that he was in no position to judge. How could he be? He knew hardly anything about her.

Sasha cleared her throat and continued. "I tell you something, one of his friends in particular became very fond of my company."

He knew what was coming next.

"My father would've had his heart attack a hell of a lot earlier if he'd known what we used to get up to."

Manny didn't want to hear any more. He smiled weakly, said nothing and looked out of the blackened window, his thoughts drifting on to the charred and ruined relationship he'd had with his own father.

"My old man's best friend was the bottle," he said in a voice he barely recognised as his own. "Still is, I suppose. I just used to get in the way of their relationship. We all did."

It was his turn to gaze into a distant memory. It was rare for him to mention anything of his personal life but he felt the confession being extracted from him. He'd heard enough to know that Sasha had also been deprived of the love of a decent father, rejected by the hands that should have 'confirmed and consoled'. He felt the urge to continue.

182

"I swore blind to my mother and sisters back then that I would look after them, we didn't need him. I used to tell them as soon as I was old enough I'd get a job, make enough money for us all."

He could have told her much more, but he didn't. Instead, he leant forward and poured out the last of the wine, thinking he'd already said too much. He was finding the whole discussion upsetting and yet strangely comforting at the same time

They sat up talking for a long time, mainly about the turbulent relationship Sasha had had with her father. She described how from an early age she felt intimidated by him. He was a powerful and widely respected medical consultant with friends in high places. She also mentioned that he'd come from a pedigree sporting background and never wasted an opportunity to express his disappointment that she hadn't inherited his sporting genes.

"He used to take every opportunity to find fault and belittle me, making it abundantly clear to all and sundry that he was ashamed of what I was… what I was becoming."

There was a willingness in her to talk about parts of her life that she'd refrained from discussing during their previous encounters. She continued to explain that her academic achievements alone were not enough to win her father's approval or respect. After he died, she admitted to becoming a mental and emotional wreck who had lost herself in a fog of drink, drugs and wild partying.

"He did keep to his word, however. We kind of had a deal. He gave me an incentive to turn my life around and be successful in my field of expertise. His will being the carrot, the promise of financial security."

Manny could see that it was more than just his money she hungered after. Her success was also motivated by the need to earn his love and pride. It helped him to understand a little more about Sasha's desperate longing and constant need of approval. He went on to learn that many of her goals had been achieved after the demise of her parents, including the sex change. The only other thing she would reveal about the change of sex, however, was that she had once been called Stephen and had felt in her very early teens that she was supposed to be a girl.

He sat forward intently, wanting to discover more, but it was something she was uncomfortable talking about. He was interested to know if she was much happier as a woman and whether or not she ever regretted her decision. But her eyes were far off, lost in a reverie of her own, not responding to his gestures. She went without talking for a long time.

Her father's harsh treatment also helped her to learn how to handle the barrage of unpleasant remarks and unwelcome sexual advances she'd later receive, especially post op. She gave him something of an insight into the vile treatment and degrading comments she'd had to endure over the years, from her peers, colleagues, old friends and strangers in the street who stared in appalled fascination. She could never get used to it but she'd learned how to handle it, was how she put it. Although she talked about the prejudice against her with good humour, Manny could see for himself that the years of pain and suffering had taken their toll. The deep grooves etched around her eyes were a giveaway. In the moment of silence that followed, he really wanted to, but couldn't quite bring himself to see her as a woman. There were too many contrasting factors, both physically and mentally.

Manny raised his brows and shook his head, both in sympathy and in an attempt to keep his eyes from closing. Suddenly he was very tired. He could also feel the onset of a headache. A combination of too much wine and too little food. He would have liked to have listened to more and even asked her a few questions, but they would have to wait. With the heat from the fire and the deep comfort of the sofa, he was struggling to fend off the hands of sleep. The one-sided conversation eventually died a natural death. Manny was ready for his bed but wasn't sure where that bed was. A churning feeling began in the pit of his stomach, like when a child first discovers that they're lost. All his uncertainty came flooding back. He thought about contacting Len and staying at his, but it had long gone 3am and he wasn't sure if he'd left it too late. For the first time he began to feel uneasy and what made it worse, he could feel her watching him.

"Why don't you stay here tonight?" she said soothingly. "I can show you the spare room, if you like. It's peaceful *and* comes with its own bathroom." Sasha noticed the uncertainty flickering in his eyes. "Don't worry, you'll not be disturbed," she added with a reassuring smile.

Manny nodded, agreeing that it was his best option, and followed her up the stairs to the spare room. She showed him in and turned on the lights so he could see inside. It was spacious, modern and clean. Like the rest of the house, it too had been given a thorough makeover. Clean white walls, inviting double bed, soft white duvet, en suite bathroom, with a huge Turkish rug that covered most of the polished wooden flooring, a writing desk and chair positioned by the window and framed by dark curtains on a iron pole. It reminded him of something from the pages of an interiors magazine, stylish comfort oozing plenty of charm.

"It's perfect," he said appreciatively, because it was and he was. "Thanks."

"I'm sure you'll sleep well in here." She was about to head off when she felt a tugging on her arm.

"Listen, I really enjoyed tonight...The talk in the study and everything... I've never really...you know." Sasha could see that he was struggling to express how he felt.

"Yes, I must say I think it helped us both in some way. Healing and therapeutic. I can see that you're damaged, too." Manny stood staring at her with a crease in his nose.

"No, I'm not. What makes you say that?"

"Oh, come on, Manny, give me some credit. Why else would you be hiring yourself out to total strangers?"

With that, she turned swiftly, wishing him goodnight, and headed for her bedroom at the opposite end of the landing.

He closed his door, shaking his head in mock surprise. It was the first time she'd mentioned anything about his being an escort to his face. *This changes everything*, he thought to himself. *I thought the subject of escorts was taboo, strictly off limits. It'll make for an interesting conversation tomorrow.*

Looking around the room, he saw, hanging on the wall above

the desk, a handwritten, glass-framed version of Rudyard Kipling's poem, *If*. With an arched eyebrow, he read aloud the last line: *'And what is more… You'll be a man, my son.'*

Manny almost laughed.

He got out of his clothes, dumped them on the floor, threw himself onto the bed and stretched out, allowing the events of the day to play out in his mind. Some moments were darker than others: the letter he'd received at work, the feeling of self-loathing he'd experienced in the hotel. He smiled ruefully because the feeling still lingered. The image of the old man with his paunch, sitting in the chair sweating, his trousers down around his ankles, would take a long time to fade from his memory.

He remembered Sasha's warm welcome and her soothing tone. Something good had taken place in the study, he recalled. A kind of unaccustomed thrill wrapped in a sense of wellbeing. At first he'd thought the heat that glowed inside him might have had something to do with the amount of money he'd made or the wine he had drunk, but it had felt better than that. Much better. A rare moment of inner peace which went beyond anything he had experienced before. He closed his eyes in hope of sleep but it was slow in coming. He sat up, switched on the bedside light and reached for his jacket, pulling out the envelope that Len had handed over to him earlier. He'd been paid in cash as previously agreed with Virginia. Including his £500 tip from Bill Smith, he'd made a cool £1,300. Not bad for an evening's work and the meter was still running. His lack of joy was understandable, he told himself, he was overtired. *Tomorrow*, he thought, *when the booking's over, I'm sure the thrill will hit me*. He spent the next hour tossing and turning in a restless depression. The feeling of disdain would not go away, no matter how many times he mentally counted his money. It was the dead time of the morning, he reminded himself. The time his darkest fears and anxieties always liked to play games with him. The time his dreams and ambitions all seemed so terribly distant. The time all his daytime defences finally grew weary, giving up on him. Leaving him exposed to the mercy of his demons.

Sasha had been in bed a short time and was about to fall asleep when something disturbed her. She looked at her bedside clock. Ten past three. She held her breath and continued to listen. It was Manny. She could hear him tiptoeing down the stairs. He was leaving, she thought. Unable to stand it any longer. She felt an ache in her heart. Then she recognised the sound of her study door being opened. She sat up curiously and got out of bed, wrapping her bathrobe around her and cautiously moving to the top of the stairs, where she stood listening. A light had gone on in her study. Slowly she crept down a few of the steps and crouched down. She could peer through the gap of the half-opened door. Manny was sitting in the chair, gazing silently at the picture on the wall. His face was alight with red and gold tints. Mystical. It was a beautiful and poetic moment. One she would never forget. The lonely wanderer in need of rest and recuperation, speaking to the beloved, in her own home. His face showing a sadness she guessed his smile usually kept in check. Fate had led him here. Now she must play her part and set about fixing his damaged soul. *For the moment*, she thought, *I must leave them. I'm intruding.* She was about turn and head back up the stairs when she heard a thud. Peering in again, she saw that he had pushed away the chair and was now down on his knees, a look of sorrow on his face.

Fighting back the tears, she carefully ascended the stairs and made her way back to her room. Before getting into bed, she paused by the mirror to examine herself. Her hands were ready, waiting, wanting to heal his soul. But she was unsure how she could reach him. Confused as to which hand to offer him: *Feminine or masculine? Discipline or caress?* She lay down on her bed, looking up into the darkness, awaiting instructions from some higher power. While waiting, she sunk her face deep into her pillow and allowed the tears to flow.

In the morning Manny showered and put on the clothes from the day before. His white shirt was showing signs of distress and his suit looked crumpled. He cursed himself for not having brought a change of clothing. *An escort has to organise these kinds of things and think them through before the booking*, he lectured himself. *I don't even have a wash bag with my own toiletries.* He sat at the desk and rubbed his face wearily, his hands bristling over his dark stubble. He debated for a minute as to whether he should ask Sasha if she'd kept her old shaving kit but soon decided it might not be such a good idea.

When he arrived downstairs, Sasha was already up and sitting at the kitchen table, drinking her coffee. She was wearing less make-up than usual. He wanted to believe that she looked better for it, but he couldn't. She smiled warmly and offered him some coffee. Her voice was deeper, croaky and hoarse. The ashtray next to her was overflowing with cigarette butts. He figured that the reason for her deep, rasping tone was not entirely down to her chain-smoking ways. There would be other factors at play. Factors he was not willing to think about at 10.20am. He wondered how long she'd been up. She looked tired and her hair was wild.

He eventually agreed to join her on her regular Saturday morning walk over the common. Sasha had offered him a get-out clause by insisting that he was welcome to stay behind and relax in the comfort of her home. He was tempted but allowed himself to be coaxed into the walk, though he soon regretted not having warmer clothing.

They meandered along a path decorated by winter trees, Sasha leading the way. The conversation ebbed and flowed. The air was cold and fresh on Manny's face and a grey drizzle was falling lightly from the sky. She would stop occasionally to point something out to him, divulging to him a little of her past. Manny listened and enjoyed seeing her through fresh eyes. They'd been walking steadily for about an hour when they approached a bench. Manny stopped to wipe the seat with his sleeve, suggesting that they sit down. Apart from the singing of the birds, the common was silent, damp and green. It was as peaceful and therapeutic as he had hoped. A couple of dogs were providing company for their respective owners. The scene held his attention for a moment. He looked on, imagining what it would be like to have a dog. Or better still, to be in a position where he could

188

keep a dog. He thought about it for a minute or two, deciding that he liked the thought.

They exchanged a few words before she asked him a question that startled him.

"Have you ever been in love, Manny?"

Jesus, he thought, *what a question to ask me*. He said nothing, hoping her question would fade away. But she didn't let it go. He paused a long moment before answering, adopting a pose that made him appear calm and collected. Names and faces filtered through his mind. Like a shopper at the sales, Lucy's image kept barging its way to the front. He debated for a short while whether to tell Sasha about his former girlfriend but, as he carefully tried composing an answer, Lucy's image pushed forward again, only this time she was with the man she'd gone off with. They were both grinning at him. He shook his head.

"No, I don't think so. That's some question by the way." He watched the leaves cartwheeling their way along the path. "I'm not sure I can define 'being in love'… Can you?"

She nodded, seeming to sense he wasn't about to reveal anything of his love life to her. "Well, I can only speak for myself, but for me being in love encompasses several emotions which are experienced together or at one time, or somewhere in between. These are feelings of fear, desire, elation, jealousy, lust, to name but a few. It's also unpredictable - I don't know how I'm going to feel until I feel it. And that's why, when perhaps I've had a few too many glasses of wine and I let my guard down, all these feelings rise up to the surface. I can't always decide which feeling should take priority because they are all so very intense… And it's these intensities of feelings which tell me that I'm not in a normal state, so I must be in love! … Wasn't it Freud who said that being in love was a state of madness?"

Manny could only shrug.

"But then again, I'm not sure if these feelings I have come from within, or whether they come from you, such as the light that shines in me now – does that come from me or from you? To whom can I attribute it? Whatever it is, I'm enjoying a warm glow, the kind of glow that I hear people talk about."

She took his hand and squeezed before continuing. A powerful wave of anxiety seized him. He couldn't help noticing that her hands were bigger than his.

"Many people put being in love down to a state of hormones and the need to reproduce, whereas I feel that being in love is a spiritual and aesthetic event. Otherwise, why would so many people write such beautiful poems and songs about it? It's difficult to describe it logically, but that's what led me to Rumi. In my opinion, he describes better than anyone what it is to be in love. The more I discovered about him, the more I wanted to know and experience the love he so masterfully describes for myself." She turned to face him. "I have been looking for somebody for some time now. Somebody who can awaken my soul in the same way Shams awoke his... I believe you're that person."

Manny's anxiety tightened its grip as she tightened hers. He wanted to say something, but couldn't. The expression drained from his face. Motionless, he sat there, eyes wide, mouth open.

The line between being a professional escort and being honest was out there somewhere, he just didn't know where. *I'm groping in the dark here, trying to find it. I have to tread carefully so as not to trample over her feelings.* He smiled to soften the rejection.

"Sasha, I'm going to be straight with you." He hesitated, remembering Virginia's words about 'making the client shine and feel special.'

"You mentioned last night, quite correctly, that I'm an escort who hires himself out to strangers. I can't deny that I enjoy your company and you're certainly opening my eyes to many new things. But I'm no Shams, believe me. I feel in your desire to find a soul mate and kindred spirit you're projecting a great deal on to me, hoping that I'm the one. I'm not."

A look of hurt entered her eyes.

"I'd be delighted to carry on seeing you now and then, but that's all I can offer ...Company. You hire me for my company. You deserve much more than that. More than a professional arrangement. We're getting along so well because of two things: I need money and you want company. That's how we came to find each other." He said the last bit with a smile in his voice.

190

They sat in silence for a few moments, still holding hands. Manny waited to see if she would add anything, hoping she wasn't about to implode.

"I understand what you're doing here and why you do it," she frowned. "Yes, I use escorts for reasons I'm not sure I'm ready to go in to. But we *have* met, we were always going to meet. How we came to meet … well, it's irrelevant. The fact being that I've found you. Destiny and fate played their part too, and as usual their timing was perfect."

Manny's eyes widened. "What?"

Her face, a mix between anger and pain, as if she'd been stung.

"Do I really need to explain?"

He nodded. She sat forward and punctured the air with a exasperated sigh, like a frustrated teacher having to explain the basics to him all over again.

"A meeting of souls is happening here. Something very special is taking shape. From the moment I first saw you, I knew. My soul has been whispering your name to me in the honesty of the night. I can't deny being a touch disappointed that you do not yet see or feel it, but in time I'm hoping you will. Anyway," she said, drawing heavily on another cigarette, "the lesson has already begun. Your soul is ready even if you're not." She noticed his face, a picture of confusion and apprehension.

"Sorry. I should shut up. As usual, I've said too much and now I'm scaring you."

"No, no, you're not," he said without any real conviction. He tried to think what else to say but hit another blank. He was dumbfounded.

Manny didn't understand what she was getting at, nor did he want to. *She's living in her poems*, he thought. Reminding himself again that he was being paid for this, he put it down to being all part of the service. Some clients hired escorts for one reason only: carnal pleasure. While others, like Sasha, had an emotional longing that also needed fulfilling. It was, he guessed, what he was being paid to do. *I need to change the topic and somehow lighten the mood. This is getting far too heavy.*

191

The two of them sat in silence for a long moment, gazing over the common. Her looking up at the moody clouds, biting on her bottom lip. Him looking down, elbows on his knees, face in hands. Sensing the growing tension, he stood up, helped her up from the bench and put his hands in his pockets, inviting her to link arms. She was happy to oblige. They continued on with the walk, only he was no longer feeling a sense of calm, just the cold and the twigs and leaves underfoot.

"I should have brought a change of clothing with me," he said, determined to divert matters back on to safer territory. "I'm cold and I think I'm beginning to smell and I must look really dishevelled."

"No, you don't," she laughed. "Anyway, I was thinking that maybe we could go into town later for a bite to eat and a drink. I also want you to take me out to a club later. I feel like some fun after a very demanding week. I'll speak to Virginia and let her know. I can't have you running off later to be with some other client. You kept me waiting long enough last night. What do you say?" she asked cheerfully.

"Yeah, I think I can manage that." He breathed an internal sigh of relief at being back on familiar ground. "In fact, I know a place along the King's Road that you might like."

He recalled being told that it was Monica who dealt with guest lists and such. He made a mental note to call her.

"Excellent. Also, I want to buy you some new clothes, if that's okay? No offence, but every time I see you you're in the same attire. And you look freezing. If you're taking me out later I need you looking your best," she added with a wink and a nudge.

He shrugged to show that he had no objections. His mind drifted back to what Louise had said about Sasha being 'a lonely fantasist'. He turned to look at her and smiled warmly, trying not to see her awkwardness, her interchangeable moods. Insecure one minute, she was a wise beacon of knowledge the next. He pulled her close to him, not sure if it was out of pity or because he was beginning to care. Probably a little of both. He felt a responsibility towards her, wanting her to feel happy. Something he hadn't anticipated. He didn't think about the extra money he'd be making that day, just ways he could help brighten her day, put a smile on her face. She had tugged on a cord that rang something inside him: *I'm a teacher who always feels for the awkward kid nobody seems to like. The odd one who struggles to fit, just like his uniform. 'Borrowed or handed down?'*

A friendly smile, a knowing nod, always at the ready, just for him. Don't wander alone looking sad, it makes me feel bad too. Watching out of windows at break, waiting, willing for someone, anyone to come along and ask him to play.

Must be a friendly face though, free of any malice, for I fear another nasty comment chucked his way and he'll finally crack. He's fragile, see, the damage has already been done... Some fathers, eh?

CHAPTER
TWENTY-TWO

They had lunch at a little restaurant not far from Sasha's home. Over lunch she was keen to probe more into his life and how he'd come to be working as a male escort. Manny began by answering in a guarded fashion, giving her an edited version of events, but the wine soon encouraged him to loosen up and be less cagey. He spent the next thirty minutes telling her about his troubles at work and how he'd become disillusioned with some aspects of his job. He also explained why Anna, his landlady, had little alternative but to issue him his marching orders, which led into a short synopsis of how he'd come to be entrenched in debt.

She'd listened throughout with genuine concern on her face, making it easier for him to be slightly more open and honest.

"Oh dear, so where are you staying now?"

"Well," he said in between mouthfuls of pasta and slurps of red wine, "I haven't faced up to it yet … so, like the fool I am, I booked a couple of nights in a hotel." She looked at him for an explanation.

"I needed some time to think and be closer to work."

"When you say work, do you mean…?"

"Sorry, yeah, I mean school. Don't really think of escorting as work."

Her eyes narrowed. "Oh?"

"I see it as a must, survival, a solution to my…"

Sasha raised an eyebrow. Instantly Manny realised his mistake. Putting down his cutlery, he looked straight at her.

"The difference being with you, Sasha, is that I actually look forward to seeing you." He measured out a short silence before adding, "Sorry, that was clumsy of me."

"It's fine. Don't worry, at least you're being honest, I like that about you. Anyway, you haven't answered the question."

"Well, Len, the driver, happens to be looking for a lodger but..." He didn't bother to finish the sentence. He didn't have to, the grimace on his face was enough.

"A homeless wanderer, eh?" Sasha looked thoughtful for a moment. She was thinking something through.

"Yeah, something like that. I'd love a place of my own really... another reason for escorting. My teaching salary alone is not enough, I'm afraid, and as I've already explained, any chance of promotion or receiving a pay rise are looking remote. The way things are shaping out at work, I'll be lucky to survive this term, let alone the next."

Sasha nodded in agreement, which kind of surprised him.

"Especially if someone in the education authority gets to hear that one of their employees is hiring himself out as a male escort outside school hours."

It was his turn to look at her, demanding an explanation.

"Oh, come on, Manny. You can't tell me that you've never considered the possible implications of what you are doing."

He had of course. The stone in his shoe.

"Teachers these days need to be whiter than white. Sensitive times... you know that! How many times have you seen articles in the newspapers or on television? Teachers who have been weak or reckless in some way... their misdemeanors highlighted in bold for all to see." To create a simulation of a headline, Sasha raised an arm just above her head, shaping her hand into a block and impersonating a newspaper vendor standing on a street corner: *"Read all about it. 'Teacher exposed as male gigolo.' Read all about it."*

The tone was masculine. Very masculine.

Manny shifted in his seat, not enjoying what he was hearing on both counts. A shiver of apprehension ran through him. He sipped his wine and sat in edgy silence, hoping that they'd soon be moving on to something more trivial like, 'Now, what clothes would you like me to buy for you today?'

"Look, regardless of how you're feeling about the profession, you're still considered by many to be in a position of trust and with trust comes responsibility. There are plenty of people out there who would object to what you're involved in."

"Would they?" he asked tamely, already knowing the answer.

"Yes," she stressed. "They would... Believe me! I'm talking through experience here. When I teach, lecture or give seminars now, it's predominantly for adults... mature students. I can't quite see parents, education authorities and the press turning a blind eye to a transsexual running amok in their schools teaching the children. Can you?"

He slowly shook his head.

"Don't worry, you're not alone. The same rules apply to police, doctors, judges, politicians, priests..." She grinned before adding, "Though some of those I've mentioned have still to master this simple concept."

He snorted a laugh in agreement. "Yeah, but I'm not doing anything illegal, am I?"

"Legal or illegal, it doesn't matter. It's news... gossip that spreads and sells... gossip that can't be managed but can certainly be sensationalised."

She paused to take breath and another gulp of her wine.

"People who hold positions of trust are not supposed to meander too far down the ... the... muddy and murky path of misdemeanors... Can't afford to get dirty, see. Society will not allow for it. Never has done. And rightly so."

A pause while she took another sip. Manny was sitting awkwardly but quietly, wise enough not to interrupt, trying to pay attention. She was back on the podium behind her lectern.

"Plato did warn us about the perils of the abuse of trust. Governments tumble. Communities crumble. It's in 'The Republic'... though I can't quite remember which chapter he so eloquently puts it in." She raised her eyes upwards in search of the answer. "Anyway, despite the declining standards of today, people still need to believe that they can trust and rely on those in a position of trust. In fact, it's most vital."

Sasha reached over the table and laid her hand on Manny's. Again, it was the size of the hand, not the deftness of touch, that startled him.

"You, my dear," she continued with a look of seriousness, "fall into that category. You must be careful. A whisper here, an insinuation there, and before you know it, you're fighting to save your career and reputation. As my old professor once told me, 'To be able to teach is a blessing, one should treat it with the respect that it deserves'."

Sasha waited a moment to allow her words to hit home.

"And intuition tells me you need that *something* teaching gives you. Am I right?"

Manny nodded in a manner that suggested she'd played a good shot.

"Don't," she chuckled with just a little too much modesty. "You forget us women can read you men like books."

He was about to grin back at her but suppressed it when he realised she was being serious.

Silence was allowed to lie between them for a minute or two. She noticed that his eyes had drifted out of focus and were now looking at something in the distant or near future even.

"Sorry, I'm lecturing you again, I have no right to. A couple of glasses of wine and I'm off, getting all philosophical. Can't help myself. You're old enough and wise enough to make your own decisions now. I'm sure you know what you're doing. I would hate to see you suffer, that's all."

Manny shrugged, tipped the glass to his lips and smiled for effect. There was plenty of truth in her prattle. However he was in no rush to shrug off the niggling doubts of scepticism. It was probable that she had an agenda. *She wants me for herself. The thought of me being with other clients doesn't sit well with her.*

He recalled Virginia's comment, "Dr Sasha Harrington is going to have to learn to share." But a part of him wanted her motives to be pure. Why? He wasn't sure. A bond was forming between them. Dare he say an intimacy? Unexpected because she was a paying client and a respected commentator, droning on at him about morals with an air of authority one would think twice before challenging. *Like a loving parent, she is warning me of the potential harm escorting could do to my reputation and floundering career as a teacher. She's looking out for me and I seem to be warming to the notion that she cares. Or does she?*

Despite his doubts, he found it refreshing hearing a voice other than his own giving some validity to this obsessive fear. A fear that regularly hijacked his mind, holding his happiness hostage. It was indeed something to be taken seriously.

Louise, on the other hand, when seeing him struggle over this dilemma, opted for a more robust approach, choosing to go on the offensive, attacking it with financial optimism. The promise of regaining control *if* he could hold his nerve.

And what were her motives? Why, money of course. Part of her job. If I'm earning, she's earning too. But her late night visit? Her tenderness? Ho hum, what a conundrum.

"How long do you think you will be escorting for? And how are you finding it?"

"Sorry?" He was miles away.

Sasha repeated herself, yanking him from his thoughts.

"Not long. Just until I've managed to put some distance between me and my debts. I've only been in the game five minutes and already I have my doubts as to whether I can do this sort of thing."

"Care to expand on that?"

The memory of the potbellied man with his trousers down around his ankles, masturbating, flooded his mind. He had to work hard to suppress a shudder of revulsion. Nina's face, already forgotten, vanished from Manny's memory, the husband's taking a little longer to follow suit.

Looking at Sasha with a fixed smile, Manny knew that to elaborate would mean digging himself into another hole. Nimbly, he changed track, searching for the right words.

"Don't get me wrong, if all clients were like you, well, I'd be okay. Trouble is they're not."

Twirling the stem of her glass between thumb and forefinger, Sasha waited to see if he would expand on that. When he didn't, she leant down to collect her shoulder bag, announcing she needed to go for a cigarette. She stood up, smoothed down her skirt and departed with a smile of sorts. She squeezed his arm reassuringly on passing.

Manny stayed at the table, running a hand over his chin, hearing the rasping sounds it made against the couple of days' worth of stubble, thinking. It felt similar to his yesteryears. Every few months he would meet up with his mother for a spot of lunch or a coffee. She would copiously pry into his life, fretting about his lack of progress and laidback approach, his lethargy. Needing him to convince her that he was ambitious, full of drive and coping. Forever warning him of the consequences of falling behind with his studies, experimenting with drugs, not finding a proper job. The final summary never lacking in dramatic effect: 'What a tragedy it would be, should you ever turn out to be like your father.' He allowed himself a dry smile in recognition that he had been a sceptical bugger back then too, questioning his own mother's intentions behind her overdue display of selfless concern. He remembered his thinking at the time: *She couldn't face the prospect of me turning up at her home, having taken a stumble along the path that leads towards adulthood and independence. She's moved on. Remarried. New life, new family. Happy no doubt. The warmth of family niceties now helping to heal her pain. What she doesn't need is me on her doorstep, lost and confused. For my failures would be her failures too. Wouldn't be just the door she'd be opening, there's her wounds of old. Father's flailing fists that I couldn't prevent from landing. I'm told that I look like him now. It's the eyes. Surely she's suffered enough. Tell her what she'd like to hear and let her get off.*

Manny tried to remember the last time they had spoke but soon gave up. He often pondered the ways in which he could help close the chasm that had developed between them over time. The answer unfortunately was always the same. Success. Something that he felt was still a million miles away. Chastising himself for this moment of melancholy, he ordered himself to get his head straight. Breathing out noisily through his nose, Manny scrunched the napkin he'd been aimlessly folding and chucked it onto his half-eaten plate of food. Yes, there were risks in what he was doing and it hadn't been an easy decision to make. But the decision *had* been made. The deal done with himself, not the devil or anyone else. He was answerable only to himself. The contract was written and stored in his head: *Do this for the next few months only, make as much as you can, then get the hell out and resurrect your once-promising teaching career …*

As usual, he never bothered with the small print.

Meanwhile, outside, Sasha had lit her second cigarette and was inhaling deeply, exhaling slowly. The thought of Manny entertaining other clients had caused a silent shiver to shoot down her spine. Only the fierce flames of anger rising in her chest prevented the chill from settling in, freezing over her heart. Again, she took another long drag before throwing her cigarette onto the floor, destroying it underfoot with a violent twist and a snarl to match. So, he had been with other clients, despite Virginia's reassurances that he hadn't. He'd let it slip himself. She was determined to prevent it from ever happening again. She had a plan. The time had now come to execute it, put it into action. His face as she left, a mixture of worry and bewilderment, suggested that it wouldn't be too difficult. The confusion in his soulful, dark eyes, the appealing look of vulnerability hidden so well behind that alluring smile: what woman, she wondered, could refuse? She, Dr Sasha Harrington, certainly couldn't.

On her return she bent down and planted a big sloppy kiss on the top of his head. This caught him unawares and for a moment his face froze. Only his eyes shifted from side to side, trying to gauge how many people had witnessed this 'touching' moment. Luckily, the other diners seemed preoccupied with the business on their own plates. He rubbed his hands over his cropped hair, swallowing hard, a trifle embarrassed, resembling a schoolboy who'd just been kissed by his mother at the school gates in full view of his smirking mates.

"Listen," she said as she settled back into her seat. "Why don't I settle up here and take you into the West End for a spot of shopping? I'd like to treat you to some new clothes. Then, later, after we've been back to mine to freshen up, I'll let you take me to that club you said I'd love... No more lecturing, I promise. We'll let things lie... for now. What do you say?"

Manny exhaled loudly, almost too loudly. A smile broke out across his face. It was what he had signed up for. He nodded in approval. This time without any hesitation.

CHAPTER
TWENTY-THREE

Sitting in the back of a black cab on their way back to Sasha's house, south of the river, Manny felt in a good place, revitalised. He was staring out of the cab's window, watching the grey of London whizzing by. He'd come to the conclusion that retail therapy did work. With money in his pocket, bags at his feet, the afternoon shopping spree had turned out to be fun. An unexpected blast.

The regular pit stops into pubs and bars, together with the thumping music played in the trendy high street stores, had also lent a hand in creating a real carnival atmosphere for the pair. Sasha had insisted that all his problems and concerns be temporarily put on hold, which after a while he eventually managed. As shopping trips went, it hadn't been too bad. Despite himself, Manny had enjoyed the experience. He'd enjoyed the time he'd spent with her and enjoyed the money she had spent on him. Even the glances he was sure they were attracting ceased to bother him. But the feel-good factor he was experiencing could not be attributed to monetary reasons alone. No, there were other underlining factors he was yet to fathom. True, her generosity had proved to be both boundless and seductive. Amongst other things, she'd bought him enough clothes to fill a decent size wardrobe. Trousers, jeans, jackets, tops, shirts and shoes. All in the plural. She'd even insisted on putting some money into his account to help reduce his overdraft. Only after giving him another of her mini lectures, of course. "Boundaries," she'd said. "Nobody's ever been in your life long enough to impose any, to help you adhere to them. That's been the problem." He'd played along with the odd smile and nod, there were moments when she made him feel like a naughty kid who'd been caught out. *Laughable really,* he thought, *I can sense a part of me almost wants to like it.*

The only things that she'd desired for herself that afternoon were his undivided attention, which she got, and what could only be described as a bizarre fairy outfit or angel dress - pink, frilly and with ridiculous wings. Manny smiled a glance at her as she dozed, head back, mouth open. From the moment she'd spotted it through the novelty shop window, she had to have it. Laughing, she'd playfully dragged him by the arm into the shop and demanded that he buy it for her. So he did. To his relief she never bothered to try it on. He doubted whether she'd be able to squeeze her frame into it. Petite, she wasn't. One thing he was sure of, though, he didn't want to be around when she tried it. Cheap too. It had only cost him twenty-five pounds. Not bad, as drunken purchases go. He smiled while leaning back against the headrest, trying to find a comfortable position to support his head. *I bet she'll never wear it,* he yawned before joining her in closing his eyes for a minute or two.

"My God, it's amazing. I never knew about this place. You're so thoughtful," she said ecstatically before hugging him in front of not only the burly doorman but the other guests who stood patiently in the queue. Thanks to Monica, Manny never had to stand around in any queues. Instead, he took Sasha by the hand, marched to the front of the line and whispered his name into the doorman's ear. At once the doorman showed them both into the club.

During their call earlier, Monica had more than done her bit by ensuring that not only were their names put on the guest list but they were given a bit of the V.I.P treatment too. Manny made a mental note to thank her. He'd also promised her that they would catch up soon.

The club itself, to Sasha's delirious delight, was called 'Rumi Bar' and was situated along the King's Road in Chelsea. Once inside, the Arabian décor alone was enough to leave her speechless.

"It's perfect," she kept saying once she'd found her voice again. "Just perfect. I can't believe it's called Rumi." He thought he saw her shed a quiet tear too when she first noticed that words from her favourite mystic were projected onto some of the walls. She was overcome. Manny congratulated himself on getting something right. He'd gambled that she had not heard of the club and it seemed to have paid off.

"My way of saying thanks. I'm sure we'll have a great time here." And he really believed that they would.

They walked around for a short while, acclimatising themselves to the setting. Her, wide-eyed in awe, succumbing to the club's eastern charms. Him, looking around for a secluded spot for them to sit. Most of the sofas and tables were already occupied. The club wasn't the biggest, so it seemed fairly busy. The cushioned sofas and surrounding candles lent the place a sense of intimacy, creating a mellow ambience where one felt safe and included.

They had arrived reasonably early so there were still one or two of the comfy sofas left to choose from. The atmosphere was simmering along nicely and Manny was in the mood to party. He found a sofa and a small table in a far corner, near to a bar and close enough to the contemporary looking dance floor. They made themselves comfortable and drank the complimentary cocktails that had been handed to them. Again Manny congratulated himself. It had been the perfect start, her face still soaking in the thrill of it all. It felt good inside for him too, seeing how such a simple act could make her so happy.

He stood at the bar feeling suave in his new suit. A lighter shade of grey than his other one with a much sharper cut and closer fit. Tie hanging loosely around his dark, open-necked shirt. More man on the town than stuck in a business meeting. Not only had Sasha shown a sound eye when it came to men's fashion but her ability to pick out his size and guess his measurements was uncanny. Only a couple of minor alterations had to be made, small enough to be carried out by the in-house tailor there and then. She wanted him looking his best that night.

The wall behind the bar was mirrored, so in between the optics, array of bottles, glasses and bartenders' heads, Manny was able to catch the odd glimpse of himself while he waited to be served. It made a change for him to like what he saw. Of course, the club's dim lighting helped, but he acknowledged that it felt good to feel good, to be winning. Optimism once again suppressing despair. And providing Sasha's demands went no further, he could see himself warming to the role as her escort. Easy money to be made from someone whose company was easy to endure. Who would've thought it?

He felt less on edge too when out with her in public places. Whenever the situation became a little too daunting, he'd use the mantra: *'Think about the money you're getting for this.'*

Other than the uncomfortable conversation they'd had on the park bench, he felt that the booking had gone relatively well. All that remained was to ensure she had a fantastic time in the club. He was on the home stretch, the finishing post in sight. Manny felt confident of clearing the final hurdle. Just as long, that was, as the night ended as it had done the evening before, with Sasha retiring to her room and him to the safety of the spare. Then he would be able to say, not only to himself but also to the girls at the agency, that the weekend with Dr Sasha Harrington had gone without a hitch. A profitable success which had caused no lasting damage to his soul, unlike the first booking of that weekend. The sudden shudder that went through him served as a sharp reminder to have those words with Virginia.

"Yes, sir?" asked the bartender.

"Same again, please."

"Bottle of Verve?"

"That's the one."

"Would you like it brought over?"

Manny turned to look over at Sasha who sat comfortably in their corner, calmly drinking and absorbing the music. She noticed him and waved. He responded warmly.

"No, it's okay, mate," he said, turning back. "I'll carry it over, no rush, take your time." He needed a few moments to himself. She had already dragged him up to the dance floor once. He'd been a little self conscious at first but the music and his mantra soon had him loosening up. The floor was bustling with handsome, young and fit-looking people. Tanned, toned and shining with health. Manny wondered if some were professional dancers, models even, paid by the club to inject energy onto the dance floor early on, accessories to match the fine décor. They certainly moved like pros. He felt like he'd walked onto the set of a video shoot for a hip up-and-coming Indy band, only he'd been paired with the eldest and least attractive person there. Cut! Manny would make sure that he danced no longer than was necessary that evening. There were drinks and a table to safeguard. It was getting busy.

Manny had told Sasha earlier that it was the best he'd seen her look. Which was true. There was an energy in her eyes and an almost girlish enthusiasm about her. Yes, the neck did slightly give away her age and the dark skirt she wore maybe clung a little too tight to her muscular thighs. She was also tall, as tall as most of the men in there. That was okay though, women were taller these days. Getting taller all the time. Some of the girls at his school were already as tall as him, if not taller.

The make-up she wore helped to soften her jawline and gave a healthy glow to her complexion. Wearing her hair pulled back suited her. The heavy mascara did a decent job in bringing out those dark eyes of hers. Nevertheless, he'd spent quite a bit of time with her of late. Times when they had been in close proximity with each other. And Manny had started to see what lay behind the make-up. Despite her best efforts, traces of masculinity lingered. She knew it and he knew it. The sensuous pearl of femininity would always elude her no matter what she or any surgeon did. Again, he'd been silently willing himself to see her as being beautiful but he couldn't quite bring himself to do so. More for her sake than his own, it had to be said. If he'd learnt anything in life it was this: *Women of all shapes, sizes and colour possess beauty. A beauty they never lose, no matter what their age. A beauty hard to erase, slow to erode. A natural beauty. A gift to be cherished, for it was delivered by the divine hand of sweet mother nature.*

Manny could not help but pity *her* for the decision a *he* had made.

Once you got over the initial surprise, you could see a face with much to admire. A handsome face and there lay the problem. *When I first saw her, I was reluctant to look, worried about what I'd see. I was being charitable in an uncharitable way in order to help me through.*

These thoughts made him feel bad. Bad, because he felt he knew more about her now. There was no denying that he'd warmed to her. She possessed qualities he admired in a person: she was considerate, intelligent and sincere. At first he'd looked on with apprehension, soon turning to admiration as he discovered the different sides to her engaging personality. *Laughable really, she's even managed to gain my trust.* Which not many had done.

Manny pulled his thoughts back before they wandered any further, ordering himself to focus on the here and now. He turned and looked across at Sasha, trying to keep the look of sympathy from his gaze, thinking that she didn't deserve the ruminations and stinging criticism rolling around in his head. *It doesn't concern me. What does it matter anyhow? And who am I to judge? What matters now is that she has a good time.*

And that, he reminded himself, *is why I'm here and what I'm getting paid to do.* With that last thought, he carried the drinks back to their table, fully intending to fulfil his role. It was the least she deserved.

The night had truly hotted up and they were getting on better than at any time before. They'd swapped jokes, shared cocktails and had even bobbed around some more on the dance floor, both of them in high spirits, jocular moods.

Back in their corner, Sasha had put down her drink, announcing that she needed to relieve herself and find a place where she could enjoy a cigarette. She added in between fits of drunken giggles that she was desperate for both.

"Don't you go anywhere," she ordered, "I'll be right back."

Manny took a moment to relax and look around, busily surveying the place, thinking what a great venue this was to meet women. The place was full of them. Stunningly seductive women had been registering on his radar many times over. Christ, it had been tough but he'd managed to show discipline. Best behaviour and all that. As tempting as they might be, flirtatious eyes had to be avoided, unfortunately. He was working and the client would certainly not approve. Only, with the client now gone, it would be a shame to let the opportunity pass. Manny allowed his gaze to roam, free from any constraints. He was busy admiring the female form in all its different guises, dazzling on the dance floor one minute, oozing sensuality the next, as they stood about laughing and chatting. Magnets to roaming eyes.

Wow! Eye candy everywhere...

He lent back and spread his arms along the back of the sofa, feeling smug and totally content, when a figure appeared in his peripheral view. The figure was approaching him, walking over with purposeful strides. He could tell by the gait that she was female. As she got closer, Manny noted that she had a pretty face. The face was beaming widely at him. A familiar face.

"Manny? Oh, it is you! I thought so..." she said, whooping in delight.

It took Manny a few seconds to place her and when he did... *Oh shit... it's what's her name... The new geography teacher.*

"It's me, Emma... You know, from school. I've just started working there."

His heart sank and his stomach churned, his composure shaken.

"Yes, of course. Sorry. It's the light in here," he said, doing his best to appear unruffled. He stood up and greeted her with a kiss on the cheek, catching a faint scent of musk. Emma Clarke wore a crop top that showed off a toned midriff and a diamond stud piercing. Her hair tumbled over her shoulders and was curlier than Manny remembered. He was back to being on edge. Every few seconds he would frantically glance over in the direction Sasha had headed off.

Emma's eyes lowered onto the table where a half-drunk bottle of champagne rested on ice, two glasses sitting beside it.

"Who are you here with?"

Manny looked stumped for an answer. "Er, just a friend. You?"

"With Phil and a few of his mates. They played football earlier. I went along to watch. They won and have been out celebrating ever since."

"Phil? Phil Young from school?" he asked, already knowing the answer.

"Yeah, he's over there." She turned and flicked her head towards the backdrop of lights and bodies. Manny followed her eyes but failed to make out Young's face or form in the club's hazy atmosphere amongst the bobbing heads. He groaned inwardly. *Oh fuck, it gets worse.*

Manny felt at a complete loss as to what to say or do. Emma sat down beside him and began to make some comments about the club, school and the game she'd been to see, but he wasn't really listening. He was looking at her and nodding, thinking of the best way to handle the situation. A verbal jousting session with Phil Young didn't bear thinking about. School staffroom? Yes. In a nightclub with a six foot transsexual on his arm? No.

"You look good, Manny. Very debonair. Sorry, who did you say you're with?"

He paused and hesitated as he thought about the consequences of each possible response. He could feel his insides churning. He needed to remain calm, disaster could yet be averted. He needed to get rid of her, and quick.

"Listen," he said eventually, "I don't mean to be rude but I'm on a bit of a promise here. If she comes back and sees me chatting to a stunner like you, well, I can see it all going up in smoke."

Emma smiled and nodded in understanding, seemingly appeased by the compliment.

"She's a lucky lady." She stood up and wished him luck, on the verge of leaving. But it was too late.

"There you are. I was beginning to think..." Phil Young never finished his sentence, his eyes and attention had shifted onto Manny instead, who had sunk his frame deep into the sofa in a pathetic attempt to remain incognito.

"Rodriguez? You old dog, what the hell are you doing here?"

Manny smiled out of courtesy but his mind was elsewhere. The two men shook hands and bumped chests, one with a little more enthusiasm than the other. Young then embraced him like a long lost friend, which they certainly weren't. Their relationship could be described, at best, as being indifferent. Young's over the top reaction told Manny that he was most likely inebriated, more than he was himself, no doubt. He possessed all the swagger and confidence you'd usually associate with a P.E. teacher, only Young had well and truly crossed that invisible line where confidence became plain arrogance. Funny really, Manny had always thought, seeing as Young had never excelled in any of the sports that he played or taught. Jack of all trades but master of none was the polite way of putting it.

Young was solid, well built. Tall with broad shoulders, in his late twenties, and with a head of fluffy, highlighted hair darkened by gel, worn in a style that was popular amongst the boys at the school. His suit was dark blue, his shirt white, reminding Manny of a male model posing in the pages of a 'Next' catalogue, a look he hoped never to replicate.

"Well, I never…" Young continued as he repeatedly slapped Manny hard on the back, a little too hard for Manny's liking. "Fancy bumping into you. Of all the clubs in London you had to walk into mine," he added, mimicking Bogart and his legendary line.

"Yeah, funny that, I was thinking the same thing."

"So," he said, looking down at the champagne, "who's the lucky girl?" He nudged and winked at Manny, none too subtly. "Champagne? I hope she's worth it." He picked up the bottle from the bucket and read the label. "Fuck me, Rodriguez, expensive stuff this. I'd have her sign on the dotted line first, guaranteeing me the bunk up." He looked up at Manny who was subtly pointing his eyes in Emma's direction.

"Oops, sorry, babe. Only pulling his plonker…" Young sat down on the sofa and told Emma to do the same, pulling her by the arm.

"No," she retorted. "We should get back to the others and leave Manny to his date."

"He doesn't mind, do you, Rodriguez? Anyway, I want to meet this hot date of his, it would be rude not to. He's a cagey bleeder is our Mr Rodriguez... I take it she's the reason you've not been playing staff football of late?"

Manny offered a shrug, sensing that his world was about to cave in. Young was hell bent on meeting his mysterious woman and in his position Manny acknowledged that he'd probably be the same. He tried to think of what he could do to avert the situation but, other than running off, he drew a blank. Alcohol, on this occasion, was proving to be more of a hindrance than a help.

"Think it's time I had a quiet word in her ear," Young smirked, revelling in Manny's growing discomfort. "I can't have her disrupting my team selections."

Emma offered him an apologetic look.

"Come on, Phil, let's go." Her plea not only fell on deaf ears, it also lacked conviction, causing Manny to believe she was in no real rush to leave herself, maybe wanting to check out the competition, as he'd been told girls liked to do.

Manny's mood had darkened. He rubbed his hand over his cropped head and loosened his tie some more. Beads of sweat had started running down his back; suddenly he felt very claustrophobic. He thought about sloping off again, but that would make him a coward and would certainly bring an end to his money-making venture. Hell, the way he was feeling, maybe that wouldn't be such a bad thing. *Damn.* It was the first time his mantra had failed him.

"Where is she by the way?" Young inquired.

Manny declined to answer. His dislike for Young was intensifying with every passing second. Emma kept offering him apologetic smiles. Well, he presumed they were apologetic. Suddenly, the brief lull in Young's self-absorbed patter made Manny look up.

Sasha's arrival had silenced him. The ordinary sounds of the club, the music and chatter, filled the void. Yet, despite all the background hubbub, Manny was able to hear Young gulp and swallow.

Sasha stood there looking strong and determined. Standing straight, inflating out her chest, face devoid of any emotion. She looked over to Manny with her dark eyes frowning, waiting for introductions. He rose to do just that. It was an awkward moment for him and she knew it. Young stood up, wide-eyed and open-mouthed, to offer his hand. Manny flinched as he noticed that Sasha was just as tall and just as broad as he was. When Emma did the same, Sasha towered over her, Emma's hand seeming tiny in hers. Both Young and Emma seemed at a loss for words.

"Would you care to join us for a glass or two of champagne? Manny seems to have forgotten his manners. Darling, have you not offered your friends a drink?"

"No, they're not my friends. They're work colleagues," he said bluntly, hoping she'd see his predicament.

"Nonetheless, I'm sure you know each other well enough to share a drink. Honestly, a few drinks and he forgets his manners," Sasha sighed and gave Manny a smile with a cold glare. *Get a grip*, the glare ordered. Then she turned her attention back to the pair. "Champagne? Looks like we could do with another bottle."

Emma was about to politely refuse but was quickly interrupted by Young who answered for them, giving the younger teacher a look as if she were a child at school who'd forgotten to bring in her P.E kit.

"That would be lovely, thank you very much. We'd like that, wouldn't we, babe?" Emma sat back down again, smiling at Manny apologetically.

"Great," said Sasha. "Make yourselves comfy and we'll go to the bar and fetch another bottle and some fresh glasses." Then to Manny, who was looking on in disbelief and anger, "Ready, dear?"

Sasha grabbed his hand, turned and headed for the bar, Manny not looking too enthralled. At the bar, he was about to furiously protest when she put her finger up to his mouth.

"Shh, don't say a word! Do you want to make things a whole lot worse for yourself?"

Manny shrugged his shoulders like a petulant child.

"Then listen and keep that hot head of yours cool, stay calm and act like we're lovers, like we're together."

He arched an eyebrow again, ready to protest, but she wouldn't have any of it.

"Or would you prefer they knew the truth? And what it is that you do?"

Manny wearily shook his head, feeling sick to the stomach.

"Right, then hold my hand and start showing me some affection." Manny hesitated and bowed his head, shuffling his feet. *Christ, this is a nightmare.*

"Manny, look at me." No response. "Manny, do you trust me?" No answer, so she tried again."Manny, do you trust me?" Slowly he lifted his head and met her burning gaze.

"I'd like to," he finally mustered in a low mumble.

"Under the circumstances, I suppose that's the best I can hope for," she sighed. "Come on, let's take these drinks over. Try to lose the look of concern on your face. The sooner we show them that we're out to have some fun *together*, the sooner they'll get bored. It's your moody strop that's entertaining them." Manny doubted this was the only thing that they found entertaining. He'd seen the big wide grin on Young's face. He knew it meant trouble. No doubt he'd find out on Monday at school what it was they found the most entertaining, along with the rest of the staff. *Fuck, fuck and fuck.*

"Jesus, look at you, lighten up!" She tutted before walking off. "And bring the drinks."

He stood at the bar for a few seconds more in one final attempt to collect his thoughts and find his courage.

"Sorry, did I hear Manny say you're a doctor?" asked Phil curiously.

"Yes, that's right," she said, knowing where this would lead. "Not a medical doctor though. The title is down to my PhD in Persian Literature. I spent many years studying the works of mystical poets from the 13th century onwards. Ever heard of Hafiz, Attar…?" Young's face went blank while he willed the cogs of his brain to work. "…Or ever read about Sufi mysticism?" Manny could see that she was losing him.

"You must have heard of Rumi?"

A light went on, a cog had turned. "Of course I've heard of

Rumi. That's easy." Manny braced himself, he knew what was coming next.

"It's this place. We're in his club or her club. Is Rumi male or female?"

Sasha looked at Manny as an understanding passed between them. She winked at him. He managed a smile, not quite feeling reassured.

Emma was looking a little nonplussed, not enjoying the lack of attention. Worryingly for Manny though, she slouched on the sofa with her gaze firmly fixed on Sasha.

"Where did you two meet?" Emma's question was put to Manny but it was Sasha who answered for him. It was obvious from Emma's face that she clearly suspected something. Manny hoped he was being paranoid but the wave of sickness in his guts suggested he wasn't.

"Manny assisted me with some research."

"Really?" Emma sat up straight, seeming alert again.

"Yes, he's a quite a master when it comes to helping me understand the words of Rumi."

"Who? Rodriguez? Are you sure?" Young looked at Manny out of the corner of his eye, smirking.

"Why do you sound so surprised? He's a very gifted individual. A little misunderstood, perhaps. That's part of his charm, a lonely wanderer who's not fully appreciated. His talents should not be wasted, teaching solely in the confines of a tough comprehensive state school whose rigid syllabus, to all intents and purposes, was surely designed to dull and darken the young creative mind. It's no wonder schools are so unruly these days."

Both Young and his partner found it hard to stifle a grin. They both looked at Manny and held their eyes on him, sensing his embarrassment, digesting what they'd just heard.

Manny could not take any more. He'd heard enough. Sasha meant well but she was now doing more damage than good. The champagne had taken over. Excusing himself, he strode purposefully towards the gents where he marched into a cubicle, sat down and placed his head in his hands, wondering what else could possibly go wrong. He would go back and tell Young to push off, politely but forcefully telling him he'd got what he wanted, game over. Then he would take Sasha home. There'd be time over the weekend to concoct a story ready for Monday. *Shit, Monday can wait...* Damage limitation was now his priority. He needed to get back out there and end this fiasco. *God knows what she's telling them...*

Sensing that their intrusion might be causing some tension between the odd couple, and having now seen and heard enough, Emma nudged her partner in the ribs, ordering him to drink up, telling him that they really should be getting back to their mates before they ended up losing them, resulting in them missing out on the pre-paid cabs. Young agreed and emptied his glass. They both stood up and thanked Sasha for the drinks. She insisted that they wait to say their goodbyes to Manny, but Emma politely declined, knowing that he'd still be a while. Phil Young leant over and kissed Sasha on the cheek, asking her how often she worked out. Emma slapped him on the back and told him to get moving. She also kissed Sasha on the cheek and wished her goodbye. Once back amongst their own group of friends, the same questions kept on resurfacing in her mind. Manny and his date, the peculiar-looking woman that was Sasha ...Was she really a woman? Those hands, that jawline. Emma had her doubts.

CHAPTER
TWENTY-FOUR

"Sorry, did I wake you?"

Manny sat up and rubbed his eyes, slowly coming to. He threw off the duvet and looked around the room frantically. It was eight thirty on Sunday morning. He hadn't made it to the spare room upstairs. Instead he'd fallen asleep on the sofa, still wearing the same shirt and trousers from the night before. It hadn't been a good sleep. Patchy, with lots of jerks, crammed with confusing dreams. *Always running, always falling. Never knowing who to trust.*

His tongue was stuck to the roof of his mouth and his head throbbed. Sasha, meanwhile, was perched on the arm of the chair opposite, dressed already and drinking coffee from a large mug.

Christ, how long has she been sitting there?

Beside him on the sofa was one of her books, *Rumi's Longing*. He recalled reaching it down from the bookshelf and asking her to enlighten him, which she did. Surprisingly, he'd found it almost comforting. Comforting enough to distract him from his troubles. Manny had listened without interrupting. Again, full of admiration at the way she'd been able to captivate her audience, her audience of one. He was beginning to understand something of the poet and found parts of what Sasha was saying intriguing. She had wanted him to keep the book. He was to read it all the way through, so that at their next meeting, they'd be able to have an in-depth discussion about it. It was homework she insisted he complete.

"Study is good for your soul, Manny. Correct me if I'm wrong but it appears you no longer feel the need?"

He nodded. As usual she was right. The thought of bettering himself was never far from his mind. The problem was finding the time to turn thought into action.

"A real teacher never stops learning. They owe it to their students. They must master their subject. Take our friend, Rumi: he was revered in his day as a brilliant teacher and scholar, yet he always regarded himself as a student with much still to learn. The day you stop learning is the day you stop living. When I hear you talk about your job, you never show any passion and that pains me. You live in a constant state of agitation, dreaming up ways of escaping from your mundane world. Open your eyes, unlock your potential; your world is full of possibilities, but it seems that you have given up already. There's still time for you to change. I'll help you."

He'd smiled in appreciation. It had been a long time since anyone had shown this amount of interest in his personal development, longer than he cared to remember. When Sasha spoke to him in this way, not only did he want to comply with her instructions and embrace every one of her words, a part of him had wanted to embrace her too.

It wasn't long before the evening's events started to unfold in his mind. *Shit,* it had been going so well. Really well. Then came the intrusion into his secret life. The feeling of dread he'd felt in the club was back again, knocking loudly on his door.

"How is it that in a city as big as London, with all its clubs, I choose the one which two of my workmates frequent?" he asked while stretching out his aches.

"I take it you didn't manage to get much sleep?" Manny slowly shook his head. The lack of sleep was making him feel cranky and irritable. It had already been quite a weekend and the longest of nights. Time to go home. Have a soak in the bath, maybe. Lounge about in nothing but his boxers watching the footie, reading the papers. Again, that nagging question though: where was home?

"Have you decided where you'll stay tonight?" Sasha asked, bang on cue.

Manny shrugged. "Not exactly."

"Oh?"

"I'll probably just stay in a cheap hotel tonight and search for somewhere proper during the week."

"I thought you said you had a place with this Len chap. You still not sure?"

Manny shook his head. He didn't feel comfortable with the idea of moving into the grouchy driver's home. *Not today*, he'd thought to himself. *Too much like hard work. I need some time on my own.*

It wasn't that he didn't appreciate Len's offer because he did and he still might take him up on it. But at that particular moment he desperately needed time away from the whole escorting scene. A bit of time to compose himself, collect his thoughts and recharge the batteries. Mentally he was shattered and he had to get himself prepared for school the following day. The escorting work had consumed so much of his energy it was time for a short break now that his money had been made.

He really didn't want to start his Sunday brooding about what would be said at school the next day. But he couldn't help himself. Manny just couldn't seem to rid himself of the image of Phil Young and his sneering grin. It was scorched onto his brain and it was troubling him. *That sneer of his: did he know something or am I being paranoid? And what about the way Emma just sat there unable to peel her eyes away from Sasha, what had she seen?* Manny couldn't be sure. But with Monday morning just around the corner, he didn't have long to wait.

"Why don't you have a shower while I get the breakfast ready? I've left a sports holdall on the bed. It should be big enough to fit all your stuff in." He nodded his thanks while still rubbing his eyes, yawning.

"I suppose you'll be going after you've had some breakfast?"

"I ought to start thinking about making a move, yes. Lots to do."

"Oh well," she sighed, "I suppose all good things must come to an end. Are you free any time in the week?"

He debated whether or not to lie. Finally, he settled for the safety of a non-committal shrug of the shoulders. "I'm not sure yet. Would it be okay to let you know later?"

She nodded as she made her way into the kitchen. It seemed

her talkative mood had come to an end. He felt a sudden pang of sadness. *This is ridiculous*, he thought. *I feel bad about leaving her here all on her own.* But she'd been good to him, and that was what made it so hard.

Manny remembered getting a taxi back to Sasha's in the early hours of the morning, drunk, and in a state of agitation. She had tried to calm him down but he was unable to sit still and hold a sensible conversation with her. Instead, he'd paced the room, fretting about Monday morning at school, worried about what Phil Young and that Emma what's her face might say to those willing to listen. *"Who, Rodriguez? He never... With who? He what?"*

It was only after some time that Sasha had been able to reassure him temporarily, with her soothing words and a gentle shoulder rub. When she'd first stood up and walked behind him, placing her large hands on his shoulders, he had almost panicked, not knowing what she was going to do. Fortunately, her actions were purely platonic. All she was trying to do, she'd insisted, was help ease some of the tension out of him. It had felt good. He'd shut his eyes and soon found himself in a state of relaxation. The back of the sofa helped, acting as a reassuring safety barrier between him and her.

Then a fuzzy blank where everything disappeared. He'd dropped off to sleep, unaware of the uncomfortable darkness that was waiting in the wings, ready to pounce. A cocktail of dread and anxiety that had seeped into his unconsciousness, causing him to toss and turn all night.

Now they both sat silently in the kitchen. Him sitting down at the table eating a bacon roll and her resting against the worktop, cradling a mug of coffee. The atmosphere was a little strained. Manny had showered, changed into clean clothes and managed to pack the holdall with all his new stuff. He'd left it at the bottom of the stairs in the hall, close to the front door. Like him, it was ready to go.

"Look, Sasha, I'm sorry how the night ended. I allowed them to ruin everything."

"Nonsense," she said sternly. "I had a great time. Yes, it was a shame bumping into your work colleagues like that and I can appreciate the dilemma it must have presented you with. But, as I've pointed out on numerous occasions now. I'm certain they just saw us as a normal couple out having fun. Where's the harm in that? You must stop fretting over nothing. There is no way that they suspected you of being an escort, no way at all. Stop giving yourself such a torrid time over it. It's beneath you. Anyway, I'm sure they're far too preoccupied with their own lives to be wasting time mulling over you and your choice of clubbing partner. You're far too self-obsessed, Manny, it doesn't suit you. What's the point in worrying? They probably won't even remember a word that was said."

Agreed, he sighed inwardly, *but I'm willing to wager my last pound they suspected there was something a little odd about you.* Cruel but true, for he'd seen something in Young's snide leer.

"Let's hope so, eh?" he said, looking up at her.

She turned her back to him and opened a window in preparation for a smoke. "Of course..." she said, putting a cigarette into her mouth and lighting it "...It could just be..." a pause while she exhaled "...that you're terribly embarrassed and ashamed at being seen out with someone as hideous as me."

Manny heard her sniff and, although he couldn't see her fact, he could tell that she was wiping her eyes. He sat there motionless, searching for the appropriate response, his delay allowing her words to linger awkwardly in the air. Manny felt himself fading away. Her words had unleashed a swirl of guilt in him. Never had he felt so shallow. A man of substance he certainly wasn't. He knew then that he wouldn't be going anywhere. Not until he'd attempted to patch up some of the damage. He owed her that.

He stood up and approached her, pulling her close and clutching her tight with a tenderness he'd never known he possessed. A lump had crept into his throat. Close to, her musky tang was similar to that of his father - tobacco, coffee and day-old alcohol - but the tears she cried were more reminiscent of his mother. *Funny that*, he thought, *the tricks scents and sounds can play on our minds*.

"Come on," Manny said gently. "Let's go for one of those long walks of yours. Then later, if you're a good girl, I'll let you shout me a pub lunch."

"I'd love to. And then, when we get back, there's something I'd really like to show you."

Manny smiled uncertainly, not quite managing to conceal the look of concern that had appeared on his face.

"I can let you scuttle off home then, knowing that we shared a special moment," she winked, doing nothing to ease his anxiety.

What is it that she wants to show me? He prayed it was nothing sordid. It would ruin everything. He smiled again, trying not to look like the proverbial rabbit caught in the headlights. *Surely she doesn't want to take things a step further? It was the way I embraced her earlier, it gave her the wrong idea.*

Trepidation kept him company all through their brisk Sunday stroll. But he needn't have worried...

"I've been waiting for the right moment to show you them. Wait there a moment." Manny stood outside the locked door of one of the upstairs rooms, trying – and failing - to guess what she had in store.

She came back out of her bedroom clutching a bunch of keys.

"I don't just show them to any Tom, Dick and Harry, you know," she said insistently, putting a key into the lock. Opening the door, she motioned for him to go on through, which he did.

The room itself was pretty sparse except for a small mahogany cabinet full of books, two leather chairs and some art prints, hung on opposite sides of each wall. The floor was pine, with a deep-polish finish. The walls were painted burgundy and white. The only light came from a small window at the opposite end of the room. Sasha pointed out why it was important that the natural light beamed from the window never managed to reach the cabinet. It would damage the books. But she needn't have told Manny this. He'd already worked it out for himself.

Manny walked towards the cabinet and browsed through the half-dozen or so books on display. It was immediately apparent to him that they were antique. The cabinet needed to be temperature-controlled, Sasha informed him, to stop them turning to dust.

He couldn't make out the titles. But, with patience, he could just about decipher the names of Rumi and Shams on the covers of two of the books, probably biographies, he thought. They stood impressively, side by side, on the top shelf, pride of place. You'd need to be an expert to identify the others. Manny banged his head on the glass trying to get a closer look. Academic texts, no doubt priceless to some, dusty old books to others. Antiques. Collectors' items, probably worth a small fortune. Manny saw that they meant the world to Sasha. Her face blazed with pride. *She's showing me her babies,* he realised. She explained, with a great deal of affection, how an old university professor of hers had spent much of his life collecting the books. His enthusiasm was most contagious, she kept saying. During his long, final illness, Sasha had continued to add to and care for the small collection. "I had to," she said. "He was the only man to truly understand me, back then."

Movingly, the professor had wanted Sasha to care for and cherish the books after he was gone. "They are there to be read, held and admired," he'd told her. "Not to be lost and forgotten in the miserly vaults of a university library."

Manny looked on and listened as history spoke to him. He found the experience intoxicating. It wasn't long before he himself fell under the room's spell. Later, he would struggle to understand how a small room which boasted no more than a cabinet of antique books and a couple of battered old leather chairs would leave him so enthralled.

"It wasn't something you could put into words," was what he'd tell himself. The smell and atmosphere in the room reminded him of an empty church, sitting quiet and still after the celebration of a mass. Appropriate really, seeing that it was a Sunday.

CHAPTER
TWENTY-FIVE

"So," Len sighed heavily down the phone, "are you moving in or not...? I need to know, otherwise I'll stick an advert in the paper... It's no problem, really."

"Can I let you know for sure early in the week, Len?

Len debated this for a moment. "Yeah, okay, make sure it is early...no later than say Tuesday evening, okay? If I haven't heard from you by then, I'll take it it's a no. Ere, what about your bags? They're still on the bed in my spare room."

"Oh yeah, I forgot about those," he lied. "Can you hang onto them until I know what I'm doing...I'm all over the place at the moment."

"Yeah, okay. If they're still here on Friday I'll charge them rent, shall I?"

Manny forced a laugh, thanked Len and ended the call. He had enough smart clobber to last him the next couple of days. What he hadn't told Len was that he still harboured hopes that Anna would allow him his old room back. He was sitting on the train, on his way to see her. Another three stops and he'd be at West Hampstead station. Manny had tried to call Anna several times since leaving Sasha's, but he wasn't having much luck. Her mobile was switched off and her landline was not being picked up.

It was late Sunday afternoon and the chances were he'd find her at home. He recalled that Sundays, for Anna, were always a day of rest. She usually liked to while the day away at home. "I'm busy doing nothing," she used to say to him, "so you'd better not disturb me," she'd joke. A nostalgic smile broke out across his face at the memory.

Manny patted his inner pocket. A little earlier he'd counted out £500 and had tucked it away in readiness to give to her. The fact that he still owed her money was enough of an excuse for his unscheduled visit.

He hoped that, with all his debts paid and providing his smile was warm and sincere, then maybe, just maybe, she'd allow him back in. He'd been keeping his fingers crossed since travelling back north of the river.

At first she'd be a little suspicious, a little mistrustful perhaps. But once he'd expressed sufficient sorrow for his past misdeeds, he could expect a softening in her stance, a welcome embrace perhaps, a chat and a cup of coffee at her kitchen table.

The sound of the train announcer pulled him from his reverie. He would be arriving shortly. Manny reached up in preparation and claimed the large sports holdall Sasha had lent him. It was full of new clothing and wash kit. Not the ideal method of transporting two new suits but it would have to do. He was dressed smart but casual. New jeans, new jumper and new black winter jacket, which he put on now. All thanks to Sasha. Although the weekend had been profitable and at times enjoyable, he was mightily glad of the change of scene. His weekend, with its escorting enterprises, had left him feeling exhausted. *Time for a little normality*, he thought as he got off the train and stood alone on the platform station. The weather outside was grey and dry with a nasty, biting wind, a typical late January day. Manny did up the buttons on his coat and turned up his collar in protection against the chilly blast that served as a welcome back. He glanced around the station, there were not too many people around. He was not a fan of Sundays. Too slow and too close to Monday mornings for his liking. Picking up his holdall, he slung the strap over one shoulder and began the short walk to Anna's house, feeling optimistic. His good mood fuelled by the money in his pockets, putting a spring in his step.

Anna answered the door. She was wearing thick black leggings, a pink jumper and an apron. Her hair was pulled back in a bun and she had flour on her hands and smudged across her face. She was baking. She'd always bake to take her mind off things. Manny would go to the gym. Anna baked cakes. It smelt good too. Chocolate sponge pudding. It smelt of home. When he was around, she'd ask him to be the official taster. He used to like scooping out the mixer bowl with a finger. If there was no bowl or mixers to lick, he would act like a petulant child.

"Manny, what on earth are you doing here?" she asked with a touch of annoyance.

"Hello, Anna. I have some money for you." They kissed as friends did, a brief peck on the cheek. She opened the door wider for him to come in before walking back down the hallway and into her kitchen. Manny saw the look on her face. It wasn't happy. He followed her into the kitchen, unbuttoning his coat. Anna then nodded with her head for him to sit down at the kitchen table. There was no offer of coffee nor any kind of gesture to show she was pleased to see him.

"I'm pleased you're here," she said.

"Really?"

"Yes, saves me having to take the rest of your belongings to the charity shop. There's a whole bagful outside."

"Oh…"

"What? You didn't think that I'd throw them out?"

Manny shrugged.

"I'm not that mean. I'll go and get them." Anna wiped her hands on a dish-cloth and walked out of the back door. She came back in carrying a black binliner full of clothes, her face devoid of any emotion as she dumped it down by his feet. Manny kept staring at her as if waiting for her to break out into a friendly smile.

"How's the new job?" she asked.

He nodded. "Yeah, it's going well. I've got some money for you," he said again.

Anna raised her eyebrows. "Blimey," she gasped. She let her eyes settle over him for the first time, nodding her approval at the new attire. "By the looks of things, you're doing okay. Pay well does it, this other job of yours?"

225

"Could say that, but I won't be doing it for much longer."

"In that case, save your money, Manny... you're going to need it. We both know why you're here... the answer is no. How could I after what you did? The trust is gone." She looked tired, her face pale, dark rings under her eyes. With her hair pulled back, the protruding silver streaks were more apparent. She needed a good meal, he thought. The woolly jumper did nothing to hide her bony collarbone and scrawny neck.

It wasn't looking good. He still had his coat on. *No need to take it off*, he thought. *Looks like I'll be going soon.* All of a sudden he felt very tired, his legs heavy and lethargic. He wanted her to ask him to taste her cake or whether he wanted to lick the mixing bowl. But she didn't. Instead, the conversation become more and more stilted.

Anna continued, "I thought about letting out your room but decided against it. My divorce settlement came through finally, so there's really no need. In fact, it's been good having the place to myself... handy, too, for when my mum or daughter are down, means they can stay over without me having to drag out that damn old sofa bed."

Manny brought his hand down on the table which was hidden beneath a pile of Sunday supplements. His earlier optimism had been misplaced.

The thud was loud enough to convey his disappointment without having to resort to words which would've been a little stronger. But she had every right to stand her ground and not to have him back, it was his own doing. Who could blame her? *Time I was off.*

He nodded slowly to show that he understood. They grimaced at each other for a long moment before Anna saw him back out to the front door.

"You left me no choice, Manny," she said, without meeting his gaze. "You do know that?"

Slowly he bent down to lift his bags. "Thanks for everything," he said

"You're welcome."

They didn't bother with the peck on the cheek this time, she didn't even bother to stand and wave him off. With a large sports holdall in one hand and a black binliner full of stuff in the other, he lumbered down the garden path. She had gone before he'd even reached the gate. Manny swallowed hard and looked up and down the road, deciding to head for the café a few yards to his left.

There he sat, staring out of the window, collecting his thoughts, hands clasped around his cup of coffee, thinking what to do next. *Len's? Maybe tomorrow. Look for a cheap hotel? Yeah, why not? School in the morning, Young's grin.* He let out a long and wearisome sigh.

So, Anna hadn't wanted his money. He'd expected to feel slightly happier about that, but it had been the same on Friday night after the *Mr and Mrs Masturbates* episode. He might well be carrying around a wad of cash in his pockets, but his heart was heavy, too. Outside, it had started to rain. *Shit,* he'd never liked Sundays.

CHAPTER
TWENTY-SIX

So the queen bee herself wanted to meet him for a drink and a chat that very evening. She would pay him too of course, 'for the privilege of his time,' was how she'd put it. Manny just had to wait for her to text him back with a meeting place and a time. Virginia had told him not to worry, she wasn't after his body, just his brain. Still, intriguing nonetheless.

The day before, after despondently leaving Anna's, he'd used his laptop to find a relatively cheap hotel. He'd called Sasha to thank her again for the weekend and then spent the best part of the night channel-hopping and scrawling down his list of contacts on his phone, wondering who he could call. In the end, he settled for a couple of beers and a hot bath, deciding it was probably better if he didn't call Louise. He was bored and fed up with staring up at the ceiling of an ageing hotel in St Albans, but boredom alone was not a good enough reason to get her over. Eventually, he booted up his laptop and prepared some lessons for the week ahead. The work seemed to soothe him and bring back some focus to the pleasures of his real job, although the problem of Young still persisted and prevented him from getting a decent night's sleep. It gnawed at him all through the night. *What will he say?*

Now, seated at his desk, he gazed at the three piles of exercise books still awaiting his attention. Putting away his phone, he rose sharply from his chair, causing the legs to scrape along the floor. Time to face the staffroom, morning briefing was in five minutes' time. Books and folders would have to wait a little longer.

Manny had arrived unusually early for work. He'd bypassed the staffroom and headed instead for the relative safety of his classroom. But he could put it off no more. It was time for the games to begin, time to let events unfold. One or two of the senior leadership team would be scrawling down the names of those either late or absent from the morning meeting, and Manny was in no position to risk further wrath. There was nothing quite as humiliating as having to walk into the staffroom once briefing had already begun. All eyes would besiege you, some with a silent snigger behind them, others with a piercing look of disapproval. Manny and Andy Moran often referred to it as 'the walk of shame', something all the teaching staff there tried desperately hard to avoid.

Manny walked down the forbidding corridor where spirits were broken as well as built with a sick feeling in the pit of his gut. The place echoed with history and squelching leather soles; that unmistakeable school smell which caused a flutter of anxiety for both staff and pupils.

Towards the end of the corridor were the double green doors of the staffroom. Outside stood two smartly attired prefects, head boy and head girl, unsmiling, with arms folded and their sombre looks insisting upon silence and straight lines. Future colleagues, perhaps, of those who were allowed through the double doors, Manny thought, while nodding a good morning to them both. They politely opened the door for him and, to his horror, Young was already sitting, big and proud, in Manny's usual seat, next to Moran who seemed to be laughing along with him, happy at the change of company.

Let Young have his moment, Manny thought, *I'll put a time limit on it though. He's got until the end of morning break, then the piss taking stops, otherwise… Well, we'll wait and see, shall we?*

Young's smirk seemed to widen the minute he saw Manny walking over, worryingly Moran's did too. *Christ, what has he been telling him?*

They faced one another for a moment, knowing smiles were exchanged. Then Manny turned and sat in the only chair available, trying valiantly to hone a look that said he wasn't bothered about anything, but his efforts only made him look petulant and sulky.

Young seldom ventured over to their side of the staffroom. Manny knew what he was doing. Young had got to Moran's ear first. No doubt painting the picture with colourful words for the art teacher to marvel at. Moran was all laughs, drinking in whatever lines he was being fed.

Fine mate you turned out to be, Moran, couldn't even safeguard your old pal's chair.

Manny tried to sit still and zone in on whatever announcements were being read out, but it was proving difficult. The first two had already flown over his head and the third was interrupted by some late arrivals. Oh dear, one of those latecomers was the new girl, Emma Clarke, flushed with embarrassment; her petite body weaving in and out like a downhill skier, desperate to find a space, trying hard not to be noticed. She finally took up a position next to Manny. She looked tired. Puffy dark circles sat under her eyes. A few days ago she'd looked keen, fresh and alert. Reality had dawned. Four years of hard study had not prepared her for the baptism of fire that greets all new teachers. Manny knew very well that, for some, the first term in teaching was the worst hell on earth.

True, there were those with angelic faces who sat still and listened to teacher. And then there were those bolshy adolescent types with their gold chains and iPods, drenched in attitude. Not really surprising that the dropout rate for newly qualified teachers was horribly high.

It seemed to him that only the slightly insane or those unsure of what else to do with their degree or those mortgaged up to their eyeballs tended to survive past their first year. Most teachers he met were dispirited with how things had panned out, forever pining for their discarded dreams.

"Mr Rodriguez...?"

"Uh...? Sorry? What was that?"

The deputy head repeated the question, only much slower, and with more condescension.

"You will be taking the Year Nines to the Globe Theatre again next month, won't you?" It sounded more of an order than a question.

"Er, can I get back to you all on that? I've left my planner in my room, sorry."

Briefing then ended with murmurs, tuts and some serious eye rolling.

Shit, it had completely slipped his mind. It was a yearly trip which he coordinated and was proud to oversee. He hoped there was enough time as well as spaces left to rectify the small oversight. Otherwise, there'd be yet more grief from those at the top. Not what he needed. *Oh well, off to first lesson.* He was about to walk away when his hasty exit was brought to a sudden halt.

"Well, how did you get on?" Emma asked, standing between him and the doors.

"Sorry?"

"With your date... Sasha, right?"

"Oh, yeah..., good. Yeah, all good. Um, I was hoping to catch up later... and talk about that."

"Oh?"

"Yeah. Could you do me a huge favour and not mention anything to anyone, just yet? It's just that I..."

"It's not me you should be talking to," she interrupted. "Phil's the one who couldn't wait to get here this morning."

"Really?" Manny was quiet for a moment. Inadvertently, she'd just confirmed his worst fears. Young knew about Sasha. He'd seen what Manny himself had reluctantly acknowledged. Her manly features. *Okay, act calm.*

In the background he could hear busy voices preparing for the start of the school day.

Think. Come on, think.

"Couldn't you have a word with him for me?" he asked in a calm undertone.

"I could do," she said, looking over towards Young. "But I don't think it will do much good. Do you?"

Fair point. Young was sitting there smirking, still enjoying his agony. He met Manny's stare and held it. Manny was first to look away.

"I can try and say something to him if you really want me to," she said, turning back around, about to put her hand on his forearm.

She was disappointed to find that Manny had already walked away.

As he marched back to his class, he was feeling adrift and a touch subdued. But his Year Sevens soon suspended all woes with their childlike brilliance: *lumps of clay yet to be formed, one hand disciplined, the other of love.*

He began by reading them a short story that made them laugh and made them jump, especially with Manny's melodramatic narrative. They laughed most when he put on a woman's voice. Manny seldom stuck to the script. He knew the texts so well he would deviate and improvise to generate more laughs, more jumps and best of all more gore. It helped keep the teacher entertained too.

The young students then had to get busy and carry on the story from where Manny left off. A piece of original writing to get the creative juices flowing first thing on a Monday morning. At this age, they'd always manage to put a smile on his face.

They had a riot when it was the students' turn to read and mark each other's work. Nothing like a bit of peer marking to help ease the busy teacher's workload. Some of the children's comments and feedback were on a par with his own, neater too.

Lesson two, his Year Thirteen (sixth form), a bright and conscientious group, turned out to be another enjoyable hour. It helped of course having the likes of the exceptionally beautiful Imani Lewis in the class. He felt wrong thinking it but she was beauty personified, her youth and vibrancy wrapped up in a grown woman's body. Impossible not to look without feeling the tremors of a schoolboy crush, he could secretly admire, knowing he'd never touch.

Imani had joined the school late after her family moved out of London. Manny doubted that he would see her in the same light if she'd been there from the start. She brought a certain something with her. Also, when she smiled, it was impossible not to smile back. She was bursting with life.

He had photocopied the front page of a tabloid with the headline 'Violent Britain' and organised the students into small groups to highlight and discuss the emotive language used in the article. Then he set them a question: *declining standards in Britain, who's to blame? Government? Parents? Or teachers?* This was proving to be a popular topic, generating constructive and mature debate among the four groups. Manny simply sat back in his chair with his hands clasped behind his head and zoned in on the debates going on around him. He listened with interest, only getting up once to explain the homework for that week and write it up on the board. Dare he say it but his first two lessons had turned out to be somewhat therapeutic.

At break he took a stroll down to the canteen and fetched back a coffee and a croissant. It was all he fancied. Again, he avoided Young and the bear pit of a staffroom. No doubt he'd soon get to hear what exactly Phil Young had been saying about Saturday night. God, he dreaded to think what was being said behind those green doors. Maybe, he thought, it wouldn't be too damaging and his reputation would carry the day. But knowing Young, he seriously doubted it.

When he arrived back at his classroom, Andy Moran was there waiting, wanting to talk. Leaning on a filing cabinet close to Manny's desk, he looked a troubled man; gone was the beaming smile from earlier that day. Nodding a cool hello, Manny sat back down behind his desk, ready to carry on with his marking. An awkward silence fell.

"So," Moran began, "I hear you were spotted out clubbing on Saturday night?"

"No crime in that, is there?" Manny replied, without lifting his eyes.

"No, not unless you see nothing wrong in being seen dating a transvestite."

Manny paused for second, lifting his pen but not his gaze from the page he was marking. He snorted. So there it was. The news was out. His worst fears confirmed

"Phil Young has been having a great time telling me and everyone else all about her or him, whatever your preference is, I guess."

"Young talks because you puppets listen. And if you're talking about my *good* friend, Dr Sasha Harrington, she'd be the first to tell you that she's not a transvestite. As usual, Young's got his facts wrong."

Moran let out an audible sigh, obviously relived to hear this. Manny almost saw the unspoken words fall from his mouth: *Thank Christ for that.*

"For you and all those others who care to know, she's a *transsexual!*"

"What," Moran said with a degree of alarm, "is there a difference?"

"Look it up," he replied calmly. "Like I did." The calmness of his response surprised him, belying the tightening in his chest and the sick feeling in the pit of his stomach.

Another pause as Moran frowned, rubbing his forehead, trying to make sense of it all.

"Jesus, Manny, how could you? We're supposed to be mates."

"No, we're not," he snapped. "We're colleagues. My mates don't let pricks sit in my chair and laugh as they go about bad mouthing me and my *real* friends." He forcefully jabbed his pen in Moran's direction.

"I was laughing because I thought he was winding me up. Never for a minute thinking it was true."

"Dr Sasha Harrington is a friend. She's an expert in Persian Literature and I've been helping her out with some research, that's all." He paused before continuing sarcastically, "There you go, something else you've learnt about me today... my love of literature."

"But... but Young said that you'd told Emma that you were on a promise. They said this... this Sasha person," Moran spat, "had his hairy hands all over you."

"*Her* hairy hands, get it right, Moran. *Her* hairy hands. And what the fuck does Young know anyway? We talked for a matter of minutes," he lied.

There was a deathly silence. Moran paced the classroom, rubbing the back of his neck and shaking his head, seemingly at a loss as to what to say or think.

Manny ate his croissant and drank his coffee, not wanting to say too much more. He thought he'd recovered well and wanted to leave things there, not start digging more of a hole for himself.

Moran wasn't his problem, he was easy to deal with. Manny knew he'd eventually win him back round, just like a soppy dog who returns to his master. He was hurt at finding out personal information about Manny third-hand, that was all. He'd always whined about how Manny never really shared anything with him about his personal life.

"Let me buy you a pint later. I'll explain everything." he fibbed again, putting a hand on his mate's shoulder.

Moran made a performance of thinking this over. "Maybe," he shrugged. "Another question, though?"

But he never got the chance to ask it. Young was leaning in the door frame, leering in at the proceedings.

"Don't go, Moran. I'll warn you now. He'll be asking you to dress up in drag next."

Manny, hands by his side, fists clenched, wondered how long the tracksuit-wearing twat had been standing there, how much had he heard? He tried to keep the fury raging inside him in check. The sneer on Young's face was not helping to ease the charged atmosphere.

The two men held each other's gaze. Manny had no intention of looking away on this occasion, this was his domain, his territory. The time limit of up to break time for Young's bullshit was almost up. Both men moved towards each other, ready to remonstrate.

"I'm pleased you're here, I heard you've been insulting my friend."

Young threw back his head and laughed menacingly. "If you're talking about the gorilla in the dress that you're shagging, then yes, I have been. Shame you're spoiling all my fun by hiding out here in the safety of your room. And anyway, what are you going to do about it, tranny lover?" he taunted, shoving Manny in the chest.

Red mist exploded into Manny's head, his eyes blazed. A desire to protect Sasha's reputation over his own won the day again and he lunged at Young, grabbing him around his throat, hissing in his face, spitting an explosion of expletives into his ear.

Moran acted fast and jumped between both men, causing desk and chairs to fly. Calling for calm, he gestured with a strained nod over towards the door. A student had entered the room. It was Imani Lewis. She'd come rushing in, in a hurry to show her favourite teacher the speech that she'd hastily prepared on 'Violent Britain'. Now she was standing there with one hand over her mouth while the other clasped at her sheet of paper, eyes open wide, looking on in sheer disbelief. She could not bring herself to believe what she was seeing or, worse, hearing. Her teachers had been grappling one another on the verge of an almighty fight. This couldn't be happening. Dropping her paper, she turned and ran back out to find her friends in the canteen. She had to get away.

Manny wandered over to retrieve her sheet of paper, worried how much she'd seen and heard. He read through her work, ignoring the shove Young gave him as he passed on his way out. He felt sure she'd be rewriting her speech later. Especially now, after seeing her teacher in a completely different light. Which was a pity, because this was good. She'd blamed the parents, in her first draft. "Teachers," she'd written, "should be exempt and praised more for the outstanding work that they do with young people. My English teacher for example..." He didn't have the heart to read any more, screwing the paper up and putting it in the bin. She wouldn't be needing it now.

After work, Manny and Moran went to a pub a little further up the road from the school. Both in a slightly better state of mind. Moran seemed pleased Manny had found the time to accompany him for an after-work drink. It had been a while.

Truth was, Manny had some time to kill before his meeting with Virginia. She'd finally texted him back. They'd be meeting later in a Mexican bar in Covent Garden, around 7.30pm.

Manny bought the drinks - a pint of Guinness for Moran and a bottle of Peroni for himself. They then took the drinks out into the garden, despite the cold. They were the only ones sitting outside. Moran, the eternal art student, wanted one of his roll-ups. He lit it, coughed, swallowed and then spoke.

"So, what on earth have you been up to?"

"Nothing really," Manny replied, looking elsewhere. He needed time to weigh up just how much he felt comfortable telling Moran. "Apart from..." And then Manny began to talk, ending up telling the whole story, warts and all. He even shared the truth of his developing fondness for Sasha: "purely platonic, of course."

He even mentioned the episode in the hotel with Mr and Mrs Masturbates, his confession managing to extract a few laughs from them both. Boy, it felt good too. An almighty relief, a huge release. Talking to someone outside, away from the agency, was making a real difference: who would have thought? Moran, his loyal sidekick, was doing his best not to interrupt as he listened to Manny's story, trying to understand the reasoning behind his controversial methods of making money, and refusing to criticise. It explained everything: the change in Manny's mood, the distance he'd been keeping of late, and his earlier outburst in the classroom.

When Manny had finished telling him the full version of events, both men exhaled loudly. Manny found himself having to hold back the tears as Moran patted his arm tenderly, supportively offering him one of his roll-ups, which Manny refused politely with something veering between a laugh and a sob, both emotions wanting to burst out from him. He wiped his nose on his sleeve, one half of him wanting to laugh out loud at the insanity of it all, the other wanting to curl up and cry. It was an emotional moment.

Manny waited for Moran to say something in response, but he was shaking his head, having trouble forming his words. In the end he gave up and settled for getting in another round. Before he headed to the bar, Manny grabbed him by the arm and made him swear to keep quiet, even to his partner at home.

Moran looked a little offended at first but soon nodded, smiling reassuringly. Manny had looked deep into his eyes and knew that he could trust him. It felt good to share, ever so good.

Taking a gulp of his cold beer, he felt the evening chill

creeping into his bones, so he went inside in search of Moran who was still ordering at the bar.

While the two men enjoyed their pints, Manny's phone rang twice, but he let both calls go through to voicemail. The caller ID showed him they were from Louise and Sasha. *They can all wait. Right now, I'm busy enjoying a beer with a mate. It's been quite a day.*

CHAPTER TWENTY-SEVEN

Manny got to Covent Garden just before 7.30pm, having managed to nip back to the hotel for a quick shower and to change into his new suit. He'd also picked out a new shirt which needed ironing but there wasn't enough time. He was running late. It looked new, out of the packet new, but it would have to do. The drink with Moran had taken a slightly bigger chunk out of his time than he'd catered for. It had been worth it, however, the long talk working wonders for their stuttering friendship.

He saw Virginia walking into the restaurant from afar and hung back, purposely allowing a minute or two to pass before he followed her in. He'd found the bar with no difficulty and he approved of her choice of venue.

Manny greeted her at the bar in the usual way, with a peck and a handshake. It reminded him a little of a meeting with his bank manager, awkward and a little nervy, concerned at what he was about to hear.

"Hello, Manny."

"Hiya, Virginia."

Virginia was certainly dressed for business, too, wearing a blue pinstripe two-piece suit with a plain, cream-coloured blouse. Her light hair was pulled back, revealing those sharp, delicate features which were only lightly covered by make-up. He was also quick to notice her heels. They gave her a slight height advantage over him. He wasted little time then in sitting down on one of the bar stools provided and looked around at the busy restaurant behind him where the diners sat and ate. For a Monday, it certainly wasn't quiet.

Finally, he turned back to the polished wooden bar. The bar itself was quiet. There was only one other couple there. A man and a woman in work suits, sitting at the opposite end, enjoying an intimate chat after a busy day in the city.

A tall, tanned bartender was polishing some glasses. Shelves, crammed with bottles, groaned behind him. Manny wondered whether all the bottles behind the bar contained drink or whether some, especially those stacked on the shelves closest to the ceiling, were there for decorative reasons only. He puzzled for a minute over how they'd be fetched down. He might find out later and ask.

Also behind the bar, mounted onto the wall, was a plasma screen displaying an image of a log fire burning crisply.

Manny hoped Virginia wasn't wanting to eat. He had no appetite and would prefer their meeting to be over reasonably quickly. He was hoping to move his stuff into Len's that night.

He'd decided it would be a good idea to call Len and arrange a time to move in. Hopefully, he could scrounge a lift while he had him on the phone and ask Len to pick him up from the hotel where his holdalls were still waiting for him behind the reception. He hadn't left them in his room for fear he'd be charged another day's rate.

"What can I get you?" asked the bartender.

"A spritza with ice for me," Virginia said.

"And a citrus vodka and tonic for me," ordered Manny.

The bartender, who sounded South African, went off to one side to prepare the drinks.

"So," Manny said, fidgeting with his collar, "you wanted to see me... I take it that it's to do with business rather than pleasure?" He was avoiding eye contact, still looking around at the bar, taking in the décor.

"Don't put yourself down, Manny... that's my job, remember?" she said in that posh tone of hers. "You could say it's a little bit of both. But, strictly speaking, you'd be right. It's more business than social, although it is always a *pleasure* to buy a drink for the week's top earner. You've made a good start, well done." She smiled but it lacked warmth. The lack of crease lines around the eyes and on her forehead told a story of vanity by injection.

Virginia looked him up and down, taking in his new attire. Pulling back his jacket so as to reveal the name on the label, she seemed impressed and nodded her approval.

"Well, well, well, I see our Dr Sasha *has* been splashing her cash, looking after her man. Who's a lucky boy? This'll come in handy for where I'm thinking of sending you."

He forced a smile and gave a shrug of his shoulder, not feeling very "lucky" at all. He looked down, fixing his eyes on his shoes.

Virginia noticed his awkwardness and smiled in return. She pulled away and sat back when their drinks arrived, allowing him to recover some composure. The bartender placed a bowl of light nibbles before them, which they both began to sample.

"Cheers," Virginia said, raising her glass to her lips. "Ah," she exhaled. "That's better. I needed that, been quite a day." She stirred her drink with the straw. No ring, Manny detected. Made sense, he reasoned. Who could possibly cope?

He nodded his head in agreement. It had been quite a day for him too. "Actually," he said, taking a sip of his own, remembering what he'd wanted to say, "I have a bone to pick with you."

Raising her eyebrows, Virginia sat up straight, ready to listen. "Oh?" she asked, a little too theatrically. The way she sat, with her shoulders back, accentuated the size of her breasts. Definitely fake, he thought to himself. He lifted his eyes to meet hers.

"Yeah, the bloke on Friday night. You told me he was just there to watch…a 'voyeur' so to speak and that he was impotent."

"I did?"

"Yeah. Only turns out he wasn't. The bloke was sitting there on a chair with his…"

She reached across, pressing a finger to his lips. "Shh now, Manny," she said, lowering her tone. "You know that we never speak about those kind of details. And do try to remember," she glowered, "you're not with your football mates now. You're with your boss. A lady boss."

"Yeah, but nevertheless, you…"

"Manny," she interrupted sharply, "have you checked your bank account today?"

He shook his head. No, he'd not had time, difficult too, without the use of a bank card.

"Thought not. Well, I'm sure that when you do, you'll find you've been well compensated for any minor misunderstandings there might have been, okay? Now," she added, glancing over her shoulder, unconcerned at the point he was trying to raise, "shall we grab a table or are you comfortable sitting up here?"

He indicated that he was happy to stay where he was, aggrieved at the swift change of subject. Still, at least he could look forward to visting the bank once more. Maybe he could even get his card back.

"I have another proposition for you, along with one or two other small matters that need to be discussed."

He frowned, feeling a knot start to form in his stomach.

"Relax, Manny, don't look so worried." She patted him on his cheek, which irked him. "You'll be thanking me later for solving your money worries. This booking is made for you, right up your street."

He looked down at the floor, grimacing inside, not sure if he wanted to hear what she had to say. Of course, there was bound to be the usual bombshell for him to agonise over. There always was with *her*. He felt the knot begin to tighten.

Virginia was certainly a persuasive lady. Self-assured and used to getting her own way. How else the success?

Her eyes were a definite asset, too. Big and blue with a cold, domineering glare that would cause unrest in the most hardened of negotiators. Some might go as far as to suggest that they were seductive, but not Manny. Not any more. Maybe on their first meeting but that was because he'd wanted the work. True, she was an attractive lady in a dominant kind of way, but she was calculating too. She was harder looking than he remembered and a little too…well, ballsy for his liking. He afforded himself a wry smile at his own irony, reminding himself for the umpteenth time that he didn't have to do anything he didn't like the sound of. *I'm free to walk at any time.*

Virginia didn't seem to him to be a woman who wasted her time and he was proved right when she cut straight to the chase.

"Manny, I have a more mature female client. A fashion critic come journalist who has expressed an interest in you, likes your profile. Unfortunately, her first choice, Martin, is unavailable this time around. There's a very important fashion exhibition happening in Madrid for three days next week. She needs someone who is discreet, charming and who'll look good on her arm. Initially, the client would like to meet up over a drink where she can observe you in the flesh, so to speak. Then, if all goes well, which I'm sure it will, she'd like to hire you for the entire trip."

Virginia saw the look he pulled. Like a petulant teenager who'd been asked to tidy his room.

"Don't fret, you'll have your own room to retreat to at the end of each night. Unless," she teased, "you both decide otherwise…"

She reached into her leather bag and pulled out a white A4 envelope.

"Now, her ex-husband, David, who is also in the fashion industry is expected to be there too. With his male lover."

She pronounced his name *Daveed,* using a heavy French accent.

Manny frowned at her, inquisitively. "Male lover?"

"Don't ask, as I said, they're in the fashion industry. No need for you to know too much except that it's very important to our client that David and others in the industry see that she has finally moved on from their acrimonious split and has found a love interest of her own." She pointed a finger at his chest. "You! We did consider other options but the fact that you're half Spanish and can speak the language impressed her."

He didn't allow the slight putdown to dent his pride.

"Here," she said, handing over the envelope. "Take this and read it later. It will stop you from getting bored in your hotel room tonight," she added, giving him a meaningful look.

Manny tried to swallow but couldn't. "When you say 'more mature'…"

"She's a young fifty-five," she fired quickly.

He flinched, knowing she'd be older, probably a lot older.

"Wealth tends to do that," Virginia remarked. "You know, keep you young."

Manny sensed that she was fishing for a compliment but he chose not to bite.

"I don't know, Virginia," he said without enthusiasm. "Depends on the dates. I have school, don't forget. I don't see how I can do it. And what about Sasha?"

"What about her?" she snapped

"I'm not sure she'll like it."

"Sasha has no divine right to you, Manny," she said sternly. "You'll do well to remember that. You belong to me, the agency, and I will use you as I see fit. We do have other clients to consider."

True, but he still felt disloyal. Like he was considering doing something bad behind her back.

"Anyway, she needn't know. And let me worry about Dr Harrington." Virginia smiled slowly, shaking her head. "How sweet, a tart with a heart."

Manny slipped off his stall, frowning at her last comment. He needed to visit the gents. He was on his way when he stopped suddenly, pausing a moment to think.

"How much?" he asked while they were back to back.

Neither of them bothered to turn to face one another. Virginia put down her drink. She was smiling as she swirled around the ice in the bottom of her glass, allowing some time to pass before answering.

"Enough to kick start your life, get yourself straight, put down a deposit to rent a place of your own maybe… Or you could find yourself with enough to take a short break from teaching."

Manny turned to face the back of her head with widened eyes, dizzy and diluted with the possibilities. He felt his heart start to race. Unable to reply, he walked away instead, trying hard to digest her words. *More like a break from this escorting lark*, he thought to himself as he broke into a smile.

In the gents he splashed his face with cold water and stared at his reflection, ordering his heart to calm down. He wasn't really seeing himself. He couldn't because he was in a state of heightened excitement. After all, this was what he wanted, wasn't it? What he had signed up for, serious cash to help him out of his wretched hole. "Play it cool," he told himself. "Remember, the ball's in your court," he said to the excited face in the mirror.

Manny steadied his breathing before drying his hands and heading back out to the bar, finding it all a little surreal. Money. Madrid. Missing work.

They sat in silence for a moment. Virginia ordered him another drink and paid up, asking for the receipt. They looked at each other and smiled. There were questions he wanted to ask but he was having trouble forming them in his head. There'd be another time, he reassured himself. He made a mental note to write them all down, when he was thinking a little more clearly.

Her body language indicated that she was ready to depart. But there was another thing she wanted to discuss.

"You and Louise."

His heart flipped and the knot tightened again.

"Who told you?"

"It's true then?"

Shit.

She glared at him with narrowed eyes, face as serious as he'd ever seen it. "Her father wouldn't approve, and neither do I. I absolutely forbid it and I'm livid with you both. Louise's father, he's the over-protective type, has been since she lost her mother. I know him well... He would inflict serious damage on anyone who'd been taking advantage of his precious daughter. Especially if he knew that person was a bit of a rogue and working as a male escort."

"How would he know?" he asked flippantly.

She fixed her eyes on him.

"Oh, he'll know," she bristled. "I'll make sure he knows. I don't want you seeing her again, amongst other things, it's very bad for business. Understood?"

He felt his hackles rising for the second time that day, tutting his annoyance while slowly shaking his head, stunned at the ease with which she had caught him out.

"With all due respect," he countered respectfully, "she's a big girl now with a mind of her own. I don't really see it's anybody else's business. You're her boss, not her keeper."

They locked eyes for a moment, neither wanting to be the first to look away.

Eventually Virginia broke off, bending down to retrieve her bag. "I don't think you grasp what I'm trying to say."

Manny picked up his drink and swallowed it in one, trying hard not to show his anger. What was she getting at? Fine, he wasn't planning on seeing Louise in that capacity again anyway. What was the problem?

"Are you still planning on staying at Len's?" she asked, placing the strap over her shoulder.

And then it hit him. His stomach churned so much that he felt winded. A surge of chaos swirled into his head, making all around him spin. Only Virginia remained in focus, standing there motionless. He could see that cold, calculating smile of hers working overtime as realisation froze him to the spot. There was no need now for her to play her trump card. He'd seen it for himself and in that moment he knew that she had him.

"Len is Louise's father, isn't he?" Those same eyes, that frown, it was all so obvious now.

"Well done, Manny. God, you're slow for a teacher. Now, the old fellow may not scare a man like yourself - but he certainly scares his daughter with that temper of his. He'd be devastated and quite maddened to hear she'd been bedding the likes of you." She spat out the last few words.

"Seeing as you're turning out to be a tart with a heart, I'm positive you'll do the right thing for both Louise and me."

He looked at her for an explanation. "You?"

"Yes, simple really. You leave Louise well alone and you focus your attention on making me and you some money. That way we'll all be happy and there'll be no reason for me to have that chat with Len, will there? Don't underestimate me, Manny," she

246

warned. "I'll do anything to protect my business - and I will not stand for your recklessness to ruin things for me or my workers. Got that?"

He nodded slowly, his frown darkening.

"Okay, good, that's that sorted," she said in a much calmer tone. "Now, this trip away would do us all a favour. The perfect solution to help defuse any rising tension there might be. It will provide an opportunity for things to blow over and settle back down as well as earning you a serious amount of money."

He looked down and blew out his cheeks, wondering when and where it would all end.

"Come on," she said. "It's not that bad."

Manny looked at her through narrowed, hate-filled eyes.

"And neither am I, so you can stop looking at me like that!"

"Give me strength," he muttered.

"I shall expect a decision from you by tomorrow and I trust it will be a favourable one. Otherwise..." She allowed the subtle threat to hang in the air.

Manny studied her, almost admiring her as much as he loathed her. He slowly shook his head and gave the beginning of a smile, thinking, *What a bitch*.

"I'll email you with further details when I know more myself. Meanwhile, think over what I've said... and carefully! You'd be a fool not to," she warned. "Don't go and spoil it all for everyone, Manny. I'd prefer to make you money than a whole heap of trouble. Though we all need to do our bit to help things along."

Manny nodded, keeping his mouth shut. She had him where she wanted him. Rattled.

"Remember why it was you came to me, Manny. Money," she answered for him. "A chance to rescue yourself. Have I let you down so far?" She tugged on the sleeve of his expensive new suit to emphasise her point. "Don't go spoiling it all now."

He shook his head, still reeling. Feeling somewhat cheated, but not quite sure by whom. "And if I don't do it?"

Virginia smiled knowingly.

She ended the conversation with a shake of his hand and a kiss on his cheek, saying, "You do look sexy when you're angry but I think I prefer your smile. *Ciao, ciao.*" And with that she departed, a smug look upon her face.

He remained there rooted to his stool, cradling his glass. Being the only one sitting there, he cut a desolate figure. Only the bartender was in view, busying himself by meticulously wiping smears from glasses he held up to the light.

Manny was having trouble comprehending it all. Trying hard to understand what it all meant, wondering what he was going to do. He caught sight of his reflection in the bar mirror. It silently mocked him. He was tempted to launch the glass he held at it. But he didn't, he resisted. There'd be plenty of time for self-recriminations and contempt later, that he could be sure of.

In the meantime, he needed to decide on where he was going to stay. It was 8.40pm and Len's was no longer an option.

"Can I get you another?" asked the bartender.

"Yeah, why not? Only make it a double."

He wanted to wallow in his mess for a bit longer.

Then,"Excuse me, mate, can I ask you a question?"

"Yes, sir?

"Those bottles, right up there on the top shelf…"

Manny arrived back at the hotel, feeling tired, disillusioned and subdued. The journey back to St. Albans had been a frustratingly slow one. Virginia's spiteful attitude still rankled, but he was less angry now. She was a businesswoman looking out for her business and he had to admire her for that.

No, he was more annoyed with himself for not making the connection earlier and for using Louise the way he had. It complicated matters. He didn't want to upset Len and he certainly didn't want to cause any trouble for Louise. And, just as importantly, he needed the work. A long way to go still, he silently acknowledged, until he was out of the woods and had reached easy street.

But why hadn't Louise told him? She'd had ample opportunitiy. Why all the cloak and dagger stuff? He didn't get it. After all, it was Louise who had suggested that he temporarily move into Len's. Manny thought about Len's huge paws and the way they gripped the steering wheel. He tried not to think of them around his neck.

"I'll have a word with him," Louise had said and, *"He'll listen to me."*

Damn it. He should have known.

Len he could understand, being the type of man who preferred nods and grunts to chitchat. But Louise...? Surely she could have said something - and how had Virginia gotten whiff of their sexual liaison? He couldn't see Virginia being the type of person Louise would have intimate chats with.

Manny pondered for a moment. *Maybe it's the murky business they're in, it's all secrets and lies.*

Whatever the reason, he needed to speak to Louise and soon, before the paranoia set in. He'd already tried to call her twice, to no avail, so he'd bombarded her with text messages instead, requesting that she urgently get in touch. He'd been waiting with bated breath ever since.

When the weary-looking woman behind reception finally looked up to see him standing there with hands in pocket, shuffling his feet, she immediately reached under the desk for his luggage. Manny told her that there'd been a change of plan and that he'd now be needing to pay for another couple of nights. Which he reluctantly did, parting with more of his hard-earned cash. The receptionist looked and sounded as if she, too, would rather be elsewhere as she sighed and mumbled under her breath.

He took his bags back up to the first floor, up the tired-looking stairwell, and let himself in with the big brass key he'd just been handed.

God, what a day.

The room was small, stuffy and lacking many of the usual luxuries he enjoyed: there was no mini bar or a decent size bath, towelling robe or room service. There weren't even any soft towels. Instead, there was a rickety single bed, a small television with a fuzzy picture and tiles in the bathroom that appeared to have sprouted mould. The white bath was looking more of a shade of yellow and the toilet smelt of stale urine. Still, it was cheap, he countered.

He didn't bother to take his clothes out of the holdalls to hang up, for fear the smell of damp and mildew would seep into the fabric.

There were, however, tea and coffee-making facilities with a couple of digestive biscuits he could savour. The water in the kettle smelt rancid, so he changed it and washed out the inside. The small packet of biscuits caused a rumble in his stomach and now he wished that he had eaten something earlier in the evening.

Manny sighed as he threw himself onto the creaky old bed and stared up to the flaky ceiling. Finding he was no longer feeling tired, he was impatient for the new day to get underway. Then he could go into his bank, check out his new balance, see about getting his card back and maybe book a night in a decent hotel to appease his bad mood. It had been a frustrating experience trying to book a room without one. Most of the upper end hotels had kept requesting a card 'for booking and authorisation purposes'. "It's standard procedure," they'd add, with a look that implied he was impending trouble.

No, it seemed to him, cash on its own was not enough any more. No longer a viable method of payment. If anything, the hotel staff had made him feel like he was trying to pay with dirty money. *Tomorrow*, he thought determinedly, *I shall get a card*. He spent the next fifteen minutes worrying whether the bank would require proof of his address. "Oh, bollocks," he shouted.

He had a shower, wrapped a hard, scratchy towel around his waist and tried to call Louise again. Her mobile was still switched off so he made himself a hot chocolate, which tasted foul. He surveyed his new home, detecting yet more of its deficiencies: musky curtains, mattress covered with stains, cigarette burns on the green carpet, skinny, flimsy pillows and noisy plumbing. Nothing like Sasha's spare room with all its unique charm.

Manny thought of her for a long moment. He missed her conversation, along with the comfort it brought him. The soothing effect it had on him when she spoke passionately of her work. The enlightenment he'd experienced in her study and the marvel he'd felt in the room in which she kept those precious books of hers. He wanted to call her, to confide in her, to see how she was and ask for her help but he didn't feel he could. He'd appreciated Moran's concerns earlier, along with the offer of a chat any time he felt in need, but, bless him, he was no Sasha with her pearls of mystical wisdom. Nobody could lift his spirits the way she could. Her words, or Rumi's words more like, would cocoon him in a state of bliss, his words, as recited by Sasha, acting as antidotes for his troubled mind.

Manny picked up his phone and scrolled down his list of contacts, pausing on Sasha's name. He wanted to call her but couldn't bring himself to do so. Amongst other things, how would he explain the trip to Madrid?

Instead, he fetched the envelope Virginia had handed him earlier and lay back down on the lumpy bed. Opening it up, he began to read the notes inside. The following points stood out:

The client went by the name of Candy Richards, a fifty-five-year-old fashion critic from Surrey (There was no photo enclosed, which worried Manny slightly).

The booking would mean him having to miss three to four days of teaching as it was pencilled in for a week's time, Monday through to Thursday.

He could expect to earn in the region of £3,000 for the booking (subject to contract). A substantial amount of money. Double what he would earn in a month for working at the school. Tempting, to say the least.

Boy, how he could have done with a mini bar. He knew then that there'd be very little sleep that night. A long, drawn-out battle was about to commence in the realms of his mind. His conscience battling against the exhilaration only money could bring.

Virginia was right. The extra cash would certainly help him get ahead and put some daylight between him and his debts. With that sweet thought, he closed his eyes and tried to snatch some sleep.

"Manny, calm down, you're over-reacting. I tried to call earlier… to let you know. Really, there's nothing to it. It's not exactly common knowledge outside the office and there really wasn't any need for you to know. Len's funny about that. We have girls who've been on our books a lot longer than you and *they* don't even know."

A drawn-out pause.

Manny had been staring up at the ceiling, hand on forehead in search of sleep, when his phone, which was perched on his chest, vibrated into life. It was Louise calling, at long last.

"But Virginia is right," she continued, "when she says he'll be angry. More with me than with you. He can be awkward when it comes to my private life. Please try to understand, Manny, there's no conspiracy. It's just a decision Len and I made when I first started working for the company. We just thought it would be better that way, honest. I'm sure if we'd met up on a few more occasions I would have probably ended up telling you... Where are you? Look, why don't I come over?"

Manny shook his head. "No. I don't think that's such a good idea, do you?"

"It'll at least give me a chance to explain face to face."

As she spoke, her naked body appeared in his mind's eye. It was soft, warm and scented.

"You said there was nothing to explain."

"There isn't but if it will help put your mind at rest, then I'll come over. Honestly, I'm sorry Virginia has found out, but it's better her than Len. Please don't do anything stupid. He can't find out," she pleaded. "He'll kill me. Len and I have been getting along much better lately. Manny, there are things you don't know, don't need to know about me."

He selfishly thought about her coming round to pay him another late-night visit. About sex. About her turning up wearing a top without anything underneath. No bra, just beautiful breasts waiting to be kissed, cupped and enjoyed, along with the rest of her divine curves. For a moment he was tempted to find solace, again, in her body. But he chastised himself and shook the thoughts away, thinking, *I'll never learn*. Part of it, he knew, was also to get back at Virginia, to show her he was his own man.

"Louise, look, it's fine, there's no need to come over." His

252

loins gave a small protest and he tried to change track. "Have you heard about the booking Virginia's asked me to do?"

"Yes, it's fantastic, isn't it? The fashion fair in Madrid... Think you'll do it?"

"Probably. Might need you to call my school and drop a sick line for me."

"Sure, no problem. Happy to help." She went quiet for a moment.

"I meant to ask you," he continued, "how did Virginia get an inkling about us?"

He heard something in her hesitation: it might have been shame or embarrassment.

"Well, we were chatting away when your name cropped up. She asked me a couple of questions and I guess my indifferent reaction told her more than she needed to know."

Louise's explanation inadvertently gave him an insight into her and Virginia's relationship. At once he felt sorry for her. After all, he'd seen for himself just how intrusive and formidable Virginia could be.

Manny could see how it would have happened. They would have been in the office one morning, he was thinking, when an innocent question or random remark from the boss would have been met with a coy response from the blushing assistant. Virginia's unblinking eyes would have then drilled into Louise while she probed further, not letting up, like a dog with a stick. Finally, Louise would have wilted under the interrogation of her more senior and tenacious boss.

There was a long silence on the phone.

"I'm sorry, Manny," she said eventually. "Hope we're still friends."

"Of course. And don't worry. It's not your fault."

He began to tell her about his own day, about his altercation at school and his meeting with Virginia, including how spiteful she had been.

"The thing is with Virginia," Louise declared, "she fears going back to her old days when she had little or no money. You should see some of the things I've seen her do. All in the name of

253

business. Don't cross her, Manny, she plays hard ball with the toughest of them out there. The only good thing being that, while she makes money, we make money too."

Manny presumed the 'we' meant Louise, Len and the other driver he was yet to meet, along with young Monica who also worked in the office. He and the other escorts, he realised, must be regarded as the manual labourers, the dispensable shop floor shelf-fillers. The thought didn't sit well. He decided to move on and try his luck by asking Louise some questions about his proposed booking.

"You can make amends by filling me in on this booking in Madrid if you like. Sounds to me that I'll need to swot up on the names of this year's top fashion designers."

A brief silence, again. "I'd rather not talk about it now, Manny. It's one in the morning and I really need to get some sleep. I've had a tough day."

Manny tried not to feel slighted.

"You've caught me at a bad time... Been a really long day and then of course I've had Virginia reading the riot act to me, so I'm under a bit of pressure at the moment, as I'm sure you can guess."

And he could. It couldn't be easy working for Virginia, especially when she'd broken one of her boss's golden rules. He was sorry he'd lumbered her with a headache and wondered whether she now regretted her actions. It sounded to him very much like she did. Again, he tried not to feel hurt.

Louise ended the call by saying they'd catch up soon for a coffee and chat. Her promises to meet up came out rather flat and a little hollow.

However, she did sound tired. Tearful, too, although she was disguising it well. But every now and then, her voice would betray her with a slight quiver. Sensing her pain over the dilemma, he again felt bad.

"Louise," he said quietly into the phone, "for what it's worth, I'm sorry too..." But she had already gone.

Sitting up on the bed, he rubbed the back of his neck, trying to put the day's events to bed. But, like naughty children, they were reluctant to go. So he stood up and crossed over to the window where he peered out onto the night-time scene below. Rows of Victorian cottages stood together side by side, lit up by street lamps. A few, he noticed, had 'for sale' signs up.

If only, he wished.

Although the streets were empty, the glare from television screens told him that there were people still up, night owls like himself probably, only they were ensconced in the comfort of their own homes, warm and safe, just like Sasha. For him, the warmest and safest person out there.

Shaking his head, Manny spent the next half hour trying to get some sleep, but he couldn't seem to wind down after the day's events. The bed was still lumpy and uncomfortable, and it didn't help when he thought of the amount of bodies who had lain where he now lay. The thought made him itch.

He sat up, gazing at his clothes, still bundled into two holdalls, and was attacked by a crushing feeling of not knowing where he really belonged. He decided to get up and do some work to kill time.

Fetching the laptop from his holdall, he started it up. Within a few seconds, he was online. He paused for a short moment, thinking again, and instead of opening his saved work files, Manny typed the name *Rumi* into the Google search engine. There were plenty of hits to choose from. He scrolled down the page until he found one that appealed.

Then he sat back and began to read.

CHAPTER

TWENTY-EIGHT

"So, you see, the final stanza really does illustrate for us the pain and longing that was tearing him apart. His emotive words epitomise the heartbreak he felt on discovering that his beloved Shams had mysteriously disappeared. It was so sudden and dramatic that it almost destroyed him. His followers, for a long time afterwards, believed that it had. Remember, he says, and I quote, *'Only those ravaged by love know love'* [9]."

Dr Sasha Harrington paused for maximum effect. As always, she had them where she wanted them: eating out of the palm of her hand.

A mesmerised silence enveloped the room where sixty odd second year degree students all sat focused. Many wide-eyed and open-mouthed, hanging onto each and every word.

For them, once again she had delivered a lecture that was moving as well as informative. Every one of the students who sat in that lecture theatre knew they were in the presence of someone special. Yes, at times she could be a little eccentric. Nevertheless, nobody could deny the fact that Dr Sasha Harrington was a well-researched academic who was rapidly becoming a leading expert in her field.

They also knew they were lucky to be able to hear her speak again with such passion. In the past, it hadn't always been the case, her mood often sombre and distant. When she was on this form though, they felt truly blessed that the controversial doctor spawned her wisdom, there, on their campus at *their* university.

"Vanished," she continued to wax lyrically, "under a cloud of mystery. Without, I might add, a solitary word of goodbye." She paused again and walked slowly away from the lectern, fully aware that her audience was wholly immersed in what she was saying.

"Now, I assume that many of you here today are at an age where you've experienced a special and meaningful relationship. With someone with whom you've shared your deepest and most intimate thoughts. If you haven't, then my advice is to get out more."

The last line was received with light laughter.

"By now, you should be at an age where emotional intelligence allows you to appreciate and understand something of Rumi's suffering. Imagine for a moment how devastated you'd be if your closest friend were to suddenly take off... to vanish... to disappear without trace... without any prior warning." Dr Harrington paused again as her students considered this.

"I would think you'd be hurt and deeply wounded, yes?"

The majority of the audience nodded their heads in agreement.

"It's widely believed that the reason Sham's sudden disappearance caused so much turmoil in Rumi is because he regarded him as his one true soul mate. A friend whose presence enlightened and caused a deep awaking within... In Celtic lore, there is a term they use: it's *Anam Cara,* Gaelic for 'the soul's friend'. This person is so special that they're able to hold up a mirror to your good self and shine that light back, into the darkest recess of your soul, while loving you all the same."

"Who's your *Anam Cara*? Do you have one, even? Or are you still waiting for him or her to grace your life? Never underestimate the power of that love, ladies and gentlemen. A love that has the power to eradicate all your preconceived ideas on the subject. A love that gives you the courage to face up to all your fears and has the spiritual tenacity to propel you onto the highest level of consciousness."

"I would like you to imagine for a moment what it would be like were you to find your *Anam Cara* only to lose them again after you'd devoted the whole of yourself to them. And, may I add, through no fault of your own."

257

A moment of silence followed as the class pondered this.

"It's quite conceivable, ladies and gents, that there may be a few people in this room today who have already experienced such a devastating and tragic loss. If there are, my heart goes out to you. But," she added with a drawn-out pause, "I envy you too."

Some gasps and disconcerted mumbles followed this comment.

"For you," she began to explain, "have had first-hand knowledge of this 'ecstasy' as well as 'agony' we have touched upon here this morning. Surely it will enable you to understand Rumi's lyrical language on love."

Dr Harrington brought the lecture to an end. There was an enthralled hush in the room, nobody seeming impatient for the lecture to be over. Again, she rejoiced in the visible effect Rumi's words had had on them all. It was what she loved to do.

"Right, for the next time we meet, I would like you to study the *Divan to Shams-e Tabriz, number 1559*. Ask yourself, what message is the poet trying to convey? And when you start planning your response," she advised, "please keep an open mind to what has been discussed here today. I want it to have come from deep within your soul. So, temporarily shut the door on the noisy world and listen to 'the hidden music of Rumi' instead. Literally and metaphorically. Sense the passion in what you read and hear! Okay, good luck with that and thank you for your attentiveness. As always, it has been a real pleasure talking to you."

A round of applause filled the room.

"I have a couple of minutes to answer any questions you may have but, please, it will have to be brief. I'm afraid we have already overrun slightly."

A mass of hands rose keenly into the air.

"Goodness me," she exclaimed. "So many of you with your hands up. I'm afraid we've only enough time for one perhaps. Er... now, let me see... Yes, the young man at the back in the red top."

"Me?"

"Yes, you. What is it you'd like to ask?"

"Thank you very much, Dr Harrington, for another excellent lecture. I really enjoyed it today and I apologise in advance if you find my question a little impertinent."

Sasha nodded her appreciation and raised her hand with a smile, inviting the sheepish student to continue.

"I would like to ask whether you've met your *Anam Cara* or 'friend of the soul' yet?"

The audacity of his question caused a few sniggers and murmurings amongst the audience. But Dr Sasha Harrington was at ease with the question and in full control of her emotions, her body language suggesting as much. Busying herself by shuffling up her papers and dismantling the other apparatus of her trade, she grinned widely, feeling ever so pleased with herself. A few weeks back, yes, the question would certainly have bothered her, no doubt producing a fierce rebuke at being posed with such an 'impertinent' query. Indeed, she would have found the question offensive and most malicious, knowing there were those in the university who still liked to poke fun at her past and her sexuality. But things had changed for Dr Sasha Harrington. Someone had taught her to like herself once more and to be comfortable with who she now was. Things were so very different today, not at all like the dark days of old when she would need a handful of antidepressants washed down with a slurp of alcohol just to give her the strength and courage to face another day.

She teased her audience for a minute or two, keeping them in suspense as she pretended to debate whether to tell them or not. An excitable noise emanated from the mass of students, keen to know what her response would be.

"Okay… okay… settle back down and I will give you my answer." Her audience complied with her request, eagerly awaiting her reply.

"I *was* starting to have my doubts. That, I must admit. But then, out of nowhere, *he* arrived," she beamed. "And that's all I'm going to say on the matter. You're not getting any more out of me," she insisted with a playful wag of her finger.

As a few wolf whistles and hoots of laughter swept around the lecture theatre, she couldn't help but wonder whether or not she was blushing. Dr Sasha Harrington silently hoped she was.

"So, I hope that gives heart to those of you out there who secretly yearn for that one special person. Until next week… and please remember to keep your heart, eyes and door to your soul wide open. Class dismissed!"

Outside in the staff car park, she lit another cigarette. One more lecture to go and then she was free for the day. The research for her latest book had also been going well and her publishers were happy. She'd been able to compile meticulous amounts of notes the previous day and she now felt that she deserved a treat, some fun maybe. She hadn't felt this good about her life for quite some time.

Sasha inhaled deeply and studied the cigarette's glowing tip, forming rings with the exhaled smoke. A warm memory was trying to force its way into her mind. When it arrived, a smile of delight broke across her face. Manny and she were dancing together in a club called 'Rumi's Bar'. How thoughtful and clever he'd been, proving his remarkable flare for intuition. *I must call him later, to see how he is… But I don't want to crowd him*, she reminded herself. She considered herself a little old-fashioned when it came to women calling men.

Sasha recalled him leaving her in a rather anxious state of mind, agitated about being seen out by those two work colleagues of his. He was a bit of a worrier, she acknowledged with a smile. But her smile was soon washed away by a wave of contempt for that Emma girl, her infatuation with Manny was clear to see. Still, who could blame her.

He was handsome enough, she admitted to herself, to cause a fire in the coldest of hearts. Flicking her cigarette on to the ground, Sasha twisted it underfoot. Break was almost over. She brushed off some ash from the sleeve of her coat while making a mental note to contact Virginia. She wanted to book up some more dates. Dates well in advance so she could have Manny all to herself again.

More to the point, she wanted to ensure nobody else could get their hands on him. To protect him from inflicting any more pain on himself. Virginia would charge a fortune, of course, but as far as Sasha was concerned, he was worth every penny. Maybe she would get to go clubbing again and get to wear her new dress. Sasha kept smiling, her mind fixed on the way that they'd danced. She believed that it was the closest their bodies were ever likely to get, in a physical sense. Other than dancing, she was unsure how to go about creating an opportunity where they'd sink deep into an embrace together. She wanted nothing more than to hold his hand and steady him as he stumbled along life's arduous path.

Rumi and Shams used to dance with each other, too, she recalled. Whirling dervishes, they were. Dancing their way into the heart of God. She began to recite part of a poem to herself:

'Dance, (Rumi says), when you're broken open.
Dance, if you've torn the bandage off…
Dance, when you're perfectly free.' [10]

And with that, she strode purposefully back into the building, feeling nothing but love for Manny. In him, she saw her liberator, salvation and true *Anam Cara*.

"You're going when?"

"Shh, keep your voice down! Jesus, someone will hear." Manny glanced around the staffroom, hoping nobody was listening in. Satisfied, he continued to talk in a low undertone. "This coming Monday." And then, "For three days, no more."

"But you can't," protested Moran. "They're school days."

Manny tutted and rolled his eyes. "I know they're school days. That's why I'm asking for your help."

"I don't know," he dithered. "My job means something to me."

"Hey," Manny frowned, "mine does too."

"Really? Which one?"

Manny stared hard at his friend, not liking his tone.

"Look, all I'm asking you to do is collaborate with my story and say you spoke to me over the weekend and that I was in a bad way then, too. You don't have to say any more than that. I already have somebody calling in for me that morning. No need for you to go screaming it from the rooftops either. Just drop the line in once or twice during a lunchtime conversation and it'll all be fine."

Moran puffed out his cheeks, not at all happy. "Okay, I'll do it this once but don't ask again. I have a really bad feeling about this. In your own time, fair enough, do what you want," he lectured. "But start taking time off work, you're simply asking for trouble."

Manny patted his arm, thanking him. He then got up from his seat and went into the staff kitchen to make them both another cup of coffee.

On his way out, holding a cup of his own, was his nemesis, Phil Young. Young said something as he passed. Something which Manny didn't quite catch. Whatever it was, he let it go. He was in no mood for another altercation. They exchanged a glare instead, both of them knowing they had to be elsewhere. Young, out on the playing fields to oversee a football match and Manny needed to be thinking about making a move back to his hotel, where he could wash and change. He was supposed to be going into London again. This time to meet the fashion critic and more mature woman who went by the name of Candy Richards. She wanted to give him the once-over before the proposed trip to Madrid.

Still, there was enough time for him to grab a cup of coffee and have a quick chat with Moran first.

The art teacher had been sceptical and not best pleased when Manny had confided in him about his forthcoming trip to Madrid, keen to point out the repercussions should he be caught out. Manny did not need reminding. He tried not to show his irritation when his colleague began to list a number of things that could possibly go wrong. There really was no need: Manny had already spent enough time agonising over them for himself.

But Manny felt that he had had very little option but to agree to the booking. And besides, he'd countered, the money he earned would mean the nearer he would be to walking away from the escorting world.

While waiting for the kettle to boil, he reached into his trouser pocket for his mobile. No messages. He peered out of the window and onto the playing fields. Young was walking towards one of the three football pitches, a cluster of boys running to keep up, kicking footballs as they went. It was breezy outside and one or two of them looked cold. For Manny's benefit, Young put on a camp walk, one hand on his hip, the other hovering limply mid-air. Manny responded by showing him his middle finger. Some of the boys clocked these acts of immaturity by their teachers and howled with laughter. Some mimicked the walk, others the finger.

Returning from the kitchen, Manny handed a mug of coffee to Moran and sat back down, all the time cursing Young's antics through gritted teeth.

"Don't let him get to you or he'll do it all the more."

"Hard not to."

"Anyway, what does this... er, Sasha person think of you going off with someone else for a few days? Won't she mind?"

"I suppose she will," he sighed. "The woman who runs the agency, Virginia, told me to leave it. Said that she'd deal with her for me. I'm sure it'll be all right. Can't really see her wanting to upset one of the clients, can you?"

Moran shook his head. He was finding all this a little strange but he tried hard not to let it show. "Nonetheless, you don't want to go upsetting her, sounds to me she's been pretty good to you."

Manny had to admit that it did bother him. In fact, it'd been bothering him quite a bit. If Sasha were to find out about the trip, it would no doubt disturb her and he didn't want that to happen, as strange as that might sound. He was hoping Virginia would come up with a plausible explanation. Were Sasha to want to speak to him or worse see him while he was away and couldn't, she would take some pacifying, to say the least.

"You'll have to make it up to her somehow," Moran said with a playful nudge.

"Yeah," he agreed. "I will. That's for sure."

* * *

263

Manny was sitting at a table in Carluccio's, in London's Christopher's Place, drinking a coffee. Virginia had chosen the venue for his meeting with the fashion critic who was already twenty minutes late. The aim of the meeting was to seal the booking that would see him escort her to Madrid the following week.

Unlike previous bookings, he was not feeling tense or nervous. Other than the money, the trip was proving to be an inconvenience. So, should the woman not find him suitable, it would bother Virginia more than it would bother himself.

The restaurant was busy with diners and those simply enjoying a relaxing drink. Manny was pleased with the setting. Conservative in its choice and not too intimate or fancy in any way. Manny was at a table close to the entrance and it was she who spotted him before he'd had the chance to spot her. He had been killing time reading the menu when she'd made her colourful entrance. Judging by the bags she held, she'd been indulging in a bit of a shopping first. Retail therapy perhaps.

Candy greeted him by pressing her cheeks to his and imitating the kissing sound with a loud *"mwah"* on each press.

Oh, fuck.

Candy Richards looked older than the fifty-five years stated on the booking sheet but she dressed and wore the hairstyle and make-up of someone thirty years younger. She had an oval face with straight, black, shoulder-length hair which Manny considered might not entirely be her own.

The make-up somehow made her look half oriental which she certainly was not, her features were far too large. Her foundation was quite pale while her eyeliner was thick, drawn on with a heavy pencil. Her lipstick was heavier towards the middle and the way it had been applied made her appear as if she was impersonating a bunny rabbit. Her outfit was made from silk, again, in keeping with the style of the orient. Colourful, too.

You'd have a job to lose her in dense fog, he thought quietly to himself while sitting back down.

For a better indication of her age, Manny needed to look no further than the loose skin under her chin, the liver spots on her hands and the glasses that hung on a chain around her saggy neck.

"Oh yes, I like the look of you," she kept saying, eyeing him up as if he was a garment in a shop window. "You'll do very nicely. A perfect cut. I gather you're fluent in Spanish, too.

"*Sí*," he said with a smile.

"Excellent."

He summoned over a passing waiter and ordered drinks. Two red wines. Neither of them wanted to eat so they got straight down to business. She gave a brief summary of what she was looking for, which was nothing too taxing or out of the ordinary. She was leaving for Madrid on the Thursday of that week. He was to contact her when he himself had landed on the Saturday. She would come to fetch him.

As she continued to talk, it became obvious to Manny that she was still in love with her ex-husband and he was being hired simply to disguise her wounded pride. To show face, so to speak.

Privately, Manny didn't mind this as he hoped it meant she'd have no desire for him in the carnal sense of the word.

She talked a lot about her profession and enjoyed name-dropping as to who would be there from the fashion world. The names whizzed over his head. While she was chatting, he noticed some lipstick on her front tooth and that her breath wasn't as fresh as it could have been. Both offences caused him to become distracted and he zoned out, no longer listening to what she was saying. He spent the rest of the one-way conversation trying to nod and smile in all the right places.

It would be a long three days, he decided. What did he know about fashion?

He shifted in his seat, trying to find a pose he was comfortable with. A pose that wouldn't reveal his boredom and the irritation building within. He rested his chin on his hands; his head was starting to feel heavy.

"You argued a lot then?" he enquired, attempting to sound interested.

She'd been talking non-stop about her ex-husband and their tempestuous relationship. Her plan was to win her husband back. Seeing her with another man on her arm might rattle him into action, she'd decided.

"Is he a jealous type?" Manny asked.

"Who, David? God, no. But his ego won't like it at all. Think about it. I'm with a man half his age and twice as handsome. I want him to feel my pain."

Manny did think about it and decided it would be unwise to fill the pause with his own thoughts. In the privacy of his mind, he didn't think her plan would work. He debated with himself for a moment or two. *Maybe she deserves to hear what I think? I know I'd want a second opinion if I was in her position.*

So he told her, straight. Perhaps a little too straight. He handed her a napkin so she could dab the dry tears from her eyes. It really was going to be a long three days.

"God, I can't do this any more," he yelled, throwing himself onto the bed in his hotel room in exasperation. "I want a place of my own... Why am I such a dick?" Candy Richards had been more than pleased with him and had agreed to the deal.

The only positive to take from the looming trip to Madrid would be the money. As Virginia had said, enough, maybe, to put down a deposit on a place of his own, something half-decent. Somewhere private where he could close the door on his chaotic world. Living as he was, was grinding him down. Severely doing his head in. He needed to act, change the pointless pattern he was so weary of weaving.

As he lay on his back, staring up at the flaky ceiling, he worked it all out.

School would provide the reference. The credit check might prove a stumbling block but by then he would have enough to put down a lump sum. At least a couple of months' rent in advance, with the full deposit, should they start to quibble.

After the Madrid trip, he'd consider doing only a couple more bookings and that would be that. *Adios* to the whole damn lot of them. He would then concentrate on what he did best. Teaching. An honest and respectable profession. Some might even say a vocation.

Sasha, he decided, would be the only person he'd keep in contact with. For him, she'd been the one good thing to transpire from the whole escorting lark. He liked her. She never irritated him the way he had been irritated tonight.

And besides, there was more about Rumi he wanted to know. Needed to know. He was thinking of asking for her advice, debating whether or not to enrol on a course.

He considered this for a moment and decided that he liked the idea of carving out a new career for himself. Something to do with Persian poetry. An expert, perhaps. Like Sasha.

He reasoned that he wasn't too old to learn. And there was still plenty of time to develop a passion for something new.

Then he could have his dream home. With a study where he would write essays to explain the most mystical of poems. He'd have that old battered leather chair and the shelves would be crammed with dusty, ancient books. Hell, he'd even have that solid wooden desk where he'd sit and write bestselling books. Far-fetched? No, not at all. There'd be incense and candles aplenty.

The desire to better himself was growing stronger. More so after a few glasses of wine. Drunken determination made it all seem achievable. Why couldn't he carry the feeling into tomorrow?

A tingle of excitement raced through him as he thought of the possibilities. Putting his hands behind his head, Manny closed his eyes for a moment and allowed himself a smile. He liked what he saw, what he had become.

He was standing proudly on stage, leaning on a lectern. Ready to deliver a talk and inform the world about Rumi's work.

Women would want to bed him, while men would want to be him.

Both Baxter and Young would be in the audience, too. Looking on, patiently waiting for him to sign their books. Books he'd have written on his desk at home.

Virginia would also be there. Offering him vast amounts of money to go on dates with lustful young women who were desperate to hear him wax lyrically into their ears, purring his magic.

Dreams, dreams, how wonderful are dreams?

Manny lifted his naked frame from the sagging mattress and

staggered over towards the mirror where he studied himself briefly before clearing his throat. He intended to recite a poem. A poem whose words had recently decided to stay with him. But something in the mirror robbed him of his moment. His eyes were almost shut and he was swaying. He took a long moment to steady himself. Shaking his head, he slowly lifted his gaze back up to the mirror. He recognised the face peering back at him. It was his father's. Drunk and with a head full of dreams. Why, hadn't his own mother once told him that his father's head consisted of only one theme? Drunken dreams.

Manny turned on the tap and splashed his face, washing both dreams and tears away. Watching as they whirled their way down the sink.

Then, with shame leading the way, he crept back into the creaky old bed, mumbling something about apples falling from trees.

CHAPTER
TWENTY-NINE

"She's adamant about it. Try and think of it as a working holiday. Honestly, you'll be fine. This booking is all about panache and class and you have both in abundance," Louise flattered, although Manny wasn't buying it. She was in work mode again, just doing her job on a busy Saturday morning.

"Ms Richards called the office first thing the following day to confirm the booking. Said you'd do nicely. So, well done on clinching the deal, you really did impress her. Easy money when you consider her requirements."

"What are her requirements?" he enquired through a sleepy yawn.

"Pretty straightforward really... Nothing too demanding, you'll be pleased to hear. The way I see it, you're an expensive piece of jewellery that's been hired to show off in public. All she asks is that, when out and about, you look upon her with affection and that you're attentive towards her without ever saying too much. You're her new lover, a Spanish toyboy. Oh, and don't forget to use your Spanish from time to time, she'll like that, especially in front of her peers. As for any extras, as always, it's down to you." The thought of Candy Richards wanting extras caused him to shudder. This time, he told himself, there'd be strict limits. Extras, on this occasion, were prohibited.

"And just think of what you can do with the money you'll be earning."

Manny already had. In fact, he'd thought of little else, but the trip still filled him with trepidation. Something didn't feel right.

He tried to sound reasonably cheerful, though. "I'd better get packing then." He rolled over and looked across at his holdalls, allowing himself a wry smile, thinking, *No need, I'm already done*. "You will remember to call in sick for me, won't you?"

"Yes," Louise huffed. "Now quit worrying! I'll do it first thing Monday morning."

He leaned back to rest his head on the pillow and closed his eyes, feeling the contradictory emotions curdle inside him. *What am I doing?* he asked himself for the umpteenth time. *Missing school so I can accompany a neurotic woman in Madrid*. The notion didn't sit well with him, despite the amount of money he'd be earning. *My life*, he conceded, *just gets more and more peculiar*.

"Oh, and don't forget," Louise added, "if you buy anything for the trip, then keep the receipts. You'll be able to claim some of it back on expenses.

"Such as?"

"You know, things like toiletries, dry cleaning, taxi rides, stuff like that."

He nodded, unconcerned. When Louise had first called, he'd been toying with the idea of inviting her out, despite Virginia's warning. In his book, she was worth another taste, another bite. But not any more. She was sounding so snooty and far too businesslike. It made him wonder whether Virginia was eavesdropping on their conversation. It would certainly help explain why Louise was keeping the call so formal. The echo on the line also made him think that he'd been put on the loudspeaker.

"Great," he replied neutrally. "I'll do that."

"What did you think of her by the way?

"Who?"

Louise tutted in exasperation. "The client of course. Wake up, Manny, rise and shine, you've a plane to catch." Then she said more lightly, "An important mission to complete. Quite a character, isn't she?"

"Yeah, just a bit. Colourful and self obsessed," he said, remembering back to the their Tuesday meeting.

"You'll have something in common then," Louise joked. The remark managed to extract a smile from him. He hoped she was smiling too. *At last*, he thought, *a piece of herself.* Louise's call up until then had been so short and to the point that there hadn't really been any opportunity for small talk.

Manny leaned forward and pinched the bridge of his nose. It was too early in the morning to summon up a witty response to her last comment. His head was pounding and his mouth was dry. Moran's fault. One quick drink, straight after work, had turned into several. The smell on his clothes and oozing from his pores told of a late-night Indian, although the fuzziness in his head prevented him from recalling exactly if he'd eaten.

The time was approaching 8.00am and he still needed to shower, dress and check out. His flight to Madrid was at 10.55am that very morning. Louise was making her usual pre-booking call. Checking up on him as she liked to do, making sure that he hadn't changed his mind and backed out.

Manny declined the lift to the airport she had offered, opting instead to take the train, much preferring his own company to that of one of the drivers. Besides, the train journey from St. Albans to Luton Parkway was only a matter of minutes. He'd already decided on getting a taxi to St Albans station and, as Louise had suggested, he'd now remember to keep the receipt.

"Best advice I can give you," she continued, "is to smile a lot, say very little and treat her really well, especially when her ex-husband is around. She's booked you a separate room in the same hotel as her. Room next to hers, apparently. She's also sending a driver to fetch you from the airport. All *you* need to do is get there. Think you can manage that?" she asked sarcastically.

"Yeah, should think so," was the unconvincing response.

"I'm sure Candy will brief you on your arrival and tell you all about her busy agenda. You'll do well to remember what it is she demands from you. She's paying a lot of money for you, so you don't forget to pack your A-game. Okay?"

"Yeah, terrific."

"Don't sound too thrilled, will you! I mean, how much are you about to earn? I hear it's quite a bit, close to three grand. That works out pretty much a grand per day. Wow, one would think you'd be ecstatic! You know, there were others we could have asked. Others who would have been much more grateful for the booking."

"Careful now, you're starting to sound like Virginia. She'd be proud of you," he said, now wholly convinced that their call was being listened to. He was thoughtful for a moment. "Look, I do appreciate it. I'm just a little nervous about missing work, that's all. And then there's Sasha's feelings to consider."

"Sasha's feelings?" she asked with a trace of annoyance. "What about her feelings?"

"What if she calls and wants to see me?"

"God, Manny, you're both as bad as each other. I wonder about you. Me thinks you like her more than you're willing to admit."

He ran his hand over his head and frowned, her comment making him feel awkward inside. Unsure how to respond, Manny remained silent, fearing that protestations at this point would serve only to heighten his semblance of guilt.

"Anyway," Louise assured him, "Virginia is speaking to her on your behalf. Christ, you're only going for a few days. Word of warning though," she stressed. "Switch your phone off while you're over there, that way she won't be able to reach you. Then call us on your return so we can fill you in on what's been said. Okay? Happy now?"

He wasn't but it would have to do. Silly as it might sound, the booking with a different client felt like an act of betrayal. It continued to weigh heavily on his mind. Why? He didn't yet know.

Manny didn't say anything for a moment and, when he did, it was to ask Louise to repeat what it was that she was going to tell his school. Inwardly, however, he was more concerned about what they'd say to Sasha. He wanted assurances that she would be okay. He suspected that she would be calling the agency soon, and he hoped Virginia would be kind to her when she did. He didn't like the idea of having to lie to her and, if he was to call her up or reply to her texts, that was exactly what he'd have to do. Maybe it was better to leave it to the girls in the office, even if it meant colluding with their lies on his return.

"I'll just say you're in bed with the flu. Don't worry, I'll make it sound convincing. Now, hadn't you better get going?"

Manny nodded. Neither of them had anything else to add so the call was ended. He was a touch disappointed that Louise had been so cool with him and wondered what he had done to warrant such a distant tone. Before, she'd been fun to talk to. This time, she'd spoken with an authority that almost matched her boss. Maybe Virginia was still making Louise pay for what she'd done. Obviously she'd be keeping a close eye on them both from now on. And that would be harder for Louise to take than it was for him.

Manny sat there for a moment, staring at his holdalls, thinking it was a terrible way to treat his new suits. Instead of being carried on hangers, they'd been folded haphazardly and forced in. By the time he got to Madrid, along with his shirts, they'd be creased to death. He'd have to get them pressed over there. Candy, he hoped, would know where. The hotel would probably have pressing facilities. He gave a close-lipped smile at all the fuss he was making, how bothered he was about his appearance. But for the next few days he belonged to the fashion world, where looking one's best was part of the norm.

He jumped into the shower where he washed, shaved and dressed casually in jeans and a light blue shirt. Then he grabbed his two holdalls and made his way down to reception where he settled his bill and requested a cab. It arrived promptly and within ten minutes he was standing on Platform 4 of St Albans station awaiting the train that would take him to Luton airport. He tried to generate some excitement for the trip but failed miserably. It dawned on him, rather surprisingly, that he craved the more familiar routine of his classroom. He could be reading stories and setting work for his students, enjoying their laughter and childlike wit. Sasha wouldn't be the only one he'd need to make it up to. He made a mental note to bring back some Spanish sweets. He could hand them out to the classes he was temporarily abandoning. Maybe there'd be enough time, too, for him to sit and pen a scary story. It could even have a Spanish theme. They'd love that and so would he. The more he thought about it, the more the guilt began to swell.

Blimey, he thought to himself, *What's happening to me? I'm actually going to miss my classes. How weird. How unexpected.* With the train approaching the platform, Manny pushed all such thoughts aside. *Madrid, here I come.*

Meanwhile, in Barnes, Sasha Harrington was sitting at her desk, working on her book. She got up and scanned along the bookshelves, searching for a book that would help her to revise and rewrite a passage that was refusing to flow. She reached up and took down a dusty old book with a damaged spine. Then, turning to a well-thumbed page, she began to read, jotting down the odd note. But it was no good. Her mind was elsewhere.

Frustrated with her lack of progress, she threw down her pen, stood up and marched straight for the kitchen where she switched on the kettle and stood for a moment, her arms folded, leaning against the kitchen work top, thinking all the time, *Why hasn't he been in touch?* It was nearing a week now and she'd heard nothing from him. And why hadn't the agency bothered to call her back? There was usually someone there on a Saturday morning.

"Manny has been awfully busy lately and has requested some time off. Said he was not to be contacted," was what they told her on the few occasions they'd bothered to pick up.

"Honestly," Sasha had fumed. "It's outrageous." With all the money they had earned from her, she expected better treatment. Much better. Her requests should never be declined. The cheek of it. When she'd insisted on seeing Manny, they'd fobbed her off with some lame excuse and offered her someone else instead. Manny was *"temporarily unavailable"* was the other lie she was being fed.

It just wasn't good enough and certainly wouldn't do. Didn't they realise the damage they were causing? Of course they didn't, she reasoned, lighting yet another cigarette. *They're a bunch of fools who deal in monetary matters alone. They know nothing of the path that leads to the beloved. Damn the lot of them!* Later, she would have it out with that Virginia woman. Tell her exactly what she thought of it all. *If* she could get through to her, that was. It was nothing short of scandalous. Strong words would be said, needed to be said. The trouble was, Virginia probably already knew just how angry she was. Hence the reason why she was being so evasive, barring her calls and ignoring the numerous e-mails that she had sent.

Sasha tutted and changed her mind about the coffee, swapping her mug for a wine glass instead. The clock on the wall told her that it was 10.35am. A bit early to start drinking but, what the hell, she was feeling depressed. Had been most of the week. She'd spent the best part of it working on her book and planning her lectures. Trying to keep herself busy. Keeping her mind off other matters. She had hoped that there would have been an opportunity to meet up with Manny, but no, not a word from him, which deeply troubled her. His silence was becoming deafening and was causing a painful sorrow in her soul. Her psychotherapist had once advised her to throw herself into her work and try to fill her days with positives when she felt as low as she was feeling now. 'Try and combat the depression by being proactive', he had said. For the past few days she had done as he had suggested, following his advice to the tee. But despite her best efforts, the advice was failing her, failing miserably.

Sasha sighed loudly and poured a healthy measure of wine, downing it in no time at all. She stopped only once and that was to wipe the dribble from her chin with the back of her hand. The cluster of bristles she felt on her chin were further evidence of her agitated state of mind. A sign that she'd given up hope of seeing her man any time soon. What was the point of making herself beautiful only to be disappointed again?

Sasha cursed under her breath. The stormy clouds of negativity were gathering pace. Every thought she had was laced with a pitiful worthlessness. Pulling on her cigarette, she withdrew deeper into her reverie.

Part of her still hoped that something could yet be arranged. But with every passing minute it was looking more and more unlikely. What on earth had happened? A quick call to say hello would have been enough to appease the longing. He couldn't just have vanished.

Thinking like this only made her spirit sink faster, when really what she ought to be doing was holding on to hope.

She'd been here before, of course, many times. Only this time it was different, far different. No, this was no meaningless one-night affair which she'd long grown tired of. For her, this was the real thing. His role was to teach her about love the same way Shams had taught Rumi. Silently. How odd that he too should disappear without warning, just as Shams, the wandering holy man often did. Her only friend had also abandoned her, leaving her alone to swim in the tempestuous sea of rejection. Like Rumi before her, she too had found somebody who represented the embodiment of God's beauty. A poem came floating to her mind.

'The friend has rejected me
He has broken my heart and shut the door.
Now my desolate heart and I
will sit patiently on his doorstep
for He loves those with a broken heart' [11]

Sasha spoke into the silence. "He does care about me, doesn't he?" And then, "Please make him care." She poured herself some more wine. Even the words of her beloved Rumi lacked their usual potency. With a glass in hand and cigarette in her mouth, she staggered back to her study, wondering why love was the most difficult concept to define and why did it cause such pain.

She tried Manny's number again, but there was still no reply. Straight to voicemail, which was another slap of rejection. She tried the agency once more, but again she only got as far as the girl on reception. According to her, Virginia was still *"unavailable"*.

On hearing this, Sasha's face creased with anger. Mumbling something inappropriate into the phone, she ended the call. Her insecurities soon began to chatter. One voice in particular was growing louder. He was with someone else. He had to be. Why else all this elusiveness?

The thought of him frolicking around and holding hands with someone else was far too painful to consider. But it was that picture that kept playing inside her head over and over again. The fact that she knew the rules of the game mattered little. The truth of it was, the very image filled her with horror. Whoever he was with, they were bound to be better and more beautiful than her. She wanted him to herself. After years of looking for that special person, she didn't have the strength to start her search all over again. There was nobody else like him. Manny ticked all her boxes. It was inconceivable that she might not see him again. She considered this for a moment. What a dreadful prospect. One that was too much to bear. Overnight, Manny had become the beacon in her desperately dark and lonely world. To lose him so soon would be a tragedy.

Knocking back the rest of the wine, Sasha decided to go upstairs to dress, already knowing which outfit to wear. It was there waiting for her in the wardrobe. The flimsy fairy costume he'd insisted on buying for her during their recent shopping trip. She felt sure it would fit and, as she had no plans to leave the house, there'd be no need to worry about the cold weather outside. Cigarette in hand, she marched up the stairs and straight into her room where she threw open her expansive wardrobe and fished out the tiny outfit. Standing in front of the full length mirror, she held it against her, vowing to make it fit.

The sound of her mobile phone ringing brought her out of her reverie. Was it him? Hastily, she shot across her room, but the caller ID soon dashed her hopes. It was somebody from the agency. Still, they might be calling with some good news.

"Hello?"

"Hi, Sasha, it's Virginia from the agency. We seem to keep missing each other. Sorry about that. I hear you've been wanting to speak to me. What can I do for you?"

"You know my problem, Virginia, so cut the crap."

There was a slight pause on the line.

"It's about Manny, isn't it?" she asked calmly.

"You know perfectly well that it is."

"Has he not been in touch?"

"No," she replied, trying to keep her anger in check.

"Well, what can I say?"

"You could start by explaining why you rejected my request."

"Look, Sasha, you know me well enough by now to know that I wouldn't lie to you. As I'm sure you're already aware, Manny is a difficult man to deal with. Now, how can I put this? He has certain issues about seeing you and he came to me asking for some time off."

"Go on." Sasha recalled how uncomfortable he had been when bumping into his work colleagues the previous Saturday. What Virginia was saying made a horrid kind of sense.

"Yes. Some time off, a chance to clear his head. And," she said slowly, "he wants to be able to work with other clients."

"Other clients?"

There was a sympathetic edge to Virginia's tone that wasn't usually there.

"Yes. I'm sorry to be the one to break it to you Sasha, but you really do have to learn to let go. He's not yours and you can't carry on acting this way."

"You nasty bitch," she spat out. "What have you told him? We were getting along just fine."

"If you're going to carry on with the insults, I'll end this call right now and wipe your details from our database. Do I make myself clear?" The sympathy in her tone had gone. "I've heard that you've been quite rude to my staff recently."

"I don't understand. Why can't I see him? He seemed fine the last time we were together."

"You have to understand that I can only go on what the escorts tell me and Manny insisted on taking some time off. He mentioned to me that, right now, he'd rather not see you."

Sasha put down her glass and wiped the tears from her eyes.

"What can I do?" Virginia asked. "I can't order him to see you. It just doesn't work that way. It's frustrating for us all. Try not to take it so personally... Listen," she said after a short silence, "why don't you give someone else a chance? I have the perfect gentleman in mind. I'm sure..."

"No," she said resoundingly. "I need... I mean, I would like to book Manny."

Virginia exhaled loudly and, after a short pause, said, "I'll tell you what, I will try and have a word with Manny. See if I can get him to change his mind. I warn you now, though, it's a big if. I'll ask him to contact you. No promises, mind. It's up to him if he wants to get in touch. You know Manny, bit of a free spirit. Don't pressure him, leave it for a short while and we will try again later in the week. How does that sound?"

Sasha pondered this for a moment. "Okay," she sighed. "Do you think I've been putting too much pressure on him then?"

"Well, perhaps. You know what some men are like though, Sasha. One whiff of a possible romance and they run a mile. Give him some time. And try to remember that he's still new to this line of work. I'm sure once he's had a bit of time to reflect he'll be okay."

"And if he doesn't want to come back?"

"Then I'm afraid you're going to have to learn to live without him. The noble thing to do is to let him go, wouldn't you say? I mean, you don't want to suffocate the poor chap."

"Suffocate? Is that what he said? Did he feel suffocated?"

"Maybe you tried to get too close, too quickly, and he couldn't cope or didn't like it. With all due respect, Sasha, the girls in the office think that you have been a little too possessive when it comes to him. Learn to lighten up. No offence but you hardly know him. I'm sure if you..."

Sasha ended the call mid-sentence. She'd heard enough. Virginia just didn't get it. She sat motionless for a moment, thinking about what had been said. There were questions she wanted answering. Only trouble being Manny was not there to answer them. She sat on the edge of her bed, still holding the dress. In her mind's eye, she could see him laughing and joking, looking becomingly svelte in his new suit.

In that moment she realised there wasn't anything she wouldn't do for him and she needed him to know this. Laying the dress on her bed, she went to sit at her bureau. She would write him a letter. She smiled thinly at the fact that she had no address for him. Of course she didn't, he was her very own homeless wanderer. He'd told her that himself. She sat there, thinking. How strange, some part of her seemed to revel in the notion that history was indeed repeating itself. The comparisons were there for all to see. She was the scholar who had finally found her soul mate. He was the teacher and homeless wanderer who seemed to have mysteriously disappeared. She stood up and started pacing the confines of her study. At last, she rejoiced, she now understood something of the grief that the mystical poet Rumi wrote so passionately about. The comparisons were remarkable. People would talk and write about them and, in doing so, would cement their relationship into the history books. They'd be mentioned in the same breath as Rumi and Shams. But theirs would have a different ending, a much more tragic ending. Suddenly, there seemed to be a great deal she had to do. In her drunken state, she set about applying her make-up.

CHAPTER THIRTY

It was a sight to behold. A hazy blue sky pierced by a round yellow sun. The sort of bright, winter day sun you could sit out in wearing just a light jacket. It was late afternoon and Manny Rodriguez was sitting at the roof bar of his hotel, enjoying a quiet beer. This was where Candy the client liked to meet before they stepped out together. As usual, he was being kept waiting while she attended to matters in her room. Not that he minded, for it had been another busy day. For the third day running they had spent the majority of their time at the Juan Carlos I exhibition centre in Madrid, which was host to International Fashion Week.

Today, though, had been the big one. The one Candy Richards and her peers had been looking forward to. Today it had been the turn of the female models to strut their stuff up and down the catwalk. The day the designers got to showcase their latest extravagant designs. A fiesta of fashion. Yesterday had been the turn of the men and the day before that had been the turn of the women with fuller figures. Manny knew which one he had preferred. Whilst there, he managed to purchase a dress for Sasha from one of the designer stalls. Black it was, with sequins and lace trimmings. He hoped it would fit. Manny was sure she'd like it and hoped that it would help disperse the guilty conscience that had been following him around for most of the trip. A guilt-driven purchase if ever there was one. He'd told Candy it was for his sister.

"Quite a large girl, isn't she?" she'd remarked.

"Yeah, she's very sporty," he'd lied. "Loves her rugby."

Later that evening, Candy and he were to attend a private viewing where up-and-coming designers would be giving sneak previews of their highly anticipated summer collection to a select few. He could hardly wait, he thought ironically. The only positive being that it was his last night on the job and then he'd be free to resume his nomadic existence.

According to Candy, the event was being staged in the converted basement of a trendy nightclub in the heart of the Spanish capital. She'd assured him that there'd be an opportunity for him to enjoy a dance and a drink before flying back to England, although she'd been quick to remind him of the role he had to play. For their last evening together, she was expecting him to put on the same polished performance he'd displayed throughout the trip.

The evening's event was for the benefit of the most important people in the fashion world and, Candy Richards being a highly respected journalist, her name was on that exclusive list with a plus one. Earlier, she'd admitted to Manny that, while she was delighted to be on the list, she was a little apprehensive. David, her ex, would also be there and, what with the club being small in size and quite intimate, crossing paths with him was an odds-on certainty. Words and glances were bound to be exchanged.

Nevertheless, with it being her last night, Candy was determined to have a good time and had ordered Manny to do the same. He was under strict orders to stay extra close to her side now that she knew they'd be in close proximity to her ex-husband and his young lover. This was the moment she'd been waiting for. A chance to show off her new man at close quarters and prove that she was more than coping with life after the split. In her colourful universe she still believed there might be a chance of reconciling their differences and of him coming back to her.

Manny sensed a problem with this and feared that her plan might backfire. From what he could deduce, her ex seemed entirely happy with his new young man; he couldn't see him wanting to rush back into Candy's arms. However, although he admired her tenacity in a way, Manny kept his thoughts to himself, quietly going about his business instead. Sticking to his brief and generally doing what he was being paid to do. The saga, however, did rather amuse him. Here was a woman in her sixties but dressed as if she were in her twenties, pretending that she had moved on and had found a love of her own, purposefully trying to wrench her ex-husband from the clutches of his gay lover and back into her own arms. It had all the conventions of a soap opera.

He lifted his bottle of beer and topped up his glass. With the late afternoon sun shining on his face, he had to admit that the trip, to date, had been an agreeable experience. Yes, he'd had the odd pang of guilt about missing work and avoiding Sasha's calls. And yes, Candy the client could at times be a little neurotic and over the top. But, generally speaking, the change of scenery with its warmer climate had done him the world of good. Something in him felt revitalised. So much so he was even looking forward to getting back to his classes and reverting back into teacher mode once again.

To date, he'd managed to smile a lot, laugh politely in all the right places and support the client wholeheartedly in her quest. He'd made a real effort to stick close to Candy's side, being both affectionate and attentive whenever it was called for and, unlike before, he did this without ever feeling out of his depth. He liked to think that he was finally getting to grips with the escorting world. Of course, having a client like Candy had helped his cause hugely. She had not placed too many demands upon his conscience and at the end of every evening he was free to retire to his own room where he would enjoy a night of uninterrupted sleep.

Also, having a room to himself in a five star hotel meant that whilst in Madrid being without a home was not such an issue. With the return to England imminent, however, the problem of his homelessness was once again beginning to dominate his thoughts. But, he told himself, with his bank balance now vastly improved, he stood a much better chance of sorting the problem out. For all her faults, Virginia had been true to her word. The money he'd now earned from his escorting work would help get him back on his feet. And the first thing he would do was find a place to rent.

Manny took another swig of his cold beer. *This is it*, he told himself, *I've now earned enough money to sort myself out*. His plan had worked. He hadn't made a fortune but he'd made enough to get him out of the hole he was in. He would tell Virginia on his return that he no longer wanted to work for the agency and that it was probably best for everyone involved if he walked away. Whisper it quietly but he felt back in control.

As a reward for his good work, Candy had allowed him the occasional moment to himself, like the one he was enjoying now. As long as he stayed relatively close by and didn't venture too far, he was free to explore the silky streets of Madrid which he'd done whenever the opportunity had presented itself.

Candy, like Sasha, was proving to be the ideal client. Louise had been right, the booking up to now had been fairly easy, without any dramas. He'd coped okay with the fact that he was supposed to be the lover of somebody who appeared old enough to be his grandmother. It was his job and out here nobody knew him, so the whispers and quizzical looks that they received were not such an issue.

The quieter moments had also provided an opportunity for him to take a step back and reflect upon his life. He'd already had a couple of internal debates about what it was exactly that was holding him back from achieving his goals. Again, with money in the bank, he could now afford to be much more of an optimist.

Earlier that morning he had gone for a stroll around the block and was sitting drinking an espresso when his attention was drawn to a line of school children walking in single file behind their proud teacher. On seeing this, he immediately felt an intense desire to return to his classroom. He promised himself that when he did get back he would turn things around at work and be a more proactive member of the much-maligned teaching profession. Being in debt, he felt, had seriously clouded his judgement and despite his earlier doubts he now believed that, for the time being, teaching was the career for him.

Also, while he'd been away, his ego had been given a bit of a boost. When wandering around the stalls in the exhibition centre, a couple of the stall holders had mistaken him for a male model. Perhaps it was a harmless bit of flattery but nevertheless he felt lifted by the compliment. It had gone down well with Candy, too. In fact, it was music to her ears. The hired piece of jewellery that she wore so flamboyantly on her arm was being looked upon with admiration. It seemed that there were many who approved of her new beau.

Manny lifted his glass and finished off his beer. As he did so, he noted a shock of pink blurring through the bottom of his glass. He put it down to find that Candy had arrived and was awaiting his attention. Standing up, he greeted her the way she liked, with a peck on each cheek and a gentle squeeze. Her perfume was strong, a scent he would long remember for all the wrong reasons. It smelt sickly sweet, completely devoid of subtlety.

"Evening, Candy. Are we well rested?"

"Yes, I feel much better, thank you."

"Come, sit down and let me order you a drink. Glass of white wine?"

"Please... No, let's have a bottle of champagne instead. After all, it is our last night and it has gone ever so well."

Manny nodded in agreement while summoning the waiter in readiness to order.

"Mind you," she said, "you're not to get drunk, understand? You have a busy night ahead. I wouldn't want you to make any mistakes later. Remember, it's an important night for me. And what with David being there, you'll need to be on top form because I know he will be. He's going to want to know all about you. So, you've been warned. If we stick to our story, then everything should be fine. Now, stand up and let me look at you."

Manny did as he was told.

"The suit is new," he said proudly. "I bought it recently in London. Hugo Boss, like it?"

Candy proceeded to eye him up and down, motioning for him to turn around.

"Good. Looks stylish and fits you well."

This had become the norm each time they stepped out in public together. She reminded Manny of one of his old aunts in Spain. Before dragging him off to mass every Wednesday and Sunday, she would make him stand in front of her so she could inspect him at close quarters, often giving him the wet tissue treatment to areas that had failed her stern inspection. He smiled at the memory. Back then, it had always been his neck and behind the ears which let him down. Fortunately, Candy's inspection was far less diligent, although somehow she managed to rekindle the same element of fear in him as his great aunt Gloria had done.

By the time he sat back down, the champagne had arrived and the waiter was ready to pop the cork. Candy gave him the required nod and he promptly began to fill their glasses.

"Cheers," she said, raising her glass. "Here's to our final night. Let's make it a good one." They touched glasses and began to drink. Neither of them spoke for a few moments. Manny guessed that Candy was busy thinking ahead to the evening's event. She adjusted herself in her seat, trying to get comfortable. He could tell that she was a little tense. He tried thinking of something to say that would take her mind off things but couldn't. He settled for complimenting both her and the shocking pink outfit she was wearing. They then sat there drinking and making small talk until eventually it was time to head for the club.

The place was busy. A selection of R&B and dance tunes were playing through the sound system. Waiters and waitresses were walking around with flutes of champagne or canapés on their trays. Everyone there looked prosperous and confidently dressed. Models dressed in outlandish designs posed on a small stage while buyers and designers discussed prices.

Manny had spotted one or two photographers shimmering about the club, taking snapshots of anybody who happened to be there. Twice they had approached him and twice he had turned his back, leaving Candy to do the necessary posing. They were seated on two stalls by the bar, observing everything that went on around them. Candy seemed to know many of the people there and was always quick to introduce Manny, explaining that he used to be a model and that was how they'd met. Manny just smiled, trying to look at ease with all the nonsense going on around him.

It wasn't long before they came across David and his lover. Candy's ex-husband had approached them first, introducing himself with a smile. Manny took an instant dislike to him and his sly way. Botox was doing its best to keep him looking young. All the usual lines and creases you'd expect to see on the face of a man of his era were conspicuously absent. His range of expressions was severely limited. In fact, with all the surgery he'd obviously had, it was impossible to say for certain how old he was. His hair, which he wore in a ponytail, was a silvery white and both he and his partner were tanned with pearly white teeth. The elder man was dressed in ripped-up jeans, cowboy boots and wore a blue velvet jacket with a heavy black outline. Underneath the jacket he wore a crisp white shirt with huge collars that made his head seem unfeasibly small.

David's partner, Freddie, on the other hand was dressed more casually. He wore the same style jeans but with a tight fitting black T-shirt that showed off a muscular frame. He had short, jet black hair and Manny estimated that he was around the same age as himself.

As they approached, Manny felt Candy's tenseness increase. In an act of solidarity, he stood even closer to her and didn't hesitate to put his arm around her shoulders. After the introductions, a fair amount of civil small talk took place between the pairs, Candy and David talking about the fashion show and who they'd met, Manny and Freddie discussing their impressions of Madrid and what landmarks they'd been able to see.

It wasn't long before David turned his attention to Manny, whom he'd been eyeing up the whole time he'd been speaking to Candy.

"Tell me, Manny, have you always been into older women?" he asked with a guileful grin.

The timing of such a question caught Manny by surprise and he wasn't sure if it merited a reply. The question was loaded with intent and Manny knew that he had to keep a cool head. Studying what little was left in his glass, he tried not to react. Candy's arm went around his waist. He felt the squeeze of support.

"No, not really," he replied eventually, looking at Candy. "Only this fine one."

David and his partner Freddie looked at each other and smiled. It seemed to Manny to be a knowing smile. He worried whether they knew the truth about him and what it was that he did for a living. He had to reassure himself that he was just being paranoid.

"Forgive me for laughing, Candy dear, I had heard the rumours but I never imagined it to be true. How on earth did you manage to find someone so handsome? My God, what a gorgeous looking specimen. Where on earth did you find him and how much was he?"

Manny's worst fears were being confirmed and Candy's plan was starting to seriously backfire. Instead of being upset or jealous as she had hoped, David's flirtatious eyes would not leave Manny alone. This made Manny feel uncomfortable and Candy prickle.

"We met at college," she lied, "where he's teaching me to speak Spanish. Then, with a tone of venom, she asked, "Tell me, David, in which men's toilets did you two meet?"

An awkward silence fell over the four of them. Manny hadn't liked what he'd just heard and made a point of grimacing an apology in Freddie's direction. Freddie appeared to be a decent kind of guy and didn't deserve the insult. Fortunately, he was man enough not to bite back.

David raised his hands in mock surrender and laughed out loud. This time it sounded much more forced.

"Now, now, Candy," he countered through smiling lips, "let's keep things civil and not allow things to turn nasty. We're all here to unwind and enjoy ourselves, remember? It has been a busy few days. I'm sure we've all done things we're not proud of." He was speaking to Candy but his eyes hadn't yet finished with Manny who by this time was hoping both men would clear off and mingle elsewhere.

The conversation soon deteriorated into clusters of catty remarks between David and Candy. Manny and Freddie looked at each other, rolling their eyes, despairing of their respective partners' childish behaviour. It was Freddie who stepped in first to gently lead David away.

With the insults over, Manny and Freddie shook hands, both mutely understanding what it was that had to be done. The club was small, so keeping the quarrelling pair away from each other would be a considerable challenge. Both Candy and David had behaved like a couple of callow youths, drawing unwanted attention to themselves. Not wanting to get involved with something that really had nothing to do with him, Manny went through the motions, pulling Candy away to another part of the club, consoling her as he did so.

It appeared that Candy had come off far worse from the verbal spat. The bitchy blows had left her reeling. She was leaning against a wall, holding herself tightly, unable to prevent the tears from falling. Manny decided to escort her back to the hotel where he tried to comfort her as they sat in the empty bar, attempting to make her realise that it was probably best if she laid down her arms gracefully and gave up the fight. She said that she would but her words lacked conviction.

"I love him," she sobbed, "and I can't live without him. My life is so empty when he's not around. One day maybe you'll understand what it feels like not to be wanted."

"Yeah, maybe," he offered by way of support. But to tell the truth his thoughts had already turned to the morning when he'd be flying back to England. Suddenly the notion that he would soon be going back to his day job cheered him no end. He led Candy back up to her room and kissed and hugged her goodnight. It was the first time he'd seen her look so beaten. She was still sobbing but there really wasn't much else he could do. It seemed reality had finally set in. Maybe now she could start to move on. Manny went back to his own room and began to pack. His time with Candy now at an end, he allowed himself a treat by drinking a beer from the mini bar. Still fully clothed, he lay down on the bed and began to think. Sasha entered his thoughts. Never in a million years did he think that he'd end up missing her. Checking his phone, he saw that again she had tried to call. He resisted calling her back. When he got back, he told himself, he would make an effort and go to see her. But before then he would need to speak to Louise. By the time he got back it would be too late for him to go into work. Perhaps he could meet up with Louise instead. A chance to collaborate their stories about where he'd been. He needed to know what she'd told both Sasha and his school. He reached for his phone and sent her a text. It wasn't long before he had his response. It was her idea to meet at Kings Cross St Pancras in the same café where they'd met before. It was where she liked to talk business, he remembered.

CHAPTER THIRTY-ONE

"He hasn't made it in again today. It's the third day running. I don't know what's up with him. Flu apparently. He's had a number of days off sick already this term. Honestly, Roger, I've been having problems with him since the start of term. The list is endless."

Maureen Baxter could have been talking about any one of her students. But she wasn't. She was sitting in the headteacher's office discussing one of her colleagues. It was 8.30 on Wednesday morning and she had insisted on speaking to him first thing. Reluctantly, the headteacher had agreed as long as she kept it brief.

"Problems? What kind of problems?" he asked wearily, glancing up at the clock.

"Calling in sick and not leaving any cover work, not turning up to department meetings, late with his grades, unwritten reports, books and coursework left unmarked... Would you like me to carry on?"

The headteacher held up his hand and motioned for her to stop, he'd heard enough.

"I've already written him a letter expressing my concerns," Baxter continued, "but it doesn't seem to have any effect on Mr Rodriguez. He's still as unreliable as ever. My concern is that it is now starting to have a negative effect on his classes." She paused, allowing a moment for the last comment to sink in. "And, as head of English, I'm ultimately responsible for their exam results. Target grades have been set high this academic year. My department simply can't afford to be carrying anyone."

The head cleared his throat and sighed. This was not what he needed.

"What is it you would like me to do, Maureen?"

"I want him out, Roger," she pressed. "I don't care how you do it but he has to go. It simply cannot carry on this way. The situation is deplorable. So much so, it's beginning to have an adverse effect on the students' learning."

The headteacher was quiet for a moment, thinking. The only sounds in the room came from the ticking clock that hung on the wall and the wheezing from his rattling chest.

Roger Wilson was seven months away from retirement. He had hoped for a quiet final year. Incident free, perhaps. A year without too many confrontations. A year where he could bow out and leave gracefully. Then and only then would he be free to work on bringing his golf handicap down. Trouble was, problems like these kept raising their heads, wanting his attention. He'd worked with Maureen Baxter long enough now to know that she wasn't going to let this go. He sighed again at the thought of the extra work this particular problem would bring.

"All right," he scowled, "leave it with me. I shall speak to him on his return. What I need you to do is to put your complaint in writing and make it official. Make a list of all the concerns that we've discussed here today. I shall then bring them up at the next governors' meeting, see what can be done. Now, is there anything else?"

Maureen Baxter shook her head, allowing herself a rare smile.

"Good, because I really must be getting on."

Louise and Manny were sitting in the café, drinks already ordered. She was dressed in her green suit, her long, dark hair clipped back in the usual way. He was disappointed to see that she was adopting the same business façade she had used on the phone when they last spoke. Keeping eye contact to a minimum, she was looking steadfastly into her coffee cup as she talked. She had already explained that the meeting would be short, due to her having to be elsewhere. Manny had started the conversation by enquiring into her wellbeing. Not that he told her as much, but he had noticed she was looking tired.

"I've had a lot on my plate," she'd replied. "Virginia's been keeping me busy."

"Does she know that you're meeting up with me?"

"Of course. There are bookings we need to discuss. She's counting on me getting you to do them. After all, business is business."

"Did Sasha call while I was in Madrid?"

"Oh, once or twice," she replied sarcastically.

"What did you tell her?"

"We told her you'd asked for some time off. That you needed time to yourself. Not sure she was buying into it though. You may well have to smooth things out for us. We can't afford to lose her business. She stamped her feet a bit and made quite a fuss. You need to be careful there, she seems to think she owns you."

"Don't worry, I'll handle it. I'll call her later," he said nonchalantly.

They discussed the highs and lows of his recent trip to Madrid. He explained that he wasn't sure whether he wanted to carry on escorting or not. Louise listened and handed over a brown envelope regardless. Manny filed it away inside his jacket pocket, to look at later.

"Don't make your mind up just yet," she said. "You might want to look at just how much you'll earn."

"Do any of the bookings involve Sasha?"

"No."

There was a pause in the conversation. Louise put down her cup and looked up.

"Why, Manny," she smirked, "is that disappointment I can see on your face?"

"No, not at all," he replied, lowering his gaze.

Louise let it go and quizzed him on his other plans instead.

"Where will you be staying? Have you managed to sort anything yet?"

"No, haven't had the time. First thing I need to do is get back to work and patch things up there. I'll book into a cheap hotel for now and start searching properly in the next few days. I can't carry on living like this. It's doing my head in. Tomorrow's Thursday and with a bit of luck by the end of the weekend I'm bound to have found something dark, dingy and overpriced."

They both smiled.

"Shame that staying with Len didn't work out."

"You mean your father. No, that would never have worked out."

Louise finished her coffee, stood up and started to put on her coat. "There must be someone you know, someone who could put you up for a few nights."

Manny shook his head. There was someone but he wasn't about to tell Louise who. They said their goodbyes and Manny watched as Louise walked away in the direction of the underground. Deciding to order another coffee, he sat there, taking his time, watching the passersby.

Staying at Sasha's for a few nights would certainly help him out and provide an opportunity for him to smooth things over with her. The dress he'd bought her in Madrid, he hoped, would see to that. He made a mental note to call her. No, better still, he would surprise her by heading to her house on Friday, after he'd finished work. He might even suggest to her that she accompany him on his mission to find a flat. Manny thought about this for a moment and wondered what it was that he missed about her the most. There was the calmness of her study, the rows upon rows of well-thumbed books, the Persian artefacts, the incense, the poetry, her generosity and, most of all, the way he'd come to feel so grounded and secure when in her presence.

For the rest of that week, Manny kept a low profile at school, throwing himself into his work by delivering excellent and well-prepared lessons to all his classes. Whenever he could, he avoided the eyes and ears of the staffroom by remaining in his classroom during break and lunchtimes, desperately trying to reduce the amount of paperwork that had built up during his time away. As expected, he'd received another telling off from Baxter for not setting any cover work during his absence and, ominously, there was a letter from the headteacher requesting a meeting on the Tuesday of next week to 'discuss certain matters that had been brought to his attention'. On reading this, a pang of anxiety filled his belly. But it was probably just a warning for him to pull his socks up. Nothing too serious, he hoped.

CHAPTER
THIRTY-TWO

For the second night running, Sasha Harrington had endured an uncomfortable night, her inner demons once again depriving her of sleep. Now she lay staring at the bedside clock which glowed back at her, informing her that it was Friday, 3.50am. Only five minutes had passed since she'd last checked.

Grabbing her phone from the bedside table, she slipped it in her dressing gown pocket and made her way downstairs to the kitchen. It had been a week now. Still no word. Not a dickey. What was she to do? Without him, everything in her life ceased to be of any importance. She grabbed the bottle of hard stuff from the larder, sat down and resumed drinking.

"A wee dram, for I feel a wee bit glum," she said in a mock Scottish accent. It wasn't long before she poured herself another. And then another.

Again, the whisky managed to warm her insides but the spirit failed to cheer her. Aggressively, she launched her glass at the opposing wall, then stood up and headed back upstairs, ignoring the lethal shards of glass underfoot. Her world, too, had been shattered. Shattered into tiny, painful pieces. "Was there no end to this suffering?" she asked herself wearily.

"Right, can you get your homework diaries out please and copy down what's on the board." The request was met with a volley of groans.

"When's it due in, sir?" Imani Lewis enquired.

"Tuesday."

"Tuesday?"

"Yes, Tuesday. That should give you all plenty of time to get it finished and copied out into neat. Remember to take more care, it's your final draft... Now, the bell is about to go so, once you have copied down the notes from the board, you may all start to pack up... and seeing that it's Friday I might even let you out a bit early."

Groans soon turned to cheers.

Manny had somehow managed to get through to the end of the week. The last lesson on Friday always managed to make life feel that much sweeter. For him it had been a short week at school but a long week in general. The trip to Madrid had taken a lot out of him. He wanted to get away quickly and go and pay Sasha a surprise visit. He was also counting on spending a couple of nights in her spare room, free of charge. Ageing hotel rooms he could no longer face, not to mention his declining funds.

He dismissed his class and noisily they began to file out of the classroom. As usual, Imani Lewis was last to leave, slow to pack up her things, hanging back so she could catch a few words with her favourite teacher.

"And what has sir got planned for the weekend?"

"Not much, Imani," he said, collecting and packing his bags with great haste. "Off to see a friend actually. The other side of London, so I really need to be making tracks."

She didn't take the hint.

"This friend male or female?" she asked cheekily.

"Er, not sure I can answer that. Private information... stuff teachers should keep to themselves and not share with their students."

"Oh, come on, you can tell me."

"No, I really can't," he smiled, taking care to avoid meeting those emerald eyes of hers, yet secretly enjoying the banter. Without the ensuing complications and if he had more time he might even have told her that he was indeed off to meet a special lady. Her good looks demanded engagement and made it hard for him to be strict with her. But he knew it would be a stupid mistake to lower his guard to such an attractive and fast maturing schoolgirl.

"Listen, Imani, I must be off. Good luck with your essay and I'll see you on Monday."

"Oh, you will be in this Monday then?" she teased.

Manny was busy looking down at the floor but now he raised his gaze.

"Yes, I sure will," he said as he made his way out into the corridor, bags in hand, en route to the station via the pub to catch up with Moran. "Have a good weekend, now."

"And you too, sir. Don't do anything I wouldn't do," she beamed.

The taxi dropped him off in the drive. He paid for the short trip from the station and waited while the driver fetched his two holdalls from the boot. Since there were no lights on in the house, he assumed Sasha hadn't arrived home from work yet. She hadn't been answering his calls either. Carefully handling the bag containing her new dress, he picked up his holdalls and made his way to her porch where he settled down patiently to wait. He wasn't sure how she was going to react to him showing up in this way. He hoped she'd be pleased. But as the minutes passed, Manny couldn't help but chastise himself for not having phoned earlier and arranged a time. He wondered whether she kept a hidden key somewhere and felt confident that she'd be happy for him to let himself in. He began to look under mats, behind bins and under plant pots but to no avail. While searching, however, he did notice an opening. It would be a tight squeeze but he believed he could get in through a small window at the side of the house.

After climbing in and walking into the kitchen, Manny immediately knew something was wrong. The broken glass on the floor and bloody footprints leading up the stairs spoke of something unpleasant. Putting the bag containing Sasha's dress on the table, Manny followed the footprints up the stairs. They led to the door where Sasha kept her collection of ancient books. He could detect a faintly unsavoury odour coming from within:

whisky and a distinct smell of stale urine. Manny paused and composed his thoughts, desperately trying to find the courage to open the door and walk in.

Eventually he did so and nothing could have prepared him for the scene that awaited him. Hanging from a solid beam in the empty room was a body, its back turned towards him. Cut and bleeding feet. Angel wings facing him. God, that ridiculous outfit.

Manny slowly walked up to the body and caught sight of Sasha's blue, swollen face.

The shock sent him crashing backwards into the wall behind him, winding him in the process. Then he fell forward, covered his eyes and lay prostrate with grief, unsure of what to do or where to look. On his elbows he slid out of the room, all the while keeping his gaze low, not wanting to witness again the image that would haunt him for years to come. With trembling lips and shaky hands, he dialled 999 and went to sit and wait in her study, stunned and saddened, eyes fixed on the print of Rembrandt's prodigal son hanging above her desk.

The sound of churning gravel and flashing blue lights brought him out of his reverie. He rushed to the door to let in the police and ambulance crew, pointing to the room upstairs. Unable to speak, he could only watch as the green uniforms of the paramedics blurred past him with great haste. Two police officers followed behind but without the same urgency. Manny was told to wait downstairs. In the kitchen he was soon joined by one of the police officers who introduced himself as PC Kendall. Kendall's manner was abrupt. He instructed Manny not to touch anything when he saw the broken glass and bloody footprints that covered parts of the kitchen floor and ordered him to stand in the hallway where he took a brief statement. Manny's lips trembled. The police officer then invited him to wait in the back of the car. Manny asked if he could go home - in his case, back to the hotel where he'd been staying. Kendall said that this would be a problem as a detective was on his way and would most likely have questions of his own to ask. More and more people seemed to be appearing around him. Some were dressed in white overalls and headed straight upstairs, carrying cases and cameras. He saw two others go into the kitchen. Another police car arrived and out stepped a large man with red hair who made his way into the house. He stopped to talk to Kendall who was still standing in the porch. Before long, they both looked over to Manny who quickly looked away. He gathered that the large, red-haired man must be the detective. Kendall then approached the car and told Manny that he would need to take him to the station where he could make a full statement.

How could she do this? Manny kept asking himself. From sheer despair was the only answer he could come up with.

"Could you tell me what your relationship with Dr Harrington is, or was, sorry?"

Manny didn't know what to say to the burly, ginger detective who had introduced himself at the station as Detective Inspector Jenkins. He was dressed in a blue suit, white shirt and a bright tie. Manny reckoned he was in his early forties.

"Girlfriend? Wife? Friend?" prompted Jenkins

"Er, friend," he eventually answered.

"Do you have a key?"

"No."

"No? So who let you in then?"

"I climbed in through the side window."

DI Jenkins raised an eyebrow.

"Was she expecting you?"

"No. I was planning on surprising her."

"The two bags in the porch, do they belong to you?"

"Yes."

"Planning on staying then?"

"Couple of days, yes."

"Have you known the deceased long?"

"No, not really. Only for a few weeks."

Jenkins raised his other eyebrow and then knotted them together.

"How did you meet?"

"In a bar," he lied

"Were you aware that the deceased used to be male?"

"Yes, but I don't see what that has to do with anything."

"Games."

"Sorry?"

"Sex game gone wrong. You'd be surprised. Happens a lot."

"We weren't having sex. We've never had sex and what you're suggesting sickens me."

"Sorry, sir, just trying to establish the facts. Why don't we sit down and try and get this straightened out. You see, I'm a little confused. Would you mind waiting here a moment while I find a room where we can discuss your statement in relative peace?"

He debated for a moment while DI Jenkins went in search of an empty room, wondering whether or not to come clean and tell him all about the escorting work.

Manny had heard or read somewhere that all suicides were treated with suspicion. This was beginning to seriously trouble him. Jenkins was soon back and led Manny into an interview room which made him feel distinctly nervous. Jenkins seemed to sense and enjoy his unease.

"Don't worry, we won't detain you for too much longer. I'm just trying to get the picture clear in my head. You see, there are some minor details that I can't seem to be able to get my head around and it's making things appear foggy."

"Like what?" Manny frowned.

"Well, to start with, there's the smashed glass and blood in the kitchen. The fact that you hardly know the person, yet break into her house, and then there's the dresses."

"The dresses?"

"Yes, the one in the bag that you say you bought for her in Madrid and then the one she was wearing when she died. The angel outfit. You said earlier that it was a gift from you."

"That's correct."

"Why would you buy her a dress like that if you weren't lovers?"

"We were drunk one day and passed a shop. It was in the window. She said she had to have it so I bought it for her."

Jenkins looked none the wiser.

"Look, I was her escort who happened to become her friend," he declared finally.

"An escort?"

"Yes, a male escort. She hired me to accompany her."

"Oh, you mean a prostitute. A male prostitute, now I get it. So I might be right about the sex game." The sarcasm in his voice was now unmistakable.

"No," Manny bellowed. "We never had sex. I was company for her. That's all I ever was. Company. She hired me for company from an agency called Perfect Company. Then we became friends. I hadn't seen her for about a week because I'd been in Madrid with another client. I wanted to surprise her. It was unlike her not to be at her home at that hour. I waited over two hours before letting myself in. I was freezing."

Jenkins rocked back on his chair, inviting him to continue.

Manny described to the detective everything he had seen once he'd entered the house. The empty whisky bottle, the shattered glass, the bloody footprints and, worst of all, the body he'd seen hanging from the beam, wearing that dress.

"How long have you been a male prostitute?"

"Not long. A few weeks."

"Pay well, does it?"

Manny realised that he had some explaining to do and that he was in a terrible mess with nobody to help him.

"That was the only reason I did it. I'm a teacher who needed money. The escorting work helped me out of a hole."

"Does your school know about your nocturnal activities?"

Manny shook his head.

"How long were you in Madrid for?

"Five days. Got back Wednesday afternoon."

"Did you go with your school's permission?"

"Of course not. I called in sick."

"Oh dear, what a pickle."

"Look, I haven't done anything wrong. I would like to go. It has been an emotional night and I've already given a statement."

"Yes, but you chose to omit the part about being a male escort. Moonlighting, eh? Working as a male prostitute. Can't see

302

your bosses being too pleased with you... and as for the press..."

"The press?"

"The thing is, Mr Rodriguez, Dr Harrington was a minor celeb in the academic world. I can see them having a field day with this one, tragic as it may seem. Are you sure that you have told me everything? Not holding back on me now, are you?"

"All I've told you tonight has been the truth. I swear. Now can I go?"

Jenkins scratched his head and read back the amended statement to himself before saying, "I think we're done here for now. Just need a bit more information, contact details and things like that. Shouldn't keep you too much longer. We'll need to speak again, so we'll be in touch again soon. Thanks for your co-operation."

Manny was finally allowed to leave the station at 1.30am. He wasn't sure where to head. He called Louise but her phone was switched off. So, carrying his holdalls, he went in search of a hotel. He felt a mess and needed some time to himself, some time to grieve. His body still trembled and his eyes watered, but it had nothing to do with the cold winter night air. In a dark part of his soul he felt partly responsible.

CHAPTER
THIRTY-THREE

Manny walked to his classroom window. From there he could see that three or four reporters had gathered outside the school gates. Bloody Jenkins must have tipped them off, he thought. Quick off the mark, he had to give them that. It was Monday, not yet midday. What did they want with him? Was it really such a big story? Christ, a photographer was there too.

A student in the class asked what they were there for and then the guessing games began. With break almost upon them, Manny was desperate to dismiss his class in order to give himself time to pull himself together. Inside, his chest had tightened. Disaster had struck. He would need to go and speak to the Head and explain the mess he was in. Something he was dreading. He could already imagine the kind of questions the Head would throw at him. Manny still hadn't got over the shock of Sasha's death and his treatment by the police had rattled him. He had thought of disappearing for a short while but decided against it, believing that school was the best place for him to start if he was to get his life back on track. He hadn't reckoned on the press turning up outside his work though, provoking further turmoil in his soul.

A little later, in the headteacher's office, the Head listened without interruption. He frowned frequently, dismayed to discover that the broken man sitting before him was not only a male escort but had also been operating his trade during school hours. Manny had confessed everything.

"So the press outside are hungry to speak to you about your

relationship with this Dr Harrington? No doubt they'll want to name and shame this teacher who also happens to be a male prostitute," he said, shaking his head grimly.

Manny didn't like the way the Head used the term 'prostitute', but guessed that was how he was going to be referred to now by all and sundry.

"Yes, that's pretty much it," he said despondently.

"It helps explain the madness on the switchboard this morning." The Head was silent for a moment. "Well, you leave me with no alternative other than to suspend you pending further inquiries. Gather your belongings and leave the premises at once. I must say that I'm terribly disappointed in you for bringing the name of the school into disrepute."

Manny got up to leave but the Head wasn't yet finished.

"One piece of advice," he barked. "Call your union and tell them about the minefield you're walking in. I very much doubt that they'll be of any use to you at this late stage though. Honestly, what a mess. The governors are not going to like this one little bit."

Manny left the office and tried to focus his thoughts. Dom Bonner, the cover supervisor, had been ordered to cover his classes until further notice. He had little choice other than to leave the building but, before doing so, he called a cab.

Outside the school gates the small cluster of reporters didn't hold back.

"Any comment to make, Mr Rodriguez?"

"A word, Mr Rodriguez."

"What was your relationship with Dr Harrington?"

"How long have you been a male escort?"

Manny fought his way through without commenting. He jumped into the back of the cab, ordering the driver just to drive while the reporters jogged behind.

"Blimey," said the driver. "You're popular. What you done?"

Manny shrugged without reply, instructing the driver to take him at once to St Albans train station.

Once there, he booked into a nearby hotel and went straight to his room, not knowing what else to do. He undressed and sat naked on the bed for over an hour, desperately trying to absorb the events of the past few days. Lost in thought, he walked over to the window and watched the people walking down below, wishing he could swap their problems for his. He could not remember a time when he had felt so low, or so alone. Listlessly, he crept back to the bed, got inside the covers and curled up, hoping to find sleep. As he waited for sleep to claim him, he thought of Sasha.

When he awoke, Manny did not know where he was. It was dark and cold. He reached over to turn on the light and looked at the clock. 6.00am. He had slept for sixteen hours. He got up and went to the bathroom where he took a long shower, hoping it would help clear the fog from his head. Then he got dressed and headed downstairs in search of coffee. The morning papers were displayed on a table close to reception. He picked one up. Unbelievably, the death of Dr Sasha Harrington had made the news. Taking his coffee and the paper back to his room, he was shocked to read, underneath a headline that screamed *'Transsexual Academic in Suspected Suicide',* a report on the troubled transsexual and leading expert in Persian Literature who was believed to have taken her own life. The authorities denied that her death was a result of auto-erotic asphyxiation, as had been suggested in earlier reports. The report also mentioned that colleagues and friends of the highly regarded writer and university lecturer had become concerned at her increasingly erratic behaviour. The paper, to Manny's horror, went on to explain that her body had been discovered at her home by boyfriend, Manny Rodriguez, a school teacher who also worked as a male escort in the London area. It concluded by saying that Mr Rodriguez was continuing to help the police with their inquiries. Glaringly, the piece was accompanied by a large photo of him outside the school gates.

Manny sat on the edge of his bed, stunned. It wasn't every day his name and photo appeared in the papers, but now his secret was out for all to see. Under a cloud of turmoil he packed his bag and went down to the front desk to settle his bill. Then he walked to the station and waited for a train to take him to central London. It was time he spoke to Virginia and Louise. In some way, he hoped they might be able to help. His whole world felt totally off-balance.

Less than an hour later, he was pacing up and down in Virginia's office, unable to sit. For once, she was sympathetic.

"I understand your predicament," she said, sitting behind her desk. "Try not to panic."

"I'm not."

"You are. Now come and sit down and let's think this through. You're still in shock."

"Have you seen the papers today? I'm in them." He opened the paper and threw it onto her desk. "Her 'boyfriend', they called me. And they've announced to the world that I'm an escort. I'm stuffed. Well and truly stuffed. My teaching career and reputation in ruins." He sat down, holding his head in his hands.

"I think we could do with some coffee," Virginia announced brightly, getting up to pour out two cups from the percolator that sat in the corner. "You need to calm down," she continued. "This doesn't reflect well on us as a company either, you know? We must keep our heads. Time for some damage limitation."

Manny said nothing, listening.

"My advice to you is to get away. Lay low for a while until all this blows over. Is there anywhere you could go? Spain perhaps, to stay with your father? If it's money you're worried about, the company can sub you some. You can work it off on your return. Things will be quieter by then. People will have forgotten all about this unfortunate business."

The thought of being in Virginia's pocket hardly filled him with joy but he failed to see what other options he had.

"We can book you a flight out today. I'll have a word with Len and get him to drive you to the airport. How does that sound?"

Manny said nothing. He got up and walked over to the window, looking down at the busy street below. Spain? His father? Maybe it was time he paid him a visit. Some time away might help. He felt nervous, frayed. A pang of guilt gripped his chest as he thought about Sasha and what it would mean to miss her funeral. It was almost as if he was shrugging off her memory in his selfish pursuit to distance himself from her and his troubles. It was a cowardly act. An act she would disapprove of.

But, after the press allegations, he couldn't bring himself to face anyone. The thought of having to face colleagues, students or anyone else who might know him filled him with dread. Having to explain away his actions to the school governors would also prove to be a humiliating experience, with only one real outcome.

Immense shame was what he felt and it pained him to admit it but he was worried about how people would perceive him for having had a close friendship with a transsexual.

"Christ," he said aloud. "What a mess."

Suddenly, Virginia's suggestion looked like a wise one.

Meanwhile, in the office next door, Louise was rather annoyed she hadn't been asked in. She was also feeling guilty because she had not contacted Manny during his hour of need. When he had entered the building, the strain on his face had been clear to see, the usual charming smile nowhere in sight. She'd seen the morning papers and knew the trouble he was in. He had confided his deepest fears to her in the past and now, it seemed, his worst fears had been realised. *The poor man*, she thought. *He must be going through hell and there isn't a thing I can do to help*. With a deep sigh, she turned back to her computer.

It wasn't long before Manny came out of Virginia's office. He walked over and stood by her desk. For a second, he seemed a stranger. Then he bent down and kissed her on the cheek and in that moment, to her dismay, she realized that she had missed him. Despite herself, she took hold of his arm.

"I've come to say goodbye," he said.

"Where are you going?"

"Oh, we decided it would be better for me to disappear for a while."

"We?" she asked with a note of sarcasm.

"Okay, Virginia thought it would be best."

"And what do you think?"

"Right now, I'm not sure what to think. Perhaps she's right."

"Where will you go?"

"Spain. Probably stay with my father."

"Oh, I see," she said, failing to keep the disappointment from her voice. "When are you leaving?"

"Later today." They both fell silent.

Virginia came out of her office.

"Louise, could I have a word..? You still here, Manny? Thought you'd be busy getting your things together. Your lift will be arriving soon."

"I'm just leaving," he said. They exchanged silent glances and then he was gone. He marched outside the building, carrying his two holdalls, and headed for the wine bar across the road. All he could do now was sit and wait for Len to take him to the airport. On second thoughts, he decided he'd rather get a taxi, so he sent Len a text telling him not to bother. Waving down a black cab, he headed for Heathrow airport, arriving just before 1pm. He had a seat booked on the three o'clock flight to Madrid. From there, he would catch a connecting flight to La Palma in the Canary Islands, home of his father and where he had spent his formative years. It was a beautiful, peaceful place, shielded from the rest of the world, consisting of mountains and splendid beaches with plenty of cafés and quiet bars in which to while away the time.

As he sat in the terminal building waiting for his flight to be announced, he pulled out the book Sasha had written on Rumi and began to read, knowing he would find comfort and strength in her words.

CHAPTER
THIRTY-FOUR

Six months later, a man carrying a black briefcase stepped down from the 10.30am train at St Albans station. He stood for a moment to allow the platform to clear so as to avoid the stampede up the stairs. It was a procedure he was getting used to, for this was the fourth day running that he had made the same sweltering journey. Today, however, he was more hopeful of tracking down the man he was having so much difficulty finding. Yesterday, he'd received a tip-off as to where he might find the elusive individual. It had come from a teacher named Moran, who claimed to be an ex-colleague and friend of the man he was trying to locate. It seemed Moran was desperate to speak to the man himself. He claimed not to have seen or heard from him for some time now and it was obvious he was keen to do so. Moran had given him his phone number and had asked that it be passed on should he succeed in his search.

The man loosened his tie a little and walked slowly through the station, keeping his eyes wide open. He paused to watch a man with dark cropped hair. Too tall, he thought, and carried on with the four hundred metre walk to the hotel where he was told his target liked to stay. Once there, he showed the receptionist his credentials, placing his briefcase on the desk. Opening the case, he pulled out a photo of the man and held it up for the receptionist to inspect.

"Have you seen this man?" he asked. "I hear he's stayed here in the past."

"He looks familiar," she replied. "What's his name?"

"Rodriguez. Manny Rodriguez."

"Rodriguez, let me see."

The receptionist tapped away on her computer keypad.

"Sorry," she said. "We have no one of that name staying here."

The man thanked her for her trouble, picked up his briefcase and headed towards the city centre, not too disappointed, for he still had a couple more leads to follow up. The second place he went to was a café called Barrissimo, located beside the taxi rank in the middle of town. Supposedly, it was another place where Rodriguez liked to hang out. Ordering himself a double espresso with a little milk and a glass of cold water, he took a seat close to the window where he'd be able to see people getting in and out of the cabs outside. It was an ideal spot for him to settle back and read the paper while at the same time keeping his eyes open for his man. He didn't have long to wait.

Manny's taxi pulled up at the rank at 11.25am. He'd arrived back from his disastrous trip to Spain about a week earlier. The moment he'd landed in Madrid he changed his mind about meeting his father and made a beeline for Tenerife instead. There he spent most of his time drinking, womanising and wallowing in self-pity, full of disgust at himself and what had become of him.

Loaded with the money Virginia had loaned him, he had embarked on several pointless journeys in the vain hope of feeling better. Wherever he ended up though, the same pattern would emerge. Time after time, he would end up drunk, often waking to find himself in the arms of some woman, each one older and more vulgar than the last.

Eventually, he was able to summon his inner strength and free himself from the self-loathing that was threatening to destroy his life. He took a trip to the north of the island where he found a secluded beach that was absent of the tired bars and nightclubs that dominated the south. There he would patrol the beach from dawn to dusk, often sitting and staring out across the blue sea, vowing to get his life back on track. If nothing else, he felt he owed Sasha's memory that much. He began to jog, swim and drink less, generally taking much better care of himself. With the money running low, he bought a ticket back home and hoped for the best, not quite sure of what he was going to do or where he was going to live. The one thing he promised himself was that he would resume his studies. Before he could do that, however, he had to find a way of paying Virginia back. She had already been in touch, demanding he return to work so he could pay off his debt. She had some work lined up, she said, clients who were keen for his company. Although he was not at all eager to resume his escorting duties, under the circumstances, Manny felt he had very little choice. The thought of burly Len hounding him for Virginia's money was hardly a comforting one. No, he decided, a few more bookings and then he'd finally be free. Free to take up his studies and do something more meaningful with his life.

Grabbing his holdall out of the boot, he walked the few short yards to Barrissimo's café where he ordered a double espresso. He hadn't been in there two minutes when a plump, middle-aged man wearing a dark suit approached him. Manny's face clouded over. Another journalist, he thought. The man reassured him that he wasn't and invited him to sit down. Manny looked at him sceptically but took a seat.

"My name is Walters, Derek Walters, and I am the executor of Dr Sasha Harrington's will. You are a very hard man to track down, Mr Rodriguez. I have been looking for you for some time." Walters looked at the tanned man who sat before him and asked him if he had been away.

Manny nodded and watched as the man opened his black leather case. He was stunned, but he did not doubt that Walters was telling the truth.

"Don't look so worried," said Walters, "it's good news."

Manny listened as Walters spent the next few minutes reading from a document that he had pulled out of the case. It was several minutes before he could absorb the whole impact of what the man was saying. And it was a lot longer before he was able to speak.

REFERENCES

1. Mafi, Maryam & Azima Melita Kolin, *Hidden Music*, Thorsons: 01/10/2001, p. 9
2. Mafi, Maryam & Azima Melita Kolin, *Hidden Music*, Thorsons: 01/10/2001, p. 196
3. Mafi, Maryam & Azima Melita Kolin, *Hidden Music*, Thorsons: 01/10/2001, p. 122
4. Mafi, Maryam & Azima Melita Kolin, *Hidden Music*, Thorsons: 01/10/2001, p. 12
5. Mafi, Maryam & Azima Melita Kolin, *Hidden Music*, Thorsons: 01/10/2001, p. 114
6. Mafi, Maryam & Azima Melita Kolin, *Hidden Music*, Thorsons: 01/10/2001, p. 16
7. Mafi, Maryam & Azima Melita Kolin, *Hidden Music*, Thorsons: 01/10/2001, p. 196
8. Mafi, Maryam & Azima Melita Kolin, *Hidden Music*, Thorsons: 01/10/2001, p. 136
9. Rumi, translated by Raficq Abdulla, *Mathnavi 1. 109: Words of Paradise, Selected Poems*, Studio: 1 Amer ed edition 10/04/2000
10. Rumi, translated by Raficq Abdulla, *Mathnavi 1. 109: Words of Paradise, Selected Poems*, Studio: 1 Amer ed edition 10/04/2000)
11. Mafi, Maryam & Azima Melita Kolin, *Hidden Music*, Thorsons: 01/10/2001, p. 130